THE DARK POOL

MONIKA CARLESS

STONE'S THROW
PUBLICATIONS

Cover design by Sue Reynolds, Stone's Throw Publication Services

Cover photographs:
    Kissing Couple by Shutterstock.com
    Misty Castle and Misty Forest by BigStockPhoto.com

Interior Layout and Design: James Dewar

ISBN 978-1-987813-12-8

Published by Stone's Throw Publications
Port Perry, Ontario, Canada
www.stonesthrowps.ca

Printed in Canada

1 2 3 4 5 6 7 8 9 10

THE DARK POOL

"I want to love you wildly. I don't want words, but inarticulate cries from the bottom of my most primitive being that flow from my belly like honey. A piercing joy that leaves me empty, conquered, silenced"

~ Anais Nin

For My Boo,

Thank you for all of who you are, you inspire me. And for your support, it means the world to me. I hope you enjoy the people in this book, They are made of Stardust + Dreams.

Mama Coyote,

Dedication

For my parents, Teresa and Ted Kozak.
You left this world much too soon, but not my heart. Thank you for
my life, born entirely of your love.

Acknowledgements

I am deeply grateful for all the serendipitous events in my life that have brought me to writing this novel.

A deep bow to my partner Steve, who believed more than I and encouraged me daily, no matter what it cost him. He is the inspiration for many of my words.

To my daughters Elizabeth and Jessika, who kept me at my typewriter by living life with passion and courage; your love is my breath.

Thank you to friends who read early manuscripts, offered much needed guidance and stood by my dream.

To Sue and James at Stone's Throw Publications; many heartfelt thanks for your thoughtful handling of my work, your guidance and the beautiful cover design. Namaste.

A very special thank you to the characters who came to me in dreams, visions, meditations and finally manifested fully within the pages of this book.

The Gift of a Woman's Voice

Woman, do you know that planets shift when you speak?

Do you know that the sun explodes fiery secrets to the Universe when you write from your soul?

Do you know that the moon's tides ebb and flow with every expression of your heart?

Do you know that with each syllable you utter, consciousness shifts and men with honor, bravery and peaceful strength are born?

Woman, your words are what stirs the cosmos...what brings men to their knees...what creates a deep knowing within The Goddess.

It is She who walks with you on the lonely road.

It is She who guides your steps when you have lost your way.

It is She who embraces you when you question your decisions.

It is She who stands by silently and powerfully when you lie on the ground seemingly defeated, screaming your pain to the silent sky and letting your tears soak the earth beneath you.

It is you, woman, whom the Goddess learns from. She and you are One. There is no sweet incarnation of the Goddess without the words that flow from your inner sanctum.

She is only because you are.

The more you learn about yourself, woman, the more Earth learns about herself. Your emotions are what feed the rainbow river of life.

When your pen speaks your truth, the world opens to possibilities of the lying down of arms; opens to the song of Shakti, ever flowing, like the blood you spill when Luna calls your name.

Woman, you have spilled your life force so that we might learn to walk the path of tolerance and love.

You have been burned, drowned, hung, tortured and spat upon.

And yet, you continue to gift us with your words of forgiveness and shower us with insights from your ever expanding being. Without your words we would be lost to the darkness of the unknown.

Once, a long time ago, in a place where light was not yet expressed, where all that could be lay still within a gossamer wrapped cocoon; Goddess spoke and her word found wings.

And since that time, it has been the word of a woman that has kept the planets spinning and the galaxies from collapsing.

From your word, your womb births realities.

Woman gift me more of your words. For I cannot live without the fruit of your pen. All that is and all that will be, survives on the ink you spill, the essay of your grace.

Excerpt, *The Gift of a Woman's Voice*, Monika Carless - originally published @ www.elephantjournal.com

Foreword

This novel came drifting to me on the wind. I'd always known that I would write one, and truly never questioned when, I simply waited for the moment when the characters would reveal themselves. When my fingers first began to type chapter one, I was unaware of who I was writing about, what the story would be, or how it would evolve. With time, I met everyone who wanted expression in the physical world and told their story as it was dictated to me.

By the end, I knew that this story was about personal freedoms. Too many of us still struggle to live our truth without fear of judgement or persecution. But we must, as a society, learn to offer the same freedoms to others that we insist on for ourselves.

This novel is not polite, it challenges conventional relationships, allows for a freedom of expression that has long been denied women and men of alternative sexual orientations and delves into the mystic. The story uses expressions that once were the domain of the Goddess, and were later used against women. The characters dare to expose their magic and be real in the face of their fears.

To create change, sometimes one has to drown in the deep end of the forbidden. Will you jump in the deep end with me?

Prologue

Medieval England

What hour was this? Brigida opened her eyes to the smoky warmth of the room. Light was just beginning to creep in at the horizon.

The mullioned windows of the bedchamber were frosted with cold, the yellow-orange glimmer of the rising sun barely visible through the glass. Her eyes lifted towards the rich canopy hung above the carved oak bed.

Her mouth was dry. She tried to move her arms from the position they were in, stretched above her head. She had always slept like this, from the time she was an infant. Open. Trusting of the world, although then she had known nothing of it. But her arms would not move, and neither would her legs. Panic set in, and then memory flooded her brain.

"Are you awake, my lady?"

The rich voice of Brigida's lover brought the memory into sharper focus. She tried to answer but her throat, parched as it was from the wine she had drunk the night before, closed to all words. She nodded, watching the handsome face lower towards her. He kissed her gently where her pulse was now beating madly at the base of her neck.

"Water, my lord," was all she could muster.

He nodded, eyes soft and hungry at the same time. "By God, you are beautiful," he whispered, and turned to the table by the bed where a pitcher of water and a cup stood ready. He poured, and lifting her head with one arm, watched her drink as if she had walked the dessert the night through.

"Untie me." Brigida, throat moistened, gathered her courage.

"Not yet, my love." A shadow fell across her as he bent down to kiss her lips. She could smell the oils in his hair, the musk of his body, the wine on his breath. It made her weak, his presence. And she wasn't sure now that she wanted to be released.

He smiled, a wicked smile, while his hands pulled up on the rich fabric of her nightdress and exposed her breasts, nipples taut; and the pink of her sex visible. He moved now to the bottom of the bed. His stare was penetrating. He licked his lips. Brigida squirmed, a flush blooming on her cheeks.

"Are you still the blushing maiden, Brigida?" he asked, untying the bindings on her legs. "After everything we have done, after all the words of love I have spoken?"

Brigida moved her legs together, and brought her knees to her chest. Her back ached and she wished to stretch the pain away. He waited, giving her a moment to ease herself back into a lying position.

She said nothing. Words were of no use when he looked like this.

"You are more to my liking like this, my lady," he growled, taking up her legs and bringing her knees once more to her chest...spreading them wide. She gasped.

His hair falling about his broad shoulders, chest heaving with desire, her lover lowered his face once more. There was no reason to resist him. She wanted this as much as he. Her body, traitor that it was to all things decent, began to respond to his skilled tongue. He looked up at her briefly, curious.

"Do I please you, my lady?" His question was madness. He knew that he pleased her.

Pleased her so well that she forgave him his requests. And his hold on her heart.

CHAPTER 1

Sahara drove into town with the things that she loved most in the back of a pick-up. Some things that had been left behind still lingered in her heart. Everything else that she would need could be bought or had been carefully packed into the moving van.

The light at the intersection turned yellow, then red. She tapped her fingers impatiently on the steering wheel, anxious now, one hand searching for the pendant at her throat. It was still twenty miles past town to the place she would call home; a property she had bought sight unseen, but one that she recognized from a deep well of dreams.

She peered through the windshield looking for the coffee shop that fronted the realtor's office.

Probably serves burnt espresso, she thought miserably.

Sahara parked in front of the cafe signed simply *Patisserie* and got out, stretching her petite frame like a cat. Already she could feel eyes glued to her. Her intuition told her that she was being looked over, if not judged. People generally disliked her or fell madly in love with her, but rarely anything in between.

Washroom, coffee and inquire about the realtor, she decided. Sahara had a habit of running the details of her day through her mind; order made her feel secure.

It was six in the evening. Before dark she would like to get to the cabin, turn on the propane, start a fire in the fireplace, and make her bed.

The cafe door screeched her arrival. A few heads turned in her direction, some nodded and smiled. Sahara did likewise, although her smile, usually so freely given, did not reach her eyes. New surroundings always unsettled her and brought out her cooler side.

With no one behind the counter to guide her, she searched for the bathroom, expecting the worst. When she found it, she was surprised to find luxurious lavender hand soap in the dispenser. She left the bathroom lost to her thoughts and walked directly into someone rounding the corner toward her.

"Oh! Sorry. Not looking where I'm going," Sahara apologized. She looked up into the face of an unexpectedly beautiful young woman, hand held out; eyes friendly and curious. Sahara felt a familiar sensation in her heart, a signal that she was well acquainted with. It always happened when she crossed paths with a kindred spirit.

1

"Hello. I'm Holly." A spark of electricity startled them as they shook hands; Sahara's heart beat wildly, her sharp intake of breath surprising them both.

"Oh dear," Holly muttered, voice shaky.

Sahara sensed from the expression on Holly's face that the splendid creature in front of her felt ungrounded in some way. Dressed in figure hugging jeans, black leather boots and a sweater that did nothing to hide her impertinent nipples, Sahara was a force field of swirling energy.

It wouldn't be the first time she had thrown someone into a head spin. Sahara knew this and had long since given up trying to figure out what to do about it.

"Hi," Sahara said; lips now curved into a devastating smile. I'm looking for the real estate agent, Claire? She mentioned that her office backs the café."

Sahara pointed behind her shoulder to the darkened doorway of a musty looking room, the closed sign offering little hope of finding Claire.

"You bought the old cabin on the edge of the ridge," Holly said, matter-of-factly. Her face had that open, you-can-trust-me-with-anything look.

"Yes. How do you know?"

"Claire asked me to look out for you. I have your keys. She had to leave. You must be running late."

"I'm not late. She said by day's end." A frustrated edge crept into Sahara's voice.

"Well, her day ends by noon at this location. Claire also runs an antique store. But as it turns out, you won't find her there either," Holly replied, eyes still wide, her voice soft, fidgeting with a loose tendril of long golden hair that was tied into a loose knot at the base of her neck. Her lips were stained red, somewhat tender in hue. She bit her plump bottom lip then released it. A sigh hit the air.

Normally such vulnerability in someone would have warmed Sahara's heart, but at the moment all she could think of was how annoyed she was to have missed the agent.

Sahara frowned. A complete stranger had her keys. She was thrown off by Holly knowing more about her situation than she did. Her skin cooled and she shivered as her emotions shifted. It wasn't her way to be rude, unfriendly. But Sahara felt herself slipping into an unwelcome bad mood.

"Hey, would you like some hot coffee?" Holly asked. "I've just ground some."

The young woman turned and led the way towards the counter, pointing to the pastries behind the glass. "Hungry?"

"You have a roaster!" Sahara exclaimed, sounding so surprised that Holly laughed.

"Small town, but well appointed," Holly offered with a mischievous smile. "You might like it here. Now, tell me what you drink." She gestured Sahara into a stool by the counter. Sahara slinked herself into a seated position, as one who felt very comfortable in her body, and with that yogic ease of movement, very aware of Holly's eyes upon her.

As Sahara looked around, slowly sipping her extra strong coffee and nibbling the flaky pastry that Holly had picked out for her, she noticed civilities that smoothed her somewhat ruffled feathers. Linen table cloths, gourmet preserves, crusty bread...she relaxed her shoulders, pendant in hand, her stillness a comfort in the new environment.

Holly had left her alone while she cleaned the tables after the last of the customers. Sahara's attention followed her around the room. If Holly was the owner of this café, Sahara was impressed. This was no ordinary coffee shop. It had flair, a definite attention to detail. And Holly was equally intriguing.

She seemed very young, but quite sure of herself tending to her chores. Yes, she must be the owner, Sahara decided. She moved like she owned the place. The coffee was to die for. The pastry was rivalled only by a particular bakery in Denver. And perhaps not even so.

However, it was Holly's bottom that held Sahara's attention longest, try as she might to pretend that she was in her own world.

"Coffee ok? I hope you like the pastry; this one has been popular." Holly's voice melted over Sahara like chocolate fondue.

"To be honest, Holly, I expected burnt espresso. And I'm pretty fussy on pastry. This is amazing, truly."

"That's good; I'm the only bakery in town," Holly laughed. "Coffee's fair trade too."

"I won't have to drive to Denver every day for my fix then." Sahara winked. Holly blushed.

"We have a good farmer's market... a friend and I go to it on Saturdays." Holly's blush deepened, and Sahara wondered about the "friend". No doubt the girl was dating someone interesting. There wasn't a ring on her finger, although that could simply be for convenience sake at work.

"Perhaps I'll see you there." Sahara said.

Holly's eye's brightened. "That would be fun... and the library is amazing too. Lots of bright spaces to sit and read. It was built by that same friend. It has a woodsy, enchanted feel to it.

That was it then, Sahara decided. The "friend" had quite the impact on Holly, beau or not. Experience as a writer ignited Sahara's curiosity for the story behind Holly's words. Interesting.

The phone rang and Sahara fell back into her own thoughts when Holly disappeared to answer it. She should be leaving, but felt oddly comfortable despite the new surroundings.

"Sahara?" Holly stood behind the counter, a cloth in one hand, the other reaching for a paper bag she had filled with a few supplies.

"Hmmm, yes?"

"I was saying; would you like me to come out with you, to help you find the way and maybe turn on the propane? I used to make deliveries to Jack..."

"No thanks, I'll be fine."

Sahara had no intention of making friends yet or letting anyone share in her first moments at the cabin. She stood abruptly; suddenly aware that she must look ungrateful for the offer. But there was no going back now, rude as she might appear; she desperately needed to greet her new life on her own. Still, she was sorry she had brushed Holly off; what a surprise she was, entirely welcoming and sweet.

"I'll get going. Thanks again." Sahara announced.

The two women locked eyes briefly. Holly looked towards the bag she was holding.

"Here, take some croissants and a bit of my special blend of coffee."

She handed Sahara the paper bag. It had a number written on it. "Here's my number, call me if you need anything. Oh, and your keys! Welcome to Riverbend."

Sahara felt some part of her shut down despite Holly's warm smile and offering of food. What the hell was wrong with her? It had been a long day, with so much anticipation of what was to come. She smiled graciously and took the bag from Holly, then walked out into the warm evening air, with one last wave to the girl behind the store front window.

That impossibly attractive girl, who turned away as Sahara climbed into her truck, and pulling her hair out of its messy knot, let it fall to her waist in a cascade of gold.

Holly watched Sahara leave, noticing every nuance of the woman's sensual, petite frame; she was utterly feminine and soft, and at the same time tough and unapproachable. It would be sad, Holly thought, for Sahara to arrive at her cabin all alone. But perhaps fitting. Sahara had definitely made it clear that she wasn't looking for company.

That mouth though, and those dark eyes under the messy crop of short hair had Holly unconsciously licking her lips.

The phone rang, breaking in on Holly's thoughts.

"*Patisserie!*"

Holly listened patiently as the woman on the other end gave strict instructions in a mix of Parisian French and English, accented by a distinctly self- important manner.

"*Oui, C'est ca.* I will send them first thing tomorrow morning. Directly to the Gallery Montfort this time? Of course. *Merci. Je comprends l'orde.*

If Holly was honest with herself, meeting Sahara had thrown her off balance, and left her heart open to a feeling of vulnerability.

CHAPTER 2

The truck radio cracked up into garbled voices and spits of country music. Sahara turned it off and stepped on the gas. Her cat stuck a paw out of his carrying case and let out a plaintive cry.

"Almost there, Willow. Almost there."

Where *was* this place? Surely she had not turned down the wrong side road? The trees seemed confining here and night only an hour away. She shouldn't have spent so much time at the café. Sahara felt herself tense and decided to sing, half to herself, half to the cat.

She longed for a hot bath, fresh white linens on a bed piled deep with pillows and a down duvet. The mountain air felt damp and chilly now despite the recent heat of the day. Still, the wind was intoxicating, Sahara felt her cheek; it was hot.

Excitement swept her body, knowing that her long held dream of life in a log cabin in the shadow of the mountains was finally coming true. She didn't have it all figured out yet, how to integrate her old life into the new, how to appease her ache for the occasional lover, but there was time to figure out the details. The truck rolled on, almost knowing the way, picking up on her electric energy.

The road widened on the last curve towards the mountain range that loomed dark in the shadows. It appeared mysterious and dangerous; yet comforting in its strength. Between her and the mountains, vast fields of waving grass. If this place were a symphony, it would reach its climax in the form of the aspen wood, where the leaves on the trees danced the enchanting crescendo.

Sahara's emotions threatened to spill over as she came face to face with her need to live in solitude. She was a woman scarred and this place would have to hold all of her. The road wound alongside a stony banked creek. Around one more corner and Sahara pulled up to the old homestead, cabin windows glowing with a warm light.

Light?!

Feeling weak now, Sahara climbed slowly out of her truck, her mind reeling with questions. The screen door gave a small protest as she pulled it open, a note fluttered to the ground:

Ms. Taylor, Welcome. Will be back in the morning with some firewood. Aiden.

The handwriting was smooth, almost elegant.

Sahara pushed the door open and walked into the place that she would call home. That she was really here felt almost surreal.

Who was Aiden? Why did he have access to her cabin? Sahara's tiredness fell upon her suddenly and completely, her squalling cat the only thing keeping her mind focused on what needed doing before she could sleep. She surveyed her surroundings.

The main floor of the cabin was dominated by a stone fireplace, a great room of pleasing proportions, extending into a cozy kitchen, which had the one thing she had always longed for, a wood cook stove. French doors looked over the plains, towards the mountains. The bathroom and an extra bedroom made up the rest of the space.

Sahara gratefully touched the massive, smooth beams making up the alcove under the stairs. She gazed out the window over the sink. She imagined dinners cooked here, using her own provisions, herbs drying overhead, candles burning, spells churning. Spells! She ran back out to the truck and pulled a large box from the back seat.

Sahara had asked the former owner for two things, the sofa and a small table and chairs. These would suffice while she waited on the delivery of her own belongings. Alright, enough thinking, she had to go to bed. Opening her box of magic tools, Sahara found her incense. She lit it and waved it in the direction of the four corners, before placing it on the kitchen counter. That would have to do for now. If there were any negative energies lurking in the cabin, they would have to wait until the morning to be cleared.

Aiden looked toward the old homestead from the edge of his property. He could barely see the faint glimmer of light coming from the log cabin. The distance, at this corner of the farm, between his house and the other, was not especially great, and a fine aspen wood grew thick enough to obscure most of the view.

When the old homestead had gone up for sale, Aiden had walked around in a foul mood for days, imagining what kind of back-to-the-landers might purchase the farm, eager for company. He had scowled at the thought as he strode up to the owner, a man of considerable years, whose wife had recently passed on.

"Hey Aiden."

"Hello. Listen Jack, any chance of telling me who's looked at purchasing the farm?"

"Sure thing. Are you worried? You live far enough away that it shouldn't be a problem. Anyway, it's a girl."

"A girl?" Aiden almost shouted. "What do you mean, a girl?"

"Well, she's a woman really, not sure of her age. The agent said she was to live here alone."

"Live here *on her own*? No family?" Aiden couldn't believe it.

"Just her and a cat it seems."

A woman. Alone. Aiden stared into the distance as he contemplated the information at hand. How the hell was she going to survive here on her own? The winters were harsh...she'd need a snowmobile to get to the road. Well, whatever, he guessed it was better than a family with six homeschooled kids who would want to visit him unannounced. Not that Aiden disliked children; he simply preferred to make his own decisions about how to share his time.

"When is she arriving?"

"End of next month. I'll be out a week before. My sons are coming to collect me."

For a month before his departure, Jack carted piles of waste to the land fill on the other side of town, and Aiden could smell the smoke from a never ending fire on which Jack burned his dreams and memories. The real estate woman had left explicit instructions that nothing could be left behind. Every room had to be emptied, every outbuilding, every piece of scrap lying on the land hauled off.

The woman who was making the purchase was very insistent on this, she would pay the price asked, but would not entertain any thoughts of having to sift through another persons' crap. And when Aiden showed up that evening to light a fire and air the place out, there was indeed nothing left. Not even the vinyl liners in the kitchen drawers.

Deep down inside, Aiden had a panicky feeling that his life would somehow change after this woman moved in. As her only neighbour, he knew that he would feel obliged to check in on her, even though work often called him away. He'd resent having to be social when he least desired it.

Even as a child, Aiden had been keenly solitary. His parents had chided him for being stand-offish. Aiden, of sharp mind, deep thought and increasingly good looks attracted many gazes, but he paid little attention. Invariably, he could be found trekking through the forest, a book and Swiss army knife in hand. Aiden lived for the written word and a piece of finely turned wood in his hands.

All those years of roaming the wilderness and working with his hands had toned his naturally muscular body. His nut-brown hair grew handsomely to his shoulders, and he developed a habit of running his fingers through it to keep it in place. He enrolled in university for architectural design, but at the last moment, his distaste for crowded environments and uniformity had called for a change in direction.

Running his own carpentry business just seemed to happen organically anyway, as word spread of his skilled workmanship.

Aiden had many opportunities to find companionship, or more to his desire, unbridled sex. Girls he had grown up with were easy to take. Women older than him sought out the challenge that he had become, if only because he craved a particular kind of lover. And they all wanted to be chosen, to say that they had been the ones he had honed his skills on.

His reputation as intelligent and brooding made him irresistible to everyone but the one girl he wanted. And she was too intimidated by the rumors of his conquests, if not his preferences.

Aiden didn't hurry when he had a girl in his hands. He would study her in the same way he would study a piece of wood before he took his knife to it. He would kiss her lips gently, his strong hands in her hair, body firmly pressed into hers, with no mystery to his size.

He made the rules, except for the few times that he was skillfully mastered by a woman who truly understood his passions. And then he would gladly take the role of the taken. Aiden's hands would explore a woman's neck, pushing her hair aside with a sensual touch, giving way to his lips. He'd touch her back with gentle strokes, his kisses becoming more forceful, and just as they were melting into his arms, he would expose their breasts to his hungry mouth, with rarely a protest.

Eventually, Aiden grew tired of life in the town of Boulder, he craved a change from his childhood home. He ended up in a quieter corner of Colorado, on a building project that would take a year or so to complete. During that year, he had found his land, bought it, and settled into a place of great solitude. And then he had met Holly. It was Holly who made his mind reel and his body betray its' usual composure.

Aside from recognizing the gentle spirit that hid behind the sometimes gruff exterior while serving him coffee, Holly didn't give Aiden too much notice. And a good thing, as he blushed when he saw her, because even he was shocked by the things he thought of doing to her. Walking back from the edge of his property to his house, Aiden felt annoyed that there would be another woman so close to his beloved woods.

Once home, he poured himself a glass of wine and ran a bath.

The languid moments of hot water and classical music soothed his soul. His tongue savoured the smooth texture of the wine, and his thoughts immediately turned to a vision of Holly on hands and knees before him, ass spread provocatively.

He longed to pour the wine down her bottom, watch it drip into her folds, and lick up every drop. He wanted to hear her beg for his hard and throbbing cock. As on so many nights before this one, Aiden's hands were his only companion; although he could have picked up the phone and dialled any combination of numbers to reach a willing participant.

The women who had their eye on him couldn't understand why he was so difficult to nail down, and he couldn't understand why Holly never picked up on his obvious advances.

———— ✳ ————

In her small apartment above the cafe, Holly sat up in bed writing in her journal. Writing kept her centered; it revealed parts of her that remained elusive otherwise. She wrote about meeting Sahara, and how she thought the woman had a certain air of mystery. Not outwardly mysterious really, just something about her that made you feel pulled in. She made a note in the margin to order some good French olives. Thoughts of France made Holly reach into her bedside drawer, for an older journal, one with a photograph of herself and a short haired young woman standing in a market square, baskets in hand, kissing. Not an unusual scene in France, but one that brought either tears or instant passion for Holly.

Tonight she recalled memories that stirred her passion, and she wondered if she would ever know such wild abandon again as she had with Julie. That girl who could convince her to do almost anything, even fingering her on a beach crowded with tourists, with just an umbrella and a small towel for cover. Holly's face turned a deep crimson as she recalled Julie's orgasm.

Julie had asked for Holly's fingers in her mouth. Holly had noticed then that lying next to them on the beach and watching shamelessly, was a man with a glass of wine in his hand. He had held up the glass to them, smiled and asked, "Some wine perhaps?" But that was Europe.

There was no point in hiding from her feelings of desire now. Holly opened her bedside drawer again and took out her collection of erotic photographs. The ache for another woman was never too far away, and these plus her magic bullet brought some relief. She shuffled through the images, and took out her favorites.

Her preference was for athletic, petite females. Small breasted brunettes, who when spread open, displayed a tight, sleek pussy. Holly thought back to the woman she had met tonight; exactly her type. She licked her fingers and ran them around her nipples, until they stood tight. She spread her legs, noticing how wet she had become looking at the photographs, and imagining Sahara's perky breasts revealed.

God, she craved the taste of a woman desperately! She licked her lips, and turned on the vibrator. Running it gently around her slick opening, she teased herself until she ached for release. Holly pulled another toy from the drawer, and wetting it with her mouth, inserted it inside her swollen, aching sex. She felt so open, so un-grounded.

The smooth toy deep inside her, Holly ran the bullet over her clit; eyes locked on a picture of a delicious woman, every bit of her exposed, and came with soft moans.

Snuggled down, dreamy and aroused still, Holly wondered what Sahara would think of her only neighbor, Aiden. Surely, a friendship would blossom? Even Holly, generally not attuned to the thoughts of men, knew that Aiden, much gossiped about in town, would appreciate the newcomer.

Who wouldn't? Sahara was unusually appealing. It must be in the way she carries herself, Holly decided, and brushed away a nagging question about Aiden's availability.

He just never seemed to date anyone, though not for a lack of offers.

Morning came as a surprise. Sahara opened her eyes and stared at the ceiling. Very slowly, her sleepy mind opened to the realization of where she was. Her heart pounded, and for one moment she contemplated the idea that she might hate the place, and that the crazy act of purchasing property from an ad would somehow sour in her heart. She felt an ache in her chest which twisted into a knot of anxiety. She hid her head under the covers and felt a rush of terror run through her.

I must breathe, she thought, panicked.

Sahara stayed under the covers but positioned herself into child's pose, her favourite yoga move, stretching and breathing, her heart and mind gradually relaxing. Sahara peered out from under the safety of the covers and a smile slowly crept to her lips. The cabin was clean and bathed in the promising light of the rising sun.

The fire was out but the massive logs still radiated warmth. Through the French doors, she could see the stretch of rolling landscape undulate its way to the foot of the mountain range. Fresh tears came quickly. Gratitude spilled its way out onto the covers. She knew she was home.

Willow scratched at the door and Sahara got up to let him out.

Outside, in her rubber boots, Sahara took in the lay of the land. To her left, beyond a small clearing, a wood, mainly evergreens and birches. Good place to gather mushrooms and kindling, she decided.

To the front, a mix of open and wood, ending in a horizon of foothills, and the stream she had noticed last night, winding its way from their bosom.

Beyond the side door, another stretch of native grass, dotted with trees, and rocks. It seemed that there was a sort of footpath winding its way towards the aspen wood beyond.

Hmmm...I wonder where that goes.

She looked with longing towards the aspens. Their magical waving leaves beckoned something very deep within her, but this was not the time for exploring. She rounded the corner to the back porch. What she saw pleased her. Here the setting sun would make its' way behind the mountains as it cradled the last of the fading light. Perhaps here, Sahara thought, she would find the peace that she longed for, where her journal would receive the best and the worst of her.

It was a great place for an outdoor dining room as well.

"But with whom, Sahara, will you share a meal?" she queried out loud.

She had made her choices. She had asked for solitude. She had longed for freedom from relationships and a heart broken by bad decisions. So why should she suddenly be saddened by the prospect of days spent alone? Yet, sad she was. Everything has its' price, and the price of her scars seemed to be eating alone.

Sahara made coffee in the French press and grabbed a croissant.

With renewed curiosity, Sahara climbed the stairs to the cozy loft. Big enough for a large bed, a desk and dressers, it overlooked the cabin's great room. She threw open the windows, one of which faced the mountains, and the other, the aspen wood.

Her mind pictured the white lace curtains she would purchase, writing at her desk overlooking the mountains, and the pillows and duvets that she would snuggle under while a snow storm raged outside.

CHAPTER 3

Aiden woke up feeling restless. He was not in a good mood. Last night's fantasies had left him less than satisfied. The prospect of meeting the woman who had bought Jack's place made him pace the floor as he waited for his coffee. He pictured a middle aged woman. Was that what Jack had said?

A sort of hardened, mannish type, who thrived on surviving in a man's world. She would drive a pick-up truck, shake hands very firmly, and would assure him that she was capable of taking care of herself. With this picture in his head, Aiden grabbed his mug of coffee, and strode off through the woods to the neighbouring farm.

The walk through the aspens was one thing that Aiden never tired of. He knew every corner, every path. He thought of it as his kingdom, his to protect and value. The trees opened up to the clearing, and Aiden could smell smoke coming from the cabin chimney. It was a comforting scent, and his shoulders relaxed a little.

Yes, he had been right; there *was* a pick-up truck in the driveway. Maybe it wouldn't be so bad after all. He would try to be friendly. He almost smiled, picturing the odd woman puttering about in her kitchen.

Aiden knocked on the open front door. He smelled incense, good incense, not the kind from the dollar store. No-one answered. He knocked again, calling out.

"Hello! It's Aiden!"

Sahara, with her head in the drum of the washer looking for evidence of rodents, thought she heard someone calling.

"Hello?" she called into the washer, then laughed to herself.

Straightening her short hair, she walked out into the yard, coming up behind Aiden standing on the front porch. He turned suddenly as he felt her presence behind him. They both stood still for a long moment, appraising each other with surprise.

Aiden's mind turned quickly from the image he had thought up to the woman who stood in front of him. Slim and well- muscled, Sahara stood just short of five foot four. Her green, cat like eyes, open wide with curiosity, wore a shadow of mystery that threw his equilibrium. Her hair, short and dark, in a pixie style, suited her to perfection. She was not odd looking, was not manly, and when she smiled at Aiden, he was charmed.

Sahara was equally shocked. This was no old man! This man was tall and well built, had long hair and hands that swallowed hers as they shook in greeting. His face was friendly and his energy was vibrant.

"Err...I'm sorry if I'm staring, I imagined someone older and grumpier". Sahara felt her blood turn hot.

Aiden burst out laughing, head thrown back, his hand in his hair. "Oh, well, I won't even *dare* to tell you what I'd imagined!"

Sahara stood rooted to the ground. His laughter had run through her like an electric shock.

"In any case," she recovered, "I'm Sahara."

"Sahara." He said her name slowly, letting it roll on his tongue.

"Have you met Holly?" he continued. "She told me that she had your keys. You'll like her..."

"I'm not looking for friends," Sahara blurted out. Aiden looked surprised but he checked himself quickly.

"*He's in almost complete control of himself,*" she observed. Still, the unruly side of him had not escaped her notice.

"*She's wounded,*" Aiden thought, interest piqued. "*Strong, but wounded. Hmmm.*"

"You said, 'hmmm'."

"Oh, did I?"

"Yes. Well, I didn't mean to be rude, about being friends with Holly I mean, I'm just looking for some solitude."

"You've come to the right place. I'm your only neighbour for miles, and I'm a bit of a hermit myself."

"I won't be bothering you, so no need to worry. Can you recommend a good carpenter though? And a plumber. I need a new bathroom, and bookshelves. Do you think I'll have any luck finding someone to start right away?"

Aiden contemplated her quietly. *She's sure of what she wants.* He liked that in a woman.

"I can do those jobs for you, if you like. I'm a builder by trade. You've caught me with a rare holiday week."

"You can? Oh," Her voice trailed off as she got lost in a thought, her lips playing with a smile. Aiden was instantly aroused by her openly sensual manner.

She pointed in the direction of a long line of unsightly electrical poles weaving their way to the cabin. "I should have those wires buried. I hate the sight of those poles."

"I know what you mean, I had mine sunk also. The utility company can run a ditch for you; it's not that big a deal. But it will cost you."

They stood on the porch, exchanging ideas. It was easy, and it seemed that they enjoyed life from the same perspective. She asked if there was wild food to forage, he offered tips on winter survival. He knew someone who was selling a snowmobile, for the inevitable weeks that she'd be snowed in. She could park her car at the end of road where the county came by to clear. She asked about purchasing a plow for the pick-up.

They made plans for Aiden to come by in the morning to begin work on the bathroom, and she asked him to make a list of the supplies he'd need.

Aiden's sharp eyes noticed that she stretched every now and then like a cat. She was very lithe, almost fluid in her motions. Her hands were small, her smile was honest. He sensed that there was something about her that seemed otherworldly, although he wasn't sure what the thought even meant.

Sahara noticed his strength and how tall he stood beside her. He was well spoken. She wondered what he read. His long hair and the way his hands ran through it made her nipples hard. Damn!

"I need more coffee. Would you like some? It won't take long to brew."

Aiden declined; he had to run into town. He would take a quick look at her bathroom and pick up the supplies he needed at the hardware store today.

They walked into the cabin, Aiden remarking what a great job Jack had done of cleaning it before he left.

"Yes, there's a bit of painting to do in the kitchen and the floors need polish, but that's about it. Once the bathroom is in, I'll be all set for the furniture delivery."

"I guess you'll want a new shower installed here?" He pointed to the corner of the room.

"No! No shower!" She realized how vehemently she had spoken. "I'm looking for a claw foot tub, as big as you can find."

"A big bath is one of my allowances for luxury in this life," she explained, catching Aiden's puzzled look.

"I won't argue with you. My own tub is a bit of a behemoth."

With this, he said his goodbyes and strode back to his side of the woods. She watched him walk home until she couldn't see him anymore. His back was broad, his hips slim, she noticed. She felt almost sorry that she had met him, but not that either, just...unsettled. She replayed their meeting in her mind.

When Aiden got to town later, he sourced a tub at the hardware store, picked up some wine and stopped in at the café.

He sat at his usual table by the window. Holly smiled up at him and he nodded. She'd know what he wanted. It was always the same at this time of day; coffee, extra strong and black, an almond croissant and the paper from Denver.

His eyes were warm and smiling when she arrived to serve him; he had that way of appearing both confident yet vulnerable. It was irresistible to most women. Aiden caught a fleeting look in Holly's eyes that intrigued him.

"Hello Holly. All good?"

"Yes," she replied. "I'm ordering some new things for the café, olives from France, cheese...have you met your new neighbor yet? Sahara." Holly's voice caught on Sahara's name.

"I was there this morning, in fact; she's asked me to do some renovation work for her." Aiden considered his next question for a mere second. There was no reason not to ask.

"Would you like to come over with me one time, for a visit? I'm sure she'd love to see you, and your croissants," Aiden laughed, his eyes locked on her face. It broke his heart just looking at her.

"Oh, that sounds good, Aiden, but I don't know when."

And Aiden knew that she was giving him the brush off. Honestly, he had never had to ask anyone more than once. He watched her run around serving her customers, flashing that exuberant smile, looking pensive as she made more coffee.

Once in a while she would glance his way, and ask if he needed anything. He wished he could say what he wanted: "Your lips on mine, your mouth on my cock, you in my bath, you sitting by my fire sipping wine, reading together in the hammock on the porch...you name it woman, I'm yours."

Perhaps Holly thought him too old for her? But even he knew that his looks rivalled those of men much younger than himself, so it couldn't be that? He stood to pay, waiting his turn at the till. Holly's hand brushed his. His face turned hard to hide his reaction.

"Meet me at market this Saturday?" she asked, innocent to the fact that he waited impatiently each week for their friendly ramblings through the farmer's stalls.

"Of course. Wouldn't miss it. I also have a new book to share with you." Aiden wanted to kiss the pout off Holly's lips as she said "Ooooh!" He left before he made a fool of himself.

Sahara unloaded the rest of the truck. Kitchen things first, then the small box of books that had made the trip with her. Now and then she looked towards the aspens, longing to explore their world, but knew that today was a day for setting up and performing ceremonies. Tonight she would look towards the heavens and call upon her spirit guides.

Here she would invoke magic in a way that had been impossible to do where she had come from. No one from her old world knew where she was. She had covered her tracks well, and was wary of making new mistakes that could cost her much needed privacy. But what about Aiden?

What about him? He lived a distance away, and had said himself that he was a hermit. Perhaps she could get it across in some way that he should call first if he were to drop over?

The cabin was now ready for the cleansing ceremony. Sahara, dressed in a plain, long, black dress, picked up her smudging stick and made the motions to cleanse her aura before she began clearing the rooms. She called upon her spirit guides and her teachers from other lifetimes. She sang under her breath in an old tongue, uttering primal sounds and stirring up the ancient spirit of the land.

Ceremonial broom in hand, she walked a circle around the cabin, creating sacred space. She walked each room and chased away old arguments and stuck energies. The cabin welcomed the scent of the sage and the light of the candles. It had been a long time since love had entered here.

By the time Sahara was done, the light in the cabin had softened. It was late afternoon. She had put on her old skin again, the one of the solitary witch, forest dweller, spirit communicator. She would leave more serious work for another day, tonight she would celebrate life!

Sahara walked to the woods beside the cabin looking for fallen wood. Her hand automatically went to the pouch she wore around her neck. She felt the stones chosen for protection and wisdom. Entering the wood would mean greeting all the spirits that dwelled there and she wanted to be prepared. She motioned a greeting in sign language to the trees.

As evening encroached, Sahara found her way to the fire. She sat on a log and watched the flames dance before her. Looking towards the cabin she noticed the calm light from within, the cabin resting in its new found energy. There wasn't a light visible from the direction of the aspens and Aiden's home. She felt confident that he couldn't see her, and took another sip of wine, her eyes now tired and heavy. But before she could sleep, she would dance to her new life. She looked to the sky and called to the stars. She howled at the moon and sang a song she had learned from a witch who had initiated her into the wise woman tradition.

At another fire, months past, Sahara had learned that a man she loved was about to leave her. He spoke of why he was leaving, but she hadn't wanted to hear, and had begged him to make love to her. And he had, roughly, with passion fuelled by rage at her denial of what was happening to them.

Sahara had let him tie her hands, and didn't object to a vigorous spanking which he later made better by kissing every inch of her, his tongue eliciting screams of erotic joy from her lips. He held her down and fucked her from behind as she came over and over, thinking that after this he would stay. She offered him all of herself, and he took everything, wishing that she would hurt as he had, when he had found her with a lover in their bed.

He didn't care that it was a woman. Trust broken was trust broken. Her apologies were of no avail. She had wept because she wanted them both. She wept because no one had made her come like he had and because he had told all the wrong people about her affair.

Sahara understood only love and abandon. Rules confused her.

⸺ ✳ ⸺

At home, Aiden gathered his tools for the next day, made a fire and started supper. There were things to do outside, but today he was in the mood for a good book, and he had many to choose from.

He loved this solitude. The ability to just be with oneself, satisfied with one's own company, was a real gift. In many ways, Aiden was happy with the way his life was unfolding. His business afforded him the luxury of being his own man.

His eyes rested on the fire, and he wondered about his new neighbour. He was not as displeased with her being there as he had anticipated.

He stood up and stretched, took another sip of wine, and opened his front door. The sky was lit up with stars. He took a few steps towards Sahara's and had a fleeting thought of bringing her a bottle of wine as a housewarming. But then again, she probably wouldn't appreciate an impromptu visit. He would bring it in the morning.

Somehow his feet took him a bit further down the path, the night air welcoming. He decided to walk to the edge of the wood. Standing

18

at the clearing, Aiden saw that his new neighbour had lit a great fire, and he heard something like howling, but couldn't be sure.

Good God! That fire is huge! I wonder if she understands about grass fires, or has built any kind of a pit. This is ridiculous. I'm going over.

He walked quickly, thinking about how he would apologize for intruding.

As Aiden made his way closer to Sahara's cabin, he realized that he was right about what he'd thought he'd heard. It *was* howling. And it was Sahara howling! Ok, so she was not going to be a boring neighbour. He smiled to himself; then stopped dead in his tracks.

Sahara danced like a woman on fire, banging on a drum wearing nothing but her jewellery which flashed each time it caught the light of the flames. Her naked body snaked its way around the perimeter of the circle, her breasts high and round, her tiny frame perfectly proportioned, having the seductive quality of a woman who knew herself well.

Aiden stood perfectly still, in awe and in unabashed desire. He didn't make a sound, and wondered why he felt like his head was about to split open. He had a sudden déjà vu moment, sure that he had stood in this spot before, watching the magical creature before him. He turned suddenly, and made his way stealthily back to his home.

There he drank some water and washed his face. In all of his wildest imaginings, he could not have come up with the scenario he had just witnessed. He paced back and forth, agitated. Several weeks of dealing with his own desires finally brought Aiden to the realization that he needed to make a phone call. He picked up the phone and dialed.

"Hello?"

"Dianne. Hi, is this a good time?"

"Yes, perfect."

"I'll see you in an hour." Aiden headed for the shower and some clean clothes.

CHAPTER 4

Dianne stood in her kitchen, her heart beating wildly. It was always a perfect time when Aiden called.

She was under no illusions as to why he was coming over. He wasn't interested in a relationship; she knew that he had his eye on someone else, and that she was where he released his passion. But he was a consummate lover, his manners were impeccable and she needed what he offered. Diane opened a bottle of wine.

The knock on the door came sooner than she had expected. Diane was still damp from the shower, her body eagerly anticipating her lovers touch.

"*Aiden.*"

He pulled her to him, kicking the door shut with force. She could feel that he was as ready for her as she was for him. His hands reached down to the bottom of her dress, and running his hands up along her body, he ripped it up over her head, pleased to see her naked underneath. She buckled a little at the knees but he held her tight against him, growling as she ran her hands over his bulging jeans.

"Aiden, I'm..."

"No! Don't speak." He kissed her on her sultry lips then buried his face in her hair, seeking out her ear and neck.

"Aiden, please don't tease me. Just fuck me."

"Take down your hair, Dianne."

"You take yours down."

Aiden loosened his hair, watching as Dianne's raven curls fell down around her full breasts. It stirred something of a distant memory that he couldn't quite place his finger on.

"And your shirt..." Dianne breathed, eyes sweeping down to his tight belly as he obeyed and slid his shirt off. She licked her lips, staring hungrily as his biceps tightened and his back widened at his armpits with his arms lifted. He grinned at her as he threw the shirt to the ground, so very aware of her appreciation of him. His hand went to his erection, adjusting it, a deliberately sensual move that he knew she'd enjoy. Dianne made a little whimper and fell to her knees.

Aiden was not shy about talking his way through sex. His hand reached for her hair.

"I love seeing you on your knees Dianne, are you offering me that pretty mouth of yours?"

He moved his hips closer, and his cock, still straining in his jeans, brushed against the soft of her cheek. She opened her mouth; her head tilted back, eyes pleading, and stuck out her tongue in a long, teasing, curve, a low moan escaping her throat.

"Good girl," Aiden said softly, imagining himself spilling onto it, running one finger tenderly along her jaw. She was so good at playing dirty, and at forty-five, her body still held onto its youthful blush, accented by a sinful dose of confidence.

They had worked out their terms long ago, when she had first hired him to build her house. She wanted him to fuck hard and leave before morning. That suited Aiden fine; Dianne was beautiful and skilled in bed and he hadn't wanted any sort of long term love affair. He had discovered that she was willing to try almost anything, and she was sure that he'd be the only lover who left her hand written notes with bits of naughty words to spur on her passion until the next time. And neither of them kissed and told.

She undid his belt and his jeans, and his hard cock sprang out. She was as impressed now as she had been the first time. There was no denying that it was large, but it was more than that, it was beautiful and tasted great. Aiden was a well-groomed man.

She gratefully accepted his invitation to suck it, lick it and devour it in its entirety. Aiden stood before her and groaned as she licked him from his tight balls to the tip of his cock, then easily swallowed his length. He gripped her hair but held back from pushing her head down. She was quite good at taking all of him, her hands working in perfect unison with her mouth.

"Stand up, Dianne." He wasn't taking no for an answer and pulled her up by her elbows as she struggled to take leave of him.

She stood and he kissed her with a seductively patient tongue, his hands rough as they moved to her breasts. He tugged hard on her dark nipples, now perking tight in his fingers.

"What I need, Dianne, is to feel your silky cunt on my fingers." And with that he slapped hard at her ass until she spread her legs wider, to make room for his hand as he slid it towards her heat, one long slow caress along her thigh before he plunged his fingers into her, chest rumbling with a pleased growl.

"Mmm, yes, that's what I wanted...you're so nice and snug, Dianne." He gave her a taste of his fingers. She felt like melting onto the floor, his presence so intense and demanding, it threatened to knock her out.

"Aiden, please." Diane was an expert submissive, it was her favorite role.

"Say please again, whore," he suggested quietly into her ear. The whisper somehow took the sting out of that word. His fingers pumped, his hand wet with her readiness, his other arm holding tight around her waist.

"Please Aiden. Please fuck me."

Dianne stumbled after Aiden to her bedroom, the inside of her thighs slippery, the muscles in her legs weak, although her belly had tightened into a hard knot of anticipation. He threw her down onto the bed, his eyes sweeping over her delightfully waxed cunt.

She spread it open for him and he slid down to lick her clit in that way that he had, first softly, then pushing forcefully with his tongue, then sucking it hard, giving her the first orgasm of the night. She writhed and moaned, tried to push him away, but he was not finished teasing her. He kissed her belly, then back between her legs....his hair tickling her skin, then softly up to her nipples.

"Push your tits together... yes, like that...I love it when you obey me!"

He bit at her, each nipple swelling to his touch, she tried to cover them when it hurt, but he bit her fingers and ripped her hands away, then, sliding himself between her velvety legs, he rammed himself inside her... and held.

She opened her eyes, stared into his, and let out an agonized moan; partly because the last inch was more than she could comfortably take, and partly because he had stopped.

"Kiss me." Aiden didn't wait for her reply, but lowered to cover her mouth with his, his cock throbbing as she tightened around him. He pulled out; his lips to her neck, leaving the tip of his erection just inside her swollen sex. Dianne tried to maneuver herself back onto him, but he kept her in place with one knee and his hands in a vice like grip on her wrists.

"Damn it Aiden! Get your cock back inside me!"

He complied. She kept her eyes open because he was beautiful to look at, his muscles working with each stroke. He smiled down at her, and she up at him, his rhythmic thrusts evoking her cries of pleasure.

"I'm taking it all today, Dianne," he informed her with that fierce look he got when fully aroused. She knew what he meant.

Aiden ran his hands through his hair, stopping his assault, his cock stiff and wet with her cum as he shifted positions. She trembled, but reached into the bedside table drawer for a bottle of lube and the anal beads. His eyes turned dark, his face determined, but his hands were kind when he turned her over onto her belly, spreading her ass and drifting his fingers along the part.

She would give him what he asked for; she always did, and was never sorry that she had. She moaned, and let her legs splay a little wider, to give him better access. Their roles were like well- practiced dance moves. Dianne was allowed to beg for any kink she could imagine, but needed Aiden to lead their play.

"Such a fuckable ass," Aiden mused, rubbing his prick, hot and hard as a rock, against her bud. Dianne beat her hands against the sheets, impatient now.

"You're so willing to take my cock in your ass, Dianne. I do appreciate a naughty girl like you." She moaned into the bed and lifted up.

Aiden opened the bottle of lube and let a dribble of it snake its way down the seam of Dianne's ass, his fingers following, and his voice rough when he told her that she took it better than anyone he'd known. For some reason, his words found their way into her heart right then, and she grasped at a sliver of hope that he might want her more than he would admit. He picked up the beads, and rolled them along her clit, towards her tightly pursed anus.

He pushed at her, ever so lightly, the beads slippery in his hand, talking her into relaxing under his touch. She waited quietly, his voice drifting softly but persistent. Aiden pushed a little harder, growling under his breath. She held her breath as he slid the first bead in, his moan sending her skin into goose bumps.

"Aiden?" she asked when he stilled.

"I wish you could see this. You're beautiful Dianne; your ass is such a turn on for me."

He pushed again and slipped in another bead, then another until she had it all inside her, but one. He slid his fingers inside her cunt, his voice reached her from far away; she was rolling towards the crest of the wave. His thumb rolled her clit, rubbing her towards the edge. Then, his fingers pumping hard at her secret place, Aiden pulled the beads out, slowly, one at a time, until she was screaming her release.

He ran his cock quickly through his hand to apply some lube, and while Diane was still in the fog of her orgasm, he slid himself inside her, his muscular body heaving with desire, roaring as he filled her ass, his own pleasure spilling onto her back when he saw that she could take no more.

She sank down to the bed, and waited while he brought a hot, wet cloth to clean her with. He was always as attentive after sex as he was before, dominant turned servant at the end of their love play.

Aiden tucked his arm around Dianne and kissed her lightly. He looked down at her, smiling.

"Delicious...thank you. I needed that."

Sleepy now, Diane ran her hand down Aiden's chest to rest where his cock lay heavy upon his tightly muscled belly. She laid a slightly proprietary palm on it and they slept in a comfortable embrace.

Aiden woke up early and slid out of bed making sure that Dianne was tucked in. Her long, black hair spilled around her and he had another pang of that elusive feeling that the sight of it evoked.

He wandered to the kitchen through the house that he had built, and put the kettle on for tea, then stepped into the shower. Morning was just around the corner. He thought of Sahara and her fire dance. He hoped that his eyes would not betray him, but he knew that he was curious to know more about her. He left a quick note, and locked the door behind him, dropping Dianne's keys into the flower pot beside the garage.

CHAPTER 5

Sahara rose early, and took her coffee onto the front porch. The stone pit was blackened from last nights' fire, but she had doused it well before she had come in to sleep. She was pleased with how it had all turned out, she knew that she was firmly embedded into the lands energy, and felt that her privacy was secure in this valley.

Sounds carried far into the night, but she doubted that Aiden could have heard anything...unless he had crossed the woods? But no. She pushed her fears away.

Aiden would be here early, so she made her bed and ate her breakfast. Then she went back outside to investigate an outbuilding that would have to house her garden things. It was empty, and didn't need any repairs. She could easily fit in winter and summer tools. She had started a list of supplies that needed to be purchased. She thought that she would hit the hardware store today, while Aiden was working and maybe visit the café for some pastries.

These she could offer to Aiden with his coffee. It was alarming how comfortable the idea of Aiden sat within her soul. Although they were strangers, she felt a kinship of spirit that she had truly not anticipated. Well, that was all good news, because she could have ended up with some kind of crackpot neighbour, someone disagreeable. That would have spoiled everything she had hoped for in this move.

Imagining a narrow minded individual coming up on her during one of her ceremonial fires made her shudder. She would make sure to show Aiden her fire pit to alleviate any worries he might have about grass fires. Yes, that would prevent any frantic visits in the night.

"Sahara."

Sahara jumped. She hadn't heard Aiden walk up behind her, lost as she was in her thoughts.

"I apologize, I scared you."

"No, no. It's ok. I was lost in thought. I might get a dog," she said, and surprised herself. She had not thought one bit about getting a dog.

"That would be good. That way, you wouldn't be surprised by someone suddenly creeping up behind you."

They both laughed. Aiden looked towards the fire pit.

"Looks like you had a fire. I'm glad you built a pit. It's pretty easy to start a grass fire around here." He ran his hand through his hair and shifted his stance.

Sahara's intuition perked up. She thought she heard something in his tone. But his eyes spoke of sincerity. Still, there was something...

"Yup, I know all about that. I thought I'd have a welcome home fire for myself. Fire is such a primal activity, it can take one back centuries in time, you know?"

"I do. Fire makes sense to our ancient selves. I know exactly what you are talking about. It's safety and comfort and a guarantee of a hot meal."

Sahara's cat-like eyes narrowed. She ran through his energy field with hers. Aiden shuddered and it unnerved him, but his eyes shut down any reflection of his emotions.

"Well, we should look at the plans for the renovations." And with that statement, Sahara walked into the cabin with Aiden following in her steps, shoulders squared, eyes firmly planted on her ass. He tried to forget the scene from the fire, but a familiar ache started to grow in his jeans. He focused his brain on the work ahead.

"I don't have a closet upstairs, so I thought we could build one here, underneath this staircase."

"Good use of space. You mentioned bookcases?"

"Yes, I'll need to span that wall with a row of them." She pointed to the wall in question.

Aiden stared at her, intrigued. "Just how many books do you have?"

"Lots. Hopefully they'll all fit there...so many poets to fit into a collection." Sahara smiled.

"Ok. What about the bathroom?"

"As I mentioned yesterday, I would like a bathtub over there. The toilet can stay where it is. I mean a new one...and the sink also, but I'll need a built-in cupboard on that wall there." She pointed again. "I don't need anything fancy, you can pick them out."

"I've ordered the tub. It will take two days for the delivery." He thought for a moment. "If you need a place to bathe, you're welcome to use my tub."

"Oh, that's ok. I've been washing in the stream, sort of. I can wait a few days. But thanks."

"Suit yourself, but the offer stands if you change your mind. I can have this taken apart today and can start dry-walling tomorrow. What about the window?"

"You pick, but not vinyl. Something in wood. I'm going to town soon; should I pick up something?"

"I have all I need for today. I'll get started."

They parted company. Sahara left for town, and Aiden took a hammer to the bathroom walls. He worked quickly, ripping out the old things and taking down walls. A pile of scrap lay in the yard. He would have to come back with his truck and trailer to haul off the debris. The room soon stood naked and exposed.

He boiled some water on the stove and found some cleaning supplies. Nothing toxic, good girl. He washed down the floors, and left the window wide open for the wind to clear the air. When Sahara got back, Aiden stood with his hair in a ponytail, shirtless and quite dusty in a room that was as clean as a workspace could be.

He smiled at her crookedly. "I guess I'm a bit of a mess, I'll put on my shirt."

Sahara laid down her supplies. "I can't believe all that ugliness is gone. Thanks Aiden. And you've washed the floor!"

"Hope you don't mind, I helped myself to the soap."

"You won't offend me Aiden. I'm a bit of a freak myself when it comes to cleaning."

He liked the way she said his name, it slipped easily off her tongue.

She watched him put his shirt on. His muscles rippled with his every move, and she could not help feeling pleased with what she saw. She did appreciate a good looking man. She wondered if he had a girl; perhaps Holly. Not that she was looking for any kind of a relationship...that wound was still raw and bleeding.

"I'll make coffee," she said suddenly. "I've been to the café. Holly sold me some almond croissants. She said you like them. I have soup that I made yesterday, with mushrooms from the forest." She smiled. "Nothing poisonous, I promise."

Sahara noticed once more, the play of Aiden's thoughts on his handsome face. He was easy to read, and she imagined it to speak of integrity, something she admired in a man. He had been about to refuse.

Aiden smiled, a flash of perfect teeth behind a sensual mouth. "I accept, with pleasure. If you don't mind though, I'll go home first and bathe."

"You can go, but first we'll have coffee and croissants. It will only take a minute."

He sat on the couch while she ground the beans and tossed them into the press.

"You could use some high stools against the counter there," he said, relaxed in her space.

"I'll have to buy some. I'm planning on a trip to Denver in a few days."

"Oh don't buy any. I can make them. I have plenty of wood at my place."

"Is it aspen wood? I would love some of the forest in here!"

She sounded so childlike and so earnest that he felt a strong urge to take her in his arms and assure her that she could have exactly what she desired. But here she was, with coffee in hand, and urging him to sit with her on the porch. He started for the front door.

"Not there, Aiden. Let's sit at the back and watch the sun settle. I haven't had a chance to do that yet."

"Good idea. You'll love the sunsets here, Sahara. They're magical."

Boom! Sahara's spirit exploded with a memory of a man sitting with her on a rocky ridge, watching the sun go down over the fields below. He held her tight and spoke of magic and ...and what? Who was that man? Why was she feeling so exhilarated and so weak at the same time?

"Are you ok? You look far away."

"Yes. I'm fine. Just thinking."

They sat in silence for a long time, sipping the coffee. There was no awkwardness. They both understood quiet and being totally alone while with someone else. Finally he stood and said that he would come back for soup. She watched him walk away. Tears welled up and she thought of the man whose heart she had broken. He had known her so well, but not well enough to accept who she was.

When Aiden came back the sky was dark, and the cabin was awash with candle light. The smell of the soup and bread baking filled the air. Sahara opened the door.

"Welcome! It's a simple meal, but it's good."

He handed her a bottle of wine and she noticed a book tucked in under his arm. She pointed to it. "Going to read me a bedtime story?"

Aiden felt extremely teased by that question. He smiled at her and handed her the book.

"No, I thought I'd read you some poetry. Do you like William Blake?"

"Yes! We have something in common."

Aiden opened the wine, while she served the soup and a plate full of Yorkshire puddings.

"Thank you, Sahara. This looks great." He lifted his glass. "To good neighbours." They drank and he added, "I really do understand your need for privacy, Sahara, you won't have to worry about my being a pest."

"I know. We should always call if we're to visit. It'll just be better that way."

Over dinner, Aiden asked her which mushrooms she had added to the soup. "Ceps," she said.

"Sooo, as promised, nothing poisonous," he joked.

"I try to keep knocking my neighbours off down to a minimum," she quipped. "This wine is fantastic. What is it?"

"It's plum wine...organic. You can have it ordered in at the liquor store. Holly likes it too, we usually share a case."

"You like Holly."

"What?" Aiden looked flustered.

"It's nothing you've said. I can tell. It's a curse."

"A curse that I like her or that you're psychic?"

Sahara's eyes narrowed again. "So you *do* like her!"

The wine had relaxed them both, and Aiden saw no harm in being honest.

"I'm clearly too old for her, and she doesn't fancy me in the least, but yes, I do like her. She's sweet... and pretty."

"Oh, you're being very nonchalant. She's not that young, maybe 26 or so? And besides, you think she is a lot more than easy to look at."

"Ok, enough of the mind reading. Let's read a book instead."

Aiden picked up the book of poems, and began to read. He fit into the couch like a lion sprawled comfortably in the long grass. His arms bulged in his well-cut shirt, his jeans accentuating his strong thighs, feet bare, hair hanging loose at his shoulders. His voice was deep and as one accustomed to reading aloud;

"Once a dream did weave a shade
O'er my Angel guarded bed,
That an Emmet lost its way
Where on grass me thought I lay.

Troubled, wilder'd, and forlorn,

Over many a tangled spray,
All heart-broke I heard her say…"

He lost himself in the poem by William Blake, and would have forgotten that she was there but was alerted by the tiniest of whimpers.

He looked up to see tears flowing down her face. "My dear, I'm sorry, I've made you sad." Aiden moved towards Sahara instinctively. His hand stretched out to take hers and she offered it without hesitation, the rest of her desiring to follow. His first thought was how he loved the way her hand fit into his. Comfortably. He was struck by how vulnerable it looked within his grasp, but not because she was weak, more because his hand spoke of steel.

Sahara's fingers warmed to his touch. Her eyes swept up towards his, and locked. He felt the sudden surge of energy that leapt from her unfathomable stare directly in his loins.

"No, Aiden," she murmured, her hand and voice now searing him to distraction. "It's not you, it's the words. Words make me cry."

Aiden's heart stirred as she purred her explanation. "I love words too," he replied. "I know how you feel."

He wanted to kiss her teary eyes, but the thought seemed out of place. Still, he couldn't deny the growing hardness of his cock and how much he wanted to pull her into his lap. Aiden set the book of poetry down to hide his desire.

"I should go," he offered. "I'll come by in the morning with my truck and trailer."

He left into the night, walking quickly. Sahara tidied up and blew out the candles. She didn't think that she had imagined it; his energy had risen with her touch. It made her curious and feel deliciously naughty. She fell asleep and dreamt of a rocky plain and a man leading a horse with a deer strapped to its back. Sahara frowned in her sleep. She could almost touch him, his essence so familiar that she woke, searching for him in the dark of the room. But as always, he had slipped away with her dream.

The next day, Aiden found a note stuck to Sahara's door.

"Aiden, I've gone to Denver, shopping. Will be back in two days. There's coffee in the cupboard. Do your thing." She also left her cell number.

He went inside, surprised by the sudden pang of disappointment that came with reading the note. When he'd woken that morning, his first thought was that he'd see Sahara, and he had smiled at the instant rise of his cock. The cabin had a very comforting smell, beeswax candles and incense; and already the scent of a woman. He unloaded his truck of supplies and began his work. Aiden had time to contemplate his new neighbour, her tastes and what life in this cabin would be like for her. He wondered what she did for work. She had certainly not divulged much the night before, but there was time for all that.

Thoughts of solitude brought him to thoughts of Holly. She certainly was one for keeping to herself. He had meant to ask her about her family, but the timing never seemed quite right. He was always struck by her air of complete authenticity. And although she was obviously well read and ran her café with efficiency and attention to detail, it was her naiveté that made him truly weak for her.

He imagined that she was not yet jaded, or prone to some women's tendency towards game playing. She seemed to him tender, but not lacking in spirit and he longed to find the woman hiding behind it all.

More specifically, he was attracted to her supple breasts, the way she smiled when she had made a joke and found it particularly clever, and always the way her bottom rounded into fullness as she bent to serve a table in front of him. Aiden wanted badly to explore her body and mind. He longed for an uncomplicated yet accomplished woman; one that he could adore and care for but who would understand his need for space.

Holly stirred his passion at every level. He had slept with plenty of women that had tutored him in the art of pleasure. But Aiden wanted to be the teacher when it came to Holly. He could almost taste her, her youth a delightful adventure in his minds' eye.

The afternoon saw Aiden trim out the bathroom storage cupboard, and installing the sink. The tub would be delivered tomorrow, and the third day should have the project finished for Sahara to paint, and have her inaugural bath. She would be back by then.

He was maddened by his attraction to her. How was a man ever to decide on one woman? Would he always crave the variety he had been accustomed to? The day grew late and Aiden drove home to a hot bath and an invitation to dinner from a prospective client. He drove back out into the night. He'd keep it short if possible. He had an idea for Sahara's bathroom that would require an extra early start the next day.

CHAPTER 6

Sahara had made the decision to drive out to Denver quite suddenly. She had planned on it anyway, but her evening with Aiden had left her hot and full of questions. Of course she had thought about the fact that she didn't intend to be alone forever. She had no intention of living life without a lover. It was just that in her imagination, her lover would not live anywhere near her.

He or she would be a sometime visitor, needing neither a commitment nor any promise of one. He would certainly not live next door. But her passion had been awoken much sooner than anticipated, and Aiden's sexual energy had her thinking naughty thoughts that simply would not go away. Shit! He was supposed to have been old and gnarly, not long haired and bound with muscle and charm.

Aiden's comfort with himself was very intoxicating. He read, his arms were strong and what she had glimpsed growing in his jeans had piqued her immediate interest. She left the house early and drove straight to the city. She had a lot to accomplish, but first she would book her stay for the night. She looked forward to a hot bath and reading in bed with room service at her beck and call. She had a list, of course, of what needed purchasing. She was always organized, always excited about the challenge of putting ideas together, especially when it involved a new apartment or home.

She would splurge on some new bath towels, candle sconces, and handmade creams from an herbalist uptown. Living in the middle of nowhere didn't mean she couldn't enjoy a few luxuries. Of course the trip wouldn't be complete without browsing the independent book stores or ethnic markets for spices and rarer ingredients.

The drive was long but beautiful. She breathed in the beauty of the Rockies, the sight of mountain goats grazing on their slopes despite the close proximity of the highway. This was God's country, and she knew it. Colorado had been a childhood dream. She had made it a reality in early adulthood. The mountains were her refuge.

She checked into her room and ran a quick shower. Her phone beeped while she was in the bathroom, and her heart skipped a little as she wondered if it was Aiden.

She read the text message: *Sahara, you can run but you can't hide. Call me, I mean it.*

It was Kathryn, her agent. Sahara had ignored her last four attempts to make contact.

The last text had said: *You have a contract. Stop ignoring me.*

It was time to face the music, she knew. She stared at the phone in her hand and sighed. She sent a message: "Can you meet tonight for dinner? My treat."

"Of course it's your treat." Kathryn messaged back. "You owe me. Good to know you're alive."

Sahara replied: "Meet me at the Moroccan Caravan at 7."

She spent the day in happy oblivion, forgetting everything that made her tense, browsing stores and making her purchases, feeling a great joy at having the resources to buy whatever she wanted. As evening approached though, she felt an old familiar ache in her heart, and wondered about her dinner plans.

"Kathryn, you look amazing as always." Sahara extended her arms and hugged her long-time friend as they met in the vestibule of the restaurant.

"Well, so do you for a person who's been missing for several months. Where the hell have you been?"

Sahara sighed. "I've been, you know..."

"No, I don't know. For heaven's sake, I've been worried sick about you. Your friends have no idea where you've moved to, that asshole you left said he didn't care, and you didn't answer any of my calls. Really, Sahara, you are maddening." But Kathryn smiled to soften her words.

"Kurt was not an asshole, I'm the one who hurt him, remember? I still love him..."

"No, you don't, you love the idea that you'd made up in your head about him, but he could never be what you wanted. I'm not mad at him for not being something he wasn't. I'm angry because he's so insecure that he had to trash your name all over town." Kathryn took a quick gulp of her wine, seated opposite Sahara and pretending that she wasn't on pins and needles to know the details of Sahara's move.

"Aren't you drinking?" Kathryn asked.

"Yes, I will, give me a minute to decide on what I want. God, you're as annoying as ever." Sahara rolled her eyes then squeezed Kathryn's hand. She ordered a glass of red wine.

"I'm so sorry I worried you. I just needed to be lost. I'm still lost."

"You working on anything right now?" Kathryn asked, staring at her drink.

Sahara glared at her, green eyes flashing.

"Working on something? Yes. I'm working on my anger, on my

feelings of abandonment, on all the baggage I'm still carting around from the mess I have made of my life." Sahara's shoulders squared.

"You've not made a mess of your life! You've loved and you've lost. That's it. Your secrets were spilled out onto the gossip page… it's not the end of the world. Surely there is some fodder there for a book; is there not? I don't mean to sound rude, but you are the one who has always prided herself on surviving. So survive!"

"Listen, I'm not writing from my pain anymore. I'm not giving you my shredded ego, or my attempt to heal myself through my work. You will wait until I feel that I have something worthwhile to share, and there will be nothing before that." Sahara's words hissed out.

They sat in silence for a moment. Finally, Kathryn held out her hands.

"I'm sorry. I'm frustrated. You left without a word, everyone was worried. I'm getting pressured from all sides about your next book. You're never going to meet deadline now. Can you tell me where you're living at least?"

"Not yet. I will, but right now I just need to hide. Please understand. I just can't write anything anyone will want to read in this frame of mind. If I try, it will be all self-indulgent drivel. As soon as I feel settled I'll have you out to my new place, and we'll have a great dinner. Just know that I'm alright. I'll be ok. I promise."

"Are you going to finish that wine?" Kathryn asked.

"No, you can have it. I'm so tired. Let's eat so I can go to bed."

Kathryn finished Sahara's wine as she had finished countless drinks for her before this. "You ever going to learn to drink properly?" Kathryn asked. Sahara just laughed.

***

Far away from each other the next day, Aiden and Sahara went to work at their respective projects at hand. She drove to the fringy part of town, where artists liked to spend their time lounging in coffee shops, resurrecting their fantasies of books written or paintings painted, or just meeting with friends to discuss their latest pet peeves. This area felt worn and familiar. Warehouses and dilapidated buildings had been converted to new life, the streets a bit narrower, the contents of the stores edgier, tattoo parlours, fair-trade offerings, music stores and plenty of vegetarian restaurants.

Sahara was headed to the magic supply store. She needed some special candles, some dragon's blood, more incense, and a few books that she had on order. A bell rang as she walked into the store. It smelled nice, comforting...to a witch.

She hoped that the girl who had served her last time wouldn't be there. She had annoyed the shit out of Sahara, rambling on about her new age philosophies, but not as one who lived them, as one who knew the lingo but couldn't be further from the walk. Her energy had been all wrong for a store that catered to the serious magic worker. Sahara wondered why she had been hired in the first place. Her mouth turned down in distaste of the memory.

"Well hello." A voice spoke from behind a bookcase.

"Hi." Sahara looked towards the dulcet tone.

"I have your books." A woman with flaming red hair stepped out into the light. She smiled. She was comfortable in her own skin.

Sahara peered around the perimeter of the room.

"Don't worry, she doesn't work here anymore. She was a desperate measure at a desperate time."

"Oh. Thank Goddess. She was frightful."

"I know. Sorry. I have your books behind the counter."

"Thanks. I'm really looking forward to reading them. I need a few other things; I'm going to look around, K?"

It was not a question really, more an acknowledgment of their comfort with each other. It spilled over from another lifetime, a powerfully turbulent relationship, but they had yet to explore what that fully meant. Still, there was a great degree of trust and comfort, of understanding. Sahara wandered around the store, picking up stones, testing their power, necklaces for protection and for holding magic, cards for reading, candles for specific spells; she could have stayed there for hours. Finally, a familiar tug at her heart centre gave her the signal that it was time to move on.

"Iona, I'm ready. I think I have everything I need. Do you have the new catalog yet?"

"I do." Iona smiled a deep smile.

She felt like the dark woods to Sahara, the place where witches lived in secret to escape persecution, where magic was a part of the scenery.

"Sahara, do you have time for a reading?"

"To give; or to have?"

"To have."

"Umm. Yeah. I think so. Do I need one?"

"I'm sure of it, your energy is quite scattered."

"Oh, well, that's my norm. But sure, I would love that."

Iona flipped the sign on the door and locked it. Her hands felt the familiar tingle of energies and heat that awoke when she was about to read. She furrowed her brow. Something in the room felt off.

"Sahara, you've brought someone with you...are you aware?

Well, not in the conscious, I really had no idea."

They sat at a small table, their hands outstretched to hold each other's, palms barely touching, but electricity flashed between them, an energy so strong that they shifted in their seats to gather equilibrium. A candle burned on the table, they both looked into the flame and breathed three deep breaths in unison. When they looked up again their eyes burned bright as well.

Smiling, they sat in a silence that spanned centuries. Their breathing was deep and rhythmic, loving and sensual, devoid of questions or answers.

"Iona." The name slipped off Sahara's tongue, it was a new name for her teacher, a name for this lifetime only.

"You have found a new place to live, my friend. Is this a place that you hope to find peace?"

"Yes," Sahara answered simply.

"Peace is not of a place. But you already know this."

"I do, and yet I hope to find it there."

"You have brought too much of your old lover to this place, so how do you plan to find this peace?"

"I'm letting him go, bit by bit, but he is a scar on my ego, and I have to do work to release him."

"Make this work a priority, Sahara, this new place is a powerful vortex; it has no room for ego or broken hearts. You like the way this pain feels, and would like to keep it alive. You're proud of the wound, and it will keep you from experiencing a new layer of freedom. Why do you hang on?"

"His memory makes me feel alive, I love the pain and the ecstasy, and it's a punishment I seem to enjoy."

Iona laughed a deep laugh and Sahara felt herself weaken. Her whole body shook with desire, and she stared into Iona's eyes.

"*Oh my faithful student,*" Iona said telepathically. "*I will punish you, and have waited a long time to do so, but today we will sit and listen to the voices. We have been apart for so long, I wish to feel your energy in mine, to hear the wisdom of the elements, let us begin!*"

Without any movement from where they sat, Sahara and Iona merged their energy fields and consulted the elders that had taught them so long ago. They stood in a forest so dark that even in the day-time, one needed a torch to keep from losing one's way. Beings emerged from the trees and linked in a sacred circle around them. Slowly, slowly, they opened their ears to the words of the ancients, soaking in the powerful essence of the Between.

How wonderful it felt to be together again, almost as if centuries had not rolled by, wars and kingdoms had not been fought for and won, lovers found and lovers spent, lessons learned and magic woven. This was the start of an initiation to their life's work together in the present. There was more work to be done, but today was purely for remembering and re-uniting.

A shadow pulled out of the tree line, at once dominant and proud but somehow tender and yielding. Iona recognized him at once. Sahara felt instantly curious, but knew she was not ready for the encounter and veiled her third eye. Intuition checked, she waited to see if her teacher instructed her to stay open. Iona, however, had grown silent in her heart space, and the time for exploring had passed.

When their eyes opened, they both knew that the time would come for them to talk about a new relationship in this dimension. Right now, they parted with Iona committing to sending Sahara the items on order, and a kiss that tasted like tenderness but promised a night of wicked pleasure. Weak with lust, Sahara decided in the last minute to ask for tea and something to eat.

"Of course," Iona purred. "Your favourite?" She opened a jar of herbs and put the kettle on to boil.

⚬━━◦❂◦━━⚬

The truck rolled down the last hill towards the driveway as if entirely possessed. Sahara sat behind the wheel completely lost in thought and with a great desire to get home, her eyes scanning the landscape. Her eyes finally found what she was looking for, the outline of the home-stead, set firmly against the mountains.

She knew that the 'Others' had arrived now. There was not time to wonder if she had made the right choices, found the right place, this was it. It was enchanted, initiated to magic. Iona had reminded her as they embraced in the last minutes, that there was no going back, if she had wanted the simple life, she should not have sought her out. But of course, both of them had pledged for this lifetime, and now it was time to go home and live the life she was born to. It would take weeks and months to discover the elementals and beings assigned to her, they would come in their own time, from the shadows, from the trees, from the hills.

Willow met her at the door, making loud exclamations about her absence.

"Sorry, Willow, you know I always come back."

The cat just screamed louder and finally ran to his dish, waiting for the inevitable treat.

She went immediately to see how much work was left on the bathroom. The cabin smelled of new wood, sawdust, and the telltale sign of incense burned. She smiled. That scent always made her smile.

Sahara swung the bathroom door open and gasped in surprise. It was finished, all of it, from top to bottom, the bathtub and all! Aiden had done so much more than she had expected. Indeed, the tub was magnificent, a claw footed, cast iron beauty, set in a corner under a window that opened to the view of the mountains!

Everything was new and clean and smelled deliciously of new wood. Nothing remained of the ghastly bathroom she had seen on the first day. It was a room fit for a queen, with gleaming fixtures and room for candles and luxurious towels. Tomorrow she would put up the sconces and fill the new linen closet, set out jars of bath herbs and oils, and thank Aiden for his craftsmanship. He had not forgotten anything, including her instructions to put in the widest baseboards. The details were what made this room beautiful.

She lit a fire in the fireplace, noticing with a smile that Aiden had arranged the firewood for her. She set some dishes out for her supper. She had missed her music while away, and now put on her favourite CD, an ethereal mix of classical and folk, played by friends from her old life. Soft and soothing, the music filled the rooms, one at a time, opening spaces for her to feel that this truly was safe and hers alone. She ate by the fire, staring into the flames. Dark was now falling rapidly, wrapping the house and the woman in it.

She should run the bath, she thought, but that thought quickly faded into a dream. When she awoke the next morning, she remembered nothing of her dream, but in the yard, edging the forest, stood an elder tree, fully grown with branches waving softly in the breeze. Regeneration and Wisdom had arrived.

CHAPTER 7

When morning broke, Aiden was up with a leap. Sleep had been fitful at best. He showered and hurried through breakfast, grinning to himself and deciding on driving over to Sahara's instead of crossing the plain. He found her busily unpacking her truck. She struggled with a large box of linens, the edge of it stuck behind the door. She looked up and smiled at Aiden. He jumped out of his truck and offered to give her a hand.

"Wow, you've brought a lot back. The cat missed you... he didn't seem to find me a satisfactory substitute."

"Oh, he's a bit of a snob, he'll get used to you."

They stood in the doorway of the cabin, Aiden wanting to ask if he was crazy or was that an Elder tree he had never noticed before. Aiden knew trees, but Sahara interrupted his thoughts with an impromptu hug that suddenly made trees an insignificant detail.

"Aiden," she crooned, still hugging and smiling from ear to ear; "that is simply the best renovation work I have ever seen, and the tub, oh that tub!"

Aiden lifted her up without thinking and swung her around. They were both surprised by his familiarity but nonetheless, it did not seem that out of place.

"Do you really like it? I mean, I hope it's what you had pictured?"

"Like it? Aiden, I LOVE it! I hoped it would be good, but you stole my vision right out of my head, it's exactly what I wanted. You nailed it!"

They laughed at her unintentional pun, and walked in to see it together.

"Aiden, where did you get those towel racks and hooks? They look hand crafted."

"Oh, that was my special surprise for you," Aiden grinned. "A local craftsman, but I promise they didn't cost the world."

"I have some new candle sconces; maybe I could you ask to put them up as the finishing touch?"

"Of course. But, have you had your coffee yet this morning Sahara? I would kill for one before I head out."

"Yes, yes, yes, let's have coffee," Sahara clapped her hands together and Aiden saw her childlike happiness through a mist that sent a shudder over his exquisite frame. But she was already in the kitchen, humming, and didn't know that Aiden had caught a glimpse of another time. And Aiden didn't either, because he was busy wondering how someone that new to him could make him feel so utterly comfortable and intrigued.

After Aiden left, Sahara finished unpacking all her boxes and putting away her magic supplies. She ran the washing machine and hung her new bed linens, then moved around her room making it cozy and filled it with her special books. She wouldn't leave her magic books downstairs for anyone to happen upon, or her besom broom, or her magic pouch. These belonged in her safe space, close to her in the night, where she could reference them in her dreams.

Already, she felt the beauty of the space, imagining her warm duvet covered bed, the windows facing the mountains, the place for her writing desk and her favourite painting facing her bed. The cabin could be bigger, but really for one person, it was enough. She ran her hand through the space where her desk would be, and felt the familiar stirring of spirit that signalled her readiness to write. She was not a prolific writer, with reams of stories to her credit, indeed, she wrote only when she knew that words would spill from her fingertips. She envied those writers who could fill notebooks with prose, sitting in crowded cafés hacking away at their computers, multitudinous story lines at their imaginative disposal.

Sahara wrote when her spirit beckoned, and that only happened when she was very much alone. Kathryn had said that it was because she wrote so very little, that her words were so much in demand, and because she shook people out of their comfort zones.

"All right," Sahara said out loud now. "Today I write. Kathryn will be pleased." She was surprised at how much work had to be done to her manuscript once she opened her laptop. It had been so long since she had dared to allow herself the freedom to live pain free. Reading over the pages, she could see that there was no magic here. All these words spoke of writing done to meet a deadline, and that deadline was already too close to work with.

In Denver, Iona worked powerful magic pulling together several dimensions to send Sahara the inspiration she knew she would find useful. They had always worked this way, one offering alms to the spirits while the other tended to the task at hand. Sahara had always been the student, even though she could easily have taught her teacher. Iona's love for her had made her strong but Sahara always felt a little bit afraid, knowing that her teacher would work both sides of magic, good or dark, according to her needs. Sahara never strayed to the dark side, at least not where magic was concerned.

"But darling, will you not follow me to the dark places?" Iona had purred when they had begun their discovery of each other in this lifetime.

"I will not, my love. But will you leave me wanting if I refuse to live in your dangerous world?"

How many times lately had Sahara dreamt of Iona leaving her tied to a bed, left her screaming for more, left her wet and aching and needing to feel her hands execute pain? Who was that man who entered when Iona left their forest home, the one who untied her and held her, kissed her tenderly and spoke soft words? The one whose large frame would envelop her and lift her onto his lap, where she would thrust herself upon him, and scream into the night? He was always so eager to give her what she needed, and she needed it from both of them.

But when Iona came back home, she was always tense and angry. Sahara would beg to know where she went or why she seemed so displeased, but all she got was silence. Still, in the next dream, they played the same game, and neither of them could stop. The lover they shared always came cloaked in a mist, Sahara never able to move through his veil. But his smell, his strength, his love were unmistakably the same in every dream. Shrouded visions like these filtered into Sahara's consciousness; there was still so much to remember.

As Sahara typed through the morning, she could feel the old energies returning, she knew that Iona was pulling magic from the dark place and wrote of things that no one would believe existed outside her imagination. The sky darkened, and the wind kept the trees moving, there wouldn't be any interruptions as long as her fingers kept typing. When she stopped to drink, her throat parched and her stomach grumbling, the day had turned to evening, the light to dusk.

At work Holly sat behind the counter and waited for the last customer to leave. She felt restless, anxious. For days she had felt a deep longing to slide into the arms of a lover, to satisfy her need for all the things that made a woman what she was. This town was satisfying in so many ways, but a same sex relationship seemed impossible. There was just no one here. Deep in thought, Holly looked up and thought that she saw someone walk by on the sidewalk with a mane of red hair, but no, there was no one out at this time in general.

It was a sleepy town really, not much happened here that didn't involve golf or skiing. It was a playground for the rich and almost famous; one of those places that seemed manufactured to fit the money that had settled in these mountains. So many new houses had sprung up, a lot of them garish, but she smiled thinking of the ones that Aiden had built. Those were thoughtfully and passionately built.

Aiden had a knack of talking his clients out of some terrible ideas, gently steering them to think that his ideas were initially theirs. And when he was not so gentle, it was to say that he simply would not put his name to the atrocities their architects had put to paper.

Aiden was one of her few true friends here. He respected her privacy. He was always eager to listen to her ideas for the café, and bought everything she recommended. Their conversation was easy, never strained, except when he asked her to dinner and she had to turn him down. She wasn't sure why she didn't tell him the truth about her sexuality.

Holly wondered how old he was and guessed about thirty two. His good looks were not lost on her; she had admired him on occasion, as he read the paper in his favourite corner of the patisserie. He was smart, that was appealing. He had a definite intensity that she found interesting. Aiden was full of charms that even Holly could appreciate. However, he was not a woman.

Finally, her last customer waved goodbye, and she walked to the door to lock it. Aiden stood on the sidewalk, pacing back and forth.

"Aiden! What in heavens' name are you doing?"

"Well..." He ran his hands through his hair. Dressed in a sharp pair of jeans and a sexy v neck sweater, he looked as darkly handsome as ever.

"Listen Holly, I'm not taking no for an answer. Would you join me for dinner? I have some new wine to try, and you're just the girl I want to try it with." Aiden looked increasingly demonic as his words spilled out.

"Ok."

"Ok?"

"Yeah. OK! Why do you look so surprised?"

"Oh, only because you've turned me down all the times before."

"Well, you've never said you wouldn't take no for an answer before." Holly laughed hysterically and asked him to wait there while she ran upstairs to freshen up.

Aiden stood rooted to the sidewalk. He felt so many things at once that he thought he might lose his mind. When she came down she had changed her mind about driving with him, insisting on taking her own vehicle even though he promised to have her back at a decent hour. They met at his door, Aiden's face arranged into a composure that he did not feel.

Holly curled up in a comfy chair. She was reading aloud, from one of his books. He was not sure which, or what she read, because his loins were on fire and his heart raced inside his chest. She looked up and caught him staring.

"Aiden, your house is so very much a man's place, and yet, it has a feminine feel."

"Yes? In which way? Tell me what you see." He poured their wine.

Holly loved that he was interested in her thoughts. Her father had been the only man who had ever been truly interested in how her mind worked.

"I see that it's strongly built, definitely with a man's sensibilities in mind. All these beams...but you've created so many lovely nooks and whimsical spaces, like the reading area under the stairs, the built in cupboards with leaded glass for your music, spacious windows towards the forest view. A man's house is often much more utilitarian. You're showing a sensitive side." She shot over a playful smile.

"Well I'm not all brute," he joked, but he kept his head down and his eyes veiled.

"So what's upstairs?"

"Upstairs?" he repeated, fumbling over the word.

"Yes, upstairs. All bedrooms I suppose?"

Aiden stared at Holly long and hard. A shiver ran along her spine.

"Oh sorry, I'm not trying to be nosy. You can give me a tour another time. Aiden?"

He snapped out of his thoughts and smiled.

"Sorry, I thought I heard something outside. Sure, I'll give you a quick tour while dinner is cooking." He led the way upstairs, wondering how many times he had imagined bringing her here. His senses were awake to the importance of the moment, he felt vulnerable. She walked behind him, wondering if she had liked men, if she would be his type. Most likely not, he seemed fierce sometimes, she probably felt tame to him.

They were both of them lost in their thoughts as he showed her the master's suite, with its massive bed backing onto a wall of windows.

"Aiden, it's so magical!" Holly exclaimed. "It's like sleeping right in the forest! I can see why you love being at home so much, it's a place fit for a king!"

Aiden held onto the doorframe with a powerful grip. His legs tensed; he could almost taste her on his tongue. He wanted to ravage her, to see her on her knees before him; to hear her say "please" before and "thank you" after. To know that she was his to own, and that he could do things to her that she would ask him not to do; to give in to her pleas, and to be on his knees before her. But for now, he thanked her for her compliments and invited her to eat.

They ate like old friends and laughed out loud at each other's jokes. She stared for a long time at his books, they drank too much wine. She asked why he had books on hermeticism, and he said he didn't know but that he found them very familiar when he had read them for the first time. She said, "Yes, I know that feeling, when I read poetry, it's like I had written it, like I had thought those lines up myself."

"Because our thoughts are part of the collective consciousness," he offered.

"Yes, just like that, as if we're made of bits of every particle that has ever existed," she replied.

"I had a friend, in France," Holly started slowly. "She loved to discuss esoteric philosophies, and I had never heard of them before. She used to laugh at me, she said that I was new and naïve to this world."

Her eyes were sad as she said it, and Aiden instantly knew that her friend had been her lover and why Holly had kept him at arm's length. His heart sank while his passion exploded and he offered her more wine.

"Aiden, you're going to have to let me sleep on the couch," Holly murmured. "I'm becoming very drunk. Do you feel like a walk, I need some fresh air?"

They walked into the darkness, and he showed her the way to Sahara's. Holly looked over the plain to where a tiny light could be seen in the distance.

"I wonder how one gets invited to there? Sahara seems like a worse hermit than even you, Aiden."

"Let's go back, it's getting chilly." Aiden turned towards home.

And indeed a chill had settled on his heart; as he felt an odd sensation of something powerful circle over their heads. A raven shrieked above them. He took Holly's hand. She didn't resist, she had felt it too.

"Shall we make a fire?" he asked.

⸙

Sahara filled her new tub with water, and added scented oils. She lit the candles in the sconces, and slid in.

She closed her eyes and thought about the last few weeks. So much had happened; meeting Aiden, re-uniting further with Iona, this place, and all the words that she had typed today. She was finally excited about this next book; her fans would not be disappointed. She was ready to share, and from the place that made her who she was.

Iona was the only person on this earth who knew who that was anyway. And even Iona did not know everything. Sahara got into her improvised bed on the sofa. She looked around the room, it felt safe and warm, her favourite things around her. The wind blew in through her window; this would be a good sleep. Her thoughts turned to Aiden, and she was suddenly aroused. Aiden awoke certain memories. He felt familiar. As complicated as this seemed, Sahara knew that her curiosity would eventually get the better of her and that she would make her move. A problem, yes, but she knew herself too well to pretend that she could just forget about his impression on her.

For now, though, her thoughts returned to Iona. Boundaries would have to be issued. In spirit and body, Sahara knew what letting Iona have the run of you implied. Tonight, she would let her in. Certainly, Iona was near, she had seen the raven sitting in the Elder outside the cabin. Uncovering herself, Sahara called Iona's name. She smiled as the powerful sorceress appeared at her side.

"Iona," Sahara whispered. "I've missed you. What have you to give me tonight? I want it all!"

"All? What I have for you is usually more than you can take, so ask wisely."

Sahara spread her legs a little and ran her hands over her body.

"Everything Iona, all of it and don't spare me. I'll give you my safe word."

Iona slid herself out of her sorcerers dress, and stood naked before Sahara. Her body was tall and slender, beautifully made; she was a stunning creature. Her hair ran long down her back, wild, a deep burnished red. Her breasts stood impossibly firm and round for their size, nipples pursed tight.

But it was her eyes that gave her a startling appearance. Almond shaped and such a light green that they almost shone opaque. Her ears were slightly pointed, entirely elemental in nature. By first impressions she was delicate and winsome, but this was purely a mask for her fire. It was easy to be surprised by her power; she gave nothing away by way of looks or coquettish manner.

She asked Sahara if her looks pleased her, and her student moaned and turned over on the sofa. Raising herself up, Sahara pleaded for Iona to come closer.

Iona watched Sahara's lithe body open in the most provocative way, then slid in beside her, gently kissing her on the lips, softly nudging her with her body.

So, this is how we're going to begin. Sahara thought. *You'll play the lamb while I'll play the lion.*

There were love words and spell words and veiled remembrances of the past. Sahara writhed under candles dripped and an expertly wielded whip by the wild eyed Iona; and wine sucked lovingly from nipples that had been worried to just the right amount of pain.

It was a celebration to span centuries and their tongues knew no boundaries. A box of sex toys provided forbidden games.

Although Iona flew away in the morning with nothing but love and tenderness reflected upon her face, Sahara knew that Iona wondered what had changed between them. She trusted Iona to never reveal her hand in the game they had played for centuries, and looked forward to discovering what their relationship would reveal in this lifetime.

CHAPTER 8

Aiden took Holly to his room.

"You'll sleep here tonight, I'll sleep downstairs. There is no way you can drive and I'm in much worse shape than you."

"Aiden, I feel bad, you sleep here; I'll sleep downstairs."

"You should never argue with the man of the house. Now get in my bed!"

Back by the fire, Aiden drained the last of the wine bottle into his glass. "What in the name of God is going on here?" he muttered to himself. He scowled at the fire which suddenly flared up. "I have fallen in love with a woman who has no hope of ever loving me back." He swallowed a big gulp of wine. "I'm an idiot, and my intuition has failed me."

But still, was she not so very perfect in a multitude of ways? He smiled to himself remembering her laughter at agreeing to dinner. She was so much a clear and open spirit. Her naiveté made her utterly charming, her mind was sharp, her curiosity about life refreshing. Aiden sprawled out onto the couch. Sleep. Yes, sleep would make it all better.

But sleep didn't come as his heart ached for Holly, and his body ached for something he knew would be impossible to attain. His mind raced to all kinds of scenarios, wondering about Holly and her French lover, he would have killed to have been a witness to their passion. He must have slept in the end because he woke up to the smell of coffee and Holly sitting in the chair beside him, watching him pensively.

"Shit! I'm sorry, how long have you been sitting there? I hope I haven't been laying here drooling and snoring?"

She laughed. "Not long, maybe an hour?"

"Impressed by my hosting skills?"

"Actually, you're a perfect host, and I would love to come back."

Aiden shot her a wry look. "You're just being polite."

"No, no, I mean it. You cook well, you serve good wine, you have a library, and your bedroom is spectacular!"

"Ok, stop teasing me; you're not interested in my bedroom at all."

"Aiden, I'm sorry, I should have told you before..."

"That you like women and are not interested in me?"

"Yes. I mean, I trust you, we've been friends for a while but you know how it is. And I really didn't think you were interested in me, I just thought you wanted a random date."

"Ok, we're going to need coffee for this conversation. Give me a minute, I'll be right back."

He ran up the stairs to brush his teeth and wash his face. As he ran the water, he looked at himself in the mirror. "Fool!" He changed clothes quickly and ran his fingers through his hair.

She had the coffee poured and set on the table when he came back down.

"I found my croissants in your freezer. I've thrown them in the oven, K? Can we sit under the stairs with your books?"

They sat opposite each other, coffee in hand, smiles on their faces, comfortable, contemplative.

"Holly," Aiden began. "I feel like such a fool. I've been trying to get a date with you for so long, and now I have to say that I am more than a little disappointed that my hopes will never be met. I mean, that is as honest as I can be. I wish we could go back one day and I could still have some hope."

"I know. But I'm such a ninny. I'm sure I'm very boring compared to all the other women you've dated, so even if I was interested in men, you've probably got the wrong picture of me anyway."

I'm sure I don't, Aiden thought. *Just how much did she know about ALL the women he had dated?*

Intensity etched on his face, eyes honest, Aiden felt Holly's energy shift and decided to just ask the question.

"So, you've dated only girls? I would have thought that coming from such a small town, it would have been frowned upon?"

Holly took a long sip of her coffee and lifted her eyes up at him over her cup. He felt that familiar tug in his loins, and set his jaw.

"To tell the whole truth, Aiden, I have only had one lover, the one I mentioned last night, and before that I dated a few boys in my home town. But they were, as I said, boys, and were incredibly dull."

His eyes stayed calm, but his jaw moved slightly as he digested what she was saying.

She read him this time and laughed out loud. "So yes, Aiden, I *have* been kissed by a boy!"

He grinned at her and nodded his head. "I'm caught, that was my next question. And... did you like it?"

"I don't know."

"What? Either you did or did not. Tell me."

"I might have, but the kiss was always followed by some ridiculous remark and then I was turned off, and that was that. So I really don't know." Her lips twitched. He laughed now.

"Ok, that's just not fair. You're teasing me."

"Maybe. How old are you Aiden?"

"Older than you, how old are you?"

"I asked first. Ok, I'm twenty five, almost twenty six."

"I'm thirty five."

"Thirty five. Hmmm."

"What does that mean?"

"It means the croissants are ready! Let's eat."

"Aiden," Holly said between bites, "Would you be willing to see me again… as friends, I feel safe with you, and I get lonely for someone I can really talk to. What do you think?"

"I think that you're going to break my heart." His words sounded bitter but his face remained soft.

She looked so startled that he was instantly sorry he had said it.

"Holly, I truly do enjoy you, you're not too young, or boring, or any of those things. I'll need some time to adjust my head from wanting to explore a relationship with you to accepting that it's just friendship. I've had a crush on you for a very long time. Maybe another man wouldn't admit that, but that's where I'm at, and I would prefer to be upfront."

She looked at his muscled body and his handsome face, how he stood leaning in the doorway, his hair spilling to his shoulders. In a way she was afraid of him. She had known only boys, and he was a wild, intense man, and she would have no idea of how to approach anything more than his friendship. Still, she was curious, but not as curious as she was about Sahara. She sighed and he ignored it. They walked through the woods; she slipped her hand in his. His grip tightened, and he looked down at her with a pounding heart.

"Friends then?" he asked.

"Friends," she replied and squeezed back. Aiden tucked the smallest sliver of hope somewhere deep in his heart.

"When is the moving truck coming?" Aiden stopped his hammering on the bookshelf and looked into the kitchen at Sahara.

"Tomorrow."

"Tomorrow? Well, not a day too soon, I'll be done, you can unload your books, and you'll be pretty much moved in."

"Yup. I'm really looking forward to finally being settled and just getting to the business of working on my book. And no, I still won't tell you what it's about!"

"That's just some ploy to sell another book, I'm sure."

"I'm sure it's not! I'm superstitious." She smiled.

"Shall I come over tomorrow to help move things around?"

"Sure, I could use a hand. Shall I cook dinner?"

"No. You will not cook dinner. You will come to my house and I will cook."

"Ok, but I'll bring the dessert. That's exciting! I haven't seen your place yet."

Well it has not been for lack of me inviting, Aiden thought, as he inspected his work.

Sahara drove to town in the late afternoon. She thought of starting at the café and moving on to the liquor store. That would cover desert and wine for tomorrow. Had she offered to bring wine? She couldn't remember.

Aiden took inventory of how the cabin had changed since Sahara had moved in. Jack had kept the place tidy, but it certainly had been lacking in personal touches. He was pleased with the new additions to the place, the bookshelves, the bathroom; it was the details of her designs that pleased him. He approved because her style spoke very much of how he would have renovated it. The cabin was modest in size but now had personality and warmth.

He could especially feel Sahara's touch in her loft. Here was evidence of a woman's softness. The room felt like dreams; those dreams that one has when they imagine something remote and wild yet cozy and enveloping. It was mainly empty still except for the soft white sheers, her personal belongings and beautiful rug she had found at the antique store.

He had looked curiously at the only painting Sahara had brought with her. Vivid in colour, it depicted a woman in a sheer chemise, wandering through the woods, blonde hair whipping about her face, trees bent with the wind. Behind her a tall horse, dark and graceful; and a crescent moon shining from behind a hill. It was not so much that the scene was so unusual, it was the colours. Reds and purples where one would expect browns and blacks and those eyes! So blue, so innocent and mild. They held him from within the canvas. He had stared at it so long this morning that finally Sahara had asked what he was staring at.

"Not sure," he'd answered. "The eyes of that girl in your painting,

I feel like I've seen them before. Who painted this?"

"I don't know the artist. The painting is old, as you can probably notice by the quality of the canvas. It's been initialled, but not signed. I found it in a gallery in Salem. It's one of my favourite things. It feels comfortable and yet exhilarating at the same time. I can't really explain it."

"No, no, I know. That's exactly it! Comfortable and exhilarating." He thought back to it now and decided that he would take another look at it tomorrow. He didn't want to go up to the loft without Sahara there.

"Hi Holly!" Sahara smiled as she entered the café. "Oh my Goddess, it smells so good in here. What *are* you baking?"

"Sahara! I'm glad you're here. Here, sit down and try one of these new cheese pastries I've been playing with. Tell me what you think? Coffee?"

"Sure. Just a bit. I need to purchase some dessert for tomorrow evening, and was hoping that I'd find something delicious here."

Holly grinned. Her eyes lit up and she waited with anticipation. "Well?"

"Mmmm. These are amazing. Sweet, but not too sweet. Creamy. Flaky. Holly, these really are too good!"

"Want these for your dessert then? Are you having guests?"

Sahara quickly checked in with Holly's energy field. Was she just curious or being nosy?

Curious...but with some motive.

"Well, actually, my furniture is arriving tomorrow, Aiden is coming to help me set up, and has offered to make me dinner after. I thought I'd bring wine and dessert." Sahara waited for Holly's reaction.

"Oh, that sounds nice. I guess you're not really that far off from his place, you could easily walk over."

"Aha. Well, I haven't been before, if that's what you mean." Sahara bit her lip.

"No, I mean, if you did go, it's not far, that's all."

"Holly, I've been rude. You've been so kind to send me lovely things to eat, and I've been so busy setting up, I haven't had a chance to invite you for a visit. Why don't you come over tomorrow morning, we can have a quick walk and coffee before Aiden arrives." She smiled, but inside she wondered why she was being so suddenly hospitable. Still, she liked Holly's easy friendship, given so freely, to someone who had made so little effort in return. Holly really was young, Sahara mused, and she didn't mean in years, she meant in centuries.

Holly accepted immediately, and offered to bring fresh goodies. They parted with Sahara running across the street to the liquor store.

<hr />

The next morning broke full of sun and crisp air. When Holly pulled up in front of the cabin, she could smell wood smoke from the chimney. She knocked on the door, quickly scanning the surroundings. It was a good place, she decided, friendly.

"Hi Holly, welcome." Sahara stood in the open doorway, offering a hug.

"Ooooh, it's so nice here. I love your wood stove! Maybe one day you'll let me bake something in it? I'd love to experiment with a bread recipe or two."

Sahara said yes as long as she could have the first bite.

"Of course, you get the first bite!" Sahara felt an instant wetness gathering between her legs.

The next hour sped by, as they shared a cup of coffee and a continental breakfast, each of them asking questions and wanting to know the other better, but being careful to not push past comfortable boundaries. The walk was completely forgotten, as they curled up on the sofa, and both were surprised to hear the knock on the door as Aiden arrived to help. In the last few weeks, he had grown to love stepping into Sahara's days.

"Two fair maidens, how fortuitous!" Aiden tripped over the doorstep.

Holly got up to offer a hug, and a smile. Aiden pulled her into him and looked down into her upturned face. "What are you doing here? Sahara didn't mention that she'd have company."

Sahara observed the two of them with great interest. She felt a twinge of intuition. Aiden looked at her, smiling. But Sahara was now focused on a feeling that Iona was present, always the curious mystic.

And indeed, far away in Denver, Iona sat up as her inner knowing was awakened. Something big had just happened. Sahara. She sat down at her scrying ball. She would find out. Sahara would have no secrets from her.

Snapping out of her thoughts, Sahara smiled at her guests.

"I've finally remembered my manners and invited Holly for breakfast and a walk in the woods. However, we've forgotten about the walk, talking all this time, and now I'm afraid the truck will come and we'll have to start unloading. I'm sorry Holly. Maybe we can have that walk another day?"

"Of course, any day that works for you, as long as I'm not working...which seems like every day. I could pack a picnic and we could have an al fresco supper in the woods?"

The sound of a large truck lumbering up the long drive ended the conversation as Sahara clapped her hands together gleefully. "My things are here!"

The morning whipped by as the three of them moved Sahara's possessions into the cabin. Boxes of clothes, kitchen supplies, bedroom linens, an antique Shaker table and chairs, a couch with many cushions, a large reading chair with an ottoman, but more than anything, boxes upon boxes of books!

"Really Sahara, this is an entire library!" Aiden exclaimed. I don't know that the shelves I built will hold all these.

"Well, you'll have to build more!"

"Yes, but where? Are you expecting to expand this collection?"

"Of course...books are my weakness."

Aiden smiled in approval.

"You're one to talk," Holly said. "You have more books than this."

"You've been to Aiden's house?" Sahara asked as casually as she could manage, her heart in a sudden flutter.

"Yes, but just once," Holly offered, and wondered why she felt like she had done something wrong.

Both women looked at Aiden as he stood with his arms full of books and licked their lips unconsciously. Both felt a bit self-conscious around him, both knew that this was ridiculous. Why should they feel anything? Aiden was a free man, and neither had any claim. Still, each felt a curiosity towards him that belied their projected nonchalance. Aiden felt some tension as he looked at the two of them. He put down the books and walked back to the truck where the driver and his helper were packing up.

The two girls smiled at each other and acknowledged their awkwardness with silence. Holly, as innocent as she was, could tell that it was almost time for her to go. She felt with an instinct new to her about these types of situations that she would be invited to join them for dinner out of politeness, but that she should not accept. Another time, she would ask Sahara to come to her apartment for dinner; but not yet. Holly ached for the company of a woman, but Sahara felt so confident, and so very much out of her league, that she would need time to gather the courage for the invitation.

"I think I'll go now," she said.

Aiden offered his hand as farewell. Holly held it and wondered how he had snuck into her heart space so easily. She let go and smiled a little smile that he tucked into his heart. Sahara gathered her up for a hug and immediately felt the electricity between them, energy coursing from her head to her toes, and places in between. She tried to shut herself down but it was already too late, her heart space longed for a kindred spirit she could trust, her body remembering the pleasure only a woman can give to another. Sahara let go of Holly and said, "Soon. We'll get together soon."

Holly said, "Yes, we'll walk." But Holly had felt her knees weaken and was sad because she was sure that she was only imagining that thing that had sprung up like fire between them.

Aiden watched as they parted company, his mind feeding on images that made him burn with desire. He truly thought that he would like to have them both as his lovers. He didn't see anything wrong at all with sharing partners or loving more than one person at once. But his ideas were not ones that he shared out loud.

Who could he tell that he could very well love and bed two women, and share his life, his mind and his passions with them? And how to make this happen; he had no idea. Sahara watched him as he pushed her furniture into place and sensed his deep thoughts. She ran herself through him. He mentioned a chill creeping into the evening air. She could tell that his feelings were in a jumble and that his sexual desire was surging through him, because a man moved differently when he was aroused. Aiden moved like an animal on the hunt. He prowled the room with intent. His faced was etched with intense concentration; and he barely looked at her as he asked directions, but she knew that he was keenly aware of her.

Finally, it was all done, the truck and its driver gone, and they stood on the porch quite pleased with their work.

"Well, it looks like you're moved in Sahara. It truly does look quite cozy and I approve of your sense of décor," Aiden mused.

"Oh you do, do you?" Sahara teased. "Well, I'm glad you like it." She wondered what explanation she could offer if he asked why she cared that he liked it. And why *did* she care?

Aiden was truly comforting to her. He made her crazy with desire and she wanted to trust it. She knew that this was hazardous and that she shouldn't go there. But she wanted to. She wanted to love him, undress him and taste his skin under her tongue. She wanted to please him and be as naughty as she could think of, doing all those things that men desire and hope their lovers will be willing to do.

She wanted to scream into the night and ride him till the morning light. But she also wanted those things from a woman. And now she knew that she was already treading on thin ice, as her lustful nature always led her down the slippery path, and she had vowed not to repeat her failures with relationships again.

They agreed to meet later for dinner at Aiden's and he walked away, turning once and waving. Sahara gave in to her needs and opened her box of toys as she ran her bath. She waited until the tub was filled with water hot enough to scald her and eased into it, delighting in the aroma of the bath oils she had chosen. She gratefully sank into the warmth and slid her hands over her breasts and between her legs, trying to rub some of the sinfulness from her being. The bath was akin to a spiritual cleansing most times, but she really didn't feel cleansed at all today. She felt like the wanton spirit that she knew she was and there was not going to be any escape from her thoughts.

She crept up the stairs to her loft and spread herself out her newly assembled bed, writhing with her thoughts, and reached for her playthings. She was tiny and tight but she could take the largest of sex toys, which always surprised her lovers. Sahara looked into the mirror at the end of her bed. She was pleased with what she saw, she had always found it easy to maintain a fit form and her skin was glowing from staying active and good attention to health. Playing with herself was something Sahara was completely at ease with, alone, or in front of others. Slipping a vibrator over her clit, she rubbed at it, and then slid it downwards, letting her wet gather before slipping it inside and turning up the speed. How widely it filled her. That always made her hot.

CHAPTER 9

Sahara thought about her new book as she walked to Aiden's. The wind, especially, made her feel ready to resume her work, which she had pushed aside when her love life had fallen to pieces. Sometimes magic gave her strength, but when she was feeling especially fragile, it only exacerbated feelings of helplessness. That was when she had usually turned to Iona, but this was only the start of their journey in this lifetime, and she was not yet sure of her footing with the powerful witch. As a last minute decision, she had brought her deck of tarot cards. Aiden had seen them by the sofa and had asked if she read. She wasn't sure if she was ready to read for him, but she had longed for the feel of them in any case. The wind played in the aspens as she approached, flashlight, bottle of wine and a book of poems in her other hand. Entering the trees shadow, she was greeted by Iona, first as a flash of raven flying by, and then, facing Sahara on the path.

"Iona!"

"My love," Iona purred.

Sahara's intuition prickled and she readied for a tense conversation. Iona's hand reached for Sahara and the younger woman fell to her knees, kissing her hand.

"Teacher," Sahara whispered. "I can only wonder what you mean by meeting me here. I am, as always, delighted to see you." She meant it. Iona melted her at her core, her hands ignited fire in every cell, but Sahara knew better than to trust her completely.

"Why do you follow me to the house of a friend, un-invited? I'm curious."

"I'm simply looking out for you my love. Shall I attend with you in spirit?"

"Iona, you and I both know that you will do as you want and that I would have to cast you out to keep you from following, which I'm not going to do. I've simply no time to engage in a battle of the wills. Don't worry my sweet, all shall be well, I do not need your protection. Unless you know something that I don't about my neighbour?"

Iona walked so lightly that she seemed to float. She rested her hand on Sahara's waist. Sahara leaned in and turned her face up for a kiss. She knew that Iona was reeling her in, putting her scent on her, marking her as her own. She must have reason to fear Aiden's influence...but why? She moaned as Iona kissed her deeply, licking her ear and holding her close, her taste like honey. Slowly and expertly, Iona probed with her tongue along Sahara's lips, licking and biting gently, moaning softly.

"I haven't done anything wrong," whispered Sahara, slipping into their age old pattern of submissive and dominant.

"Are you still mine?" Iona asked with a husky voice. "Give me promises."

Sahara gave all the promises, as she always had, her resolve weakened by Iona's touch. Iona left on a high wind, shrieking into the dusk filled sky. And that is how Sahara arrived at Aiden's, now on guard and wondering what Iona had to fear from him and with her whole body ready for play. She stood at his door quivering and trying to regain her composure, ears and eyes fully engaged in her surroundings, she had left her house as Sahara the neighbour and arrived as the Mystic.

She stood on his doorstep, her soul registering the beauty of the forest glen in which Aiden's house was built. Wave after wave of familiarity washed over her. The house was deeply beautiful. Dark, carved out of the forest itself, with an aura so strong that it almost felled her to her knees again. She could see Aiden moving about in the kitchen, preparing something, listening to music that crept out of the slightly open windows. Sahara held on to the door frame, feeling herself receding to another place, another time. Slipping, slipping...

"There you are! I thought you might have gotten lost. I was just going to come out and meet you on the path."

Sahara slammed back to the present. She looked out at Aiden with eyes half closed, like a sleepy dragon.

"Hey, you ok? Here, give me these things. Come in. You look like you need to sit down."

"I'm ok," Sahara said. "Maybe I should sit down, I could use a drink."

He was already in the kitchen, pouring some wine, and returned quickly to sit her on his man sized sofa, into which she sank gratefully.

"Umm, my sofa seems to have swallowed you up. Supper is still a ways off. We have time to relax."

"Aiden," Sahara interrupted. "Your home is, well, I don't know, I feel like I've been here before. It's familiar in some way."

"It's probably like a lot of homes in this area, you know, open concept, lots of wood, windows..."

"Mmmm... maybe." She suddenly realized that she was in a very vulnerable position emotionally, feeling light headed and on the verge of returning to another time. This certainly was not the place to go exploring past lives. And she never did this anyway, give away secrets to strangers.

She took the biggest drink of alcohol she had ever taken, in one big gulp. Kathryn would have been proud of her.

Aiden asked "How was your day?" and they both laughed at the domestic nature of the question.

"I'm feeling quite settled now, thanks to you. I've been looking forward to this evening Aiden, I've spent so much time lately with my nose to the grindstone getting myself set up and writing, that I've forgotten how nice it is to share an evening with a friend.."

"I thought you were going to stay committed to hermit-hood?" Aiden quipped.

"Very funny. Well yes, I still am, but I'm starting to see that you're not altogether un-trustworthy."

"A high compliment from you, I'm sure, my lady."

"My lady". The words resonated within Sahara's memory. She reeled back once again, ripping through time, slipping into the mist.

"Sahara! Now you've truly got me worried. Give me that glass of wine," Aiden commanded and reached for her glass.

She handed it to him eyeing him through a veil of mist while he got up and moved closer to her. He took her shoulders in his hands and leaned her into a corner of sofa cushions.

"I think you need an evening of rest. Now just sit here, take this blanket. For heaven's sake Sahara, you must have overdone it today. You're pale as a ghost and your eyes look positively possessed."

She smiled a weak little smile that melted his heart. He longed to scoop her up and hug her tiredness away. They sat in silence for a long while, she regaining her composure, he thinking about what a strange little creature she was, all a bundle of fire and at the same time softer than a spring rain. The music flowed all around them, the darkness settling in outside. He looked at her book of poetry, and read some of it to her. She fell asleep as he read and later woke to find the table set for two, candles lit, the fireplace blazing.

"Awake at last! Not a moment too soon, because I'm ready to put our supper out. Hope you're hungry?"

Sahara was hungry indeed. Hungry for knowing more about Aiden, hungry for the comfort he offered. Hungry for a lover who could stir her soul. She knew that she was once again on thin ice, that she could barely trust herself to not cross all the boundaries of a new friendship. But she wanted this man, and she would have him.

They ate amidst laughter and stories shared, then moved to the alcove of books.

She ran her hand along his book shelves, perusing the titles, interested in what moved him.

"Hey! You didn't tell me you had one of my books!"

"What? I do? Show me."

She lifted it off the shelf. "Here, *Magic and Alchemy, Doorways to Within*. It's my only non- fiction work."

"I'd forgotten...what a buffoon!" Aiden laughed at himself. "But looking back now, I remember reading it and thinking that I was drawn to the title even though I barely understood the text, it was like reading it with the wrong strength glasses. I'm not sure why but I'm drawn to things that are old, things that cause men to lose their minds over figuring them out. When I was quite young, I had that same pull to the woods, and there I would feel some kind of connection to, well, I don't know what. But trees have always been a sort of kindred spirit to me, they talk to me." Aiden tried to gage Sahara's reaction to his words. "Do you think that's crazy?"

"Wait, I'm still trying to forgive you for forgetting you had one of my books!" she teased him. "But no, I don't think it's crazy. I talk to trees all the time."

"You do? I mean telepathically."

"Exactly, they're conscious, like you and me, and their voices can be heard by some."

She stared at him. Did he know what she'd said? That she was asking him to reveal his magic, if he practiced it at all.

Aiden's eyes pierced hers, his eyes flashed green. It was his spirit's natural response to something he was familiar with but had forgotten. Her breath quickened. She waited.

"I don't know if we all hear nature in her true voice, although I'm sure that what I hear is not usual, at least, you're the first to speak of it to me."

He hadn't answered as she would have hoped. Still, he knew something; maybe he was not to be fully awake to magic this lifetime. But magical he was, of this she was sure.

"Aiden, we all hear what we need to hear, and it's for all of us to figure out what that means. You have quite a few books on the mysteries of nature...have you really read all these?"

"No," he admitted. "I have them because they looked as if they belonged in my library. "I'm sounding idiotic; you don't have to deny it."

"You'll know when to read them Aiden. Everything is revealed to us in good time. The Universe is never too early or too late in its judgements of timing."

Aiden remembered the night he had silently witnessed Sahara's fire and the naked, sensuous dance she had performed, very much a witch at a private ceremony. His eyes raked over her, his blood running hot at the memory. She noticed the fire in his eyes and squirmed under his gaze, he looked as if he could see her naked.

"May I admit something to you?" Aiden took a step toward Sahara and she felt the air around them shift, as if he pushed it along with his body, his legs stunningly powerful, his scent in her nose.

"Of course." She wondered what it was, but only briefly, because she was caught staring at the obvious growth in his jeans.

"You can tell me anything," she mumbled, her eyes darting up to his, noting that he was not perturbed one bit by his bold display of arousal.

"I'm not angry anymore that Jack sold his place. When I imagined who my new neighbour would be, I didn't imagine this conversation, or that you'd hold my attention like this...I want to learn from you."

He stopped there but wanted to add that she held his cock's attention as well, that his weakness for brainy women made him hotter than hell. Aiden was indeed willing to be the student with Sahara; she had awoken his desire to be led into pleasure by an intelligent woman.

Sahara had a weakness of her own, for well spoken, well read, well-mannered men. Aiden's approach to life left her breathless. She asked for more wine. He gladly obliged. They moved back to the sofa where he asked if she would be opposed to smoking a small joint between them.

She said she wouldn't mind, as long as she could ask the plant's diva for wisdom. His cock stirred once more. She ignited a furious need in him that he knew came from admiring her mystery. He went to the bookcase and returned with a box, while Sahara explained that everything on earth had a spirit of its own.

"Everything?" he asked.

"Everything," Sahara said.

She watched as Aiden expertly rolled a joint. His hands were strong and muscled, dark from being out in the sun, his fingers almost caressing the paper as he smoothed the finished product. Sahara's breath caught watching his tongue slide over the joint to seal it tight.

"Now what?" he asked as he handed it over to her.

"What would you like to take from this experience? The herb holds wisdom and healing, I've always been careful not to abuse it. I use it more to meet up with my guides."

Aiden looked greatly intrigued.

"To be honest, I've never approached smoking in this way," he said. "I've always used it as a way to reach deeper into my mind, but not consciously. It was just a natural way for me to think less and just be."

"That's a very revealing statement Aiden." Sahara was impressed. "*Being* is a state where you're totally in the moment, not worrying about tomorrow or agonizing about yesterday. Being is where we all want to exist. So you DO know something of the sacred mysteries!"

"Perhaps... why don't you guide me through this? You provide the ceremony, I provide the herb, and we'll see where it takes us."

Sahara got up and drew a circle around them with her dominant hand, calling in the four directions, the wisdom of the plant they'd be using, her incantations oddly familiar to his ear. He was fascinated by her energy, which grew from her like a serpent un-coiling, her eyes like stars in the dim light of the room. Then she asked him to draw and release three breaths with her, one for guidance, one for clear intuition, and one for clearing away anything they didn't need on their quest. In silence, they each pondered what visions they were seeking. She asked Aiden to light the herb as she drew in her breath, her mouth around it. He was as tense as he could be, excited to learn and intoxicated by her power, not to mention what the image of her lips tight around the joint did to him. She of such small build could command so much energy with her words and intent.

They sat smoking together, the music drifting into their consciousness in soothing notes and undulations of sound. She drew tiny drags, needing very little to find sacred space. She asked him if he would do ceremony next time he smoked. He said he thought that the next time he would like to experience it with her again, the old way felt thoughtless now. Yet thoughtless seemed to be where he was headed.

He took a long deliberate drag and, leaning in towards her, feeling absolutely no indecision, he found her lips. As they opened to his approach, he blew a breath of smoke into her; then moved back to his place on the sofa, a satisfied look in his eye.

Sahara breathed him in. She felt his energy mingle with hers; dizzy with the pheromones he exuded. He sat watching. She leaned back into the couch and breathed out, releasing all her anxiety about what she hoped would happen between them. He was very, very sure of himself in this moment. She liked that very much, a man in control, but one who she could also hold under her spell. He smiled at her, a slow and decadent smile.

She was lost to his beauty, his ease with himself, his powerful build, his kindness. She wondered if Aiden understood the alchemy of sex, of the soul connection that happened in times of ecstasy.

"More wine Aiden?"

Aiden was slow to move but got up to pour. When he sat down again, she spoke.

"My dress, Aiden...help me." She pulled the bottom of it up along her legs, and his eyes immediately followed the direction of her hands, desperately hungry for her to reveal her tenderness to him. Sahara felt the surge of power that came with knowing what it would do to him to see her slick folds for the first time. She knew that Aiden would stare blatantly, and it made her tighten with longing.

He asked if she would like to stand up. She did. He approached her slowly, deliberately, with every confidence in his power over her. She silently asked for help from her guides. She was so very good at making mistakes with men.

He wrapped his arms around her, found the buttons at the back of the dress, and undid them. He ran his hands down her back, fingers tender but sure, feeling back up to her neck. He turned her head and kissed around her ears. He growled as she pushed into him. Her dress dropped to the floor and they sat back down, facing each other, she bare - breasted, her nipples pointing her arousal, begging his attention. He stared at her breasts and longed to bring his mouth to them, but she, knowing what he was thinking, shook her head no.

So we're to play games, he thought. He smiled at her, amused, his tongue slipping over his lips.

She admired him openly when he took his shirt off, a hard knot of muscles defining his middle, his chest groomed, and it whet her appetite for the rest of him. He smelled as good as he looked; a mix of herb and that musky fragrance that she recognized from the first day they'd met.

It made him hot as hell knowing that she found him wildly attractive. Sahara drew a line of descent with her eyes: from his broad shoulders to the swell of his biceps, along his chest to his slim waist, finally settling on the growing bulge in his jeans. He was happy to let her eyes take possession of him, to watch her mentally marking the places where she wanted to press her lips. They sat by the fire for a few moments. By now, they had left their ego selves far behind and took each moment as an eternity unto itself.

He undid his belt as a cue for her to show him more, and it was obvious that she was curious to see his growing weapon. She had only her black lace g string, but wasn't ready to show it all yet. Instead, she dipped her finger in her wine and circled it onto her nipples, then gave them a bit of a tug. She smiled a deep smile and lay back on the sofa, her hands cupping the round of her breasts. They weren't in any hurry, both of them relishing these first moments of discovery.

Aiden lifted himself towards her, his lips feather light on her breasts, kissing them tenderly. Then, finding her pursed up areola, he sucked hard on her nipples until she cried out. He moved his lips to hers and growled into her mouth: "A bit of pain with your pleasure?" He ran his hand towards her panties, his fingers demanding, but she snaked away from his grip.

She guided him to drink some wine, she took hers, and with tongues still wet with it, she kissed him long, her lips at once soft as velvet and demanding a hard kiss back. Aiden was having trouble thinking straight; he struggled to keep his hands from her throat.

She felt his strength and it brought her close to the edge of release, her clit throbbing as he rubbed himself all over her, his belt biting into her skin. She loved the feel of his hard-on in his jeans, it felt immense, but then, she had always enjoyed a challenge. Sahara was a confident lover; she could be shameless in bed. But now, as she stared into Aiden's intensely focused eyes, she wondered if she had met her match.

"Take off your jeans," she commanded, her body shaking with a deep need to fall before him with her mouth ready for service.

"No," he replied, feeling the tension building between them. He'd have it his way, and had a hunch that she knew all about being submissive; if he played the game right.

He moved towards the fire and reached to take hold of the massive cut of oak that made up the mantle with one hand, his other hand pulling his belt free. She understood immediately, and crawled over to him on her hands and knees. It made him insane to see how well she understood his cues.

"You know what I need, Sahara, I don't even have to say it, you know that I need you to beg on your knees."

A strangled cry left her throat. He stood strong and confident; his waist such a tease where it met his lean hips, his face dark with greed for her obedience. She looked up at him and slipped her arms towards his waist, then pulled down on his jeans.

"Jesus. Aiden," Sahara whispered.

If he was any bigger, she would have had to decline. He took his cock in his hand, guiding it towards her.

May I?" she asked, as she nudged closer, her breath a fiery inch away from the smooth velvety tip.

"Say it again." He bit out the words.

"May I suck your beautiful cock? Please, Aiden."

"Only a whore would say that so easily. You *are* a whore... or am I mistaken, my lady?"

"I am *your* whore, my lord."

Aiden almost came when she said that. "Why do you call me 'my lord'?" he asked, tension rising in his chest as he tried to make sense of their words.

"Why do you call me 'my lady'?" she countered.

"I don't know..." he answered, his voice agonized.

She saw the muscles in his jaw working as he pondered her question. She contemplated his expression; he was ever so beautiful with his vulnerability showing. Lightly, ever so lightly, she nuzzled him, licked under his tight balls; then looked up at him with a smile.

"I'm hungry, Aiden."

"*Sahara.*" He shoved his hips towards her; his hands reaching to grasp her. She stood up and asked him if he would take her g string off. Aiden did as he was asked, on his knees as she stepped out of her lace. She stood bare before him, her cunt tight and quivering under his gaze. He admired her smoothness, her cleft completely exposed; she was groomed in the way he preferred. Aiden was used to seeing beautiful women naked, but Sahara took his breath away.

Her eyes taunted him; she touched herself and licked her fingers. He wanted so very badly to taste her, his eyes communicating his thoughts to her. She shook her head no. Once more, he forgot to ask how she knew what he wanted because she was on her knees again, licking him from bottom to top, then sucking on him with great vigour and making such delicious sounds that he had to steel himself to not come in her mouth.

She realized that he was too tall for her to keep him in her mouth as his erection stood to its fullness. She looked for a pillow for under her knees and he adjusted his stance, his leg muscles locked, toned ass in her hands.

"Fuck. Sahara. You suck my cock like it's always been in your mouth." She moaned; his words pleasing to her. She felt her wet sliding down the inside of her thighs, the fire warming her.

"I can smell your sweet pussy from here. It's mine for tonight, Sahara."

"Tell me that that's not negotiable, Aiden. I need to hear that you want to possess me." She moaned onto him, his cock stretching her mouth, the feel of the tip of it against her lips making her sex ache.

He pulled her up and kissed her brutally, tasting himself on her tongue. His hands found the roundness of her bottom, he moved on to her clit, giving it a small nudge. It throbbed under his fingers.

"Think of anyone else and you'll see that I mean it."

His hands tight on her shoulders, he pushed her down to the carpet and spread her legs. Aiden always loved seeing everything that he was getting.

"Wider," she said, her fingers reaching to ease the ache in her clit.

He felt that powerful tremor again. She rocked his world with every word that she uttered. At first, he just looked at her, and she trembled as he feasted on her loveliness, legs spread so wide that he could see every hot bit of her, her engorged clit, her tight opening.

"My lady, you're so very beautiful, but you're impossibly small, how will I fit my cock inside you?"

"Your tongue, Aiden, please!"

She almost yelled it, impatient to see his handsome face lower toward her, to see that way he had of pushing his hair aside, to see his tongue against her.

She lifted up towards him. Her clit throbbed as he leaned in, his arms powerful as his muscles locked. He licked her delicately, one small touch, so light she almost couldn't feel it. She pushed against his face. He licked again, on each side of her clit but not quite over the top, he kissed the inside of her thighs, on the tender skin where her thigh met her sex. He bit her there, paying careful attention to her breath to guide him to her most pleasurable spots. He kissed all around her folds, drowning in her scent and flavour.

Sahara cried out when he licked her fully from her tightly pursed bud to her clit, his tongue wide, holding her open with his hands. He pulled her tender and swollen clit into his mouth and sucked expertly, her voice urging him on, until she let herself fall under wave after wave of release, finally plunging his tongue into her as her muscles worked the force of her orgasm. He lifted himself to kiss her once more, his cock resting against her belly, hard, insistent, the wet of her cum on his lips.

She rubbed her hand over her clit and spread herself for him to have another look. "Fuck me Aiden." She stared at his raging erection. "I need that inside me."

"I think that I might hurt you, but I *am* going to fuck you Sahara."

She turned over like a cat, and shoved her ass towards him. He looked so large and dangerous behind her, his hand in his hair, his eyes contemplative of the task before him. She knew that she needed to drive him to the wilder parts of her desires; she needed him to punish her for being so easily taken. He was looking at her ass like a man possessed, his eyes devouring all her crevices, wondering how in the world he would be able to fuck her without breaking her, but wanting so very much to hurt her at the same time. She glistened from the licking he had given her. He ran his fingers over her ass, along her back entrance, and pushed lightly against her bud. She moaned and opened up a little.

"I need you, Sahara. I need to fill you. I'm going to fill your cunt with my very hard cock, if it pleases you."

Aiden pushed her pussy open with the head of his cock, letting the thick crest rest just inside her opening, his hands holding her still to prevent her pushing back on it. She moaned with frustration.

"It pleases me to please you my lord." She laid her forehead down on the carpet, her hands flat, submissive, back arching towards him. "Give me all you have."

With that bit of encouragement, Aiden took a chance and smacked Sahara's ass so hard that she cried out and fell hard to the floor. He froze; surprised at himself, poignantly aware that he had not asked permission for rough play. He tried to clear his head but all he could feel was an intense need to try it again.

"Again!" Sahara cried out. "Please Aiden, again!"

She waved her delicious ass, and Aiden, ecstasy rolling over him, spanked her hard, every strike determined; then dropped a series of tender kisses where his hand had caused her pain. She reeled between sensations, pain and pleasure so closely united that she couldn't decide which she craved more. He licked her perineum softly, now and again thrusting his tongue deep inside, before returning his punishing hand to her bottom. She was crying from the sting of it, tears streaming down her face. He asked her for a safe word, knew that he should insist on it when she begged for his hand once more, but he pressed on without it, even though he was now leaving welts.

She tasted better than anyone he had ever known, and he just wanted to keep his mouth to her sex. But she kept screaming, "Fuck

66

me Aiden," and when he did, she was filled so completely, so deeply, Aiden hitting all her best kept secrets so powerfully, that she sobbed tears of joy. She felt his movements in her soul, and responded with an orgasm from her very core, drowning in the magical abyss of feeling everything and nothing.

He held her hips in a tight grip, pulling her in as he pumped towards her, her cum soaking her legs and his rigid stomach. He pulled out for a moment and teased her ass with the head of his cock. He pushed at her gently, and she pushed back. He had to use all of his will power to not force his way in. Sahara was wet enough for him to slide in with one thrust. She yelled at him to get back inside her, needing to ride to the crest of the wave she was on. He was incredibly hard; she didn't have to coax that out of him. He pounded at her yielding cunt as fiercely as he dared, knowing that it hurt her, but unable to stop.

She asked for kisses, and he turned her around, guiding her to mount him. She tightened herself around him, rising back and forth, feeling his energy shift. She offered her nipples to his mouth. He loved the way that they stuck out enough for him to get a good grip with his lips and tongue. He pulled a little harder, moaning into her, his hands still gripping her waist, his prick so fully engorged that she had to spread herself wider. He pulled some of the wetness dripping down her legs towards her back opening, pushing at her bud, one finger making its way in easily. The tight ring of muscles clamped down on him, but he had no problem moving his finger gently in and out.

"Sahara," he groaned. "So tight. I want to hear you say that you like it." His eyes tore into her, his need savage in his stare.

But she couldn't speak; being filled this skillfully by a man this gorgeous was almost more than she could bear. Her moans as he teased her back entrance left him on the verge of release, and she felt it as his cock suddenly thickened and throbbed.

She pressed her mouth to his ear and whispered, "Would you like inside there, Aiden, to come in my tight little ass?"

With great satisfaction, she heard him roar, calling her name, calling her a whore, exploding his heat into her, his prick pumping out all that he had. There was nothing between them but the need to feel each other as one. His cock stayed hard for a time as she lay on top of him, Aiden holding her in a tight embrace, easing her down from the thresholds that the pain had surely taken her to.

She felt her energy pouring into him, infusing him with her gratitude. They lay in front of the fire, void of thought. Aiden eventually brought some ice wrapped in a soft cloth, and soothed the skin on her bottom, ending with some gently massaged in salve. Sahara had never been taken care of so tenderly after rough play, and certainly not by a man this delicious. She whispered things under her breath. He heard a name he thought, but he wasn't sure. She curled up into him.

He'd managed to hurt her and make her feel completely and utterly safe at the same time. And *that*, she knew, was one of her biggest addictions. Trusting a lover that way spanned dimensions that she usually only accessed in her dreams.

"Shall you stay?" he asked. "I'd like you to stay."

She nodded as her eyes searched his face, and her body trembled for more. He carried her with a steely grip up to his room and laid her down in sheets so cool they made her shiver. But when he lay down beside her, kissing her hair and apologizing if he'd hurt her, she fell into the mist again, without wanting to return. Aiden stayed awake for hours, watching her sleep. He didn't know who she was. Not really. They were so new to each other, yet how was it that they understood each other so well? Still, he knew that he wanted to please her and hurt her, and he wanted to love her.

She woke to him kissing her belly, kissing down to her bruised sweetness, his heart pounding hard in his chest, he felt lost to her scent and her magic, his mouth hungry for another taste. Sahara moaned his name over and over as his tongue licked possessively over her wet opening. Aiden slipped himself inside her. She winced but spread wider to accept him. He loved her tenderly and she cried as he did.

She knew that she was broken and that no-one could fix her. She needed a lover like Aiden to make her love and to make her hurt. And she was afraid because she could tell he needed the same. She'd been here before, in the place where two passionate people found love. She'd promised herself that she would be careful. But it was already too late. It was always too late. She always crossed the forbidden boundaries. She had no resolve when it came to love or sex.

"Sahara."

She looked at him with clouded eyes.

"Sahara."

She smiled. He needed to say her name. To hear it on his lips and on the air, to understand how her name felt to him. To think about what her name evoked in his soul. She stretched and turned over, away from his eyes.

He rolled her back towards him and smiled his most charming

smile, his tongue slipping over his sinful lips, looking for the last of her taste.

"Sahara. I'm going to go downstairs, put the coffee on, and take a walk in the woods. Make yourself at home. Do you have time to eat with me or do you have to get back to that mysterious book you're writing?"

"If you don't mind, I'll shower and wait to have coffee with you. K?"

"Yes. Wait for me then, I just need a bit of time to myself."

"No need to explain, Aiden, I need it too."

She wound her arms around his neck and nuzzled around under his hair, kissing towards his ear. He gripped her arms tightly and pulled her down so he could see her.

"Sahara, you're casting a spell on me. How will I ever escape your charms?"

"You won't," she said, her words light, but she felt troubled. Had a spell, indeed, been cast? She could smell magic on him but he felt bound. And she had an idea of who might have bound him. There was no going back now. Sahara would take Iona to task, and if it took her forever, she would find out what her interest in Aiden was all about.

⋯ ⋯ ⋇ ⋯ ⋯

Aiden opened the front door and breathed in the cool forest air. It was damp at this time of the morning. The sun was filtering in between the branches; it was his favourite time of day. He padded barefoot towards an opening where he had set up a series of props to work out on. He sat down and put his head in his hands.

My God, Aiden! He thought. *What are you doing?*

He had always been a considerate lover; he knew the rules of rough play. Always ask for safe words *beforehand*! Always establish the boundaries...*beforehand*! Ask for what you need but respect the needs of your playmate. Don't push past pain thresh-holds unless asked. Fuck! He knew he had hurt Sahara uninvited at first. Not quite sure why he had completely lost his head and all his bedside manners, he turned his mind back to the night before. How completely she had taken his lust to the very edges of sanity. He was certainly not without experience in loving un-inhibited women. But this! He did not alto-gether trust himself with her, nor did he trust her either. Lost to his thoughts he pushed himself through a workout. His arms bulged un-der the pressure, but he ignored the pain, he was used to much more than this, and not all of it administered by his own devices.

Aiden Halloran also loved to be taken, tied and whipped. He required a courageous lover, who could play both the submissive and the dominant.

Walking back to where his home came into view, Aiden was greeted by the smell of coffee. He had never had a woman stay overnight at his home. That had been a fast held rule. Before Holly, there hadn't been one woman visitor. Home was sacred ground, even if he did not verbalize it as such. He walked into his house savouring the image of Sahara at his counter, cup of coffee lifted to her lips.

She smiled a mischievous smile. "Sorry, couldn't wait..."

"I see." He smiled back. "I'll have some."

What he really wanted to say was that he needed to fuck her again, to feel himself stretching her tight around him, to demand she say that she was his.

"Aiden, it's ok," Sahara began, feeling his need to apologize for hurting her. "I know what you want to say, and it's truly ok. I wanted it, the welts are all but gone."

"It's not about the marks," he replied wryly. "It's about breaking boundaries, about not honouring a woman's right to feel safe. I never do that. I mean, until last night, I have never hurt a woman... well, unless we had agreed on something she wanted in bed."

"Until last night, Aiden, I have never been so completely satisfied. You hurt me, yes, but I wanted it more than you could have known, and I think you felt it from me before it happened. I also am sorry, for pushing you to those places. We went somewhere last night that...I don't know...it's almost like we'd done this before. I'm not afraid of the pain..."

She looked at him with hope in her eyes; hope that she hadn't scared him. The last love of her life had run away because she had given in to all her desires. And the last time she had not asked for the boundaries. It seemed that she hadn't learned a thing.

Aiden tried to take in all she was saying. That thing about more pain, my God, he would have to take this slowly, ask more questions. His pants bulged with new desire. He sat down to hide it.

"Sit with me Sahara. I'm curious about something."

"What makes you curious, tell me?" Sahara felt a twinge of apprehension.

"I'm curious to know what you think about re-incarnation."

CHAPTER 10 - ENGLAND - 1405

"All Shall be Well, and All Shall be Well, and All Manner of Things Shall be Well" ~ Julian of Norwich

Arinn stood in the doorway of her dwelling with her face to the gathering wind. Dagr was on his way back. The wind told her so. The wind carried his scent, sweeter than any she had ever known, and the promise of his blinding love for her. Dagr, like his name, was meant for a new day, a new earth that the two of them had often dreamed of.

"What else," she asked the wind. "What else do you bring with Dagr? Be it not danger," she chided the wind, her friend.

What kind of a double edged sword might Dagr have for her? She had known from the beginning of their life away from all the others that there would come a day when Dagr would long for his dreams and visions. He talked of it in his sleep. He called to his previous lovers, and the man he had counted as more brother than friend. He dreamt of peace and swords set aside from the work of gutting men on the battle field.

One day not long ago he had risen from their sleep pallet and whispered softly in her ear; "It is time, my love. I must be on my way."

"Will you go to the Dark Pool to seek answers?"

"Yes. Provisions are plentiful now. You have enough firewood to keep the hearth and you can snare a rabbit as well as I. Your larder is full of herbs and roots." Dagr had run his hand softly across her cheek then, reminding her to keep her sword by her side, his eyes tender upon her.

"Will you be long?"

"I will not stay away longer than the season of the harvest moon."

She knew that she could trust his word, saving he be killed or captured on his travels. This was a troubling and fearful time of men that knew no honour, whose word meant nothing, whose mouths spoke vile curses that were best left unspoken. Arinn thought back to the time when Dagr had been the respected lord of the manor and she, his lady; when he had been the skilled knight whose sentiments about the human condition had chafed against the life that he was born to.

He had been naïve, her Dagr, insisting on incorporating the magic his mother had taught him into life on the demesne. What he thought would bring stronger community, instead had brought grief and death.

Dagr's magic took time. It was watchful of the seasons, it called on co-operation with the Fey. And that was how he had run the manor lands, urging the people to stay tuned to the whispers of nature. But that had been bad advice to the superstitious among them. There had come a day of reckoning for all of them, when it had become obvious that Dagr had no intention of changing his ways. His stubbornness had brought them all down. Even the Earl Richard Dumont, whom Dagr loved far more than was customary between men, could not convince him to temper his practices.

Still, Arinn loved the man that Dagr was. He had conviction, a kind heart, and a love for the natural world. Challenged by the law of the land, Dagr had stood firm in his beliefs. He would always be the one who kept asking questions when everyone else thought they had already arrived at the answer. But that was how they had ended up alone in the Oracle Wood. When the fight had come to him, Dagr had tried to lead the villagers to the safety of the trees, but none had followed. And now it was only him and her.

Arinn turned into the simple wattle and daub hut that was now their home and stoked the fire. She threw on a bundle of sweet scented herbs. She brushed her golden hair until it shone and left it loose about her shoulders. Dagr liked to hide his face in her hair when he held her; he said it made him feel safe. She stirred the rabbit stew in the cauldron. He would be hungry. For food and for her.

She shifted on her heels, smiling to herself as she thought about Dagr in her bed. Brave and battle hardened, he had turned her heart over towards love of a man as she discovered the soft parts of him, his dreams of peace and honour a powerful aphrodisiac to her soul and mind. He had always been admired by women, and some men had also lusted for his attention.

Dagr was taller than most, his long fair hair braided at times, held together with beads of bone and wood. He exuded power when he walked into a room, his large frame outsized only by his confidence. Dagr was not afraid to be different, to own a distinct style, though it made others wary of him. He weighed the opinion of men and women equally. He crossed the boundaries between the world of the Fey and human kind without ever being lost. Dagr, from a long line of magic workers, and closely nurtured by his Irish mystic mother until the age of seven, had the best of both male and female sensibilities.

He had set his eye on Arinn when she was still a girl of fourteen, blossoming and being readied for marriage to an older, lesser noble. Arinn, who had come to him in friendship, had sat on a stool in the stable and confessed that she did not want to marry.

"Oh?" Dagr queried as she followed him around the courtyard as he saw to his affairs, while her mother, Dagr's chatelaine, worked inside the house.

"Should you not be inside, helping your mother?" He winked, knowing that she would rather be in the barn with horse and leather smells than anywhere else.

"Dagr, I do not *like* the man I am betrothed to...he smells of cabbage and garlic." She curled up her nose in disgust but that had only made him throw back his head with laughter.

"He is terrible and rough and has rotten teeth! Dagr, tell him that I *will not* marry!"

"Arinn, you know the way a woman needs a man to give her a home and you have nothing to say about it. It has been decided."

"Well, it is wrong that I have no say, and I hate him. I will not marry him!" And she buried herself in his strong arms and cried. "Dagr?" She finally looked up from her tears and sought out his kind countenance.

"Dagr...if I tell you a secret, will you keep it for me?"

"Of course, my sweet. Anything for you."

She looked up hopefully. Dagr had looked out for her since her father had fallen in battle. At twenty four, Dagr was the man she had always counted on for advice. She hadn't known yet that Dagr was also the man who lusted after her emerging womanhood, and who had fallen in love with her.

"Tell me your secret. It is safe with me."

"Dagr," Arinn whispered, "I love Brigida."

"Brigida! The sister of my bailiff? I can see why. Brigida is sweet in look and spirit." He turned away.

"You do not think it is wrong? That I should not love her?" She tugged on his sleeve so he would look her in the eye.

She was confused by his easy answer.

"Not love her? Arinn, you should be free to love whom you wish."

"Then you are the only one who thinks so," Arinn observed with a downturned mouth. "I can tell no-one else."

"Tell me, does Brigida know that you love her?" Dagr took a deep breath and faced her once more.

"Oh yes! And she loves me too! We have vowed to be together.

But nothing will come of it, I know."

"And have you thought about what this would mean, Arinn, a love with Brigida? I mean..." And here he fumbled.

"Dagr! Of course we have thought about it. I am not a child." She pouted her lips and fixed him with a stare of her grey-blue eyes.

"So then, how would it be that you would have young ones? Have you thought of that? Or maybe you do not desire to have any?"

"Oh, I do not, but Brigida does. I have attended too many births to desire children, but Brigida said we would find a way."

Dagr looked at her and scowled.

"Are you angry with me Dagr? You are wearing your fearsome face."

"No, Arinn, I am not. But I am upset that at your tender age, you are already afraid of men."

"I am not a little girl! Brigida and I have lain together! And I am not *afraid* of men, I simply do not *like* them in that way...you know, the way..."

Dagr raised his eyebrow at Arinn and she blushed profusely.

"Arinn, I truly do not think that you are a child."

"Do you not want to know about my lying down with Brigida?" Arinn offered provocatively.

"You *are* trusting, Arinn. Your secret is safe with me, but I would suggest that you not tell anyone else, it would not bode well for either of you."

"I trust you," She said with all the innocence that youth afforded her. "Brigida is a little bit older. Her brother says that her black hair and ruby lips will one day bring her ruin, but I think she is beautiful. Your bailiff has never liked how much time we spend together."

Dagr kept brushing his horse so vigorously that Arinn was tempted to stay his hand.

"Well, once, when she and I were at the sea side, laying in the long grass and enjoying the heat of the summer sun, she kissed me! And before that I did not know that a girl could kiss another girl, but it felt so nice and she was so soft and she held me. And I felt a funny thing in my stomach, like a tightening, and I longed for her. She told me she loved me and that I was beautiful. But I know that it is wrong."

Dagr walked to the back of the stable.

"Dagr. Are you listening?" Arinn demanded.

"I am listening, but I just do not see a way for you Arinn. You run the risk of being flogged."

"But you would not have us flogged. You would allow it? We'll run away, Brigida and I," Arinn declared.

"Come here, you fool." Dagr gathered Arinn up again and held her close. "You will *not* run away, and if you do, I will follow."

They grinned at each other, partners already in the secret of forbidden love.

"Will you always protect me, Dagr?" Arinn asked with her upturned face, soaking up all of the safety of his embrace.

"Always Arinn. But you must remember to address me as 'my lord' when we are around others. And you have to stop hiding in my arms whenever you have a problem. You are betrothed."

He held up his hand as she opened her mouth to protest once more. Arinn decided that changing the subject was best.

"Why did your mother name you Dagr? It is not a Christian name." She followed him now to the back of the stable, where he found a store of bruised apples and taking her hand, placed it in her palm so she could offer it to his horse.

"It means 'new day'. My mother had a vision for me. I can only hope to live up to her dreams. She believed that men could learn to forsake war...and live peaceably."

Dagr did not bother to hide the mist in his eyes.

He smiled when Arinn lifted the apple to his horse's mouth.

"Like velvet," she murmured, her hand opening to the horses nibbling, her face lit up by her love for the huge beast before her.

———————

By week end, Dagr had made an offer so generous to the noble betrothed to Arinn that the man could not refuse. Dagr then paid the fine required for the break in betrothal, and offered himself to Arinn, while explaining that she had no choice, she had to marry him, if she wanted any life with Brigida at all.

She agreed, on one condition. Brigida would become her lady in waiting. She needed her close.

Dagr agreed immediately. The rest, like their obvious confusion about obligations in the marital bed, was left unsaid. Arinn offered her tearful gratitude to Dagr with a soulful press of her lips to his. He took what she offered, her hands in his as she stood on tiptoe to reach him, not surprised that her mouth didn't open to invite his tongue in. And in that moment, it was enough.

Dagr received word the next day that he was to meet Earl Richard Dumont. He was to leave for battle. There was no indication for how long. The implications of his leaving hung like a dark cloud over Dagr. Leaving Arinn seemed impossible. Arinn could barely make sense of what she was feeling. Brigida's arms were her only place of solace.

What little time there was to prepare for his and Arinn's wedding, Dagr spent in making sure that his bride would have every comfort that he could afford. Brigida helped Arinn make her own preparations, packing up her beloved's few belongings, and delivering them to the small chamber connected to Dagr's solar.

Dagr passed Brigida in the stairwell. She looked at him with anxious eyes. He was entitled to his husbandly reward, he told himself. One could hardly blame him for wanting to bed his own wife.

Brigida's legs seemed to tremble as Dagr stood towering over her on the narrow stairs.

Dagr looked at Brigida with compassion. Every fibre of him wished that he could claim Arinn for himself. If he had been anyone else, he would have done so, and without apology to Brigida. But it was not his way.

"I will leave her for you, I will not touch her," he said simply.

His loins were on fire, he tried desperately to will his cock into behaving. Brigida held on to the wall for support as he leaned into her and ever so lightly moved his face through her hair as he spoke.

"Thank you, my lord," she curtsied, head down, acknowledging his kindness. It only made him want her more. If only he could dare to have them both. The thought brought him pleasure and rage at the same time.

Dagr wondered if he had finally lost all his good sense, for what good could come of this arrangement? Arinn was safe now from a life with a man who surely would have killed her spirit, but how could they manage the charade that their union surely was.

Brigida had a bath poured for her beloved on her wedding day, fragrant with herbal oils, and washed her tenderly, kissing her lips, her hair, her breasts. They shed grateful tears knowing that this was the only way they could ever be together, under the protective arm of Dagr. It was a flawed plan, but the only one they had.

Brigida and Dagr's eyes met as Arinn stood on the church porch in her marrying gown, her hair brushed to reflect the radiance of the sun. She looked more beautiful than either of them had ever seen her, her eyes calm as she took Dagr's hand. In that moment, the groom and the lady in waiting acknowledged their mutual longing for the bride, and it was he who lowered his gaze first. Dagr made good his promise to Brigida and slept alone that night. The two women shared the small bed in the antechamber of the solar. And from that day on, something began to build between them, silently and powerfully, as love sometimes does.

Dagr relieved his desires with a woman almost twice his age who had skilled him in the ways of the bed chamber. She was not surprised when he showed up at her door the night before he left for battle, but accepted his explanation that his bride was young and naïve in bed, and that he needed a bit more of a tussle than Arinn could offer him. Teresa, a widow and an exotically colored beauty, could take Dagr to places he would not dare go with another. She was the one who had taught him about tying her without bruising her wrists, about pleasuring her back entrance with oils and patient strokes, and to ask for the same from her. These things she was sure he could not do with a girl of fourteen.

Dagr could release a degree of his strength on her knowing that she would keep him in check. He was lovely to watch, when he struggled to escape the tight knot of rope around his wrists, begging her to desist her painful attentions. She knew when he really meant it, and then she would take him gently in her mouth. She was wicked and kind; and he repaid her attentions with freshly caught venison.

Arinn and Brigida fell into a gentle rhythm of life at the manor when Dagr rode away, his promise to return tucked deeply into their hearts. Arinn learned to supervise the servants and to run the household under the skilled tutoring of her mother. She took pride in knowing that when Dagr came back, all would be well at his hearth. Brigida's brother Mark, kept order on the demesne, and a keen eye on his sister, who was determined that nothing should befall her lady, while her lord was away.

The two women soon learned that it was Dagr who kept the peace on his estate, his diplomacy and reputation as wise and fair no exaggeration. As good a bailiff as Mark was, they noticed that he could not quell all the bickering among the farmers, he simply did not have Dagr's touch.

It was also while Dagr was away that Arinn found her way to the Oracle Wood, in need of the wise woman. Of course she knew of her, she had been the shadowy figure at difficult births, and the one the villagers sent for when in need of a skilled herbalist.

After she had made the trip once, nothing could keep Arinn from going back to soak up the old woman's teachings. From decoding plant lore to the magic of tree spirits, the old woman held a treasure of knowledge in her head and her hands, and she delighted in her young student. Arinn was a natural, not surprisingly to the crone. Dagr had spoken of her often, his heart spilling out with his words, and the old woman had known even then, that a man who held magic so easily in his hands, could only fall in love with a maiden who could work it.

CHAPTER 11

Arinn and Brigida set up a still room at the manor and spent many happy hours preparing tinctures and salves. The room was a place of solace for the two young women, so desperately in love. No one ventured there, save for the occasional visit from the gardener, who brought them bundles of herbs for drying and flowers for soaking in vinegars and oils. The rest of the time, the room, which opened up to a private walled garden, became their favourite place to pass the hours waiting for Dagr's safe return.

If not for the kitchen boy, and his fervent conversations with the village priest, no-one would have known about the stolen moments of lust that Brigida and Arinn indulged in while the cauldron of herbs boiled over the open fire. Or that Brigida wept a confession to Arinn one day about her love for Dagr, and her fear that he be killed at war. Even the kitchen boy could not believe his ears when he heard Brigida say that she'd repay Dagr on her knees for the chance at love that he had afforded them.

They were witches, trying to catch lord Dagr into a sinful ménage, was how the priest explained it to the dull witted boy.

"You would repay him on your knees?" Arinn asked incredulously. "Would you Brigida? Do you know anything of these skills?"

"I would, and I don't, regrettably." Brigida replied. "Only what I have heard from the village wenches and it all sounds rather ghastly. But what I think about, what I think would happen between a woman and a man; I would be willing to try."

Brigida took Arinn in her arms, and kissed her softly.

"But only if you let me, he is yours, after all."

They blossomed into women in the year that Dagr was away. There had been chance to lie together and explore their love. It looked good on them. And it was the first thing that Dagr noticed when he rode into the courtyard of the manor.

He jumped off his great horse to greet them, but checked himself as he reached for Brigida when Arinn left his arms. The whole of the household was turned out to welcome him. He handed his horse to the stable boy, and looking about him, expressed his pleasure to be back.

"How have you fared in my absence, my lady?" Dagr took Arinn's hand in his and led the way into the house. He felt her warmth against him and his love for her ripped him apart. Dagr was hungry for home and his wife.

Brigida followed behind, looking lost and bewildered. Would Dagr take what was his tonight, and would she lay in bed alone after all this time of feeling Arinn next to her? She could not help but grieve the loss of her time alone with Arinn, although her body hummed with desire, as she locked her eyes on Dagr's wide back, his step powerful, his hair spilling long down his back.

Dagr sent the kitchen boy to prepare his bath, and pulled the women aside with a grin.

"I bring you gifts, my lady." He bent low over Arinn's hand.

"May I have them now?" Arinn asked with a sparkle in her eye. Dagr laughed and pushed back his hair, now knotted in places.

"I have missed your outspoken manner, my lady. Take Brigida to your chamber. Let me bring them to you." He did not miss the shadow in Arinn's eyes. He knew that she would be protective of Brigida's feelings, and it made him love her more.

"There are some things for you as well, Brigida." He winked at them both, a smile on his handsome face.

"Thank you, my lord." Arinn stood on tiptoe and planted a kiss on his lips, her arms loose around his neck.

Dagr's arms went to her waist instantly, and he pulled her in for the embrace he had longed for all these months. She had never felt such heat, such hard muscle set so intently against her soft breast. Arinn pulled away, her eyes confused, and looked towards Brigida, who stood with tears welling up in her eyes.

"You will be proud, Dagr. We have taken the liberty of setting up a still room."

Arinn burst into chatter. "I have even visited the wise woman. Brigida and I have been making tinctures and teas."

"I am well pleased and surprised my lady! I will come to the still room tomorrow, when you may show me what you have learned. But were you not afraid to walk the wood? You know the superstitions of the village folk. And was the good priest not outraged at your visiting the wise woman for instruction? He has never been fond of my close ties to the crone."

"My lord," Brigida answered, "Your lady has proven to have a gift for plant lore, and since the priest had a bad humor, even he was forced to call upon us for a healing tea. There was no avoiding going into the wood, we were told that if you were here and there was need, that you would have fetched the wise woman yourself. The responsibility fell to my lady upon your absence."

So much had happened since he had been gone. He could see that his household was no worse for wear with these two at the helm, however unconventional their partnership was in keeping the manor well cared for. He knew that Arinn would have leaned on the older and wiser Brigida to help her work out tricky details and that they must have had to be clever not to reveal their love.

He bowed his head to Brigida. "I am grateful for the good care you have given my lady."

They were in the hall outside Arinn's chamber now. He would go in for his bath soon, but was hesitant to leave them.

"Does your chamber offer you comfort, my lady?" Dagr knew that now that he was home, things would change for them all.

Arinn nodded in answer.

Weary from the road and anticipating his hot bath, he bade them farewell until the evening meal. He looked forward to hearing how they liked their gifts.

Lying in the welcome hot water, he could hear their whispers and smiled when he heard them exclaim over the fine stockings he had brought from France for Arinn, and enough material for a new chemise and tunic for each of them. He closed his eyes. The sound of their voices brought delight to his heart. He called for the kitchen boy sitting outside his chamber to fetch more hot water, and waited contentedly until he heard the knock on the door.

"Come!" He answered, drawing his legs in so that the water could be poured.

To his surprise, it was Arinn who walked in carrying the heavy bucket. He sat up, his heart pounding.

"My lady?"

Arinn poured the water in, keeping her eyes on his chest, her face burning with their sudden familiarity.

"I would wash your hair, my lord."

She moved to his head and put her hands in his hair, massaging through the tangles with shaking fingers and falling tears. She had willingly put herself in this position, wanting to attend to his needs, but now fear took over her previous determination to make all things appear normal between them.

Dagr, overwhelmed by her courage, fought to keep his cock from rising as her hands sent deep shocks of energy through his muscles.

"Arinn." Dagr's voice broke. "Attend to me only if you truly desire to do so."

He caught her hands in his and held them tight, hoping to stop her shaking.

"Dagr. I want to, it pleases me."

He sank down under the water and wet his hair thoroughly, scrubbing out the worst of the sand and grime. Arinn watched as he moved in the water, it was difficult to not appreciate his fine form, as much as she usually delighted in the more refined beauty of a woman's body. Everything about him spoke of excellence. It seeped out through his pores.

"Your hair is longer. And tangled!"

She lathered up her hands with the soap she had made as a gift for him while he was away.

She was good at this, he discovered, feeling how her fingers scrubbed at his scalp. He complimented her on the scent of pine in the soap. She said she'd made it with him in mind.

"Should I cut my hair back to its usual length?" he asked.

"No!" She exclaimed so vehemently that he laughed. "Brigida would hate that," she said. "She loves your long hair."

What was a man to make of such a statement, which incriminated his lady of discussing him with another woman, one they both knew harboured a desire for him. This was a strange circumstance indeed. Arinn worked on the tangles in his hair, and when her hands brushed his tense shoulders, Dagr shuddered in response. He truly feared for her safety, his passion rising swiftly and violently. He clenched his fists under the water, stilling the powerful urge to drag her into the bath on top of him, and find the soft flesh under her clothes.

"I would like to rest, my lady, before we eat." He choked out the words as tenderly as possible.

He was sending her away. It did not occur to her why, but she was glad to leave his chamber, his energy too intense for her to bear any longer.

"Thank you for my gifts, Dagr," Arinn said shyly, lingering at the door. "For Brigida's as well. It was thoughtful of you."

She did not have to thank him. Gifts would have been expected. But she thanked him anyway. It was part of what made him love her to distraction.

"I have something else for you," he replied. "Come back to me before we eat."

She nodded and left. Dagr got out of the bath and dried himself off. There was no ignoring his persistent erection. No-one heard his low growl as he found the release he was craving, an image of Arinn and Brigida in his bed fueling his passion.

⊷ ⊷✖⊷ ⊷

Brigida took Arinn in her arms and held her tight.

"You are shaking."

Arinn shook her head and pushed her lips to Brigida's.

"I am scared. He is ever so beautiful...and...big! He requested my return to his chamber before our evening meal. Do you think...?"

Brigida looked at her, eyes wild, trying to comprehend the image of a naked Dagr before Arinn, wishing she had been in her place, to see those broad shoulders bare, his manhood rising.

"Brigida!" Arinn shook her lover.

Brigida stared at Arinn vacuously. "No, I am sure that he will not ask; he would not. He knows..."

"One day he will have to ask. You know that he has to!"

"Call for a bath Arinn. I will help you get ready."

"You are avoiding my question."

"We will face it when we have to. Tonight, we celebrate our Dagr's return."

"You said, 'our'." Arinn kissed Brigida hard, she knew that her friend was burning up for the kind of love that she could not offer her.

"Yes," Brigida answered simply.

"I love you Brigida. I would give you anything you asked for."

They fell to their bed. Next door, Dagr closed his eyes to the muffled sounds coming from their chamber, as he laid desperately seeking rest. They would have to learn to be more careful, he thought, and wished that he had the ill manners to break through their door.

He presented Arinn with a jeweled brooch for the belt she wore around her tunic when she came to greet him in his room that evening. It was extravagant, like his love for her. Embracing her to him, he whispered in her ear, creating a sensation that surprised her along her spine.

"I will not have you worry, Arinn. You will sleep in my bed tonight, I have to insist. But I give my word that I will not touch you," he said, though he had no idea how he would have the strength to make his promise true.

She could only nod. Her body betrayed her as his warm breath washed over her, and the steely grip of his arms circled her waist.

CHAPTER 12

In time, the villagers said amongst themselves, Arinn would give Dagr an heir. He was clearly besotted with her, as she accompanied him on his rounds of the demesne; a stunning sight beside her handsome and enigmatic lord. At night, Dagr would see Arinn in his chamber for a game of cards and quiet talk in front of the fire. When it came time for sleep, he would release her to Brigida, but leave the door adjoining their rooms open.

How many times had he ventured over to their bed to tuck them into their covers and furs? They slept like kittens in a bowl of finely spun wool, he thought. Their covers askew, their arms around each other, they were as desirable in their sleep as when they were awake. One night, as he dropped soft kisses on their foreheads and whispered goodnight, Brigida opened her eyes. He stared into their dark depths, caught in the web of her blatant desire, before returning to his dimly lit chamber.

With Brigida's curious gaze upon him from where she lay in her bed, Dagr shed his hunting shirt, his necklaces and bracelets, and stepped out of the leathers he preferred over the customary hose, turning towards her.

Dagr was no small man. His battle hardened and scarred body, his hair spilling over his shoulders, made her breath rush out suddenly. He was naked, erect; his skin glowed with scented oils. He ran his hands absent-mindedly through his hair, smiling that lazy smile he sometimes teased her with. Brigida was now sitting in her bed, her exposed breasts pointing at him, willing him to come nearer. Unable to resist her seduction, yet mindful of his love for Arinn, he stood rooted to the ground, one hand on his thick cock, stroking deliberately.

This, my sweet lady's maid, he thought, *is how I would like you to please me.*

Her eyes were as rapt as a cat on a mouse, her fingers tugged on her nipples to urge him on. Then, turning away from him in presenting position, she arched her back gracefully to show him the sweetness of her folds. Dagr came with a shudder, and a groan. It had taken all his will to not come bounding towards her. Arinn stirred in her sleep and fumbled around looking for her lover's body, pulling her in, murmuring endearments. Brigida, now fully swollen and seeking penetration snuggled into Arinn's arms and pulled her hand between her legs. Arinn smiled, eyes still closed, and slipped three fingers in. Brigida sighed and asked for more.

Dagr watched as Arinn, sleepy but aroused, slipped out of the covers and exposed her naked body. He licked his lips involuntarily as he saw her ample breasts, nipples long and erect, her hair spilling down her back, the delicious round of her bottom. In the last two years that they had been together, she had grown into a truly remarkable beauty. Arinn fell into Brigida's arms, rubbing her breasts in her face, Brigida eagerly taking Arinn's nipples in her mouth, sucking hard. Dagr stayed in the shadows; unable to turn away, desperate to join them in their caress. Women truly were the best of creation, of this he was convinced.

Brigida presented to Arinn, swaying her hips, exposing herself with her fingers. Their kisses and caresses flowed with unrestrained passion, words unnecessary, as they knew each other's bodies well. And now Dagr could see Arinn unfold before him, as she bent down on hands and knees to taste her lover's sex, her tongue teasing Brigida's engorged clit, then suddenly plunging into her depths. His cock strained to its fullest height, desperate to pump them both, needing release as he watched them pleasure each other. He dared not touch himself again, because he knew that they would hear him from his place in the shadows.

He would have to wait a long time that night, because Arin and Brigida were insatiable, starting over when they were finished, with more kisses and caresses, until they fell fast asleep tangled up in each other. Dagr found his cock throbbing and his mind exploding with desire. He tightened his hand around himself once again, coming swiftly and silently, knowing that in the morning, he would have to face them with innocence in his smile.

Before the women woke, he was already gone. He rode off as the sun rose, to where the river bent into a swirling pool, and strode into the cold depths. His desire still held as he remembered the love he had witnessed. He knew that he loved them both, needed to bed them both. The river ran around him whispering to his stirred up soul, soothing his anguish, the living water taking in all that he was feeling. He felt the love of the river, and wept silent tears for his hopes that all would be well between them, that Arinn would accept his love, that he could keep the women safe from being discovered as lovers. There was no way for him to deny what he was feeling. He lay in the flow for a long time, his arms extended, floating a ways, looking to the sky for courage. When he was spent, he lay down wrapped in his surcoat and the heat of the warming sun. He fell fast asleep, his beautiful body stretched out for much needed rest.

It was deep afternoon before he woke. His horse had found him and stood a small distance off, tearing at the grass where it stood sweetest. Dressing, Dagr made up his mind to visit the wise woman in the woods, and led his horse in that direction. If he was to bed the women he loved, and he was determined to do so, he would protect them from the child he knew would be created. He would not dishonor Brigida with a child out of wedlock. And for that he needed the herbs that the old woman had gathered and dried. He would think about an heir later.

⸺⸻⸢⸣⸻⸺

Arinn woke first and looked to Dagr's bed as she did every morning, anticipating his ready smile. She frowned when she saw that he was gone, and pouted. Brigida was fast asleep, snoring lightly. Arinn traced her finger around Brigida's nipples. They stood erect. Arinn woke her with a gentle tug to one of them.

"Early morning walk?"

They dressed quickly and set out for the village. All around her, they could see the collection of small wattle and daub dwellings open to the morning sun, women up and around, stirring up their outdoor fires, children running and laughing. It was comforting to see the chickens pecking about, the animals being tended to. After the morning chores, the gardens would be the place of activity, and the older children would be sent to gather from the wild fruit bushes and trees.

They walked in silence for a while, contemplative.

Arinn was misfortune's girl. There was no rightful place for her, and the place she wanted wasn't allowed. They greeted the villagers as they went with smiles and kind words. She was loved, and it was good, but Arinn knew that had she the courage to reveal her true nature, they would turn on her and leave her to her fate.

Brigida motioned that they start for home, and their conversation turned to Dagr. Arinn said she thought Dagr had gone out hunting, and Brigida understood in that moment that Arinn had been looking for him. It was one of many small things that showed Brigida how Arinn's heart had filled with Dagr, as much as her friend denied it. They talked about all the things they'd learned from him. He knew which roots made good tea, which ones shook the contents out of your

86

stomach if you ate something bad, which ones made you sleepy, which ones kept you up at night and wove rich dreams; but these powders Dagr kept in a pouch on himself and was strict about how much they could take. He had taught them about powders for pain.

Arinn had helped grind these with the old woman in the woods. The old woman was well cared for by the village to Arinn and Brigida's surprise. The survival of them all depended on her as much as it did on the farmers and the hunters. She was solitary, she wove magic and she spoke to the spirits on their behalf.

Now Arinn was being trained to be a wise woman in secret. As much as Dagr understood the magic and mystery of plants and of calling down the energy from above; and as much as he had been initiated into the sorcerers role, he could not serve the village in this way, that role was reserved for a woman. When Arinn had asked him why, Dagr had said that a woman's womb was like the ocean, the place where God and Goddess stirred all of creation, and only a woman had the magic to bring something forth from Spirit to the physical world. Therefore, only a woman could call in specific healing powers. This was not the way of the new religion. In the new way, only men could speak to God. But Dagr did not agree with this, and insisted that the wise woman take Arinn on as her apprentice.

In the afternoon, Arinn, still restless, let Brigida know that she was going to walk out to look for more herbs and roots to dry and set out across the fields. She practiced her incantations that the wise woman had taught her, what to say if someone was shedding their mortal coil, what signs to draw over a woman's belly as she laboured in childbirth. She welcomed the play of the wind in her hair, and laughed as it whispered to her, bringing joy to her heart that she could hear such things. Her small basket filled with sweet grasses to burn in their room for scent, she ate berries from the brambles that scratched at her legs, and now and then dug up a root for tea or for healing. She saw Dagr's great horse standing under an ancient oak at the edge of the Oracle Wood, Dagr nowhere in sight. The horse whinnied in greeting. Arinn laughed and stroked his velvety nose.

"Where is your master, Handsome One?"

The horse shook his head and stamped his massive feet.

"Oh, so you will not say, you beast!" She laughed again and looked about her.

Dagr, happened upon her as she stood stroking the horse's mane. "Arinn! What brings you here?"

Arinn jumped, hand held to her heart. "Dagr! Were you visiting the wise woman?" Suddenly fearful, she asked..."Are you hurt? Did you need pain powders?"

"...in search of answers, but no, I am not hurt. Are you out in search of me?"

"Yes, I awoke before sunrise and you were not there." Her words hung between them, a diminutive accusation of his failure to advise her of his affairs.

"Before sunrise?"

Dagr fumbled over his words, but his eyes remained calm.

"Ride home with me, Arinn." Dagr held out his hands.

He lifted Arinn onto the horse's back, then jumped up himself.

She was proud of his graceful strength. She looked down at how his muscular hands held the reigns. His arms and chest hard as rocks, his hair whipping about him in the wind....she had no way of avoiding his charm. She looked up at him and he smiled down, pulling her into him, grateful for the warm light in her eyes. They rode contentedly, each lost to their own thoughts, she, feeling how his body protected her from the wind, now chilly; and he, how it felt so right to hold her in his arms.

Finally, decision made to speak plainly, Dagr stopped his horse, his hands at Arinn's waist, preventing her from turning around.

Arinn felt the rush of heat in the firm determination of his hands.

"Dagr? What is it?"

"I have something to confess my lady." He breathed the words into her neck, his body close, the rise of his cock hard against her back.

Arinn shuddered, anxious, but covered his hands with hers. Dagr's fingers laced between hers.

"Arinn...last night, I watched you and Brigida.... I was witness to the love you made. I should have made myself known."

She stiffened, her breath out in a rush, her mind racing to recollect the pleasure she had taken with Brigida.

Dagr leisured through her hair, breathing in her scent, his lips brushing against her skin.

Silence.

Arinn could only sit and allow the sensations that travelled like rapid fire from the heat in her head, down her spine and ending in a sudden rush at her sex.

Dagr pushed a little with his hips. "Are you very angry, my lady?"

Arinn found her voice. It whispered out of her in threads of confusion and lust.

"No, my lord." Her head leaned back towards him, sinking

against his chest. "Was watching to your pleasure, my lord?"

Dagr's hands went to her hair, he heard her gasp.

"Arinn, I love you." He nipped at her neck. She cried out.

Dagr adjusted himself in his leathers, his cock aching. She felt his hand behind her, touching himself but also brushing against her bottom. Her eyes opened wider. His touch was firm, so unlike the soft lingering of Brigida's hand.

"I have loved you for a very long time, my lady. Last night...I could not tear my eyes away, I wanted you more than you can imagine. I know that you love Brigida, and that you do not desire the touch of a man. Still, I want you, Arinn, with every part of me."

"But, I thought you liked *Brigida*," Arinn countered. "She desires *you*. Sometimes she watches you as you prepare for sleep. I knew that she would need a man one day. She speaks your name in her sleep. I thought it was *her* you desired...that way."

"Arinn. It is true, I do desire Brigida. She is part of you and now part of me. But it is you that my heart breaks for. You haunt my dreams, and my waking hours. I desire you above all, and wish that you were towards men inclined, because I desire to own you with my body. *Arinn.* I beg you, say something!"

Arinn had never seen him this way, not only as a warrior and her lord, but also as a vulnerable man, whose heart was now betraying him to her. She wondered whether he did truly love her, or was he like every man, only intrigued by the roundness of her breasts, the velvet between her legs.

He sat stock still, his body rigid, heart pounding. Arinn pulled his hands to her breasts, nipples pert through her kirtle. She turned her head to look him in the eye; his eyes were tortured and hard with lust. She glanced at his leathers, they were straining. She was no longer a child, she was expert at tantalizing a lover.

"My lady, please do not mock me. I mean what I say. I love you and I want you. *All of you.* I am half mad with lust for you and I would like to know that if I ever have you it is because you want me also."

His fingers locked over her nipples, expertly rolling them through the thin fabric of the kirtle, Arinn's breath coming fast now. She struggled to speak.

"Dagr I do love you. I love the husband you have been to me. I know nothing about loving you with my body. I have only known a woman, and she has all of me. You have always been my protector. I simply do not know anything about loving a man."

Dagr's tongue licked along his lower lip. Her gaze followed it hungrily. She'd given herself away.

An age old instinct washed over him. He jumped from his horse and pulled Arinn after him.

"*Arinn*. Allow me to kiss you."

"I do not know how,' she stammered, head down.

Frustrated now, he lifted her chin. "You do know how. It is like kissing Brigida."

"Still..."

He put his finger to her lips, silencing her. Her lips seared at his touch and she felt a deep urge to slip her tongue out and lick him. He leaned in towards her and found her lips, soft, yielding, her eyes open, she let him into her mouth, his tongue gentle, delicious, his smell enveloping her. Then harder, he kissed her with a man's ardour. Her eyes closed. He withdrew his tongue, he licked her lips; he nipped at her ear. His hair tickled her neck. She shuddered and opened her eyes.

"Now you. You kiss me." Dagr so very badly wanted to lift her kirtle and slide his hand along her thigh.

She looked down at his leathers again. He followed her gaze and his hand pushed down on his cock, she was intrigued at how huge it looked beneath the leather, and in his hand.

She leaned into him now, on tiptoe. He smiled down and moved toward her. They kissed with their lips closed. Over and over, they kissed as tenderly as Dagr knew how. She sniffed in his hair. She put her hand to the back of his neck. She pulled him in and opened her lips, her tongue slipping out over his, feeling his sharp intake of breath. She kissed around his jaw. He pulled her in by her waist. She pressed his lips open and thrust in her tongue, kissing him hard, then, rubbing her face into his chest, she bit at his nipple, hard. Arinn felt something awaken in him. It hit the air between them.

Dagr grabbed her by her hair and kissed her with force, his tongue lashing hers, sucking on it, moaning into her mouth. He pulled away and stared into her eyes, now wild, on fire.

"Arinn," he groaned out her name.

"I'm wet," she said simply. "Wet like when Brigida kisses me."

He laughed. He laughed with relief and with happiness. She pouted, looking once again like the little girl who had come to him for comfort in years past.

"Dagr," she breathed, swaying back to lean against the horse, her legs weak. "You can have me. Brigida too. I..." Her voice trailed off. She looked up at him, then closed her eyes, his look so intense that it filled her with fear once more.

"Home, Dagr," she muttered, turning towards the horse. "We need to tell Brigida."

He lifted her on and placed himself behind her once more. His knees dug sharply into his startled horse. Arinn soothed his hands on the reigns, white knuckled, as Dagr fought to control his need.

But she shook her head to herself. She knew that none of what he felt about bedding both Brigida and her could come out in the open, and that she would one day have to bear him a child. His dreams were just as impossible as hers. They would *all* be flogged and cast out.

She urged the horse on, tucked into Dagr's large frame. He loved her. There would not be another woman then, she had always half thought that he would leave her for someone who could return his love in the way he needed. She felt his hardness against her back. He didn't try to move back, he wanted her to feel his desire. And she felt that tightening in her stomach again, her nipples pursed tight. She guided Dagr's hand up to feel them once more.

This was new, this ability to make a man lose his equilibrium, a power so heady that it made her clit throb into an orgasm, the horses back grinding beneath her, his warmth between her legs. She smiled. All would be well. Dagr felt her release as they rode on, but said nothing. It seemed that Arinn knew a thing or two about seduction, because she was not acting the shy young girl right now.

<hr />

Brigida stood with her hand shading her eyes as she scanned the road beyond the manor looking for Dagr's horse. When she saw them coming over the rise towards her, Dagr's arm wound protectively around Arinn's waist, and she waving delightedly at Brigida from her seat on the great horse, she knew that something had changed. So, he had finally told her.

The young women greeted with a silent embrace, Arinn shaking in Brigida's arms. Arinn put away the roots and sweet grass for drying in the still room. She made small talk with Brigida about the evening meal, asking if they would take a walk afterward. Dagr met them in the garden as they picked flowers for the table.

"We shall eat shortly," he announced gruffly. The women exchanged looks. They nodded at him and bade he sit in the garden with them, but he disappeared as quickly as he had appeared.

When they sat down to eat, they could see that he had ordered a good wine to be served, and pouring himself a liberal amount, asked them if they would drink with him. He sent the server away, scowling at him so fiercely that they were sure he would stay away until morning. The women sat in silence, aware of his attention upon them and his agitated mood.

"Shall we have some music, Dagr?" Arinn chanced a question.

"As you wish my lady," he replied, hands gripping the edge of the table, looking as if he might leap up at any moment. Brigida called in a young man from the kitchen who played the recorder.

Dagr relaxed somewhat as the sound of the music drifted in from the corner of the room, and ran his hands through his hair. These women would be the death of him, he was sure. He would set his house in order, and this would be the night. He was sorry that his mood had made their meal so tense, but he was raw with nerves as to how to proceed.

"I promised my lady that I would escort her on a walk after our meal," Brigida said.

He nodded, his eyes piercing through her. "You will return her to me before dark."

"Yes my lord," Brigida answered, eyes cast down to the floor. They left him with legs stretched out in front of the fire, kicking the coals that spilled from the hearth with his boot.

Once out of sight of the village, the women held hands and walked without direction. The evening light bathed the plain with an incandescent orange hue, the wind rolling the tall grass into smooth waves, their hair whipping around them. They smiled impishly at each other, then ran at full speed until they collapsed, shrieking, into the soft meadow.

Brigida rolled over to her side and dropped a small kiss onto Arinn's lips.

"What is it Arinn? What has happened? I've never seen Dagr so impatient with us." She squeezed Arinn's hand for reassurance.

Arinn hid her eyes with her arm.

"Dagr has confessed his love. I was worried that he would one day need someone to love and that we would have no place in his home, that this charade would end. But he loves me and he loves you, and he wants us for his own."

Brigida sat up, looking at Arinn with tears in her eyes.

"Arinn! This is good news! I was hoping that he would tell you one day!"

"What do you mean... *you were hoping that he would tell me one day?* Has he told you that he loves me?"

"No!" Now Brigida was laughing. "No, he has not said with words, but I've seen his eyes follow you around. He never stops watching you. He has always wanted you. Why do you think he found a way out of your betrothal for you?"

"But you never said!" protested Arinn. She sat up, and pushed her hair from her eyes. "I thought he was interested in bedding *you...*"

"Arinn, I am sure that he is interested in bedding me, as I am in him, but for you my love, he has reserved a piece of his heart..."

"Brigida!" Arinn interrupted. "If you knew, why not tell me?"

Brigida hung her head and held fast to Arinn's hand. "Because, my love, I am jealous. I would like the love of a man like Dagr. And I also want your love. Perhaps one day you will love him so much that you forget about our love. What if you grow to like the touch of a man so much that you no longer desire mine? And how will he be able to love us both?"

"Dagr will find a way! He said that he loves you also, because you are my beloved."

Brigida took Arinn in her arms.

"We cannot be so naïve. There is no other home that holds one man and two women, not as lovers. What will the others say? One of us will be the wife and the other will be the mistress, and I will have no standing. No man of my own... if Dagr tires of me, no other man will marry me."

"No Brigida. That is not Dagr's way. I know his heart. He would not abandon you because if he did, he would have to abandon me too."

Brigida saw hope in those words. Dagr's love for Arinn might hold them together. There was still one question:

"Arinn, when you and Dagr came home, he was...has anything happened between you? Has he shown you his love?"

Arinn blushed and her nipples pricked up.

"Yes."

"Yes, and?"

"And that is when he told me that he loved me."

"That is all? Just like that? Just, 'I love you' and then you rode the rest of the way home?"

"No... he was...oh, you know how he is when he is intent on

something. I could feel his heart pounding, and he mumbled about how he has loved me for a long time, and I was so scared. But also, *Brigida,* he was so beautiful sitting there like that, strength and softness all mixed up together. I was confused by my feelings... I let him touch my breasts."

"Touch your breasts!" Brigida laughed. "You wench!" Brigida could feel the wetness gathering between her legs. "Then what happened?"

"Then," Arinn said as she slipped up her kirtle and gown, her nipples already pert... "Then, I asked him if this was what he was after and he looked like he was going to expire, and his leathers stretched to monstrous proportions, and he looked more miserable than ever."

Brigida stared at Arinn's breasts and moved herself over to take her nipples in her mouth, sucking gently as Arinn gripped her hair. "More, tell me more Arinn!"

"And he felt his manhood through his leathers and I was wet, and then he kissed me. Brigida, he tasted so good, not like you exactly, different, but so delicious and you know how he smells, and he did things with his tongue that made me want to cry. I do not have any desire for any other man but I do desire him Brigida, *I do.*"

Brigida moved her lips along, nipping Arinn's neck and making her writhe. "Kiss me like he kissed you Arinn. Show me."

She moved her tongue into Arinn's mouth and kissed her gently. Arinn, remembering Dagr's mouth on hers, gripped Brigida by the hair and kissed her hard, grinding her lithe body in, moaning into her mouth. Brigida felt a rush of heat up her spine, her folds were soaked and throbbing, her clit engorged, she slipped her hand under her kirtle and rubbed herself hard. Without warning, she let out a loud primal scream, voicing her excitement to the evening sky.

Arinn stared at her lover and trembled, she had never heard a sound like that escape Brigida's lips before. "Brigida, my sweet...what can I do?"

Brigida's eyes were covered in haze and she held fast to Arinn's body, clutching to the only lover she had known, awakened to an unknown power inside her.

"Arinn, I need Dagr's love. I do not know what is happening to me, I feel something so big inside, a strange feeling. I need you both!"

Arinn held her fast. "Today, every day, you can have him. I love you and nothing changes. I want to see your love, to learn how to love a man."

Brigida pulled Arinn to her feet.

94

"Home, Arinn!. We have enough time to bathe."

Arinn nodded, almost struck dumb by what the evening might hold. She grabbed hold of Brigida's hand and dragged her along behind her, Brigida stumbling as her love for Dagr and Arinn overtook her.

CHAPTER 13

When they returned, they were surprised to see Arinn's bath filled, steaming hot, which dispelled all questions about what Dagr had planned for them. They bathed quickly and rinsed their hair with fragrant oil, donning their best chemises.

They peered through the open door into Dagr's chamber. He was dressed in clean leathers, shirtless, his feet bare; lighting the candles and torches affixed to the walls. His room was warm and welcoming. They saw a new jug of wine and a plate of sweetmeats out on his desk, and could tell by Dagr's stance that he had gathered his courage and his thoughts. He looked very much like the man that he was, wise beyond his years, his powerful arms adorned with silver bracelets, rings on his fingers, his waist small and chiselled against the breadth of his shoulders. His hair shone clean with colourful beads holding small braids here and there. He was known to hold magic in his hands and tonight he had the power of the Fey about him. Neither Arinn nor Brigida were immune to the picture he presented as they walked in. Dagr was handsome beyond words.

He greeted them with serious eyes. His love hung around him like a cloak. He dropped to one knee before them and the women understood that this was his gesture of loyalty and servitude and their hearts filled with love at the sight of this warrior humbling himself before them. He waited for their hand on his head by way of accepting his gesture, and they both laid hands on him, Arinn murmuring words of blessing.

"My lord," said Arinn, using the title she had used for him at their wedding.

"My lady," he answered, and looked at her as she pulled him up, tears in both their eyes, remembering the day they were married, he knowing that she would not join him in his bed, she grateful that he would not ask.

He looked towards Brigida who, with clear envy for the tenderness between her lover and her lord, lowered her eyes before him, and waited for his signal.

To her surprise, he asked for her forgiveness.

"Forgiveness...for what?" she muttered, perplexed.

"For not allowing you the dignity of knowing that I love you as well, and that in my eyes, you are an equal partner to the home that we share."

"My lady," and he knelt at her feet, waiting for whatever she might have to say, hoping that he was not offending the bond between himself and Arinn. This was not as easy or as forthright as it had seemed to him in his dreams.

"My lord." Brigida addressed him as her own, and the three of them understood in that moment, that they had all been handfast, bound to love and honour the truth in each other, come what may, and that both women were the keepers of the fire, at home, in his heart and in his desires.

Feeling his strength now, Dagr led them both to the furs by the hearth, and offered them a cup of wine. Brigida brought over the honey and sweetmeats for them to eat. The wine made Arinn bold, she glanced at Dagr who was watching her hungrily. She tiptoed to the small herb cupboard by her bed. If she was to share her lord, as she knew she must, then she wanted to bless them all, and ask for courage. As she lit the crushed herbs, she was aware of Brigida's energy rising. Dagr was offering her honey on his fingers, Arinn smiled at him, reassurance soft in her eyes.

He pulled Arinn down beside him and offered her some honey as well. She licked it off his fingers and her lips, watching him watching her, her heart curious to know him more. She could see that his leathers were straining already. Her head spun a little and she fell into his scent, clean and musky.

He leaned in to kiss her; she offered her mouth, soft and young, anticipating his taste.

Brigida had waited for Arinn to receive the first kiss. She watched as they kissed tenderly, a witness to Dagrs' love so plain on his face.

He was aroused as any man could be, but he held back his desire to ease Arinn into a man's touch. Arinn's nipples strained in her chemise, she tugged at them a little, by habit of pleasuring herself in front of Brigida. Dagr moaned, kissing Arinn harder.

Arinn reached for Brigida, she wanted her close. They kissed passionately, hands held, while Arinn teased Brigida's chemise off. Dagr was bound as tightly as a coil, his cock demanding release from his leathers. As eager as he was to love them, to taste them at their most aroused, he was more curious to learn from them. Their hands knew exactly where to touch, what pleased the other, how long to stretch a tender stroke. They reached for each other with an innocent sureness. Yes, it had taken generous practice to know each other this well, he could see with some envy. Now, seeing his lady's lover naked before his very eyes brought Dagr to his knees once more.

He took another sip of wine and passed around his cup. They took it obediently, watching his every move, feeling his power fill the room.

He remembered himself suddenly, and took a pot of tea from the hearth.

"Tea, my lord?" Arinn found it odd as they were already drinking wine.

"Herbs to prevent a child from growing." He looked at Arinn. "I remember what you told me. I have other herbs for later as well."

Brigida drank right away, watching Dagr over her cup, sending him a clear message of her intentions. She laid herself down on his bed, touching herself as she held his rapt attention. Her small breasts were oiled and fragrant. Her legs spread; he caught her scent and touched her gently on her inner thigh. He looked so big towering over her. She moaned and spread a little more, showing him the pink beneath her soft dark tuft. Dagr, overwhelmed, kissed her forcefully, sensing her willingness, and asked her if he could taste her, his fingers tugging at her nipples, touching the tender skin of her stomach, touching her everywhere but where he longed to touch.

Arinn came close searching for Brigida's lips. Dagr watched and waited, spell bound. The women were bathed in the light of the fire, resplendent in their love for each other.

"Will you open her more for me, my lady?" Dagr asked, trembling at his core, his inner serpent rising along his spine.

"Is she not beautiful, my lord?" Arinn asked. He nodded, his words lost to him. She caught his eye as she bent over Brigida, bolder now, her tongue flicking along her lips.

Arinn licked gently along Brigida's clit, then sucked vigorously as Brigida lifted her hips up towards her. They were free now to love each other openly before him, to be as wanton as they pleased. What power, sending a man to his knees!

There was no holding Dagr back. Arinn's bottom spread prettily before him as she bent over Brigida. His moistened fingers explored her tightness, gently, listening to her cues as her face pressed into her lover. His manhood was aching in his leathers and he swiftly undid his ties.

They looked at him with startled eyes. He grinned at them and shrugged his shoulders. Arinn doubted that either of them would ever be able to accommodate him.

He bent his handsome face over Brigida and as the scent of her arousal rose towards him; he let his tongue fall on her slit, licking like a man who was quite familiar with the intricacies of a woman's sex. He knew when to be gentle and when to be rough.

Brigida writhed her pleasure, he fought to hold her still with his hands. Arinn leaned in to take Brigida's moans in her mouth.

Dagr moved his hands to Brigida's breasts and twisting her nipples hard, he drew her cry for more. His cock stirred in anticipation. Perhaps the lady could take some pain. He was willing to test the boundaries of her love.

Arinn was not sure where one of them started and the other ended, but she could see that Brigida was in ecstasy. She pushed Dagr aside, encouraging Brigida to get on her hands and knees, pressing her to stretch her back into a splendid curve that could only open her more. Dagr's sculpted body tensed with desire, hand firmly grasping his cock.

Arinn spread Brigida's folds open, and offered her to Dagr.

"Please, my lord," she said.

He got on his knees and came closer, Brigida begging now for his cock, she craved it without shame, or worry. She had loved Dagr in silence, and now the time had come for her to express her love freely.

Arinn dipped her fingers in and spread Brigida's wetness from her opening to her clit, massaging her folds, making sure that she was ready, Dagr's heat gathering as Arinn's fingers slipped in and out. They were so sure of their love, so innocent in their sharing with him, not at all shy as he had imagined they would be, but daring and lustful, urging him on.

He licked at Brigida again, savouring the softness. He wondered if she was intact, but was distracted by Arinn pushing her fingers inside herself then offering them to Brigida's mouth. He slid the head of his cock into his lady's lover, gently, his voice escaping from deep within his throat. When she moved back on him impatiently, Dagr gave in to his need and plunged into her with force. Brigida cried out, the sudden penetration the deepest pleasure she had ever known.

"Tell me you want me, Brigida! Tell me that you are mine. I need to hear it."

"I am yours, my lord, I am yours! The words fell out of her mouth with longing. "I want...more my lord!"

She orgasmed as he filled her; fucking her with deliberate strokes, her sex convulsing rhythmically around his rigid cock. He told her how beautiful she looked as he penetrated her, holding her open with his thumbs. Brigida felt his cock touch her in a place that was a mystery to her, and with it, raised a wave of heat that swallowed her whole.

Arinn's body screamed for release, aroused by the fierceness of their coupling, she slipped her fingers inside herself, her juices dripping down her legs. She was afraid of what Dagr's cock would do to her, but she knew she had to have it, to feel what Brigida was feeling.

"Take me too, my lord," she said, as she rubbed her swollen nub.

Dagr stopped dead in his tracks. Brigida lay spent under him, calling his name.

"My lady," he said to Arinn. "Are you certain? Will you not drink the tea?"

She shook her head. Dagr's heart jumped in response to her decision, his eyes misting with understanding.

Arinn laid herself down on the furs and held Brigida's hand.

Dagr bent over her taking her nipples in his mouth and almost came as he tasted her. "My love, my love," he whispered as his lips moved on to part the fair hair on her mound, sucking on her clit now, licking all around her quivering slit, he felt his tears come down. She tasted like she had in his dreams, sweet and welcoming, he probed with his tongue and she gripped his hair. "I am ready," was all that she could say; thrusting her hips in his face, needing him to possess her.

Dagr lifted up and entered her with care, pushing as much of himself in as he thought she could take, but she pushed back at him, willing him to fill her, her breasts bouncing as he dared to fuck her harder, thrusting deep at every stroke. He felt every ripple inside her, his nipples stood erect, surely he wouldn't last long.

Arinn held her breasts in her hands, her tongue darted out to lick at her nipples, so impossibly long and hard; eyes spirited.

"Is this what you have waited for, my lord?" she asked. "To see your lady act like a whore?"

He roared.

Dagr came with a vigour he had never known, spilling his seed, unable to last through her tight grasp on him.

Arinn came all over his huge cock, covering Dagr with more wet than she had ever imagined she could hold, spurting out of her like the love she felt for them both. They lay in an embrace, overcome by their emotions, their hearts pounding with love for each other, eyes closed, softly breathing.

Arinn asked Dagr shyly what had happened, she had never released her passion like that before. He smiled his lazy smile.

"You have showered me with the waters of the Goddess, my lady, and I am well pleased."

Before he lay down to hold them for the night, he brought a warm, wet linen to wipe them with, which he did tenderly and with a fresh erection.

They let him stare at their bare beauty, as his fingers opened and explored them for one more intense look, bold and brazen in their power over him.

He asked them if they were sore. He told them that he had never wanted anyone as he wanted them, and that he was sorry if he had hurt them in any way. They were so young and tender, Dagr fully aware of his responsibility to treat them with care. Then he blew out the candles and arranged cosily in the linens and furs on his bed, he voiced his love once more, lying on his prick to try and make it behave.

They lay tangled with the women stroking his skin. He moved gently once to try and roll over, the women curling up around him, Dagr's erection hard against Arinn's back. She whispered something taking him inside her as she slept. He lay with his manhood filling her, listening to her breathe, Brigida's light kisses on his back. He hoped that day would not come. Nothing after this would be simple or safe. He would have to claim Brigida as his own. Arinn felt him tense. She mumbled in her sleep. She cast her spell, and he was asleep at once.

Outside Dagr's chamber, the stable boy slipped quietly down the stone stairs. He ran on swift feet directly to the house of the steward. There was much to tell.

CHAPTER 14

Sahara unloaded the rented roto-tiller from her truck. She looked at it dubiously. The guy at the rental place had assured her that once you got the hang of it, it was easy to operate. It looked bigger here than it had at the store, she thought to herself. Maybe for today she would just push it over to the place where she planned to plant potatoes and squash. She scanned the sky. No chance of rain. She could leave it in the field.

She would need to have some manure delivered, to prepare the soil for spring planting. She would plan a ritual, anoint herself with smudge, and give thanks to the Goddess.

Having moved the machine towards the desired location, she thought about making a talisman to wear around her neck as she worked the soil. Shaking some dirt off her hands, Sahara made her way back to the cabin. Today would be a good day to work magic, to connect to the Earth Mother. She had no other plans. Perhaps Aiden would carve her a talisman.

Sahara heard her phone ring as she made her way back from the field to the cabin. Was it Aiden? Her heart skipped a beat, she felt instantly aroused. By the time she reached her kitchen, it had stopped ringing. The display showed the number from the café. Not Aiden after all. The phone rang again.

"Hi Holly."

"Oh, hi. I just called you, but there was no answer."

"I know; I was outside. What's up?"

"I've got some time off this aft, how about that walk you promised?"

"Ummm, ok, I have some work to do later, but if you came over right now..."

"K, I'm on my way!" Holly had hung up before Sahara could say another word.

Sahara opened the cupboard door and pulled out the bodum. She put some music on. She could use a walk, and a bit of Holly's baking. She knew her well enough by now to be sure of a treat. Holly never came empty handed.

Sitting on the front porch, Sahara drew in a breath of fresh mountain air. She smiled. Home. It was safe. She knew that she had let her guard down more than she had initially meant to. Aiden was no longer someone she could avoid. He was obviously part of something she had known before. Iona had said that this place was a powerful vortex. Sahara would need to protect her heart from making a mess of things. Her body was another matter altogether. She would seek Aiden out again.

Holly honked her horn as she rounded the bend in the drive.

Sahara stood and waved at her. Holly got out and shook the bag of goodies.

"Hope you have the water on!" She called. "Wait till you try THESE with coffee!"

They embraced, and went into the cabin, Holly exclaiming over the music.

"Is that your mailbox at the fork in the drive Sahara? The flag is up. I guess you've got mail," Holly said.

Before Sahara could answer that question, and focus on the excitement that gathered in her heart on assuming that she had mail from Aiden, Holly was already asking about the rototiller.

"I'm going to grow my own food. That will be the place for potatoes and squash. I'm also planning a kitchen garden a bit closer to the cabin. You know, herbs, greens, tomatoes."

"Sahara! Let me help you! I've been dying to have somewhere to grow things that I could use at the café. Lavender for scones, herbs for the bread. When I was in France, I visited some community gardens that supplied the local restaurants. Besides, gardening is always more fun with a helper."

"Ok," Sahara answered, a bit surprised. "I'd love that. I mean, I intended to do it all myself, but we could plan what we needed..."

"And," Holly interrupted, "we could put up preserves, and I could sell some at the café. Oh, I'm so excited!"

Sahara laughed out loud. "Holly, I think that would be fine. I really had no idea that you knew anything about growing food..."

"I don't," Holly admitted. "But I do have a few books on the matter, and if you know how, I'll provide the labour." She thought for a minute then added shyly, "Shall we grow enough for Aiden?"

"A community effort? I like it," Sahara agreed. "I wonder if we can get him to do the rototilling if we grow the food."

"You're a genius, Sahara! A trade, and a good one. Let's ask him."

"We will, but first we'll have to nail him down. I think he's gone to a job site for a few days. Not sure. I haven't heard a peep out of him for days."

She stood with her back to Holly, making the coffee and putting out the pastries. For some reason, she couldn't share anything about her feelings for Aiden with Holly yet. He had admitted to liking Holly, but did Holly like him in return?

They walked a little later on, in the woods where Sahara gathered mushrooms and firewood.

"So, what were you doing in France?" Sahara finally asked, as they picked up sticks for a bonfire.

"I took a pastry course. And, I needed to break away from the small town that I grew up in. I guess I needed to learn about myself."

"I've not been to France, but I've been to the UK. I can imagine that it was a bit of a culture shock from the mid-west?"

"Yes. Not only in what it offers culturally, but also morally. You know what I mean?"

Sahara did. She felt a ripple of apprehension from Holly and offered a smile.

"Well, I think I do. Society's a lot freer there."

"Hmmm. Yes. Hey, shall we turn back? You mentioned that you had work today. I should go."

Sahara shook her head. "It can wait. Stay...if you want. We could make plans for the garden; have a bite, maybe a little fire outside? I can write later tonight."

"Ok, if you let me help make the meal," Holly smiled a shy smile and Sahara felt something of the sadness that Holly wore on her heart. Maybe today would not be the right time to ask her about it, but Sahara could offer her friendship.

With books and paper and pencils out, the two women mapped out what the garden should hold, who needed what and how much. They decided to scale back a bit once they looked over their plans, laughing that they could feed an army on that amount! Too late to do anything this year but prepare the soil. Holly would ask around at the market to see who had extra manure or straw for mulch.

"Summer can be pretty hot here," she added, "so mulch at least for the kitchen garden would be useful."

"We can also rake up leaves and make leaf mould, that would be good," Sahara suggested. "Holly, I'm imagining an evening in January by the fire pouring over seed catalogs..."

"And dinner, and a blizzard and I might be stranded!" Holly offered, eyes sparkling.

They laughed and laughed, thinking about future adventures, and finally admitted that they were starving, and that someone should make something to eat.

"I have soup," Sahara said. "We can have that for now."

"Sahara, I am so glad we've become friends, it's been a long time since I've felt this easy with anyone. I think we have a lot in common."

"I know, thank you Holly." Sahara eyed Holly with an appreciative glance. "I'm usually pretty private, and as a confession, I can tell you that when we met I was determined to keep my distance. Just my own shit, you know? My own fears."

"Yup, I felt that. Maybe my baking won you over?" Holly winked.

"That, and you feel real, which is rare."

"Like Aiden," Holly said. "He's real. What you see is what you get. He's a good man."

"Aiden?" Sahara's heart pounded. She had to ask.

"Are the two of you friends or more than friends? I'm asking because he's pretty private himself, and I don't want to step on any toes. I'd like to respect anything that the two of you might have." With irony, Sahara thought about how it was so very late for that.

Sahara watched Holly as she twisted and turned in her chair. She curled a wisp of her golden hair around a finger. So there *was* something.....

"We're friends. At least I think we are. Remember when Aiden told you about the dinner I had at his house?"

Sahara nodded. Holly's energy felt conflicted, but not insincere.

"He admitted to liking me, and I had already known that, but he couldn't figure out why I had never accepted a date before."

"Yes, why not? I'm curious myself now. I'm sure half of Colorado would like to have him." Sahara laughed.

Holly smiled. "Because I'm not really into men."

And there it was. Just like that. Out. To someone she barely knew. Somehow it didn't seem so bad.

Sahara's eyes flew to Holly's. So she hadn't been wrong when she had felt something between them at that first hug. She organized her face towards composure.

"Except for someone that I was seeing in France, and now Aiden, I haven't told any other living soul." Holly looked both triumphant and apprehensive.

"Oh Holly, I'm so proud of you! Honesty brings such freedom. Thank you for trusting me."

"You know, it's not that bad. I mean, I think you'll be the only person I tell, and Aiden already knows." Holly looked at Sahara and hoped that she hadn't made a mistake.

"Your secret is safe with me Holly. I truly do know what it means to have your secrets spilled."

They sat in silence for a few minutes. Sahara felt the shift in their friendship. Holly felt the shift in Sahara's view of her. A sigh hung unreleased on the evening air.

"So, tell me, how did Aiden take your news?" Sahara hid behind her coffee cup.

"Not so well, I think he hopes I'll change my mind."

They laughed. So like a man.

"It's not that I'm immune to who he is, I'm sure you know what I mean Sahara. He's beautiful in so many ways, but I'm kind of afraid of him; his intensity. He's the only man who's made me question my sexuality though...I thought I had myself all figured out already. What about you?"

"What about me?"

"Do you have someone?"

"No. Not right now." Sahara did her best to look honest. "I had someone, but he left me." She paused. "I'm still a bit raw," she added. "So, that's where I'm at."

Sahara allowed a fraction of her sexual energy to escape through her smile, a hint of her interest in Holly to breathe freely between them. Holly's body language relaxed, and Sahara's nipples perked. Holly's did too. Sahara poured more coffee.

Sahara wondered about Aiden, and how difficult it must have been for him to hear Holly's confession. This was truly a bizarre turn of events, but she was too smart to think that any of it was a coincidence. Life always brought together the loose ends of one's subconscious.

Aiden was having trouble keeping his focus as he listened to the ramblings of a nice young couple who were trying to impress him with their plans for a house. He had already tried to get them to agree on something smaller.

"There's not enough frontage to display the design, it will look bigger than it should on a lot this size," he insisted.

"Listen, do you want this job or not?" The young man sat up taller in his chair, his hand covered his keys. Aiden recognized the man's move towards asserting his power.

This again, he thought, already bored.

"I prefer to build houses that fit their environment." He shot a charming but persistent smile towards the man's wife.

The wife gave her husband a small nudge, smiling brilliantly at Aiden. They would be willing to discuss changes after all. He shoved the contract across the table towards them and specified that once they had agreed to the final work order, there would be little room for revisions.

"I heard that you were strict with changes, but really...there's bound to be some."

"I want to build something that you will be proud to own. Changes in the middle of things mean that we have planned poorly in the first place. So let's take our time before we agree to the final process. Look over everything again, go over your initial dream list and then we'll settle on the final design. I'm sure your architect will agree with me."

The architect had, in fact, already agreed with him. They would meet in the morning; Aiden would assemble his building crew, and manage the build himself. He ran a tight project; he was precise and organized, almost military in his orders to the crew. Not disrespectful, but firm. He never had trouble finding good workers. They could be sure that he would look after their interests well. He outworked all of them and they found security in his commitment, to them, and the client.

When clients suggested hiring cheaper workers from across the border, he offered them the opportunity to work with someone else. If he did hire someone from 'across the border' as the client had suggested, they would not be paid any less. In most cases, he was free to do things his own way. His reputation had cleared the way.

Later, he sat at dinner alone, in a corner of the restaurant where there was less chance of being noticed. He had talked all day, and now he just wanted to eat in peace. His book sat open in front of him, a journal beside it. He cut into his steak and wondered if the letter he had left had been read yet. Sahara sometimes stayed put for a half week without venturing out. She wrote, he knew that, and she was still organizing this or that. The last time she'd called him to ask for a clamp, he had discovered that she was pressing flowers and leaves from the forest, and making wild blackberry jelly.

"Now you know what you're getting for your birthday from me," she had laughed.

"What? No! I have no idea," he had laughed right back. "I'll be appropriately surprised when that time comes."

He thought back to the hand written note he had left her...

Sahara,

I hope this note finds you well. I will be away until Friday of this week. If you need anything in the meantime, you can reach me on my cell.

I won't pretend that I haven't been thinking of you, and the night that we shared. I'd like to see you again, and this time, I have a few things that I would like to tell you...to keep things between us real. In the short time that we have known each other, I have come to respect the boundaries of our friendship, and would like to continue on in this vein. If this sounds like something you would like, leave me a note in return, and we can make plans from there. I will call you once I've picked up your mail.

Aiden.

p.s. call me if you need anything picked up from town or beyond. I'm in Telson.

It was to the point. He'd not received a call from her, and assumed that she would do as planned, and leave him a return note. Still, he found himself longing for the sound of her voice and hoped that she would indeed, need something picked up. His thoughts turned to Holly. He would have to tell Sahara how he felt, but he wouldn't disclose Holly's secret. This was the first time that he was faced with needing to share his feelings about open relationships, and his desire for multiple partners. Some feelings ran deep with him, so deep in fact that he was not sure of their origin. A part of him felt familiar with having multiple loves and a type of communal life within a village that came to him in dreams, but he wondered if that was his sub-conscious mixing his wants with things he'd read, or seen in movies.

The dreams had intensified since he had seen Sahara dancing at her fire. Then, after their dinner, they had intensified again. He had a lot of questions and longed for some quiet time with Sahara to talk over his thoughts.

A waitress suddenly stood at his side, asking about dessert.

"No, but thank you," he replied graciously and smiled warmly, appreciating good service.

Would he like a sherry? Aiden replied no to the sherry, yes to the cheque.

When he folded the receipt into his wallet he noticed that the waitress had left her number. His cell phone also registered a call from Dianne, and although he would send a warm reply back, he knew that he wouldn't spend the night at her house this time.

He walked the few blocks to his hotel. There he ordered a cognac from room service and sat on his private balcony, overlooking the Rockies, and the lights from the village below. He loved it here as a getaway while working. The hotel catered to his privacy and his love of mountain views. He thought about Sahara's view of the mountains. Really, between them, they had the best of all worlds. The forest and the mountains, water at their feet and miles of solitude. He would be glad to return.

CHAPTER 15

Holly sat in a chair by the window and read while Sahara prepared a light supper of salad with grilled forest mushrooms. The light was quickly fading and Sahara lit the candles in their wall sconces. A small fire burned in the stone fireplace.

Sahara glanced at the girl lost to her reading and not for the first time noticed her natural beauty. She felt a warmth spreading in the pit of her stomach, and found herself in deep longing for someone she had once known. Holly's golden hair spilled over her shoulders, her lips moved now and then as she read to herself, her feet dangling over the arm of the chair. Sahara longed to kneel before her and kiss her lips, so perfectly pouted and soft. She poured some wine and brought a glass over to Holly.

"I think you'll like this," she offered, voice soft and seductive.

"Oh yes," Holly stretched out her hand for the glass. "Let's have some wine, I am parched."

"Are you feeling anxious to go home soon Holly, or are you still up for that bon-fire we prepared?"

"I cannot tell you how long it's been since I've sat at an outdoor fire Sahara. I'll stay."

"What are you reading?"

"Something about the seed of life. I'm not sure I understand it all, but it's intriguing."

"Mmm. Yes. Sacred Geometry. How Consciousness discovered itself and realized one day that what was above, was also below. The sacred meeting the mundane. I haven't read that in a while, but it opens up beautiful corners of the sub-conscious, I find."

"Also, it talks about using water, fire, air and earth to sustain ourselves, and I started thinking about the garden, and how we'd be doing that ourselves."

"It's a full circle, you'll see, Holly, when you grow your own food, you'll discover the mystery of the cycles of the earth. Time will look different to you after that, you will grow to appreciate the natural rhythms of our existence. Nature teaches us to respect the wisdom of oneness."

The fire rose quickly from the dry branches that Sahara and Holly had gathered and arranged into the pit, later in the evening. The night sky glowed orange and pink, sinking into black with only the smallest crescent of the waning moon left to light the dark. Slowly, the stars came out, Venus first to show herself, then Orion and finally the Milky Way. They sat in silence for a long time, Sahara longing to weave some magic before the dark moon came, and Holly lost in the beauty of the night. Sahara offered to pour more wine for Holly.

"Aren't you having any more?" Holly asked

"I don't drink very well," Sahara admitted. "A little bit goes a long way for me."

"I've drunk too much already myself," Holly replied.

"Drink away, Holly, you can crash here for the night, don't drive if you don't feel that you can."

"I have to go, I had only planned on staying for a few hours initially. I'm baking at four a.m."

"Yikes! That's an ungodly hour. How do you do it?"

"I'm used to it. And I love it. It's quiet then, and I can just lose myself in what I do, the best of me probably comes out when I'm baking."

"It's your magic. What you create out of your love for your craft. You're very good Holly, we're all very lucky to have you." Sahara stood. "I'll be right back with some water and blankets."

Holly watched her walk away and noticed how small she looked. She finished off her wine. She felt jittery, the fire made her want to howl. Holly wished for Julie's small hands exploring between her legs, kissing her mouth and whispering words in French. Sahara had small hands...

She felt Sahara standing behind her at the fire.

"Here," Sahara said softly. "Wrap yourself in this."

Holly turned as Sahara lifted the blanket up to her. She leaned down slightly to allow Sahara to place it around her shoulders, Sahara's breath close to her ear. Holly tensed as she felt Sahara's lips graze by. Then, surprised, her lips parted as Sahara moved to place her lips on hers, kissing her deliberately full on the mouth, delicious tasting kisses, deep and soulful, making Holly weak from the sensual contact.

She kissed her back, bringing moans to Sahara's lips. They continued to explore with lavish strokes of their tongues, curious, tender but hungry. Sahara moved herself closer to Holly, hands searching for the buttons on Holly's blouse.

Holly's stare upon Sahara's face remained curious as she allowed her shirt to be opened, Sahara's lust confident. They simply allowed what would happen next, Holly taking her turn to slip off Sahara's shirt, losing the courage to utter a word when she saw Sahara's nipples stand hard in erotic defiance.

"Are you cold?" Sahara whispered.

Holly could only shake her head. She kissed Sahara again, harder this time, falling into the joy she felt mounting, taking hold of Sahara's nipples and rolling them between her fingers, nipping around her ears, and placing Sahara's hands on her breasts to hold. Somehow it seemed natural to be this familiar with each other.

"Sahara...that other lover you mentioned, the one that caused your break-up, was it a woman?" Holly trembled and moved in closer to be embraced.

Sahara nodded. "Holly, if I'm assuming too much..."

But Holly was already laying the blankets down on the cold ground. She pulled Sahara down beside her.

"Look at the stars Sahara. Look! How beautiful. I'm so happy right now, that I am sharing this night sky with you, and that you trusted me enough to kiss me. I've been longing for a woman for so long...too long."

"Do you want to go inside... the ground is cold."

"No Sahara, I want to stay here, I want to be naked under the stars; I want to know the wind on my skin!"

Magic whipped up around them. Instinctively, they threw off the rest of their clothes, excited to feel the night air, made bold by the wine and the primal need to feel skin on skin, nipples straining and sudden wetness releasing a surge of hormones that drew them together as they held each other by the now roaring fire.

They looked up at the stars, their hands entwined. Holly languished in the freedom this night brought her; she had been so lonely for adventure.

Sahara turned to Holly and rested her eyes on her beauty. Her breasts were ample and firm, youthful and defiant of gravity, stomach muscled as one accustomed to physical fitness. Holly squirmed as Sahara's eyes locked lower still.

Sahara's finger traced a tender line from Holly's face to the softest part of her shoulder, to her breast and beyond.

Holly gently moved her face towards Sahara's breasts and Sahara moaned as Holly's mouth pursed up and sucked on her hungrily. Holly's golden hair caressed Sahara's skin.

A woman's kiss was so different than a man's. It was in the softness of her lips, the way a woman liked to play the kissing game all night, the passion of experiencing something different yet the same.

"Sahara?"

Holly turned in for more kisses, her lips lush and demanding. Sahara's wild side awoken, she whispered into Holly's ear, naughty desires and promises of delights that made Holly moan. She rode the wave of wild abandon, not pulling back at Sahara's words, as shocking as they were to her at first.

But as much as Holly was ready for whatever the night would bring, her sex tight and swollen, Sahara led their play to a torturous end. Holly fell naturally into Sahara's will.

They lay silently for a spell until the cold wind shook them loose of their embrace. Struggling through their goodbyes when Holly left for home, each wanting more, the two women let their hearts unfurl to new dreams.

"*Je ne veux pas quitter, Sahara.*"

"Soon." Sahara replied, surprised by her hearts sudden decent into trust. She watched Holly drive away, cast a quick spell for her safety, and ran her bath, Holly still delicious on her lips.

⁕

On his way home from work the next day, Aiden reached the fork in the road where his lane turned to the left and Sahara's to the right. He looked to the mailbox and saw that the flag was up. Hopping out, he peered inside the box and found his letter gone, a note from Sahara left behind.

He shoved it into his pocket and drove home. He was surprised how nervous he was of her reply. He wanted good things to come from their friendship, and hoped that they had not already made a mess of things.

He opened his windows at home to the afternoon breeze. He drank some water and decided to shower. He stood under the water and let it drain away the last few days, the driving, the stress of the meetings, his anxiety. Wearing clean jeans and shirt, he found the note that he had folded and sat down to read.

It was short. Sahara hadn't wasted any words.

"Aiden, come soon. Come now."

He grinned and released a breath that he had not been aware of holding. He strode through the forest towards the clearing.

He could see her struggling with something, seemingly un-aware of his approach.

As he came nearer, she straightened and raised her arm to wave to him. He waved back and could tell that she was smiling.

"Sahara, for the love of God, what are you doing with that monster of a machine?"

"Yes, hello, it's a roto-tiller."

"I know what it is, but what exactly are you doing with it? It looks ancient! Does it even work?"

"Dunno. But we can talk about this later. How are you? I see you got my note."

He wanted to move towards her and pick her up, swing her and nuzzle her neck. But she should have the first move. He didn't want to be overwhelming.

"I got your note and here I am. You up for some coffee; or in this case, making me some coffee? I can offer an exchange. I'll see if I can get that beast to start for you later on?"

"I'll take that trade, I'm glad you thought of it. Stay for dinner?"

She turned towards the cabin and he watched her lithe little body sway along in front of him. He smiled. Somehow he was not so sure that she had not planned for him to wrestle the roto-tiller. But no matter, he was in her hands, and pleased to be there.

They sat on the sofa, knees drawn in, cups in hand, no words, just breathing in each other's presence, Sahara stretching out her toes in his direction. They laid down their cups and snuggled down into the pillows, Aiden let out a sigh.

"What is it Aiden?"

"I'm just so exhausted by the meeting process before the build. I keep thinking that I'll get used to all the backing and forthing and incessant chatter about details that really make no sense, but I never do get used to it. I felt ok when I got home, but now, here with you, I just want to close my eyes and sleep and let go."

"Sleep. Let go. I could nap. I've been tense too, and up all night writing."

He nodded and smiled, reaching for her hand. Pulling her in, he nested her into him, against his chest, and the hardness growing in his jeans. He wrapped his arms around her and let out another sigh. He felt an energy running through her that hadn't been there before, she felt tightly coiled.

"Sleep Sahara. That's what we need. I'm a mess right now, to be honest, I want to rip your clothes off, *and* I want to rest in the comfort of your arms. And I don't know what to do first. But sleep makes more sense."

He kissed the top of her head, while she purred and snuggled in against the warmth and hardness of his legs.

114

Their breathing slowed down as they gave in to their tiredness. She wanted to tell him that his body felt like she had known it forever. She wanted to say "I Love You Aiden, I have missed you this whole life time." Although she was waking up to the dreams that brought her closer to knowing who he had been to her before, she knew that the time was not yet ripe. But she said her love words in her heart and as she did he hugged her so tight that she couldn't breathe.

He finally fell asleep and relaxed his body, his hair a tangle over his shoulders, his hand wrapped protectively around her waist. Then she too dropped off to a deep and familiar dream, of a man on a horse, with a deer strapped to the back, holding her hand and leading her down a forest road. She was home.

When they woke, it was already dark.

He kissed her face and sought out her breasts. She slid her shirt off and lay in his arms as he touched her lovingly, tugging on her nipples, playing with her hair. Her nipples made him insane; they were such forward little things, jutting out further than they had any business to.

"I could lie here forever," he whispered.

"We'd starve," she answered.

"Get up then. I'll start the fire, you start dinner," he offered.

"K. But run upstairs first and get my slippers, my feet are freezing!"

She drank some water and opened the wine.

Aiden called to her from the bedroom. She stood at the bottom of the stairs and said that the slippers were by the bed.

He said, voice a little strangled, "Sahara, come up!"

She ran up and found him standing white faced by the painting she had bought in Salem.

"Aiden, what is it? You look like you've seen a ghost."

"It's Holly." His hand touched the canvas, fingers tracing the outline of the woman in the painting.

Sahara stared at it a moment..."I have felt this painting so familiar but I hadn't realized...I mean, before meeting Holly I wouldn't have known it, but even now, I didn't put it together". She stared again into the canvas.

"The girl in the painting is very ethereal. I'm just so struck by how it captures Holly's essence, it's not just the look of her, you know, it's her inner self that comes through. And it's what I've always been attracted to in her, her softness and her light."

He suddenly remembered himself and said; "I'm sorry Sahara;

that was very inappropriate."

"No Aiden. It's all right. Come down with me. Let's eat, and you can tell me all the things that have been on your mind. I have things to say, too."

He built a huge fire and lit some candles, asked her what she wanted to listen to, then sat on the sofa watching as she moved about preparing their meal. The cabin gathered up their energy and breathed in their scent, infusing itself with the magic they made together. Aiden looked to the ceiling beams to see the herbs she had drying. He saw several new hooks, she must have added those, Jack had never dried anything there. The hooks stirred something in his loins, and he looked away, the color rising in his face.

"Are those wild herbs?" he asked.

"Yup. I've found a lot more in the wild than I had anticipated. I'll grow more next year, in a kitchen garden. These are for tea, although I gathered them a bit late in the season, they should do."

"So the roto-tiller... for your kitchen garden?"

"No, for potatoes and squash, onions, garlic...the kitchen garden will be close to the door. Will you help me open the ground Aiden?"

Her question, innocent as it was, made him think of opening her to his mouth. His cock stirred.

"Of course, anything you need. The ground here is soft, kind of sandy, except for all the rocks and boulders."

"Mmm, those would make a nice stone wall to build around the kitchen garden."

"We've lots of rabbits and deer," he advised.

"I usually make a pact with them, allowing them a portion and I keep the rest. It's worked before."

"Sahara, I have a confession to make," Aiden drawled, wine in hand, coming closer to the kitchen counter.

"Oh, only one?" she quipped.

He winced. She noticed.

Aiden took a deep breath and began. "One of the first nights that you were here, maybe the second night, you had a fire."

Sahara looked up sharply. A familiar fear rose instantly, and her stomach clamped down with nausea.

"I understood that we had an arrangement not to drop in on each other," he continued, "but I had been walking the wood as I do most nights, and saw the fire blazing and became concerned about a grass fire. So, after some deliberation, I came a bit closer to warn you to be careful, and saw your dance and heard your chanting. I've felt very guilty ever since about it mainly because I broke my word to you and imposed on your privacy."

He watched as she went from looking stricken to regaining her composure.

"Sahara, I apologise. The next day I realized that you had made a safe place for fire, and felt like a fool." He waited, his hands tight.

"I can't be angry Aiden," Sahara finally said. "I understand your concern about fire. I came here, to this place, because I need to be able to do my work in privacy, in safety, and to know that I can be myself without censoring my actions. I still need those things, very much."

She looked forlorn and scared now. He felt her sadness deep in his heart.

"By 'work', I'm assuming you mean more than your writing. You're a wise woman. Am I right?"

"Yes." She came closer. The fire of Aiden's lust began to burn. "I'm a Solitary, I prefer to work on my own. What do you know about wise women Aiden?"

"Mainly only what I've read. I was once invited to a women's circle on a summer solstice. They were holding a healing ceremony between the masculine and the feminine, and I was the token male. Afterwards, they held a feast, and I was able to stay and ask some questions. It was very moving."

Aiden kept his eyes down, not sure how much he should tell of that night.

"Was there more?" Aiden wasn't surprised that Sahara had read him.

"Yes. In fact, they invited me to another circle, another time, where they taught me about sacred sex and still in the intention of healing and with full consent, certain rites were performed that, quite honestly, made me wonder about how truly un-conscious we are in our daily lives." He paused.

Sahara smiled. "I'm sure that that coven will never be the same, it is rare to find a man like you to participate in sacred sex ceremonies, one who will understand the intent and enter into it consciously but also one who is so easy to perform on. The High Priestess must have had every confidence in your honor towards women."

He nodded. Sahara was easy to talk to. It made him horny as hell.

Sahara sat quietly. She licked her lips. He saw it and came forward. He took her in his arms.

"Am I forgiven my lady?" he asked.

"Please, Aiden," she moaned, "please call me that again."

"My lady." He repeated, this time whispering it into her ear.

"Tell me I'm forgiven." He insisted.

"You're forgiven, many times over. I like the openness between us Aiden. Sometimes I hide things, because I'm afraid, but you're showing me how to have more courage." She hugged into him, smelling his scent, rubbing hers into his shirt.

"Let's eat," he said. "I'm so hungry."

CHAPTER 16

Iona looked over at the man lying in her bed, his black hair tousled, morning stubble framing his face perfectly, his chest and arms covered in tattoos. He smiled at her. His confidence was palpable.

"You look like pirate, Richard." Iona said.

"I am a pirate," he said. "And you like it."

"Yes, I like it. But this is my ship and I make the orders here."

"You can order me around all you like. I'm not afraid of you, never have been."

She ran her hand over his inner arm. His nipples stood. He put his hand to his cock, rising under the sheet.

"Iona, I don't have much time to play games with you today. Work calls. Have a heart and get on your knees. I'm famished for your mouth on my cock."

He laid himself out in the center of the bed. Iona slid onto her hands and knees. She lapped up all his deliciousness, and knew that she'd be well rewarded. But her Fey ears prickled as she picked up messages from the Under World.

Work called her as well today. She stopped her deep sucking motions to loudly voiced protests and turned around to expose her silkiness to her lover. He ran his finger over her swollen clit, expertly bringing her to as close to orgasm as he knew she wanted, then rammed himself inside, the view of his thick cock stretching her stoking his fire. He played with her ass, lubricating her with her juices, pushing his thumb in as she opened. She had not expected that extra little pleasure, and came in great spasms that clamped down on his stiffness.

Richard came in hot spurts, Iona's purring her pleasure at his release.

Knowing Iona well, Richard held her firmly against him, his lips to her ear, whispering his hopes for her attentions later on. When the energy of her orgasm waned, he let her go, and got up to shower, Iona's eyes on his spectacular ass, and the tattoo of a medieval coat of arms covering his back.

"By God, you are beautiful, Iona!" he told her as he held her at the door. "How many lifetimes will you torture me through?"

"All of them, my lord. All of them." And she watched him go out into the world, the only man she would bow her head to, although thoughts of Aiden still brought tears to her eyes.

❊

"Wine, Sahara?" Aiden asked. Dinner done, they sat facing the fire, Aiden shirtless at Sahara's request.

"How about I share yours," she smiled wickedly at him.

"Take some," he offered. "Do you have more?"

"There's always more," she replied. "Anything else you want to tell me before I begin my own confessions?"

The room was quite warm but Aiden's nipples stood hard.

"First, I'd like to say that it was terribly insensitive of me to say what I did about being attracted to Holly."

He held up his hand as she started to protest. "Hear me out. I know that this is not going to be the kind of conversation one has with a woman that they're hoping to bed..."

"Oh, you're hoping to bed me?" Sahara laughed.

"Stop teasing me you wench! I'm trying to be serious. Anyway, here's the thing. The women who invited me to the ceremony I told you about awoke a longing in me for living a polyamorous lifestyle...you know about it?"

"Of course I know what it is. I invented it," she announced.

"Are you going to settle down and let me get this out?"

"Probably not."

"I've always had trouble with the premise of being able to love only one person. I mean, how can there only be *one* for each of us, it seems improbable."

She nodded.

"When I moved here, I fell hard for Holly, and spent a whole lot of time trying to get her to see that I was worth falling for myself. But it never happened, and although we *are* good friends, and share a lot of interests, I'm afraid that she doesn't find me very appealing."

"I don't know, maybe she's just not sure how you feel." Sahara baited the trap.

"No, no, she knows. I told her one night and then felt like a complete buffoon after she explained that I was really not her type."

"Well, what type does she like, did she say?" Sahara began to reel him in.

"I don't know what exactly she likes, but it's not me."

Good man, she thought. You won't betray her secret. She let out her breath.

120

"But," Aiden continued, "That still left me with the feelings that I have for her, which have not abated, instead, I am more intrigued; although I'm sure that I'm wasting my time. Not to mention what I feel for you."

She sat looking at him impassively, not revealing her true thoughts yet projecting a feeling of intrigue. He moved a little closer. Her breath caught. She wondered if he knew how incredibly sexy he was.

"Sahara, I know boiled down it sounds quite crass, but I find a lot of beauty in loving more than one person... that's my dream, in any case."

She watched as he scowled at the fire. He had a habit of twitching his jaw muscles when he was deep in thought.

"Ok, Aiden, time for me to tell you a story."

Aiden looked slightly perplexed. Sahara did not comment on his confession although she had a feeling that he wanted her to.

"A while ago, I was in a relationship with a man whom I loved very much. He was everything I thought I wanted at the time and he loved me well, or as well as he could. Everything was great until I decided to be honest with him one day and tell him that I'm bi-sexual."

She stopped to let him digest what she was saying. He remained silent. His intensity made the room seem suddenly smaller. Her nipples stood as if on command and he fixed his stare onto them, his tongue slipping out to wet his sensual lips.

"After a while," she continued, feeling weak now, "I fell in lust with a woman, and we entered into a physical relationship. I needed her love and I needed his love, but although she was willing to try to have something with both of us, he was unwilling and asked me to stop seeing her. So I did, but soon could not stay away from her, and eventually, he caught us in bed, after which everything un-ravelled and I was left alone. The whole thing fell apart because I wasn't honest with myself or with him."

Aiden reached out to take her hand, his eyes dark. She was arrested by the set of his jaw, and wanted to bite along it.

"I'm so sorry Sahara, sounds like it was very painful. But knowing oneself is a process."

"Aiden, I *long* for what you're talking about. I crave it deeply, and frankly I don't know that I haven't lived it before, possibly in another lifetime. I'm not so good at rules"...she trailed off.

"I think that you and I want the same thing," he said slowly. You need to honour your sexual preferences and I need the freedom to love the women that stir my soul; to live authentically. And then there is my need for enough space to just survive each day, as do you, I think..."

He looked at her, tears glistened in her eyes, she was trembling and he knew she was split open by her honesty with him, and that she was afraid.

He stood and pulled a small packet of herb from his pocket.

"Here." He offered it to her. "It's exceptional. Let's make some magic Sahara, I want to learn from you. Enough confessions, I think we each need some tenderness tonight and to learn to trust each other. We've shared a lot for such a short friendship."

She let her breath out and relaxed her shoulders. She felt safe, even though it made no sense; they had a connection that left her with an impulse to just let him in. Everywhere.

"When you talk of magic Aiden, do you feel that although you might know more, it's kind of stuck in a haze somewhere?"

"Yes!" he said, surprised. "I've had dreams since I've met you. And sometimes I feel that I'm being circled when I'm in the woods, but then realize that it's just a raven. Only it feels like something much more than that."

Sahara shut down her eyes. She took the herb from him and went to find her papers. He poured more wine into their communal cup and sat back down. He had till tomorrow, there was nothing to hurry home for.

"I'll be right back," she said. Aiden nodded and added some wood to the fire.

He had rolled their joint by the time she came back, dressed in a long black gown and carrying a box under her arm.

"You look amazing!" he exclaimed. You look different every time I see you. What's in the box?"

"Some things that we'll need to raise magic. And some things that will help us know each other better."

She smiled at him and he felt the earth move. After this there wouldn't be any going back. The room glowed with firelight and the candles in the sconces.

Aiden resisted making a move. He knew that she was in charge and that he was the student. For a man who was almost always in control, always keeping his world ordered, it was a pleasure to open up to a woman's lead.

Sahara blessed the area that they were in, calling out to the four directions, inviting her guides, asking for guidance about new social

122

experiences, those that created borders between women and men. She moved with grace and with experience and there was not a word she uttered that was not intended. She understood the magic she was working and Aiden relaxed into her wisdom, waiting to be summoned to her work.

Finally she sat down beside him and placed a tender kiss on his lips. She felt his energy rising to meet hers.

"The circle is cast, we're between worlds Aiden. As above, so below. You and I will be the altars tonight. You will be the Wand and I will be the Grail."

She lit the herb and passed it on to him. They took turns filling up on the life force of the powerful botanical, calling to the plant world for hidden insights.

"Drink some water, Aiden," Sahara advised. "Keep fluid, keep your emotions open."

She passed a glass to him and he drank deeply, then lifted it to her lips.

Once again she noticed his riveting male essence, the graceful strength of his arms, the way he commanded space.

She took his hands and looked into his eyes. They got lost in the realm of the others' soul. Fire spirits danced up in the flames, igniting their passion. Sahara led them in three deep breaths, calling to the Sacred to fill them and connect them to Earth energy. She invited the Green Man to guide Aiden's journey, and Venus to guide hers.

Aiden covered her with his body and kissed her, holding himself up with his arms, only once letting his weight crush her, before he moved off again. She mourned the loss of his weight upon her. His mouth on hers tasted like honey, she felt herself melt into the earth beneath her. Holding onto his flexed biceps, she let his mouth travel to her neck, to her ears. His tongue, warm and probing, left her soaked.

Suddenly, she smelled the forest on him. He was Pan, the God of the natural world, walking lightly on the mossy forest floor, shaking his horns, with a gleam in his eye. Tonight she wouldn't be afraid to be herself. Pan receded into the shadows and Sahara opened her eyes to her lover's intense gaze.

Aiden took off his jeans and stood naked, towering over her, sweat adding a shine to his sculpted body, his cock hard, demanding attention. But it was not yet time. She bid him lie down.

She pulled his hair up, taking a bite of his ear, whispering to him in the language of the Divine. He tried to take hold of her dress. "No," she said, "I will do it." And now she stood over him, a Priestess in charge of her circle, the sacred masculine in her care.

She asked him if he was open to an encounter with the Sun God. He nodded, not knowing what she meant but sure that he was ready. She opened the box of tools and took out a wand, then, gently, starting at his third eye, invoked a pentagram on his body.

They embraced and she felt his heart pounding as he held her, his fingers splayed possessively over the small of her back.

Sahara lifted her gown over her head. Aiden's eyes riveted to her clit. She wore a loose silver chain around her waist, and attached to it, another chain that curved around her bottom and between her legs, ending in a smooth clip pressed to her erect clit. It seemed to bind her, pleasurably.

"Jesus. *Sahara.*"

He shuddered, not sure if he was dreaming, falling between here and there, a man on fire with lust and love. He thought he had seen her like this before, but of course, he had not, maybe in a dream? She asked him to pull lightly on the chain. He did, curious to see her reaction. Her knees buckled a little, she moaned and asked him to pull a little harder. She fell before him. He cradled her in his arms, hoping that everything he did was for her pleasure.

"Sahara, before we start down this road again, I need a safe word. Please give it to me. I need to know when to stop, if it's pain that you seek. Or we can play at something else."

"I need the pain, Aiden; to know that I can trust you, to learn to trust myself; to get past needing pain."

"Safe word, Sahara, please!"

His voice was softer than ever, she knew that it was the Goddess working her magic, teaching him restraint of his warrior side. She gave the word. Mercy.

"I am yours," he said, and laid her down before the fire.

"Sahara, you're..."

"Kiss me, my love," she said, daring to expose her emotions.

He kissed her tenderly and ran his hands over her glorious body, his tongue smooth on hers. Sahara knew that he was holding great restraint, because every muscle in his body screamed tension.

"Lick my nipples, but don't bite."

He licked softly, kissed her small breasts, rolling her nipples under his thumb. Aiden loved instruction, though he hardly needed any.

"Suck them Aiden."

"Harder," she said. He sucked harder, his rock-hard cock rubbing against her leg as he hovered over her, his mouth hungry and accommodating to her pleas.

"Pull on the chain Aiden. No, harder!" Her legs spread wider as she pushed her hips towards him, the chain lying cool against her wet slit.

His hands warmed. A sudden need for violence swept over him and he groaned to still it.

Sahara moaned as he pulled the chain harder. He looked hungrily at her spread legs. He found her openness such a turn on, she intoxicated him with her willingness to be this wanton and unreserved. Her nipples beckoned and he took them in his mouth.

She pulled on his hair, guiding his hand to play with her nub as it swelled under the imprisonment of the clip.

Aiden licked at her, finding the flesh around the clip, she was writhing under his tongue, spurred on by his tight grip as he held her hips down, owning her.

"I'm so hungry for your cunt, Sahara."

His hot breath left her panting and she felt her clit throb under the clip, the first wave of orgasm mounting. Sahara had been mistaken when she'd thought that her previous lover knew how to tease a woman's sex. Aiden laid a flattened tongue directly over the silk of her opening.

"Don't stick your tongue in," she pleaded, "Oh God. Aiden, don't!"

He resisted. She had read his mind. He continued to torture her swollen clit with a soft tongue. She shuddered under every lick. He let his tongue circle all around her opening, along her perineum, venturing towards her tight, pink bud. He knew that it would make the first thrust of his cock all that more delicious.

They felt themselves hovering between the layers of time. Only her voice kept them in the present as she continued to instruct him on how to take her to the edge of letting go, using the chain, a rhythmic orgasm rising towards her. When she finally gave him permission to slip it off, she fell mindlessly into the burst of pleasure while his finger gently smoothed the tortured hood of her clit. Aiden inserted two fingers, hooking under her pubic bone to find her secret place for ecstasy and pumped vigorously. She exploded into orgasm as the relief of receding pain hit her, squirting along his hand and arm, her legs spread wide, hips pumping towards him.

"*Sahara!* That was beautiful. I want to make you come again!" Aiden ran his hands through his hair, his cock straining, Sahara's abandon in her release a powerful aphrodisiac.

She smiled hazily and kissed his mouth, her tongue warm and her lips trembling with the after-shocks. He longed to hold her like this forever, but she was already asking for more.

Sahara asked to be put over his knee. Aiden did so, hands and eyes worshipping the smoothness of her curves, he touched her tenderly, waiting for the inevitable. His stomach was tight; he was exhilarated and frightened, afraid of hurting her, needing to hurt her.

"Lightly," she said.

He laid his hand on her, softly, a caress in between. He wanted to get on his knees and kiss her there, but she wanted something else. He would have been content to caress her for hours.

"Harder now Aiden! Oooh, you're so good at taking instruction."

He thought of coming in her mouth, of filling her with every drop that he had. His chest rumbled with the possibility.

He put her down on her hands and knees and positioned himself behind her. His hand came down and she felt the sting, a slow fire starting to build in her inner core. She instructed him towards delivering more pain, then layering it with his kisses, then harder yet and begging for his tongue on her slit. He groaned his obedience to her will.

He wanted to trust Sahara, trust himself. He asked if she was ready to say the safe word when tears filled her eyes and she asked him to stop.

"Say the safe word, Sahara."

He wouldn't break her trust, he would not cross the boundary of their agreement. She begged him to desist. He insisted on the safe word, and kept his hand to her ass, stopping only to lick her again, opening her with his thumbs and kissing her quivering cunt. She asked him to open the box. She pointed to the small whip.

"No," he said, his voice raw, his whole body shaking.

"You have to," she said. "I haven't said the safe word. You promised, Aiden."

Aiden wanted her to use the whip on him, he longed for it, but she insisted that it was her night, not his. He looked at her fiercely, his eyes as tense as the rest of his body, and gripping the whip, he offered what she'd asked for. With great precision he laid it down, she tested him with tears. He teased her by running the whip gently along her slit, nudging her nub with the handle, then returning with a solid hit, his jaw set...waiting, waiting for her word. She pushed him until he grew angry.

"Say the fucking safe word, Sahara!"

His words dripped out of his mouth tersely. He let the whip fall harder than even he thought he had courage for.

She said it. Mercy.

He let his breath out, grateful. She pointed to the box again, instructing him to a small tool.

"Woman, you are going to kill me," he muttered. He wouldn't last if she wanted his cock inside her.

He slid his fingers over her slippery bud and inserted the sex toy, opening her slowly. "Sahara, I'm falling to pieces here...this is...let me kiss you."

"*Please Aiden...*" Sahara pushed back.

She moaned as he continued, harder now. Aiden was mesmerized by the sight of the vibrator's smooth slide into Sahara's tight little ass; his cock throbbed terribly, his heartbeat loud in his ears.

She stopped his hand and turned around to meet his lips, kissing him wildly, begging for his cock in her mouth, in her cunt, in her ass.

"Mouth," he whispered, broken to her passion.

She slid her mouth down on him, slowly, allowing herself several delicious thrusts up and down before turning herself around again, on elbows and knees. He ran his fingers along her slit long enough for her to start bucking her hips, slipping two fingers in, offering them to her eager mouth to taste. She licked them top to bottom then sucked hard.

"Sahara, I don't know how long I can last. You're torturing me."

"You will last, Aiden, you have the Goddess to guide you. Ask for her help."

"I am sure that the Goddess is not so pleased with my treatment of you," he said, bewildered by her ability to focus on their spiritual connection while all he could think of was sinking himself deep inside her cunt.

"You have been faithful in your promise to me, Aiden, to keep to my safe word. I asked for a lesson in trust, and you delivered well. I felt your tenderness through every bit of it."

Aiden touched her gently, still so hungry to see her every fold. He held her open with his hands then slid in fully, without a word, in one forceful move. She convulsed around him but didn't let herself reach full orgasm. She waited a moment then moved back and forth on him, softly, tensing when she was near the throbbing head of his cock and pulling back hard. He called her name.

Onwards and onwards, she guided him to use his breath to keep his flow in check. It felt so damn good inside her. When she couldn't stand it anymore herself, she commanded him to fuck her hard and he did, thrusting into her with groans and incantations, fucking her until he felt her arch and heard her scream, and then, only then, he allowed himself the release he craved, filling her with his seed and his love.

He laid his tired body down beside her, holding her close, feeling her hands roam his back, her kisses on his chest. They were deeply spent, physically and spiritually.

She got up presently and moving widdershins around the circle she had cast, she thanked the directions, closed the portals, and offered libations to the deities. Aiden felt something lift from him and he closed his eyes. He stayed there until she led him to the bath she had run for them; and the mugs of sleepy time tea by the tub.

They lay in it together, she held in his arms, his size and his strength a comfort. She turned now and then, to kiss him softly, tears in her eyes, gratitude on her lips. Pain delivered by the hand of such a stunning man was a major turn-on for her.

"Thanking me for making love to you or hurting you Sahara?" Aiden grazed her neck with his teeth.

"Both. For trusting me. For hurting me. For taking me to the places I need to go."

"I meant it when I said I wanted to learn from you Sahara. About magic, about what you need. I feel so completely at ease in your bed, as if we've been together for ages...perhaps we have. I'm surprised at my own words as I say them. Could we find out about past lives?"

"*Aiden.*" Sahara's words came softly. "I'm overwhelmed by my feelings for you. I'll need some time to process. I promise that we'll talk it all out and do the work that needs doing to make sense of it all. But tonight I just need to feel you around me. I came to this place thinking that I would live here quite alone and never imagined meeting you or feeling the things that I'm feeling. I hoped that being alone in the wilderness would keep me safe in practicing my magic, that no-one would know me and that I would not have opportunity for friends...I have hurt a few people with the way I want to live my life. So this is quite un-expected. But not unwanted Aiden, not unwanted, now that you're here."

Aiden's arms tightened. He lowered his head to her face and kissed her cheek.

"I have a very intense desire to protect you," he whispered.

Sahara moved to the other side of the bath. She stared at him with her cat-like eyes scanning his handsome face, his hair wet, pushed back from his face, muscular arms draped along the edge of the tub; powerful legs drawn in to give her room. He smiled rakishly and asked how she thought he would make it home tonight, after she had wrung all the strength from his body.

"Oh no, my lord." Sahara purred. "You will be a guest in my bed tonight. I'm looking forward to seeing you sprawled out naked on my softest sheets, and reserve the right to take every advantage of your spectacular physique. There will be no going home."

"As you wish, my lady, I am at your service, in bed and other-wise." He pulled her over to his side again; his mouth nestled in her hair.

"I'm too old to play games anywhere but in bed, Sahara," he whispered.

She twisted her neck to look up at him, eyes clouded with feeling. Sahara let her tears fall.

"I'm falling in love with you Sahara. I think it started the day I met you. You were like a fresh autumn wind after a long hot summer. And I can't stop thinking about how your sweet pussy feels under my tongue. I dream of licking you constantly. Of making you come while my mouth is still on you."

She buried her head in his chest, her sex tight again with longing. She kissed his eyes. She rubbed her breasts close to his lips. He sought them out and rolled her nipples with a skilled tongue. There was so much to say, but tonight he wanted to be lost to his feelings. To be free.

Sahara put her arms around his neck. Grazing his ear she whispered her love words. She fell under the spell of his honesty and hon-our. He had courage, more than he knew. There was a darkness that he drew on from another lifetime. She felt it in his hands when he ap-plied the whip; there was no doubt that those hands had killed. The energy of abandoning himself to the battle hung around him at times; he must have been a warrior.

Sahara had some memories already, but they were scattered and she needed Iona to access more. Iona. She knew Aiden in some form. That was why she was trying to keep Sahara from going too deep with him. She would have to confront Iona, and find out what she knew.

CHAPTER 17

They slept deeply. Dreams escaped them. Pan, Aiden's protector in the past, was once again at his side. He guarded Aiden's sleep, aware of the raven that sat perched on the Elder outside, commanding her silence and her obedience. And she would obey, at least in this moment.

Iona dared not enter Sahara's dreams either. Deep rest was what they needed, sustenance for another day, when secrets and old wounds would be revealed. Pan left with the morning light, to nether regions that called his attention, leaving the scent of the forest behind as a gentle reminder to their sub-conscious of where they had once trod.

Iona flew away to raise energy for Sahara's work. She loved her. Loved her like the unshakeable addiction that she was, and was still committed to teaching her whatever she needed to know. They were a team, and passing centuries had no effect on their relationship. Or so Iona desperately wanted to believe.

Aiden woke to the dawning light, turning his head to look out the window facing the mountains; they were still covered in a dark haze, the sun not quite reaching their peaks at this hour. The cabin was silent, a safe haven for the feelings that rose instantly when he looked down at Sahara sleeping soundly in the crook of his arm. Looking very small against him, a smile curving her lips, she stirred a love in his heart that he welcomed with longing and desire. His arm tensed to hug her. Her eyes flew open; her smile deepened as she looked upon his rugged face, and she ran her fingers over his chest, relishing the muscular strength, and the warm light in his eyes.

"You look good in my bed, Aiden," she said. "I'm happy that you're here."

"I'm happy to be here. Sahara...you've thrown my world upside down. How did you find me?" He pulled her in, needing to feel her fully against him, his cock rising instantly, his kisses on her face urgent.

She wanted to say things, to reply, but could not. Sometimes, when she needed to speak, her spirit would command silence, and she struggled between giving him an answer and heeding her instincts.

"Aiden, I don't always have the words...please understand."

He understood, his heart beating fast, he spoke her words for her. "I think the forest has called us in, I think we've walked a forest path together before, I'm a bit more awake today to the past. Asking Pan to come in last night has given me the tiniest bit of insight, but it's still nothing that I could really put my finger on. Sahara, do you smell that faint scent of damp forest floor in the room?"

She nodded, still unable to speak.

"You and I know that scent. Pan was here, I felt him last night. And I didn't dream. I haven't slept that soundly in years. I think that we were under his protection. But we can save words for later. Do you have time to spend with me today?"

"I have to get back to work, it's calling me, but not till later. I need you in my arms for a little while longer."

Aiden smiled his devilish smile, dropping kisses on her breasts as she straddled him and leaned over his face.

He moaned as she turned around on him, facing his erection, her bottom spread so that he could see every hot bit of her. She lowered herself down to place a delicate kiss on the tip of his cock. Her lips parted and she offered a tender lick, then two, then three. He held on fiercely to her hips, mesmerized by the tenderness before him, just far enough away that he could not reach her with his tongue. She smiled as she sensed his frustration.

She took him fully in her mouth then, expertly sucking his length, using her small hands to pull at the base, where he was too thick for her. Aiden lost himself in her motions and the sounds she made as she went down on him, the reverberations of the noises mounting his pleasure. He could see her wet begin to flow as she became more vigorous in her tongue play, and his finger slid over her slit rhythmically, nub to her tight pink bud, but resisting the urge to slip in. Her hips started to push back on him, she was fully wet now and her clit engorged.

"Pull on it, Aiden," she pleaded, breathless.

He took her clit between thumb and forefinger, difficult as it was, her bits almost too small to fit into his large hands. He pulled it delicately first, then more forcefully, in the way she was pulling at his cock with her mouth. She moaned her pleasure onto him, sucking more enthusiastically; they rocked together towards their combined ecstasy. He wanted to find release, her mouth hot and tight around him, but waited until she gave the signal. His eyes remained hungrily on her pussy, her wet lips hypnotising him as he continued to work her clit. He felt her tense, she uttered a deep groan, and he watched her folds spasm into orgasm, all her muscles working; he had his signal.

He didn't hold back but came with loud moans, calling her name, spilling onto her straining nipples as she pumped his cock with her hand, his fingers now wedged deeply inside her. She yelled into the rising sun, not caring how much noise they made, they were safe here, wild abandon their only care.

—————— ❀ ——————

They both frowned when the phone rang, interrupting their lazy morning in bed. Sahara checked the caller ID, then, motioning her apology to Aiden, picked up the call.

"Kathryn?"

"Sahara, hi! I'm hoping that we can meet in Denver next week. I have to say, this is the best you've ever done. I'd ask if you were in love, but I know that that's impossible."

"Well *that's* good," Sahara replied, ignoring the last remark. "What news from the publishers? How much of an extension can I get?"

"Well, the answer was 'none' the first time I asked, but then I sent them what you'd sent me, and they almost went out of their pro-verbial minds reading it. Now we've got two months. Good, yes?"

"Yes! I'll have to work night and day, but I'm feeling inspired, so I think we'll be fine."

There was a silence on the other end, Sahara tried to pick up on Kathryn's energy.

"Kathryn, I know I've been difficult. More than difficult. And you've done all there was to do to keep me in the game. I know how hard that was for you. I haven't been a good friend. I'm sorry. It was all I could do to keep myself sane the last six months. But I'm good now, this place has been healing for me, I'm finally home."

She heard Kathryn shuffling about at her end.

"I needed to hear you say that, Sahara." Kathryn replied, blowing her nose and wiping her tears. "I've spent months worrying and won-dering. It's not like you to be this insensitive. I knew you were hurting, but still, I missed my quirky friend."

"We'll see each other soon then," Sahara promised. "I'll send more of my work ahead."

"To work," she announced as she hung up the call.

"To work," Aiden agreed, and rose in all his glorious nakedness from Sahara's bed. She sighed.

She was broken by him already. She'd had such plans for loneliness. Had hoped for the punishment of being cast out, friendless, undesired; to be lashed by long days of hermitage. Instead, she'd been lashed by the hand of a desirable man, one who had no intention of entering into monogamy with her. It was what she had secretly wished for and had so handily manifested. Alright, she conceded to the Universe. She'd play her cards and hope to win at her own game.

Later in the day, Sahara recalled how Aiden had looked saying his goodbye's. Easy in his movements, his frame so pleasingly strong, face unshaved, his hands keeping his hair back as the wind picked up. He had smiled at her in that teasing manner he had, asking her to be well while he was away. It had been easy to fall into something comfortable with him. She wondered about his dark side, the one she'd glimpsed as his eyes fell into a haze when he'd gripped the whip from her box of sex toys. He had held back, but she knew that there had been times when he had not. In this lifetime, or last, she wondered? She was also sure that he had been on the receiving end; his energy had betrayed him when he had asked to be the one to be punished.

She had stood with the wind whipping about her as he left for his place, the grass in the distance dancing to some silent orchestra, remembering the day she'd met him and how his laughter had pierced her soul.

CHAPTER 18

Dagr woke up early, the sound of horses in the courtyard sending a warning that something was afoot. He dressed quickly and checking that the women were tucked in and still asleep, he slipped out of the house on silent feet, sword at his side. His bailiff stood holding the reins to a tall black stallion. Dagr instantly recognized the steed belonging to his overlord, Earl Richard Dumont.

He picked up his pace, and gestured to Mark to stand back, wondering about the whereabouts of Eric, his steward. He bowed on approaching the Earl, but noticed that he was not greeted with the usual warm reception he could expect from his friend.

"My lord," he said as his bow was acknowledged by the briefest of smiles. "Is anything amiss? If I may be so bold, where is your guard, did you ride out alone with no one to protect you?"

He noticed the changing colour in Richard's eyes. He felt his sword, out of habit, when he sensed a dangerous moment.

The stable boy had brought forth Dagr's horse, evidently at Richard's request, and was handing him his reins. Dagr took them and again looked towards Richard for an answer, but knowing that none would be given until they were alone, away from everyone. He wouldn't be able to go back to give the women any warning that he was riding out. He looked to Brigida's brother, who understood immediately and gave a slight nod of the head. The Dagr leapt up onto his horse and turned to follow Richard. They rode away, towards the fortress ruins that faced the pounding, unforgiving ocean.

Dagr watched his friends back, straight as an arrow with shoulders squared. The sky remained poised for rain, the wind raw and sharp. They stopped at the water's edge, old castle ruins in the distance. Dagr turned his horse to face his overlord. The other man looked toward him grim faced and angry.

"Do you know where your steward lies?" Richard barked.

Dagr remained silent, his face twisting into impatience.

"He is dead; struck down on the road between my castle and your miserable little village. He was on his way home after spreading news of your maddening refusal to follow the faith of the land."

Richard waited to see if Dagr would speak. He did not.

"Therefore, now forced to keep peace and unity, under scrutiny of all those who would have me killed for my friendship with you, I must ask you to promise me that you can, at the least, pretend to drop all this damned sorcery you practice."

Dagr continued to stare him down, anger plain in his eyes.

"Well? Answer me, as a knight and my friend!" Richard roared.

"Who killed Eric?" Dagr sat gripping his reins with fists meant to control his rage.

"*I* killed him, you fool, to keep him from spreading more lies about you being handfast to two women at once. I have never heard such nonsense. And that was the least damaging of his lies."

Richard stepped his horse closer to Dagr, the wind making it difficult for him to keep the conversation heard.

"I *am* handfast to two women at once!" Dagr roared back. I owe you my life Richard, but I will be damned if I let even you tell me who to love."

"You are? You will not?"

Richard jumped off his horse and came to pull Dagr off his. Dagr beat him to it and jumped down, facing the Earl with all the courage that he knew he would need. Richard loved him as a friend, and also owed Dagr his life, but he was still his superior.

"Dagr, for the love of all that you hold dear, explain to me what you are talking about. I understand you less as time goes on...must you always try my patience and the limits of my protection?"

They walked down the steep hill towards the water. Dagr faced Richard on the beach and told him about Arinn, Brigida, and the circumstances of their arrangement.

"My lord," he said, knowing that Richard had a special affinity to being called 'lord' by him. "I am incapable of following a God that has been forced down our throats. We had our own ways once, and I have been taught those ways since the day I was born. The religion England follows is not my way. I cannot give you a promise that is not mine to give."

"Dagr, there is no other way. I am pressured from all sides to keep my manor lands united. I have my enemies, like you. You, Dagr, are one of the biggest thorns in my side. It matters not what I believe or want. You know this. I have my station in life as you have yours. Why can you not obey?"

"It is not my way, and never will be," Dagr replied. "I will die for my beliefs as I would die for you. But I cannot do this thing you ask...and I understand that you cannot protect me, but will you protect my women?"

His friend looked away.

"Richard! I need to know that you will keep them safe."

"So you would rather die and leave the women you love in my care, than make an effort to appear compliant? You are an idiot. I cannot promise you anything as you cannot promise me anything. You are going to be stripped of your knighthood and lands, you know this, and that's if you survive at all," Richard spat out.

Richard's jaw was grinding his disappointment. He could see that Dagr would pay a high price for his strange ways.

Dagr looked at Richard's dark and chiselled face, so much harder than his own, he was truly fierce when angry, and looked not much different when in a good mood. He remembered all the years they had had as young boys growing up, attending sword class together, their fathers' knights at the royal court. They each admired the other, they had shared lovers, meals, faced death together on the battlefield. They were brothers by circumstance if not by blood.

Richard, who easily found love at the hand of a woman, had never made a secret of his desire for more with Dagr. When sharing a lover, it was always Richard's eyes that looked for permission to include Dagr in his embrace. But permission was never granted.

Dagr had seen every part of Richard in intimate detail, and he could not say that he had not enjoyed watching his friend perform in bed. Indeed, Richard had caught Dagr staring with eyebrow raised as he filled some wench with all his force and skill. The Earl was a dark horse with specific tastes in bed. Still, they had not crossed the boundary Richard wanted to push. Now Dagr had one chance to beg for the protection of Arinn and Brigida, if he fell to the hands of fate.

"I want to swim," he said, and stripped off his clothes before the astonished gaze of Richard.

"It is bloody fucking freezing!" Richard yelled, but Dagr had already braved the cold surf. Richard followed him in, swearing at every stroke, muscular arms and hard stomach tensed to keep himself from succumbing to the frigid waters.

They could not last long, but Dagr had needed the shock to formulate his thoughts and to prepare a response. The wind made all thoughts of extended banter impossible. Both men gasped as they left the waves. Out of habit, Dagr decided on the cave they had used since childhood to warm up in, perhaps there was some drift wood left in there to start a fire. When he turned to pick up his clothes, he found Richard on one knee in front of him, looking as intense as he had ever seen him, forcing his body to stillness, even though he was shaking at his core from cold and lust, wet hair clinging to his shoulders.

"My lord, get up!" Dagr commanded with brows furrowed, forgetting his place.

"A cruel twist of circumstance, brother, me on my knees before you." Richard started to lose control of his emotions, and his great body shook with some force.

"Get up! Richard, you will die of cold." Dagr gripped Richard by his arm and pulled him to his feet. "Follow me!"

Dagr led the way to the small cave that held remnants of a long ago fire, and using the flint he carried in his leathers, he worked at lighting the small pile of tinder to warm them by. The sun was now climbing in the sky, but the wind made small of its power. They were both drunk on desperation. They sat in the quiet until they could say they were not frozen to the bone, adding more drift wood to the now decent blaze. Their eyes met, both intent on meeting their needs. Richard scowled into the fire.

"I cannot protect you, you know this. So what else is there for you to ask me for? You know my price, in any case."

"I would rather give you what you want without pressure."

"I could say the same. I would rather ask you for what I want without forcing you into it. But here we are. Both needing something that forces us to beg."

"I want my manor to go to Arinn if I am killed."

"She cannot have land title, if she's accused of the same sorcery as you! Why do you always ask for the impossible?"

"You are asking for more than I would normally give, my lord," Dagr pointed out, miserably.

They looked each other square in the eye, and neither would look away.

"I give my word to protect your women as best as I can." Richard finally conceded. "I'll find a way..."

"Find a way. Give them a home, no matter what." Dagr's heart beat wildly, imagining Arinn and Brigida having to be at Richard's mercy, imagining not being able to love them until their dying day.

"Brigida is with child, Richard," Dagr added, without any joy in sharing the news. "We only just celebrated." Dagr choked on his words. He had been afraid many times in his life, but never like this. Brigida's sweet face came to his mind.

"A fine mess you have made Dagr," Richard said, the gravity of the news shaking him.

Richard considered his friend. There were many things about Dagr that he would change, but not his enthusiasm for life; even if it did cause him peculiar obstacles.

"I admire who you are Dagr. I wish I could be like you, leading this irreverent life. But my position lies heavily on me. I wish I could save you from what is coming. All I can do is warn you, and beg you to save yourself. But I know you, you will not be saved. You are breaking my heart. I think you know how I feel."

"And you know that I feel the same." Dagr shot Richard a concentrated look.

"Not *precisely* the same."

"No, but I will give you what you want. A barter, we can call it that."

"But you will hate it?"

Dagr looked at Richard with sincerity in his eyes. "No, I will not enter into it like that. I will enjoy it also, on my terms."

"And what *are* your terms, pray tell?" Now Richard allowed himself a wry smile, removing his shirt, his chest a rock of muscle, his cock straining.

Dagr removed his clothes also. His cock rose easily, Richard was stunning in his desire. "I will stand. You will serve me on your knees. You know how I like it, Richard. You have watched me on the receiving end many a time. Then, I will have the pleasure of seeing you finish yourself off. That way I will not have to wash my hands of you, and we can remain friends till the end."

Dagr's eyes clouded. "And for the record, I do love you still, even though you must throw me to the wolves."

"Why can you not just let the King send you away to battle until all this is forgotten? Renew your place in the King's favour," Richard asked, hungrily eyeing Dagr's impressive size.

"Because I will not leave my women. They will die for the life they need, and I will fight for their right."

"You are stupid. You will be dead and this will mean nothing."

"Enough talk, my lord. On your knees. Suck my cock and do it well." Dagr stood firm, his hand in a tight grip of Richard's raven hair. He closed his eyes. Richard did indeed know how to please him.

Dagr rode home at breakneck speed. He needed to warn his people, he needed to find a way to hide Arinn and Brigida. His heart broke remembering his and Richard's parting embrace, each of them wondering if they would see the other alive again, their love for each other undeniable.

138

But how to convince a whole village of danger when none of them would understand the reasons why. He wouldn't put Arinn and Brigida in harm's way by divulging the details of their love. He couldn't explain what went on at the manor of their lord, nor that the religion they followed was ever hungry to sacrifice heretics. All he could tell them was that the king had found displeasure in his service to him. And that was not enough to lead them to the safety of the forest. Oh no, not to the Oracle Wood! They would wait it out with him, these simple, superstitious people who trusted his love for them. The priest couldn't be found, Dagr's kitchen and stable boys missing from their duties as well. He waited into the dark of the night, having instructed everyone who could swing a weapon to keep it by their bed.

Dagr knew the pattern of destruction well, to his complete despair. First the edges of the village would be set on fire, soldiers keeping villagers from running. Everyone must die, in case what the lord had practiced had filtered into his demesne. Women, especially, were a target for slaughter. It was women who, by Eve's example, were the ones to stir up sinful trouble.

When night fell, Dagr, on horseback, with wife and lady's maid hidden at the edge of wood, stood waiting for evil to arrive.

He had always hated the absolute silence that preceded a battle. He hated the stealth and premeditation that went into killing innocents. Being an honored knight in the king's court was a double edged sword. The honor that had been bestowed upon Dagr hung on the lives that he had taken. And now, with only his bailiff by his side, Dagr detected the first sounds of horror.

The shrieking of mothers, the plaintive wail of babies torn from their arms, the shouts of men as they were pierced where they stood, protecting their own; was hauntingly painful.

Dagr motioned his bailiff to circle to the left of the village, sure that he was sending him to his death. He prayed that one day Brigida would forgive him.

He braced for battle, his body hard, breath suspended, pulse racing. He had done this many times before. The first man to attempt an ambush on the Lord Dagr Bretel lost his head. After that, Dagr stopped thinking and thundered through an impossible stream of men, slashing limbs without mercy, blood dripping from his sword.

He had never been this alone in battle, with only his horse as a trusted companion. This required more strategy than he was capable of, but had to employ nonetheless. Even though it tore his guts out, Dagr knew that escape was his only option. There was no way to save his people, nor his pride.

From the edge of the Oracle Wood, Dagr could see the village in a consuming blaze, his manor also. Life as he knew it was over, but Dagr was not sentimental about possessions and privileges.

Suddenly, from the edge of darkness, a group of soldiers rode into Dagr's sight. Standing this close to where he had hidden his loves, Dagr knew that he had put them in danger of being discovered. With a quick stab of his heel into his horse's flank, Dagr rode in the direction of the oncoming bloodshed, sword high, a murderous cry on the air.

Richard sat in his castle drunk out of his mind, banishing everyone from his sight, weeping in his chamber for one who would not be saved. He hated himself and his cowardice, the pleasure of Dagr groaning as he came in Richard's mouth a bitter memory now. Tomorrow he would search for what was left of Dagr's demesne, if any of them had survived. Dagr was the smartest warrior he knew, and Richard felt the slightest, most brief sliver of hope. Then he fell into the dark stupor the liquor had the grace to afford him.

CHAPTER 19

Dagr ran through the darkness. His heart was bursting with effort, his leg muscles on fire. In his arms, the sobbing Arinn; screaming for Brigida now and again, fighting his tight embrace. There had been no good reason for Brigida to leave her hiding spot and run towards the manor, with Arinn screaming after her, to no avail. And there had been no way to go find her, without risking Arinn's or his own life.

He ran blind with sorrow towards the cottage of the wise woman. Here he would ask for sanctuary, he knew that it would be granted. The Fey had answered his call, and made entry into the woods impossible for anyone other than those who listened to their whispers.

Dagr had favours to call in with the Fey; he had always been a strong ally of their kind. While so many were denying their existence, Dagr had remained steadfast in honouring their traditions. He heard the sound of Pan's hooves as he pounded the ground beside him, taking him down the easiest path to the little forest home. He was given energy to continue on, although he wished to lie down and cry a river of tears for the fate of Brigida, whom he loved with every ounce of his being. She had taken his seed, and joining it with a spirit from the Upper World, had begun to knit a child in her womb for him; for the three of them.

Dagr had promised his undying devotion, and her safety, he wouldn't hear of her using the purging herbs, and had failed to protect her. He felt anger like never before, the battle he had just waged the most satisfying he could remember, the heads that had rolled were not enough to soothe him.

He could never accept this God, who inspired war on innocents. He had been party to killing in His name before, he could not deny it. He had been called to battle by his country and his King. He had cursed his ability to protect his liege with sword and with arrow. He had been lucky to have lived this long. But what was life if one was not free to live as they believed?

Dagr rounded the thick clump of pines that hid the cabin from the unfamiliar eye. The windows were glowing with light, the old woman must be asleep by now, far from the sound of battle...still, she would have known.

He gave an abrupt knock, and swung the door open, to silence. Looking around, he could see that the woman was gone. There was mead on the table, a fire in the hearth, a loaf of bread laid out. Pan stood in the doorway, shaking his horns, his eyes glowing red, one hoof raised ready to paw the ground.

Dagr turned and questioned him telepathically. Pan shook his head, gave one heave of his mighty hoof and was gone. He had taken the old woman to the land of Fey. She had agreed, her time had come. She would guide them from the other side, if they needed her wisdom. The forest home was now his and Arinn's, as was her magical practice.

He laid Arinn down on the simple bed and forced her to drink a swig of mead. He too drank, a long and bitter gulp. Arinn lay on her side, her eyes wide with grief, trembling in her dismay. Now and then she let out a haunting scream, unable to contain her emotions. Dagr sat by her side, her head in his lap, stroking her hair. The screaming was good, he thought, release of any kind healing at this point. His blood still coursed like a raging river, he had never felt such an overwhelming desire for brutality.

He wished for opportunity to slit more throats, to sever more heads, to spear through more hearts. Adrenalin had given him power to spare, and a voice that roared his pleasure at the kill. There were not enough dead men on the village green to make up for the loss of Brigida. Arinn could not stop shaking. He would have to warm her with his body heat. The fire in the hearth did nothing to offer her comfort.

Both of them stripped bare, they lay under a thick fur, silently, there was nothing to say, and too much too feel. She turned towards him and buried her head in his chest. He kissed the top of her head, murmuring a spell over her, asking for a dose of forgetfulness from her memories of the night. She finally melted into him, her small frame a reminder that she was still a young girl. Too young to have to feel such loss, Dagr thought bitterly.

His strong legs against hers, his hard chest against her face, brought her some respite. She did not doubt that he had done his best to keep them all alive. She had watched from behind a stand of trees as he had swung his sword and cut down warrior after warrior. She had not imagined him to possess such fierce abandon in battle. Of course she knew that when he went to fight for his king, that there was bloodshed and gore. But somehow she had imagined him to hate the kill, she hadn't ever thought that he would look so possessed, that his arms could swing with such precision, that he had such strength in his hands. He had looked unremorseful when he had cut through their bowels, chopped through their limbs. She smelled blood on him suddenly, and heaved to spill the contents of her stomach, but there was nothing there, just bitter bile.

He offered her water and wiped her face with a cool cloth. He stood naked and dirty before her, his erection a desperate grasp at some semblance of normalcy between them, his eyes spilling over with the tears he needed to shed. She lifted one tired arm to him, pulling him in. He knelt gratefully beside her, seeking solace in her arms, needing the energy of the feminine to cleanse him.

"Love me, Dagr," she pleaded. "Love me like a warrior, not like my handfast, I need to feel your strength, to know your anger. I need this sadness pounded out of me. Bring the battle to me."

He recoiled at her words. "My lady, do not ask me for this. No...I will hurt you."

"I want to feel your rage. I saw you...you were possessed, I do not even know who you were back there."

"I do not want you to know me like that, Arinn. That is not the man I want you to love."

He looked so desperate to her, she trusted that he meant what he said, but his erection betrayed him, he had grown to his utmost, as he contemplated the violence she begged for.

"Shall I bring you to your knees then, my lord, if you will not give me what I ask for?"

He turned towards the fire and she knew that she had hit the mark. He wanted to be punished for his failure to rescue Brigida. If this was to be the only way he could sleep tonight, then she would bend to his will. She prompted him to go look for a switch, and took a long drink of mead. She would need strength. How did one hurt the one they loved?

Dagr looked at this broken woman before him, offering him forgiveness at her hands. He pulled on his leathers and walked out into the darkness to find her a weapon.

She stood trembling all over again, fear and desire a strange opiate for her broken heart.

He offered her his back. She thought that she had never seen him more beautiful. He neither tensed nor flinched as she made a pattern of blood on his skin. These would be his most painfully remembered scars. His legs rigid, his hands gripping the beam overhead, he stood humbled as she pulled on his leathers and exposed his raging lust. She kissed him and slid her mouth down his taught belly towards his manhood. His back would be aching from the onslaught, but Arinn quelled the desire to bring him relief from his pain.

He shook as she took him ever so gently in her mouth, all of him, her face pressing into his muscular core. He cried out, wondering at how she didn't gag. She pleasured him on her knees, slowly, listening to the cadence of his moans, his fierce words as he called her a whore and a bitch in heat. His words had no sting; his vile references to her womanhood only made her drip her pleasure down her legs.

He could smell her, like a fox on the hunt after a rabbit. He commanded her to present, and she did, exposing herself as wide as she could, begging him to fuck her, to make her hurt. He forced his way in, no thought to her pain now, pounding her soft and pliant opening, ignoring her pleads for mercy, his hands digging into her hips, and waiting for what he knew would come, her goddess water in a puddle beneath her, his cock drenched in her juices.

She screamed as she allowed herself release, the forest absorbing the sound. He pulled out and taking himself in hand, he sprayed her quivering ass with his seed.

He stumbled to the hearth to boil some water for their tea and a quick wash. There were herbs for cleaning the cuts on his back, but nothing for the pain in his heart. They would have to wait till tomorrow to pour a proper bath, one they would share, lying wordless in each other's arms, taking days and weeks to do nothing but follow the simple routine of waking, eating, and sleeping once again.

It was months before either one said her name out loud. And that was only in their sleep, when she would come to them in whispers and cloudy images. Snatches of precious memories was all that was left of her.

Dagrs great horse showed up one morning, standing in the mist some distance from their hut. His head hung low, his wounds beginning to scab. Arinn brought him in and tended to his pain. She boiled water and herbs for poultices, and found him wild apples to eat from her hand. She brushed and brushed, the rhythmic strokes a meditation in kindness. No broken bones, she could tell, but alas, much of a broken heart hung about him and she knew that he carried his masters' emotions as a way to help him heal. She spoke to Dagr one day about his horses' burden.

"You must find a way to lift this from him; he will die to keep you alive. Ask the Fey if they can tend to his spirit, and hard as it is for us, we must release some of our sorrow. Otherwise, your companion will take your sorrow to the Other Side for you. And you will have lost a good friend."

She knew that if he were to listen, she would have to do the same, and so as the days rolled by, she would force herself to hum as she cooked and the humming turned to whispered songs, then to dancing by the outdoor fire.

Dagr watched her with anger at first. He feared for his horse but did not want to feel joy. His heart, for the first time, was openly pessimistic and shut down to hope of any kind. But as Arinn spent days ministering to his animal, setting aside her sorrow and offering unconditional love, he grew to admire her wisdom and her courage. Like any great warrior, she used loyalty and love to access strength to go on.

He joined her one day as she stood joining third eyes with the tall beast, who had gently turned down his head so she could reach him. The horse snorted softly, she stroked the velvet of his nose, talking to him in soft whispers, guiding him towards healing and strength. Dagr stood behind her, circling his arms around her waist. She moved her body to fit his. They stood like this and breathed in unison, Dagr, his familiar, and his woman.

He found peace in the moment, not enough to release him from his own prison of violent memories, but enough to signal his horse that he was on the mend. From that day, on, Dagr ventured out as far as he dared, to find provisions and retrieve anything useful from the carnage.

Richard had been here. He had left a clue, drawn with his own hand, a place to pick up supplies, the cave. Dagr felt nausea gathering as he recognized the symbol he and Richard had always used to mark the place they could meet in private as young boys looking to escape the glare of their elders. It was the mark of the cross. But although he found things in the cave that could not be gotten had Richard not been the supplier, he never waited to meet him. Richard now knew that he was alive, and Dagr knew that his pain was even worse. Richard would gladly have been speared by Dagr to erase his self-loathing.

They made much magic in those lonely days after the slaughter. Dagr immersed himself into the teachings of Pan, meeting him in meditation and often on his walks through the Oracle Wood. He introduced Arinn to his work. She had many questions.

He explained to her that from the beginning of time, the Fey worked in unison with humans to keep the Earth vibrant. In perfect communion with the living, breathing planet, they would instruct humans on how to live harmoniously with the rest of creation. People could gather wisdom from plants and animals, often speaking to them telepathically, making for a copacetic existence where man was part of the whole. But as time had passed, and the feminine energy had waned to be overtaken by the male, all kinship with the Fey had ceased, and the image of Pan was slandered into an image of a beast called the Devil.

"But the Old Religion does not recognize an image like this," Arinn had said, confused. "Pan is the God of the Green Earth, protector of all of nature. How did he come to be something to be feared?"

"By men who found a way to rule through fear and exclusion, instead of love and tolerance." Dagrs words were bitter, his heart more so.

Dagr held Arinn to him. She was eternally curious, of quick mind and excellent memory. She meditated every morn to meet with the wise woman whose practice they had overtaken. Soon, Dagr would ask permission for her to meet some of the Fey, one in particular wished to be her guide. Arinn was attractive to them, having an ethereal look by birth. Her eyes carried that glow, usually granted to those who could be trusted to honour the work of light beings from other dimensions. But he waited until she was more mature, he knew that the Fey loved mischief, and Arinn young enough in spirit to fall for their games.

She knew now how to cast a circle, how to call in the energies of the four directions, how to empty her mind and invite her guides in. There were many; towering angels who followed her every step, light beings from other planets. She was innocent and filled with love. All her hardships had not dispelled the joy in her eyes. She fed on Dagr's strength, his devotion to her education. She could count on him.

When Dagr returned enough times bearing parcels of warm clothing, mead, and luxuries like soap, she began to wait for his explanation. She would not press him if he was not ready to share. If he was anything, he was forthright. They shared their usual simple meal of rabbit, mushrooms, and bread. Arinn mentioned that their supply of grain for simple bread was almost gone. Dagr recognized her hint.

As per their evening ritual, they sat by the fire, she sitting at his feet, he brushing her hair. He had always done this, since she had been a small child. Her long blond tresses made him weak, and he loved serving her in this way. They passed their usual cup of mead between them. Dagr shifted his long legs to sit up straighter on the bench. Her nipples perked as she felt his leg brush by hers, it was an unconscious response, but one that she looked forward to. He pulled her hair back in one hand, to place the brush against her neck, running it through to the end. She closed her eyes, enjoying the pull on her scalp, she must remember later to play with Dagr's hair, he deserved a soft touch after all the hard work he did each day to keep them fed.

He lowered his head towards her ear. His breath was warm.

"Shall I tell you where I get the supplies, my lady?"

"If it pleases you, my lord," she replied, tingling at his touch to her neck.

"Are we ready to retire to our bed?"

"If you are, it would be my pleasure."

She made a pretty picture, lying in the furs, her bare body curled into a comfortable position. Dagr stoked up the fire and looked at her smiling face. She watched as he stripped off his shirt and leathers, standing proud before her, enjoying watching her eyes travel all over his frame. He sank to his knees and kissed her lightly, the sound she made as his lips touched hers a deep purr. She put her hands in his hair, and bit around his ears. He moaned, and slid into bed with her, pulling her on top of him.

They lay like this for a long time. Their breathing became one. His hardness pushed against her, her breasts crushed against his chest. It was the best part of the day, knowing that they were together, safe, able to enjoy the simplest pleasures in life. They shifted to their sides, and lay with their faces close, looking into each other's eyes. Arinn wondered when she had fallen this deeply in love with a man when once she could only imagine a woman's touch. But Dagr had given her the pleasure of his kindness and softness. He had spent long nights learning from her. She had extended his pleasure by teaching him how to touch her for hours without giving in to her pleas for penetration, waiting until he was sure that entry would bring immediate release. She could count on the most tender of kisses, the lightest of licks, the intense moments of his face brushing lightly against her inner thighs, her nub throbbing as he blew his warm breath over it, his long hair tickling her legs. He looked so huge beside her; his hair spilling over his shoulders, arms bulging; his mighty chest a mass of muscle.

"My lord," she said as his eyes closed and his breathing grew softer.

"Yes, my love." He smiled at her hazily, having grown tired while lying in the warmth of her body.

"Will you tell me about the cloaks, as you promised?"

His eyes flew open. "Yes...now, my lady?"

She moved her lips to say 'yes', but he was already asleep, his beautiful face serene in his rest.

Arinn ran her hand down towards his cock. It stood again on command, Dagr moaned in his sleep. He would perform if she asked, but tonight she was content to just caress him as he slept, to drop kisses on his chest. She watched him sleep and wept. Brigida had often told her that she could never get enough of looking at him. And now, as her tears fell on his skin, she let herself remember the woman who had loved them both. She turned away from Dagr, her grief spilling out in great silent sobs.

Dagrs' arm hooked around her, pulling her in, her sobs waking him from sleep.

He did not speak, just lay with his heart pounding in his chest, wishing that he could take this pain away from her. And, as she often did, Arinn pushed her hips back towards him, and fell asleep with his manhood buried deep within her.

Before first light, Dagr slipped out of bed to stir the fire and bring water to boil. It was one of the many things he did to make Arinn's life easier. It gave him great pleasure to soak the herbs for their morning drink and to serve her in bed. He liked the smile she gave him when the fire was brisk in the hearth, the room warming after the night chill. She almost always greeted the morning with joy, happy to be in his arms again as he slid back in beside her, hands hot from the cup he handed her.

Some mornings they would ride out to the edge of the wood, on the side where it ended abruptly at the edge of a great cliff. Sitting on the rocky ledge, they would face the rising sun, calling in the energies of the East, the powers of Air, of clarity and re-birth. There Arinn would un-wrap a warm loaf of bread, apples and some cold meat. It was the one place they could go to see the big sky outside the forest and feel safe. No-one ever came here, the only access through the Oracle Wood, and superstitions ran too high for anyone to brave it. Here they could dream of a new life, of a peaceful world where they were not hunted down for their adherence to the Old Ways.

Dagr looked over to where Arinn lay sleeping. The cloaks hung on a hook by the door. He would have to explain those. The other supplies he had brought back could easily have been found in the wreckage of their village...he had not bothered to explain them, and she had not asked. Richard had, in his usual way, provided him with finery usually found at court, not thinking to leave them cloaks more appropriate for a forest life.

Arinn sat up in bed now, watching him circle the room as he

made things comfortable for them. He opened the door and whistled softly to his horse, at the same time airing out the cottage; he believed in clearing old energies out after the night. The great beast appeared out of the mist, shaking his head and pawing the ground. Dagr reached out to kiss him on his third eye, stimulating the horse's pineal gland, a loving and healing gesture easily recognized by animals.

Arinn was already aroused, Dagr's energy field a surprising mix of male and female energy. She had never known another man like him. Indeed, she was sure there was none other.

"Thank you, my lord," she whispered as they sat opposite each other, leaning against the walls of the alcove, cups in hand.

His eyes considered her, her fair hair spread around her shoulders, eyes a mix of yellow and green flecks, her face a bit too slender now; he worried that she did not eat enough. In the months spent alone with him she had taken on the appearance of the spirits that guided them. He recognized in her the propensity for walking both worlds. The thought disturbed him. The Fey loved her. She was easy prey for the taking.

There was no point in delaying. He reached to pour himself more brew, offering her the same. She declined.

"The cloaks, my lord," she began, as she saw that his words were not readily available to him.

"It is not my intent to keep things from you," he answered.

"I have no fear of that," she countered.

"They were left by my friend, the Earl Richard Dumont." He let his words sink in. She would know that Richard would have sanctioned the burning of their village, the murders of the villagers; the capture of Brigida. She would wonder at his term 'friend'. Her eyes swelled with tears and he saw the pain of her heart reflected there.

"Your 'friend', Dagr... a curious term for someone who has torn our hearts from our breast?"

"I will explain, my lady."

He wanted to be on his knees before her, to lay his head in her lap and beg for understanding. She sat still before him. Her eyes now a silvery haze, her heart shut down so that she could bear to hear his words.

"When I was quite young, a boy," he began, "I was introduced to Richard as a sparring partner." His hands tightened around his cup. "My father was a warrior at court in that time, and it was expected, as my talents with the sword were discovered, that I would continue on in the tradition of my father." Dagr grimaced. "For reasons unknown to me, the Gods had favoured me with fighting skill, and as a young man I never questioned this, although my mother had tried her best to keep me in the work of her magical practice. The old Earl then had need of a wise woman, and my mother was well protected by him. Outwardly, of course, he denied any knowledge of her art, but he was not the first noble to employ intuitives, astrologers or alchemists.

Arinn nodded her head, she was beginning to understand Dagr's position at court.

"Of course, it was out of the question for me to remain under my mother's instruction outwardly. I still took my lessons from her when all my other duties to the Earl's son were complete. I was young Richard's playmate, his confidant, and his protector when he was old enough to be sent to battle. I was knighted after saving his life on more than one occasion. Richard was not always the most careful."

Dagr looked at Arinn, so deathly still, so cool of eye. He continued.

"Richard and I developed a great bond, as friends and as men. We shared the ravages of battle, as well as the spoils of life at court, as I was his constant favourite. I sat at his table, shared his meals and his indulgences. Richard has always worn his position at court heavily, he often said that I had infected him with my dreams and ideals and he wished that he could be free to live a private life.

"We are none of us free, my lord," Arinn offered. "Not in this kingdom; nor in this time."

He smiled a wry smile at her, knowing what his dreams had cost her.

"The morning of the attack, Richard had come to our village to warn me that news had spread of my stubborn adherence to the Old Ways, and that I had taken two maidens as my handfast."

He looked at Arinn with sorrowful eyes. She would, by nature, blame herself now, being young and naïve.

"Arinn, the problem is not that you wanted freedom to live with another woman, or that I wanted to live with two, and not even that we observed the Old Ways. The problem is that men in power have forgotten to honour the magic of women, and that power and greed has disabled them from seeing how oppression brings about misery."

Arinn lowered her head. Dagr wanted to hold her but could feel her resistance.

"I went with Richard to a place that we used as children to hide from our elders. A cave by the ocean..." I asked him to protect you and Brigida, should anyone survive."

"Why Dagr! Bending your knee to the man who would have your loved ones slaughtered? Still harbouring love for him...I do not understand."

She shook her head at him like an innocent child trying to make out the world of adults. She frowned as he set his face into the fearsome look he sometimes wore.

"It was not I who served on bended knee that day, my lady," Dagr replied, now tense and agitated, having to tell her the worst of it. He hoped that she would not be repelled by him after this. That would be more punishment than he could take.

"I do not understand," she repeated, hugging her knees in to herself, she rocked a little as she felt herself grow cold.

"During our years at court, Richard and I had shared more than just meals and camaraderie. We also shared the love of several women."

Arinn's eyes grew wide. She was not *that* naïve; she knew that there had been plenty of women before her, but not like this.

Dagr drew in his breath to go on. "It is not unlikely for men to enjoy the pleasure of more than one woman at once, or to share one between them, and for someone like Richard, this was easily available. I do not mean taking women against their will, I mean willing partners who found Richard and I pleasing to bed."

"Did you enjoy it my lord?" Arinn's eyes narrowed and her breath came quicker. She leaned in for his answer.

"Yes," answered Dagr, surprised at the shift in her energy. "I did."

They sat with electricity coursing between them now, their conversation having taken a decided twist.

"As time went on," Dagr continued, "I came to realize that Richard loved me more than his brother in arms and all other matters. I caught him looking at me with lust in his eyes many a time, waiting for the right time to include me in his embrace."

"And did that time ever come, my lord?" Arinn asked; her voice barely above a whisper.

"It did not, although I do appreciate Richard's beauty and strength, I was not drawn to men in that way. I enjoyed watching him giving and receiving, I was aroused by his skill and his ready smile. But that was only fuel to my own lovemaking with the women of my choice."

Arinn shrank a little at Dar's words. "I do not know what to think my lord. I am betrayed by my own feelings...this tale of lust at court. I am confused."

Dagr wished that he was drinking mead instead of this herbal brew.

"When I met Richard that morning, I had one chance to ask for what was most important to me; protection of my women and my lands. If I was to perish, then I needed to know that Richard would take care of you and Brigida, and that my lands would revert to you."

"You asked him to look after us? The man who would have killed us and have the man closest to his heart cut down? Are you mad? We never would have gone with him!"

Arinn was rarely angry but as Dagr looked at her now, she was flaming in her rage, her eyes sparkling fire.

"If you had been captured alive, I would have hoped that he would take you into his care, under whatever pretense, it was the best I could do under the circumstances." His voice soft now, Dagr looked truly miserable and lost.

She looked at the sadness in his eyes and her anger receded as fast as it had come. She sat quietly and waited for him to finish.

"I invited Richard into the ocean for a swim. I knew that I would be at my most convincing with Richard if I was vulnerable. I was not wrong. He went down on his knees before me and I had only one thing to trade for your safety. The one thing that I knew Richard wanted, and could not get."

"Your body," Arinn whispered. She looked him in the eye; Dagr looked down at her nipples straining in her shift.

"You are not angry with me," he said. It was not a question, but something he realized as he watched her face flush with curiosity.

"So between men," Arinn questioned, her wetness gathering, "Is it like between two women? Forbidden and hidden?"

"More so than for women I think, my lady." She would ask for more detail, of this he was sure. She was simply taking a breath to give him time to relax, his body now a tangle of nerves and sinew.

"And did he please you, Dagr?" He realized then that she made no distinction between the love of two men or two women. To her, love was love.

"He did, my lady, he pleased me well."

"But you had said that you were not drawn to men in that way?"

"I am not. But since I had to take his offer, I refused to dishonour myself and him by not enjoying it. Richard is beautiful to me in many ways. It was not that difficult to look past the fact that he is a man. I chose instead to look at his desire to please me."

"And how did he please you my lord?"

Dagrs cock strained. He also felt betrayed... by his memories. He should have nothing but remorse for his actions that day, but his morals were not that tight that he could not justify what had happened. In battle, you do what needs doing to survive.

"He served me on his knees. He had never been subservient to me before, and this was an exciting new game for him." Dagr paused, and pushed his cock down in his leathers under Arinn's fascinated gaze. He would need release soon. Arinn tugged on her nipples, feeling her wetness starting to run.

Arinn gasped lightly, imagining these two men who had shared their fill of women now exploring this new passion. She imagined Dagr standing firm as he always did when she was down on her knees before him, his intensity etched into his handsome face, Richard the servant to his knight.

"Was like it is with me, when I take you in my mouth, my lord?"

"No, my lady. With you it is exquisitely tender, with Richard I could be rougher. He can take a more forceful cock."

Dagr untied his leathers to expose his hardness to her, she parted her shift and showed him her nipples, long and tightly erect. Dagr moaned and began to pump his cock in his fist.

"And what else, Dagr. Tell me!"

"And to make my release greater, he performed a trick that he often asks for from the women he beds."

"A trick, what trick, do I know it?" Arinn lifted her shift and exposed her wet cunt to Dagr's hungry eyes.

"I can easily teach you, another time, when we can take our time to give each other the same pleasure."

She pouted. "But you can tell me, can you not, my lord?" she asked, as she slipped herself onto his manhood easily, now fully aroused and dripping her juice down towards his tightened balls.

"He sucked my cock as well as any woman had, and while he did, he inserted his finger here"...and with this he slipped his finger into Arinn's already lubricated bottom, massaging her gently in and out. She cried out and bucked her hips wildly, he meeting her with hard and fast thrusts of his cock.

"And where did you release my lord?" She was grinding herself into him, relishing the sensation of his finger in her pink bud, Dagr watching her intently.

"Into his willing mouth, my lady," Dagr groaned, and gave one more hard thrust and they came together, hanging on to each other, their love growing with this new confession. Arinn held tight to Dagr's tangled hair, whispering love words.

"And did Richard find release at your hands Dagr?" Arinn asked at last, her face buried in his chest.

"No, at his own hand," he replied. "I gave him what I could."

And now he is remorseful for his cowardice and he supplies us with these sumptuous staples. I do not hate Richard, Dagr, because of your love for him. But I do have one more question."

"What is that my lady?" Dagr whispered into her ear, his love for her exploding.

"If he had Brigida captured, does he have her still? Does he provide her with safety as promised? What if she is alive still? Because if he does have her; I will find a way to go to him and ask him for her return. No matter what it costs me...or you!"

He stared at her, surprised by her vehement tone. And he felt fear for her, because she wouldn't count her safety as part of a bargain with Richard, he could tell. Dagr held her tight until she cried out in pain.

"He cannot have you too, my love, he will not!" And with that Dagr stood to his feet and threw her to the bed. Arinn looked at him with all the defiance she could muster.

"I will do as I see fit, my lord," she hissed, "and I will not take my orders from you." She turned away from him and put on her robes.

He was sorry for his anger, but he would not take it back this time. He would kill all of them before he shared Arinn with Richard. And he did not know if he wished more that Brigida was alive under Richard's care or dead, and spared his propensity towards loving what was not his.

CHAPTER 20

"We change the world not by what we say or do, but as a consequence of what we have become." ~ David. R. Hawkins

The night stretched on with no promise of light for hours. Holly looked at the clock display, only two in the morning. She could sleep for two more hours, if sleep would come. She had fought her passion all night, Sahara's kisses still burning on her lips. The familiar ache between her legs begging for her touch, her clit tingling as she brushed it with her fingers; her pussy slick and tight, growing swollen until she gave in and pulled out her toys from the bedside drawer.

She slipped off her t-shirt, and glanced down at her breasts, tender with desire. She touched them, aware of how pretty they looked, supple, a little heavy as she approached her cycle on the coming full moon. She pulled on her nipples, a little moan escaping her lips. Slipping out of bed, she sat on the floor in front of the full length mirror. She spread her legs and opened herself further with her fingers. Julie had said that she had never seen anything prettier, Holly wondered if she had said that to all her lovers. Still, she *was* delicately made, her folds a tender picture, as she slipped one moistened finger from her mouth over her nub. She could take her time, there was no going back to sleep now.

Her eyes were curious as she watched herself slip her vibrator in, and her thoughts turned to Aiden. His handsome face came to her as he had looked standing in the doorway to his bedroom. He had held great control over his emotions, she knew; she had noticed his tight grip on the doorframe, his jaw working in that way he had when he was fighting something inside. Did it feel like this to be filled by a man? Sahara knew how it felt... she wanted Sahara's hands to guide the vibrator in, to fuck her hard until she came. Her movements faster now, she pushed her hips up as her hand pushed the vibrator in. Her breasts moved rhythmically as she took herself towards release, wishing for Sahara's lips on her nipples, her swollen clit. She switched toys to one bigger, first running it over her nub, anticipating the release she knew would come soon. The vibrator in, filling her well and reaching her deepest places, she let her lust spill over, her clit stretched with every movement, Holly allowed herself a loud descent into ecstasy. She lay spent on the floor.

Holly heard the light tap on the café door as she prepared the ovens and pastries for baking. It could only be Aiden, stopping to purchase a bag of French roast, ground for the press he always took for his hotel stays, and a supply of her croissants.

She gave him an expansive smile that made his heart leap as she opened the door. Still warmed by her memories of the early morning hours, Holly left a stream of electricity as she led Aiden to the counter for his first cup and to grind the beans he wanted.

"How long will you be gone, Aiden?"

"A week, or a bit longer, depending on how things turn out. It's a big project, and we're starting at an inconvenient time of the year. It's all up to the weather."

"Why did they start now?" Holly wondered.

"God only knows," Aiden replied, his face turning down into a scowl. "I have long stopped trying to figure out my clients." But now he was smiling at her, happy to be watching her work, her long hair still loose down her back. She would put it in a ponytail before her doors opened.

"What you thinking?" Holly asked, as she watched him give in to his ever active mind. "Wait," she said, "I have to get the beans from the back room."

He glanced up to see her disappear around the corner. His decision was made in a split second, and he stood up to follow her, determination in his step.

She stood with her back to him, on tip-toes, searching an upper cupboard for the bag. His eyes swept over the curve of her back and the swell of her bottom as she stretched to reach the beans. In an instant, he was behind her, one strong hand gripping the counter on one side of her, the other reaching into the shelf beside hers. His lips were in her hair, his voice a whisper in her ear.

"May I?"

She shuddered as the smell of his musky cologne reached her nose, the one he always wore, a mix of essential oils that smelled of forest and patchouli.

He felt her energy coursing, she leaned her ear into him, his lips now moving ever so gently along her neck, his body careful not to touch hers, his cock hard in his jeans. Holly's arousal, and he was sure that that's what it was, took Aiden by complete surprise. She shook her head a bit, searching for his lips once more on her neck, struggling to control the weakness in her knees, giving in to the rush of desire that tingled at her clit.

Aiden spoke softly to her, his hips moving in just once to push against her bottom. His hard on made no small impression on her, brief as the touch was.

"Forgive me, Holly. Ask me to stop and I will."

His breath washed over her in sensual waves, and she was too aroused to ask him to stop. She felt the wet between her legs; he kept searching for the weak spots on her neck. She felt his strength behind her, the power of his arms as they trapped her between him and the counter. Holly had a fleeting moment of fear as she wondered how to kiss a man so intense, then turned into his arms, lips open, face turned up for his kiss.

"*Holly*," was all that Aiden could say, his voice tortured. His eyes were dark and his body leaned in to allow her the pleasure of feeling his passion. Holly broke open to his desire, and set herself free to explore this new adventure. Aiden's kisses were tender and curious. She let him explore with his tongue, to taste her lips fully. His groan as he kissed her deeply sent waves of desire that reached like an electric shock from her clit to the crown of her head. She kissed him back, delighting in how good he tasted and how hard he now pressed himself into her.

He pulled back from her suddenly, and let her go, watching as she tried to gain control of her emotions. They stood studying each other's eyes. She could swear she saw love there; he was hoping he saw nothing but happiness. She glanced down at his jeans. He smiled, and pulled her into an embrace. He wanted to say many things, but could only hold her to his heart.

"I'm ok, Aiden." Holly finally said. She looked up at him, like the girl that she still was in so many ways, looking shy but not sorry that she had let him in.

"I've taken more than I should have, I know," he answered. "Are you sorry you've kissed a boy?" His smile was mischievous, daring her to deny that she enjoyed it.

"I've kissed a man," she replied. "And no, I am not sorry, I'm not sorry at all."

She laid her head to his chest, his heart was beating like a war drum; he kissed her hair and said he had to go. She let go of him but held on to his scent; and the feeling of a man's kiss on her lips.

Holly locked the door behind him. He turned once with a smile. She watched his broad back as he walked the short distance to his truck. Self-assurance...that is what she liked in his step, his knowledge of who he was.

As he drove away, Holly realized that she trusted him and he trusted her. She *was* his friend, and surprising as it was, she was not overwhelmed by his forwardness this morning. Indeed, she was intrigued by the desire that had leapt up with his closeness behind her.

Without their trust of each other, it might have made her less receptive, given the nature of her natural desires, and knowing that he knew them as well. These last two years of serving him, meeting him at the book store, rummaging about at the antique store had served as the foundation for her comfort with him.

She turned towards her work in the back room. She was almost there when she heard a small knock at the door. Sahara stood at her doorstep, waving a small pile of books at her and pointing to the lock.

Holly laughed. It was going to be this kind of day then. She unlocked the door and walked into Sahara's embrace.

"I'm interrupting, sorry." Sahara offered this most brief of apologies, while having no intention of leaving. "I'll be really quiet," she laughed, and Holly laughed with her.

"No you won't," Holly replied. "That's ok, I'm glad for the company"....and then, on impulse, she added, "Aiden just left here."

"He did?" Sahara sat down at the counter, face flushed, hands clasped together.

Holly's heart leapt with a twinge of anxiety. What had she done? Maybe she should have not said...

Oh, this was all so complicated. Holly made a gesture towards the ovens. Eyes confused and heat gathering on her face, she offered her explanation about Aiden's work habits, purchasing her coffee when leaving on a trip, etc. She voiced her frustration with being behind in her work and finally walked away from Sahara feeling completely ungrounded, like some imaginary blanket had been ripped away from her, leaving her feeling cold and a little bit nauseous.

Holly's unease spilled from her heavily; she looked utterly miserable. Sahara found Holly standing with her face to the hot ovens, tears spilling down her cheeks.

"Holly," Sahara whispered softly. She put her arms gently around Holly's waist and pulled her in. Holly continued to cry; head down and heart even lower.

"I think I've made a mistake," Holly said. "I feel that maybe you and Aiden actually do like each other, and I've been thinking of you and me...but today, I felt something for Aiden...I'm so confused, I'm sorry, I don't even know how to say what I want to say." She turned and faced Sahara, whose own eyes were glowing and unfocused with a mist of unshed tears.

"Holly, we have things to discuss, for sure. Right now, let me help you; you're got to open the bakery. Tell me what to do and we'll talk as we work, but we'll leave the bulk of it for later, when you don't have to face your day on top of all that we need to go over. K?"

Holly looked relieved and a sliver of a smile crept onto her lips.

"Thank you. I need help, there's still so much to do, and now I'm feeling all frazzled."

She slipped trays of bread into the oven and did a quick scan of what needed prepping for the next batch of baking.

In the end, they did not talk at all about what lay between them, or that Sahara had come to drop off gardening books and had hoped to sit quietly writing while Holly baked and prepared her a coffee. The books lay on the counter where Sahara had left them and now she moved them to the back room, tidying the café and making sure the counter was clear for early clients. Holly had instructed her on how to make preparations behind the counter, and she ground some coffee, looking forward to her first cup. The bakery smells brought comfort to her heart space. She wandered back and took Holly in her arms once again.

"Listen, Holly...I'm not angry with you or upset or anything. I was just surprised by your words; that is all. I'll explain why later, but as far as you and I are concerned, there is nothing wrong between us."

"Yes, but there will be once *I* explain myself, you don't know the whole of it. Sahara..."

"No. Ssshhh." Sahara put her fingers to Holly's mouth, feeling the electric shock that sprung up between them. "No, it will still be fine."

"No, you still don't know, it won't be fine!" Holly looked so disarmingly tender in her emotions, Sahara thought, so pretty in her distress.

Sahara put her lips to Holly's and whispered as she kissed her.

"It will still be fine, even if you tell me that Aiden has kissed these lips."

She looked into Holly's eyes, now wide and full of alarm. Holly's mouth opened to let Sahara in and they kissed with new desire, each of them remembering the quiet strength of Aiden's touch. Holly took Sahara's hands in hers. She lifted them to her lips and kissed them.

"Sahara, I have no idea where this is going, but I am so grateful for you; and for the fact that you have just shown me a great deal of what your friendship means to me. I'm going to make us a coffee, and then I'm going to try to get through the day. Are you staying here a bit or do you have to get somewhere?"

"Oh no, I'm not leaving yet," Sahara laughed. "I'm going to stay right here, I think I'd like to torture you some more. I'm dying for some coffee, and I'm starving... you do know how to keep a girl waiting."

Holly sought out Sahara's lips again; she was a bundle of raw emotions and anticipation. This was a breaking through point, she knew that much. Her life had just made a pivotal turn. And she was not going to stop the direction it was going in. Some things were meant to be.

Aiden drove towards Telson without noticing any of the scenery that he usually found so captivating. His mind wandered between images of Holly this morning and his memories of adventures in Sahara's bed. He suspected that he could ask Sahara for all the things that made him smolder, reservations thrown to the wind, and that she would oblige fully, if not give him more than he hoped for.

Holly, on the other hand, was to be opened like a present wrapped in the most fragile of tissue paper, bound by a ribbon of spun silk and tied in a bow. He wanted her on his tongue for hours before he was given permission to enter. He could wait, he *would* wait, until she gave him the signal to take things further...today he had made his move, but the next time perhaps it would be hers.

He replayed it all in his mind's eye, her smile, her scent as he moved his lips through her hair, her sudden leap into desire...how *had* she come to accept his kisses so easily?

Aiden strode into the hotel lobby and greeted the desk clerk with a charming, if hurried smile.

Upstairs, Aiden checked the time and set down his bags. His mind was scattered; not the way he liked to begin a job. He was definitely ungrounded, and caught himself pacing the floor. There was time to make himself coffee and eat in his room. He needed to satisfy his erotic hunger as well. His mind raced to the whip he had once bought for Dianne, his memories of her raven hair around her shoulders as she had tied his hands, promising him his due punishment and the feel of her lips travelling down his back towards his buttocks. He dialed her number and unbuckled his belt. She answered immediately.

"Diane, I have no time, I'm due at work. It's just the phone call. Do you need a moment to get ready?"

"I'm ready," she breathed. She felt between her legs, and whimpered as she touched herself, imagining Aiden's face there, his hair loose, his shoulders wide and tense.

"Fingers in your mouth, Dianne, tell me how you taste..."

He called her later once more. He went to her house and told her that this would be the last time, and did she still have that whip he had bought her? He made love to her with an intensity tempered by his sadness to be leaving her friendship. And she cried when he left because she loved him and his darkest requests. It was all so sudden, this ending. But they had made this agreement from the first, not to love, and not to get attached to the games they played.

Except that Dianne had lied when she had said that she did not want more than a romp; still, she was not sorry that she had been his lover. She had the memories; she had this house that he had built for her. But she doubted that her next lover would be as accomplished or as desirable, or be so considerate.

At the end, Aiden had held her to him and thanked her for the discretion he could always count on with her, and told her that she had satisfied him greatly... was there anything he could do for her before he left? But of course, short of staying, there was nothing he could give her. She had to let him go. He noted her tears in his heart, wiped them off her face with his kisses, and left for good. As much as Aiden loved women, he hated hurting them more.

He dreamed fitfully that night, of a dark, low ceilinged cottage, a fire in a crumbling hearth and a woman with raven hair tying his hands to a hook in the rafters above. He awoke in a dreadful mood; unable to shake a feeling of despair and thinking he could smell burning flesh. He sat before the fireplace in his room, poking the fire and trying to reconstruct his dream. What had he read in his book on alchemy? How to return from a vertical experience in the dream world? Sahara had lent him a book on just this very subject.

He arrived at work looking so fierce that everyone left a clear path for him till the day was done. When Aiden was this quiet, he needed a wide berth. It was just as well that one of his men had not shown up, Aiden was only too happy to take up his place on the crew and worked like the devil was on his heels. In his heart, he ached for Sahara's arms around him and her soft voice speaking words of comfort.

Sahara checked the tree mailbox on her way back home. The flag wasn't up but she thought she would check anyway. Yes! There was something...an envelope. Inside, Aiden's house key, and a short note.

"Sahara, if you need me, you are welcome in my home. I know that you'll find the essence of my love for you lingering there. I'll see you soon." Aiden

Aiden was perhaps inadvertently telling her that he understood, on some level, the mystery between taking something unseen and formless, such as his love for her, and offering it as something she could feel and use in the physical world to comfort herself; of transmuting an essence into a valuable, tangible gift. Sahara recognized this upon reading his note, the wizard in him was awakening.

Her eyes welled up and she tucked the envelope into her pocket.

"Oh Aiden, you are filling my heart so quickly", she thought. "We are starting a dangerous journey, you and I".

She realized that she was shaking; she was scared but knew that she wouldn't turn from this fork in the road. She would take the plunge into the fantasy she had nurtured for years; come what may. There was no denying that she was who she was, and past mistakes only made her more determined to make this work.

She needed to make some magic before Holly came, there were rites for protection for all of them that she would work, and words to write in her journal. But first, she would pick up something from Aiden's, to have as her talisman of his powerful lust for her. She wanted that by her bed. She needed his energy close.

CHAPTER 21

Iona ignored the persistent ringing of the phone as she checked inside the pile of delivered boxes. She should have called her part time helper. Perhaps there was still time to catch her at home? There was much to prepare in supplies for several important clients. Iona would be the only one to touch the wares, as was expected by the hermetics and alchemists who ordered from her, and who regarded her as the best in the magical supply business. She could be counted on to keep her word about purity, intention and the very serious matter of discretion. Iona had their names, phone numbers and addresses memorized, there was not one list where these things were itemized, nor could she be blamed if a strange energy arrived attached to the magical ingredients. It would not have come from her.

She cleansed before handling anything, only worked on one order at a time, and she didn't speak to the contents or ask anything of them either. When orders came in they were dispatched the same day, nothing was left to chance. She called her assistant and left a message. Next, she called three numbers and left a simple coded voicemail. They would all arrive in sequence, on time, as requested.

This was Iona's favourite time of day, as the sun rose, and her favourite part of the store. The back room had two access points; one from her apartment upstairs and one from the store front. There was a cupboard that only she had the key to. This held extras of the supplies she would unpack. Although her clients tended towards the strict in discipline, even they sometimes made a mistake in judgement and late into their work ran out of a critical ingredient. And then again, she might be tempted to look back through the centuries and try to reproduce an especially satisfying bit of alchemy.

Iona was Wednesdays' child. Ruled by Mercury, she possessed a cunning intellect that had gathered with time. She knew things, yes, but she also remembered. When she had met Richard, one evening as a guest at one of his art exhibits, she had clearly seen past a multitude of veils into the century they had shared before. He was blissfully unaware, in that moment of meeting. None-the-less, he had been drawn to her like a bear to honey, her aura and scent pulling him after her.

She had noticed that he was dark in colouring, as he had been before. Olive skin and hair as black as coal, his face marked by intensity, and something else...perhaps the aura of a complicated personality.

She had been told that he was someone to be wary of; his businesses took him away on somewhat secretive expeditions. An acquaintance had suggested that she might like his art for her space, and so she had prepared herself carefully for the evening ahead. Anointing herself with oils for protection, she chose a dress that although demure in the front, exposed her back beyond the curve of her spine. Her hair cascaded in fiery waves and gently swayed across her skin, her green eyes a pair of smoky magnets.

For his part, Richard had felt her before he saw her, and when she appeared out of the mist of his heightened senses, he had a sense of his world shifting within that precise moment. There was a feeling that came over him when he met someone who piqued his interest, and he could feel it now, as he saw her gliding on slippered feet towards the bar. Interestingly, she was the only woman there not wearing heels. And such a self -assured set to her shoulders, without losing her softness. Was she floating?

Don't be absurd, Richard had chided himself. *Nobody floats.*

She moved past him, her scent trapping his arousal. She had forgotten to wear a bra, he noted, her breasts a sensual tease underneath a dress that hugged and covered her from neck to toe. He turned to watch her pass, and his breath caught in his throat when he saw her naked back caressed under the fall of her hair, pointing the way towards a tantalizing bottom.

Richard was struck down by the spell she had cast on him. And he didn't care to be released. She felt his eyes on her, but avoided making contact. He would come to her. She would open to him. She would make sure that he couldn't live without her before she allowed him in. She had magic on her side. He had memories, but she would decide when he would access those. Iona wanted a devil of a man, one who could travel the sensitive boundaries between should and should not with her...one who could survive her desire for wicked pleasures and trips to other dimensions.

The trouble was that when she entered into the realm of Richard's essence; all that he was and all that he had been, she also entered into the remnants of what clung to him of Dagr. And Dagr was someone she had to forget. But maybe that was part of Richard's attraction, his connection to the past and the person she had been back then.

By evening's end, after she had been approached by every man, single or wedded, as well as every interested woman, Richard stood by her side, a glass of champagne in his hand, a determined look in his eye. She had turned to him and smiled. Her hand extended to take the drink that was clearly his, and watching him over the rim of the glass, she had sealed his need to know her. He insisted on dinner the following night. She congratulated him on his art, and bought a piece that he was astounded she could afford. Was she from town? Yes, from the shop for magical supplies. Magical supplies, had he heard right? Yes, magic, she said, as if everyone shopped there, as if everyone knew her store. He had never heard of it, and he was sure that he knew the district well. Some things stay hidden until it is time for them to be revealed, she countered.

"Well that explains it," he said.

"Explains what?" she asked, all innocence and wickedness combined.

"Explains how you have bewitched me". Richard took Iona's hand and kissed it, his loins on fire and his mind alert.

She had laughed a silvery laugh, and slipped away from his gallery but not from his thoughts. He would have her; of this he was intent and reasonably sure.

She thought of him now, and how big a part he had become in her business. He could import things that she would otherwise have to do without, as would her clients. They never asked her how she laid her hands on certain precious ingredients, but they suspected that Richard was her keen ally. And Iona didn't ask either, she simply didn't see the need to know the details of Richard's affairs. Richard had slipped so easily into her world. He was, as was Sahara, a portal into the past, unwittingly bringing centuries colliding, unable to escape the role he played as her capturer and captured.

Had he had any chance of escape when they met for dinner the night after? As the meal had worn on, neither of them really eating anything before them, her invitation for him to see her store a weighted question barely needing an answer. She had worn her hair up. He could see the way her ears turned up in that elfish fashion, her neck an exposed canvas awaiting the strokes of his tongue. He had rolled up his shirt sleeves, his forearms an interesting relief of art work themselves. The bewildered server had taken away their dishes, stashed away the hefty tip, and shook his head over how some people wasted food.

Iona opened the doors of her store, and let the cool air in. She was all warm with memories of her first time with Richard. Oh, he had been in awe of her and undeniably smitten. But not so much that he had not taken charge, or reminded her of the castle chamber where he had exacted his will on her. It's just that he didn't yet know his power over her, or why she needed him to play his part.

Jessika, her helper, rushed through the door in a flap. Iona smiled. Jessika's energy tended towards the erratic, but it was genuine. Her smile and happy exterior made for happy customers. And she brought food. Good food. In Jessika's opinion, Iona could put on a few pounds.

"Why, you're likely to be blown away by the west wind," Jessika had once remarked.

"The west wind and I are friends," replied the witch.

"Still," Jessika had said, rolling her eyes. "I doubt that he would not carry you away, just to prove a point."

All three customers came for their parcels. Jessika knew them by sight and guided them to meet Iona in the back room. She loved this store. It was comfortable, dark, soothing. She loved to unpack the stock, touch all the items and ask questions, make notes in her book. It wasn't like work really. Iona had taught her much, and was beginning to give her more responsibilities. There was a place to make tea, and she knew which regulars would appreciate a cup and a chair by the counter to have a chat.

The dried herbs were Jessika's favourite area perhaps, if she absolutely had to choose one. When the bags came in, she was responsible for filling the apothecary jars. They lined a sturdy shelf behind the counter, and, at Iona's strict instruction, were polished of dust every other day. Jessika loved the gleaming jars, with their antiquarian labels. Beside them, a variety mortar and pestle's, some wooden, some marble, larger and smaller. Iona had insisted on paying for an herbalist course for Jessika, and when it was slow in the store, Jessika would pour over her books, soaking up as much as she could in her free time. Best of all, was creating tea mixtures and making up the little sample bags for customers to try. She had an uncanny gift for putting together exotic blends, and the samples turned into regular purchases. Iona always looked so pleased at her interest in becoming an herbalist, and had said on more than one occasion that knowledge of plants and their properties was an essential part of a wise woman's training.

The door creaked open; the slim string of bells attached to it sang a merry welcome as they swung. Jessika looked up.

"You must have some kind of radar, the herbs just arrived yesterday." Jessika waved to the young woman walking through the door.

"Yup! I couldn't wait any longer anyway, I'm making soap tomorrow." Mary made her way over to the counter, her long blond dreads

166

gathered into a loose ponytail. Jessika already had the kettle on for tea.

"Your soaps smell and look so yummy, Mary, I take baths just to have a chance to use them!"

Jessika would have gone on but the door was thrown open and Richard stood framed by the entranceway.

He entered somewhat abruptly. Quickly scanning the store, he flashed a grin at the girls, muttered a perfunctory hello and strode across towards the back room.

"Iona here?" he asked, then, seemingly forgetting to wait for the answer, he was gone. The girls could hear him taking the steps to the apartment above.

Mary sat wide eyed, her mouth open with questions lined up for the firing.

Jessika looked at her and laughed. "Don't even go there. That's Richard. He belongs to our Iona."

Mary swallowed, her throat suddenly dry and thirsty. "He's spectacular!" she whispered. She was suddenly dismayed when she realized that her nipples were pushing at the fabric of her shirt. Thank goodness she was wearing a thick sweater over top.

"Well, never mind about that," Jessika whispered back. "I don't think Iona is the kind that shares. And anyway, he's ten years your senior, at least. Come on. Let's see what else is on your list."

Mary hardly noticed the pile of rosemary, chamomile, calendula flowers, lemon verbena and bergamot that Jessika had organized before her.

"Hey lady, snap out of it! Don't you have a man of your own?"

"Yes," stammered a flushed Mary. "But he doesn't look like that!"

"Anything else before you completely lose your mind?" Jessika asked, but not without laughing. This was a side of Mary she hadn't seen before. Usually, she was the picture of collectedness, a girl who surely could seduce any number of men. She had that earthy, natural look that didn't need any embellishment at all.

"Do you have any patchouli oil and lemongrass?"

"Huh? You've never bought that before."

"Oh," Mary said, hands touching her cheeks. "What do you think about a soap for men?"

"I think that you're a naughty girl, and that I'll mail you your order next time."

Mary giggled. "This is ridiculous. Ok. Let's see the bill, Jessika. I've got to get out of here."

Upstairs, Richard took Iona into his arms and buried his face in her hair. "You always smell so divine."

Iona pulled away from him to kiss his lips.

"How are you, my love? All well in your world?"

"All well, or as well as can be in my line of interest." Richard held Iona to him, closing his eyes.

"Her name is Mary," Iona purred. Richard tensed, but wasn't really surprised that she'd read him.

"Is she to your taste, Richard?"

"She is, in that natural, peasant girl, ripe for the taking way. I'm not quite sure why that's feeling very attractive to me now; she's not my usual type."

Iona stayed curled into him, his arms a sanctuary to her heart's sudden wild leap into a memory she did not relish. She had taken Richard into the past, one night, when he had insisted on knowing about another life together. He trusted the journey and the vague details she had allowed of a previous century. While it had stoked the fire between them, he was reluctant to comment on a particular aspect of his love life, or the brutal decisions he had made. Richard had a soft side, an underbelly of sensitivity, which he denied vehemently. His image was calculating and cunning. But it was his dark side that drew Iona to him; the side that she felt could be counted on in times of need.

He needed her for fulfilment but could live without her if pressed. He had said as much, in their early days, when they were exploring the boundaries around their relationship. Although she made him weaker and more vulnerable than he was used to, he would never let himself drown in her.

"Maybe we could find a peasant girl or two for you. I think I'd like to see that. My pirate having his way with a wench." Iona offered.

Richard's grip tightened, the tension rising between them.

"Iona, of all the women I have met and could have met, none could be more perfect for me."

He held her tight, she melted into his love.

"I love your strength, Iona, the way you know who you are, your wicked ways, your willingness to share me. It's rare."

"Richard, could you share me with another man?" Iona asked.

He searched her eyes, one hand under her chin. "I don't know...is there a man you'd like to have?"

"Not now. I mean, I know we can share a woman between us, I have no worries that someone would steal you away." She gave him a

168

winsome smile. "But if there ever was a man, do you think it would make a difference to you?"

"Possibly...probably. I'm not sure. If it was a man I trusted, I think I could. It's easier to share you with a woman, even if you loved her, you'd still need my love." He winked.

Iona sank back into her memories, the times that she remembered of love complicated and love lost. Of a man that they had both loved. She was afraid, even now, to test those waters. But in the end, she knew that she would. She had to.

Richard kissed her hair. How he loved the shock of red colour, her long limbs and slim waist. She looked so very breakable, so unlikely to stand at his side. But he loved her ethereal, wispy look. And she was stronger than anyone he knew. He had seen her work magic, and she was never alone. Her eyes were sharp as a ravens and could be equally as cold.

"I'll be home by midnight. Wait up for me, Iona."

"I'll be ready," she replied. Her hand caressed his face, pressing his image into her memory; one never knew which moment would be the last. She wanted to remember the shirt he was wearing, his preferred white, sleeves rolled up, exposing his tattooed arms; the way his chest and shoulders filled out the fabric, his eyes impenetrably dark, and always, the most fashionable and well-kept shoes. He was striking, because he was so well kept, and so attuned to what suited his body. He so very much still held the energy of a man accustomed to finery, to life at court. She missed his long hair from before.

One day soon, Richard, we will journey to the place and time that binds us together, she promised him in her heart.

She needed him to find the way back. Not to remember, because that had already painfully occurred for her. But to walk those days again, to relive the nightmare she had fallen into by an unfathomable mistake in judgement. To find Dagr and experience the love that broke her. And that broke everyone in her damned past.

CHAPTER 22

Holly packed her bag with care. She would need overnight things, or rather, she hoped that she would. She rarely wore perfume, but today she dotted some at the base of her neck and on her wrists. She had found some delicious essential oils at a store in Denver where she had bought soap for herself. She would have to remember to tell Sahara about that place. A magical supply store...Sahara would love it.

The café was in the hands of her part time girl, Lilith, all the extra things that had needed preparing had been taken care of, and she could call her if she had any questions. Holly was filled with excitement and nervousness. It had been a while since she had given herself fully to a lover.

Holly took one more look through the café, just to make sure then picked up the box of pastries, some coffee and bread, turned off the lights and locked the front door.

She drove the distance to the farm, and taking the fork in the road where Sahara's road turned away from Aiden's, she once again wondered about that mailbox. Everyone picked up their mail in town. So this must be something between Sahara and Aiden, she presumed. The thought of facing Sahara with her feelings for Aiden made her wince and shift in her seat. Hopefully, it would not make a mess of the evening, but it had to be discussed.

Her heart warmed as she saw the cabin appear in the distance and the lights within it, a welcoming beacon for her soul. Friendship. That is what she had missed most. Someone who understood her, who could hold her in heart space without judgement, whom she could share her dreams with. The soft touch of a woman's lips on her breasts, another thing she had despaired of ever finding again.

She parked her car and got out, the smell of fire burning in Sahara's fireplace so pleasant it made her smile to herself. Should she take her overnight bag in, she wondered, or get it later? She decided to throw caution to the wind and bring it. She had to get a grip on all this second guessing.

She looked through the kitchen window as she passed it, and found Sahara waving her in. They met at the door, Holly releasing a grateful sigh when Sahara took her bags from her and enfolded her in to a long, warm hug.

"So glad to see you, Holly." Sahara murmured. "I can't tell you how much I've looked forward to this evening. I'm glad you brought your overnight bag, there's so much to catch up on. Wine?"

"Yes, please!" Holly relaxed her shoulders. "Wine would be great."

"I hope you're hungry, I've made lots of food. You might have to stay a week!"

"Hungry? I'm starving! I forgot to eat today getting ready to leave the store with my part time girl. I always get so anxious..."

"It will be fine, Holly. Don't worry, all shall be well. And if not, we're not that far that we couldn't dash in and fix whatever had gone wrong."

Holly liked the way Sahara said "we". Already, she could sense that their friendship had taken leaps and bounds, otherwise, would Sahara offer to be part of her problems?

She sat at the counter and nibbled on olives and cheese while Sahara added herbs to a giant pot of stew on the cook stove. Several bunches of drying plants hung from the kitchen beam. The kitchen looked so cozy, with candles glowing on the window sill, dinner on the stove, and Sahara's array of mortar and pestles tucked into a corner of the counter. A hint of music filled the spaces between them.

"What is this music Sahara? It's positively medieval."

"Yes," Sahara agreed, but she was regretted putting on this CD. It was pulling something deep out of her sub-conscious.

She caught a wisp of memory; a room, walls draped with tapestries, an immense stone fireplace, notes of music drifting in to soothe the very familiar and disturbing scene. She lay naked on a bed of exquisite linens, legs spread, breasts heaving. Someone moved about the bed, she grasped at the memory to see who it was, but failed to see his face. He. Of this she was sure, she could easily feel his presence if she couldn't see it. He felt like the horror of war and the tenderness of an early spring day colliding into the same moment, a frightening mix of power and need.

His gaze focused intently on her spread legs, she moved to close them, but his look stopped her and she knew that he would tie them open if she tried that again. She recalled the feeling of wet trickling down her legs, as he willed his stare to stimulate her, touching her with a look so bold, that she worried it would cause her to pee from fear right there in his bed.

Holly's hand on hers brought Sahara drifting back, her senses on alert, her body responding to the memory with waves of surging electricity pursing up her swollen, aching nipples.

"Sorry, lost in thoughts." Sahara smiled weakly, her heart still pounding. She had to find out who that was. Who made her feel so intoxicated with lust and so terribly afraid?

"You seemed far away." Holly smiled.

Sahara pretended innocence. "The music took me away. That's all."

She poured more wine into Holly's glass, and got up to poke the fire.

"Ready for food?"

"Ready!" Holly stood as well. "What can I do to help?"

"Want to set the table? I'll do the rest."

Dinner was delicious and fun, Sahara had a way of making Holly feel relaxed. Still, she couldn't entirely enjoy herself, knowing about the confession she had to make. Holly waited until they were curled up comfortably by the fire.

"Sahara," Holly began, taking a rather large sip of her wine. "I want to explain about the other day. I've thought a lot about it and would just like to get it out of the way.

"If you want. We don't have to yet..."

"No, no, I want to," Holly sighed. "Aiden and I kissed the other day." She paused, searching Sahara's face for a reaction. "I know that that sounds confusing because, well, you obviously know now how I feel about women. You said you wouldn't be angry even if I told you that he had kissed me, but I somehow get the feeling that the two of you might be more than friends?"

Sahara took a deep breath and shook her head as if she was shaking loose some invisible cobwebs, looking for a way to make her words acceptable.

"I know, Holly. I know because Aiden told me about his feelings for you. And I didn't tell him that I knew what he already knew...about your sexuality. But the truth is, Holly, I'm falling in love with Aiden, and he with me."

Sahara let the weight of the words settle; then continued on. Holly sat very still, on the brink of tears.

"Aiden isn't anything if not honest, Holly, and he knows that I'm hoping for a relationship with you...but also with him...and to complicate things further, he is definitely in love with you, and wants you still. He's been completely forthright with me."

Holly slowly sifted through everything that was being said. A part of her was elated over Sahara saying she hoped for a relationship with her. But now she was confused, was Aiden hoping to bed them both?

How could she have a relationship with Sahara if Sahara wanted to be with Aiden?

"I'm not sure I understand, Sahara."

Sahara got up and came over to her, lifting Holly out of her seat, pulling her towards the fire. She had drank much more wine than was advisable. Her body was alight with longing for Aiden, for Holly, for the three of them in bed. Sahara hugged Holly to her and met her mouth with kisses sweet and urgent, whispering her name, opening herself to Holly's passion.

"Aiden kissed me, Sahara." Holly moaned the words into Sahara's mouth.

Sahara kissed Holly forcefully, unable to hold back.

Holly, completely undone, fell to the couch, tugging at Sahara's hand to follow her. Their lips and tongues exploring, Sahara asked if Holly had liked it... and would she do it again? Holly replied that as surprised as she had been, Aiden was stirring something in her heart, and finally letting her tears spill, she asked what good could come of this, how could this craziness work? Wasn't Sahara jealous? Shouldn't she be jealous?

Sahara buried her face against Holly's breasts, seeking out her nipples to grasp through the t-shirt she was wearing, biting down a little, sucking harder when Holly gasped and thrust her hands into Sahara's hair.

"I want you *and* I want Aiden." Sahara found Holly's ear. "Take your t-shirt off," she commanded.

Holly pulled her shirt up over her head, her breath came fast as she reached to unclasp her bra.

"My goodness, woman, they're beautiful," Sahara breathed, staring at Holly's breasts, now heavy with lust.

"Suck my nipples, Sahara. Pull on them!"

Sahara pulled hard on Holly's nipples. She was now dripping wet, her energy rising hot up her spine, and the need to feel pain at her lovers' hand. She cautioned herself, to take it slow, to keep herself in check. But it was hard. Holly was opening Sahara's shirt, her mouth demanding yet soft on Sahara's impertinent nipples.

They slipped off the couch onto the carpet by the fire, grasping at each other. Slowly, with curious eyes, they exposed their tenderness, lips and fingers exploring. Dizzy with wine, Sahara let her mouth make its' way from Holly's neck to her breasts, along her stomach, towards the soft skin of her inner thighs. Holly was thrusting her hips up, begging for Sahara's mouth on her, asking for her touch, impatient to be licked by Sahara's hot tongue.

But Sahara only kissed at that most tender of spots where Holly's folds met her thighs, waiting for the exact moment when she knew Holly could wait no more. She let her tongue slip lightly toward Holly's swollen and throbbing clit, then thrusting her fingers in, felt Holly's release hot on her hand. Sahara waited out the rhythmic movements on her fingers as Holly gave in to her orgasm, and then pulled her clit into her mouth once more, sucking with increasingly more pressure as Holly's breath quickened again. Now and then she gave Holly's quivering slit a sound spanking followed by shallow thrusts of her tongue. Holly came once more, Sahara's mouth sealed tight over her tortured clit.

"You taste incredible," Sahara murmured. "Kiss me, you can see for yourself."

"I want to taste you too, Sahara," Holly mumbled though a haze of pleasure. I want your clit on my tongue. Get on your hands and knees for me."

Sahara obeyed, shaking as she waited for the feel of Holly's tongue on her. She laid her head on the floor, shoving her ass high in front of Holly. She felt Holly's fingers take a slow swipe from her ass to her clit. Holly took her time admiring the view, she loved the way Sahara opened so fully, all of her visible and spread like a flower in full bloom.

"Do you like it, Holly?" Sahara arched her back hoping to give Holly a better look.

"Beautiful. It's...mmm."

Sahara felt Holly's mouth tenderly kissing her bottom, slipping closer towards her tight bud, gasping when she felt Holly's tongue hot on it, then slipping down through her inner lips. The girl had no reservations. Holly probed every bit of her with her tongue and mouth, expertly taking her clit in her lips and sucking softly, moaning her pleasure as Sahara rocked on her knees, waves of ecstasy washing over her. There was no hurry, they could explore and enjoy each other all night. She stayed as still as she could when she felt Holly's wet fingers push their way inside her, gently first, with Holly's teasing words about how her cunt fit so snuggly around her fingers, that she tasted delicious, how much she was enjoying seeing her spread so wide.

Sahara motioned under the sofa for a box. She pointed to a toy, amused at Holly's expression as she saw the other items.

Holly passed the dildo to Sahara who wet it with her mouth and, handing it back, gave Holly a wink. She faced down once more, anxious now to feel it inside her. Holly slipped it in, biting her lip as she saw it stretch Sahara fully, with slow, deliberate strokes before placing it to Sahara's mouth again. They met for more kisses, their tongues colliding as Sahara asked Holly to try the toy in her mouth, both of them aware of its insinuated meaning.

"I need this inside me some more, Holly, please."

"Not yet." Holly said as her hand came down lightly on Sahara's ass.

"May I do this Sahara...touch you this way?"

Sahara cried out, she had not had to ask, Holly had found her weakness. Holly rubbed the dildo along Sahara's clit, nudging it gently, along her folds, and allowing herself a few more delicious licks of Sahara's pussy before plunging it deep. Sahara bucked back to meet the vigorous thrusts, calling out her desire, Holly thrusting harder and harder, surprised at the words that spilled from her mouth and the intense pleasure of seeing Sahara take the dildo so deep.

With the briefest of thoughts about whether Holly would mind, Sahara gave in to the heat that spread like fire from her crown to her toes, and let herself descend into a full body orgasm, Holly's voice dimmed now, fully engaged in her own experience. Holly sat back wide eyed on her heels, fingers grasping her nipples, her clit throbbing with new expectations. Sahara offered a weak smile as she turned over and lay by the heat of the fire.

"Sorry, I should have warned you."

"That was spectacular! How do you do that?"

Sahara pulled Holly down towards her.

"I'll show you...later...are you happy?" Her mouth looked for Holly's.

"More," was all Holly could say between kisses and satisfied embraces.

The fire played with shadows on their skin as they lay before it. Holly traced the tattoo on the small of Sahara's back with her finger.

"Tell me about this...the pentagram? It's beautiful."

"It was my first tattoo..."Sahara stretched contentedly. There's a lot of imagery associated with the pentagram, I can give you the edited version of what it means to me?"

Holly nodded, and stroked Sahara's back.

"It speaks to the Divine Feminine," Sahara said. "The motion of change. Purity, secrecy, adventure into the unknown. Did you know that it represents the elliptical path of Venus around Earth?"

"I didn't know! Wow, quite different from what I learned about it at school, which generally centered around the occult, I'll admit. I'd read somewhere about the meaning associated with Pythagoras, his use of the pentagram to represent a sacred harmony between the five elements, and the body, or something to that effect."

"Then you know a lot more about it than most," Sahara said wryly as she sat up. "What would you say to a hot bath, and some tea?"

Holly made steaming mugs of tea while Sahara ran the water. They lit candles and poured some oils, the room infused with the heady scent of herbs and almonds.

"This is heaven," Holly murmured, easing herself into the hot water to sit opposite Sahara, who was running her hands over her breasts, her nipples sticking out from between the lather of soap.

"Mmm. Delightful," Sahara said. "I'm sleepy."

"I'm hungry."

"We could have a snack when we get out," Sahara suggested. "I have some berries and some wild nuts I gathered."

"We can cuddle up by the fire. I'm not sure if I can even express how amazing I feel, lighter, centered, alive," Holly murmured.

"I'm feeling like I want to be in your arms again. I might not be able to get enough of you."

Sahara shifted herself to sit closer to Holly, their legs intertwined, their mouths eager. It had been so long.

They spent the night talking. They ate, they sat by the fire, they went for a walk. The path to Aiden's was lit by the harvest moon, they held hands and giggled as they snuck around the aspen wood, feeling like wood nymphs on the prowl. The forest was awake, alive to their play, the Fey following them, whispering their delight.

They had been told that the new forest witch would be coming, and had been anticipating her arrival for years. It had been more than a century since they had first heard of her. They had heard from the Fairy King, who had knowledge of her, but that had been a very long time ago. He, the King, had said that she was especially kind, especially empathetic to the Land of Fey. She would bring a special blessing to the land, something that humankind had lost the gift to do...and the desire, for that matter. But now she was here, and she looked just like a fairy, tiny and light, she wore her hair like the pixies do, her laughter was kind and her heart was intent on respecting their ways.

But who was the maiden at her side? Her hair like spun gold, her face innocent like a child's. The King was especially interested in her.

He had known a golden haired maiden once. She had come and gone in the flash of an instant, but he had never quite forgotten her; or the mark she had left on his lustful heart.

"Do you see the phosphorescence in the woods, Holly?" Sahara whispered, clapping her hands.

"I do! What is it?"

"Fairies! The wee folk. They're happy to see us."

"Fairies? I've never seen it before...how beautiful." Holly's eyes misted, her heart softened and expanded to accept what Sahara was saying. Somehow, if Sahara said it, it didn't seem so strange.

The fire had died down to a few hot embers by the time they got back. Sahara stirred it up once more. They turned off all the lights and lit some candles, the diffused light bathing the cabin in a warm glow. Blankets and pillows were piled by the fire, so they could watch the fire sprites play.

"I don't want this to end." Holly said. Sahara nodded agreement.

"Shall we make coffee? How about a croissant?" Holly suggested. "I've built up an appetite running around in the woods. Coffee and Bailey's by the fire? How about it?"

"I hope you're comfortable here, Holly, and know that I am happy to share this space with you tonight, my home is your home."

"I am comfortable, which is strange, because I've been alone for so long... but you've made me feel so welcome."

"Me too." Sahara said. "I usually don't enjoy company in my home. I'm more of a 'let's meet in a restaurant' kind of person. But it's nice to feel your energy here. You know, when I first met you, I was determined not to be your friend, despite your best efforts. But you've worn me down, you wench!" Sahara laughed and hugged Holly close. "Aiden will be jealous that I've had this much time alone with you."

Snuggled down into their blankets by the fire, Holly thought about what Sahara had said earlier. She knew that people sometimes invited extra partners into their bed, but she didn't want to be an extra, and she didn't think that she wanted to become part of a swingers tryst. She sipped her coffee and whisky for courage.

"Sahara, can you tell me more about what Aiden and you are hoping for? I'm not sure that I know what you mean by it all."

Sahara smiled sleepily and took her hand.

"Sure, of course, but this could take all night," she warned. Holly leaned in for a touch of her lips. "And I can't be expected to concentrate with you kissing me."

"Try. Here, lie down in my lap, I'll play with your hair, and you can tell me all your secrets."

Sahara had never felt this safe with another woman. She had always been the one who took charge; who made all the rules and ended the game when she'd had enough. With Holly, it was different. She was relaxed and content. Holly didn't have one manipulative bone in her body.

"Ok, my sweet, where to start? I guess by telling you that in my world, it's pretty much all or nothing. I'm determined to live my life as authentically as I can. I'm attracted to women and men, maybe not entirely the same, I mean, if I *had* to choose only one person to spend my life with, I'd choose a man. Having said that, I've never felt totally happy without a woman to love. But as you can imagine, it is quite something to find a man who can live that lifestyle gracefully. When I moved to this valley, I was looking for a place where I could be alone and write. I was still hurting over the breakup I had, and in a way, wanted to punish myself for hurting my partner. I never anticipated meeting you, nor Aiden. The odds of finding someone as compatible with me as Aiden are not great. I think you must know that he is a very special man."

Holly nodded.

"Meeting Aiden was like falling asleep and finding oneself in the very best dream," Sahara continued. You know the kind, the one you never want to wake up from. He got me at my core, with his looks, his laughter, and his mind. I think he didn't expect to find what we have discovered in each other, either. And it's all very new, but in a sense, we know each other well."

Sahara paused, waiting for a response. Nothing.

"Are you going to stay this quiet for the whole talk?" Sahara asked.

"No, not the whole talk."

"Ok. Well, while Aiden and I were getting to know each other, we discovered, or at least, I discovered, that he had feelings for you. He admitted that he had cared for you for a long time and that he was not exactly your type." She smiled. "He was quite good at not giving away your secret."

"I know, I asked him not to tell. I remember when he told me how he felt and I told him about myself... he looked so dismayed, his heart was completely on his sleeve. I think that was the first time I felt something for him, because he was so desperately honest and shattered. He can look so fearsome sometimes, and so much taller than he really is, and on that day he just looked so broken. But growing up, I had little attraction to boys, although I did have a casual boyfriend here and there, you know, to keep up appearances."

"Still, you and Aiden were friends already, right?"

"Yes, we were. He's always been someone I could talk to, share some interests with. It was very easy to be his friend, but I spent a lot of time making excuses about not dating. And then one day, after you arrived, I decided to end the madness, and tell him the truth. I kind of thought that he would gravitate towards you; and it felt safer to be honest. And I'd been lonely for a friend for a long time. I kind of thought I'd never find someone here...and then I met you. When Aiden kissed me, I felt like I'd lost my balance. It felt so good to be in his arms, so safe. But I was having some pretty strong hopes for friendship with you. I'm exhausted just thinking about it all."

"And now, I've thrown another wrinkle into it, haven't I?" Sahara sighed. "I think that Aiden should be the one to explain how he feels. He has room in his heart for both of us, and he truly does want to lead a polyamorous lifestyle."

"Poly who?" Holly sat up taller and put down her cup of coffee.

"Polyamorous. Meaning, he loves us both, we love him and each other...to simplify it greatly."

"Is this done? Who does this? I mean, how would we do this? Is it legal?"

Sahara brought over two glasses of water. "I'm probably assuming too much, because right now, Aiden and I know that we love each other. Aiden knows that he loves you, and I know how I feel about you, but we don't know how you feel."

"I'm feeling like I've landed on the moon and have finally found my tribe, that's how I feel!" Holly exclaimed. "I've always been kind of a cast out, never really fitting in, knowing that I somehow could not be truly myself. But now, I feel that with you and Aiden, I can just be free. I don't know how all this works yet, but I suddenly want to stretch my wings and fly. I can't even believe that you're interested in me!

Sahara smiled. "You have no idea how beautiful you are or how talented, do you?"

"I'm just me."

"An amazing you. Do you have any thoughts about our age difference?"

"I have no idea what age you are, Sahara! I'll assume early thirties because of what you've accomplished, but that's just a guess."

"I'm 34."

"It doesn't matter, anyway. Remember the day you walked into me at the café? There hasn't been one day I haven't thought of you since then."

"I don't want to talk anymore, Holly. Let's go up. I want you in my bed." And with that, Sahara reached under the couch for her box of toys, and pulled Holly to her feet.

CHAPTER 23

The sheers swayed gently to the breeze through the open window. Sahara opened her eyes and snuggled around under the generous duvet, the feel of Holly's warm body next to her a pleasant newness.

"Hey," she whispered, "you awake?"

"No...yes. Maybe."

"Are you warm enough?"

"Yes... come 'ere."

Turned towards each other, Sahara noticed the intense blue of Holly's eyes, and the unspoiled nature of her youthful heart shining out. Holly's breasts pushed against hers, nipples perking. Sahara put her arms around Holly and let out a soft sigh.

"All good?" Holly asked.

"All good, with you in my arms. This is nice. New. You feel nice."

Sahara let her hands roam, eyes closed, her fingers tingling as she swept them over Holly's body. "I might have to kidnap you, would you mind?"

"No, but who would make you croissants, and those cheese pastries you're so fond of?"

"You could bake them here."

"What about the rest of the town? Should they go hungry to satisfy your lust? And how would I earn my living?"

"I don't care about the town, and you could work for me."

"Work for you? Doing what?"

"Feeding me, making love to me...kissing me whenever I wanted?" Sahara slid herself down under the covers.

"I'll do that for free. Hey! You're fresh!"

"After last night, you can no longer pretend any modesty, my love."

Sahara's tongue marked the spot that she knew Holly had a weakness for.

"Ok, kidnap me. I'm yours," Holly moaned.

Breakfast dishes done, and morning chores attended to, they decided to take a walk through the swaying grass towards the mountains.

"I wonder how far it really is." Sahara said.

"We could make a day trip sometime," Holly suggested. "It's further than you think. There are bears and cougars in this area, you know."

"Hmm, yes, but I have a gun."

"You have a gun?" Holly shouted.

"Yes. I have no intention of ever using it, but we could bring it, for safety."

"I seriously doubt you could kill anything, Sahara."

"Well, it's just in case," Sahara pouted. She wore a pendant that had been infused with a spell for safety, and touched it now.

"Aiden will be home today."

Holly's heart leapt. "Yes, will he?"

"He'll want to see me."

"I have to be gone before dark, anyway."

"I thought it would be fun if we invited him over for lunch, and I don't want you to leave just because he's coming," Sahara suggested.

"Well, I'm not sure how these things work. And I don't know if he's regretting kissing me."

Sahara let out a whoop. "Regretting? Regretting? He's probably been on fire for you all week! Let's have him over, Holly. A bit of torture never hurt anyone."

They let their hands glide over the swaying grass, the wind biting at their ears. They walked in silence back to the cabin, each lost to her own thoughts.

———————✳———————

Aiden looked down at his phone as it rang. It was Sahara, he noted with a smile. He was almost at the checkout of the grocery. He'd always hated the bright fluorescent lights in stores. "Uncivilized," he muttered to himself. "Hello!" He took the call. "Are you ever a welcome voice. I've missed you, and I'm not ashamed to say it."

"I'm not ashamed to invite you to lunch, can you come?" Sahara laughed.

"Yes, God yes. I need to be in your space. I'll see you in a couple." Aiden hung up, excitement mounting.

He opened windows when he got home and made preparations for an evening fire in the hearth. He put his groceries away, unpacked his bag and hung up the new clothes he had bought while away. He picked out a bottle of wine to bring. Suddenly, home felt like it needed more than just him in it. It was not quite lunch time yet, but he couldn't wait any longer. Closing the downstairs windows, he walked out into the woods. The air was brisk. Winter was making its first tentative attempts at arrival, but the sun shone brightly and threw spectacular shadows on the swaying grass. Bottle of wine held fast in his muscular hand, Aiden looked towards the cabin, anticipating seeing Sahara. He squinted to look at what he thought was a second car in her drive. Yes, and not just any car. It was Holly's Bug.

"Wench!" So that was what Sahara's laughter had been about. He was not sure what to pay attention to, his sudden desire or thoughts of how to manage his feelings for the two women he loved.

Sahara, you've thrown me into the fire, Aiden thought, but not without some pleasure.

Sahara was in the kitchen when he arrived. Holly answered the door. He stood in the doorway letting in the cold breeze, breath suspended, Holly blocking the way anyhow.

"Holly, what a pleasant surprise."

He bent down to place a kiss on her cheek, Holly's eyes sparkling. She stood looking up at him, noticing with a new awareness just how attractive he really was, and powerful. And not only because of his build.

"May I come in?" Aiden asked with some amusement.

"Oh! Yes. I'm sorry. I don't know what I'm doing just standing here."

She moved aside and smiled at Sahara in the kitchen, who was wiping her hands on her jeans and approaching Aiden with a mischievous glint in her eye. Holly watched them embrace, Sahara melting into him, Aiden burying his face in her neck, his kisses immediate and unrestrained.

After a long and heartfelt hug, Sahara let go of him and turned towards Holly, her smile reassuring.

Holly took her cue and stepped into Aiden's arms, her head down in his chest, her own heart pounding. Aiden held her to him, and looked over her head at Sahara, who nodded and mouthed a silent "love you."

He lifted Holly's chin and looked her in the eye. They shone with unshed tears, a shocking blue. His lips found hers, and he kissed her long and deep, his tongue insistent on hers, holding her up when he felt her weaken. Then, taking her hand firmly, he led the way to the sofa; to the blazing fire.

"Open the wine, Sahara, would you please? Aiden's voice broke gruff and commanding. "I know it's still morning, but it's been a long week."

"Of course, Aiden," Sahara purred. "We have time to sit, lunch isn't quite ready."

He gave her a look of gratitude. He'd need a few moments to arrange his thoughts, and his lust.

"Have you been here all morning, Holly? It's good to see you finally take some time off."

"Nope, since yesterday," she replied, a small grin playing on her lips.

It took a moment, but he realized what she had said.

"Oh. Well, that's...that's even better." He took the glass that Sahara handed to him and took a big gulp.

"You must be thirsty," Sahara teased. "Relax, Aiden, we've had time to talk some..."

He stretched out his legs towards the fire and let out a sigh. "Have some mercy and pour me a little more Sahara..."

She poured for him and filled Holly's glass as well. Then very deliberately, she bent down to kiss Holly on the lips.

Holly looked at Aiden and shrugged.

"I've been kidnapped. I'm to quit the café, stay here and bake her treats as she pleases."

Aiden ran his hand through his hair. "I can see that the two of you are determined to have fun at my expense. Can I at least have some lunch before we open this discussion? I am beginning to feel like the boy who's been caught with his hand in the cookie jar."

As last time, Aiden felt a deep desire to fall asleep, to rest in the energy of the cabin and Sahara's presence. It was like falling under a deep spell, where his mind and body could find respite, listening to Holly's and Sahara's voices as they put out the food, the sound of the crackling fire soothing and warm. His eyes closed and his breathing slowed. This was what it was like to be intensely content. He fought to keep his eyes open; surely he should not be feeling sleepy in the company of the women he loved?

Sahara came over and pulled on his hand.

"Are you going to sleep, Aiden, with all this food and women in your reach? Come, lunch is ready."

"I think it's the wine," he offered the apology. "Although there really is no excuse for this, is there?"

He walked towards the table to share the meal with them. But his legs were weak, and his heart turning over with questions.

"Maybe after lunch we could have a nap?" he queried. Aiden shook his head and rubbed his eyes. Outside, a raven screeched. Sahara noted the cold feeling run down her spine.

"There won't be any napping, Aiden, sorry. Holly only has until early evening."

"I was kind of hoping we could meet for dinner at my place," Aiden suggested.

"I could," Holly said. "But not tonight. I could come back out tomorrow after close?"

"How about I go home after lunch and start a fire, and we finish this meal there with coffee and dessert?"

"Do you actually HAVE dessert?" Holly laughed.

"Well, no, I was going to offer myself, in fact...of course I have dessert!" Aiden feigned indignation.

"Is this your way of sneaking away to gather yourself? I'll admit that this was a bit of an ambush."

"Oh, will you?" The prickle in Aiden's tone was undisguised.

He stood after his meal and gave them each a crooked smile. This was the day. There would be no turning back from the words they spoke to each other. Today they would mark out the boundaries to start out on. And although he wished that he could have had more time to work out the details, or been in charge of the situation, it was as it was, and he had to accept the terms the day had handed him. He looked to Sahara who stood so small yet sure of herself, and Holly who seemed to have blossomed overnight, holding tightly to Sahara's hand. Courage. It would take courage to see them all through this.

"If you'll excuse me ladies, I'll make my way home and prepare our dessert. One hour." And with that he was gone, the raven flying in his wake.

"He's angry," Holly whispered, seeking solace in Sahara's embrace.

"Not angry, Holly. Frustrated. He doesn't have to worry about how I feel, but he'll be anxious about your feelings. I think he hoped there would have been more time to ease you into it. But I had a hunch that if you found out later about him and me...well, you already knew that there was something there. It's better to be honest. I've found that out the hard way."

Holly nodded and nuzzled in for a kiss. "What I do know of Aiden, is that he pays attention to detail, he's meticulous, even in his thoughts. He probably had something else in mind, you know, to bring me along slowly, and now we've gone from a stolen kiss to him admitting to wanting two women. He doesn't know me well enough to know whether I could even go there. A week ago I was still someone he couldn't have."

She slipped her tongue back into Sahara's mouth, unable to stay away from the kisses Sahara was so expert at. Sahara gave in before pulling away.

"It's going to be lonely without you. Will you really come back tomorrow night?"

"I will. But you won't be lonely tonight. Sahara." Their lips began to explore once more. "I'm curious about you and Aiden."

Sahara melted into her. There was no point in trying to escape Holly's sweet mouth.

They decided that Holly should drive over to Aiden's first. Sahara would tidy up and bank the fire, make some preparations for tonight. Willow needed feeding, and she wanted to air out the space. She threw open the windows, lit some incense and spoke some words for protection over herself. She packed some overnight things. All that time, the raven paced back and forth on her front porch. Calling, calling. But Pan had made his intentions clear. Only when Sahara was ready, and only at her bidding, could Iona materialize.

As she set out over the path towards the aspens, Sahara opened her hands to the wind, and called to the raven stepping obediently behind her. Her heart space open, well protected by the magic she had worked at home, Sahara welcomed Iona into her arms.

"I'm in love Iona."

Iona shrieked her protest to the sky.

"I'm in love and I want you to leave me to it. It does not break the bond between us, and we still have our work to do. But I want to have your blessing, to know that my lovers are safe from your tricks. Can you promise me?"

Iona, torn with love and jealousy, had never looked more alluring. For a brief moment, Sahara wanted to lie in the tall grass with her, to forget all this and return to whatever they had known before. But that would mean leaving this lifetime and never returning. That much she could not give her. Their arms encircled each other and their lips brushed.

"I don't want to remember, Iona. I know that something went wrong between us. But I don't want to know. I want to leave it behind."

"It can't be left behind!" Iona insisted. "Even if you never remember, I do, and cannot forget."

Electricity sparked between them, their age old passion just under the surface of their skin.

"I'm going to Aiden's Iona. I don't know why you hate him so."

Sorrow flashed across Iona's face. Sahara felt instant dismay. Iona was in love with Aiden too. Hate would have been better.

"How have you come to love him...Iona, tell me!" Sahara's heart split with pain. But Iona was gone. A dark shadow on the sun splattered sky, leaving more questions than before.

⚬⟫✵⟪⚬

It seemed like mere moments before Aiden heard the knock on the door. The grip of his emotions grew into a tight knot in his chest. He was as scattered as the stars in the Milky Way, as tense as a tightrope, burning with love from both ends. Nothing he had dreamt before, or imagined about a time when he would be holding Holly in his arms had prepared him for this moment. So many things could go wrong with this scenario that he could hardly stand straight.

The possibility of loss after such a brief glimpse into a future with her produced a deep growl in his throat. And now she stood at his door, her smile a little tentative; her hair spilling about her shoulders, the sun catching the edges like a lambent flame.

He extended his hand and pulled her in, fighting to re-arrange his face into something less intimidating. She stepped in, and began to explain how she'd ended up at his door without Sahara.

Aiden covered her mouth with his, extinguishing her words, lighting her sexual energy. Tears were falling down her face. He pushed her up against the wall, his hands in hers, lifting them up over her head, she had nowhere to go but to fall into his need to love her. He could taste her tears now, and let his own fall. There were a million things to say, but neither could find any words. She responded to his kisses with little moans that pushed his lips to her neck, and towards the strain of her nipples in her blouse. He fought the desire to rip it open. She pushed herself into him, her eyes intent on his face.

"Sahara will be along..." she gasped. "I thought you might like to talk."

He stopped and looked at her, confused in the moment, then relaxed his grip on her and smiled a smile so charming that it made her head spin.

"Of course. Talk. We need to talk." He smoothed her hair and helped her stand straight. "I'm sorry Holly, I'm not much of a gentleman these days."

"I thought you might be angry."

He steered her towards the island in the kitchen. "Water?"

"Yes, thank you. *Are* you angry, Aiden?"

He handed her a glass of water. "I don't know what you know of angry men, Holly, but did that feel angry?"

She laughed. A clear, familiar laugh.

"No, I admit, *that* did not feel angry. But at Sahara's…"

"At Sahara's, I was worried. I had just taken the chance to kiss you the week before, and suddenly, I realized that you had probably had the pleasure of …yes?" Holly nodded, blushing.

"And that the two of you had most likely discussed my dreams of loving both of you, which I admit, might not sound appealing to the average person." He brushed his hair back absentmindedly.

"*Aiden.*" Holly's voice soothed. "Ok. It was a bit of a shock, but then again, not really. I told Sahara that in some way, I felt like I had been lost and had finally found my tribe; that all my strangeness had finally been understood. I was confused because I was so sure that a man was never going to figure in my future, and I had some secret hopes about Sahara. *Then you kissed me.* I was suddenly opened to a new desire, and our friendship had truly primed my heart towards you. To top it all off, Sahara admitted to me that she already loved you, and there I was, exposed in so many ways, a thousand questions to find answers to."

It was difficult to listen when his eyes were caught by the heaving of her breasts, her shirt dishevelled. He held fast to the counter, averting his gaze to her face. He so very badly wanted to see her naked.

"Aiden, say something!" He looked so raw and impossibly gorgeous, his muscles clearly outlined through the finely knit sweater he wore, his forearms thick, his hands tense as he gripped the countertop.

"I don't know what to say right now, Holly. I'm so overwhelmed just by your being here; you know how long I've been nurturing feelings for you. But when Sahara showed up in our lives…well, she was a surprise gift that I couldn't resist opening. You do know what I mean?"

"I know. She turned my world upside down as well. I'd been waiting for someone like her to walk through my door."

Holly watched Aiden throw great pieces of wood in the fireplace now, her eyes sweeping his back, the way his jeans outlined the strength of his legs and buttocks. She thought of Sahara and smiled. There wasn't one bit of jealousy that she could point to, her heart was clear.

He caught her looking at him, just as Sahara poked her head in the door.

"All safe?" Sahara joked.

Both Holly and Aiden noticed that she had brought her overnight bag. They didn't look at each other, but knew what the other was thinking. Sahara was the one that bound them together. It was her strength that would take them through navigating their feelings for each other. Sahara was the glue.

Sahara held herself well. Her encounter with Iona had set her back on her heels, but she dared not show it. The wind had whispered to her through the aspens. She was safe here, there was magic in these woods, and in Aiden's home.

So it was over, her time of respite. From now on she would be fully engaged in her magic, all her guides would be called in; there would be no more hiding from the past or the future. Sitting gratefully at the table, tea before her, Sahara talked herself silently into relaxing. Tomorrow would have enough trouble of its' own.

"I'll be heading for Denver day after tomorrow," she confessed. "I have a date with my agent."

Holly looked up and caught Aiden's eye. "Oh. But we'll still have dinner tomorrow night?"

Aiden kept his eyes on Sahara, sharp as a hawk.

"Of course, I wouldn't miss that for the world!" Sahara gave Holly's hand a squeeze. "I have work to hand in, and some meetings with the publishers, yada, yada. I'll also pick up some supplies, and before you know it, I'll be back. Two days at most."

"Oh! I meant to tell you Sahara, I know of a magic supply store in Denver, I think you'd like it, they have the best crystals." Sahara paled. "You probably already know it?"

Aiden's fist clenched as a feeling of unease washed over him. He tried to look into Sahara's eyes, but she would not meet his stare. He was quick, she noted. He'd become better at sensing her energy shifts. She had better diffuse this right away.

"I do know it. I shop there for all my supplies. The owner is a friend of mine. I'm kind of surprised that you know of it as well Holly, it's in a very out of the way part of Denver, unless you're looking for that sort of thing."

There was no fooling Aiden, however, Sahara saw by his face. Obviously he sensed her tension.

"Well, I'd asked someone where to buy some good soap, and was looking for antiques. The cab driver took me to that part of town. You're right, it's quite hidden. The owner of the store is stunning! If she's your friend, I might be worried."

"Nothing to worry about, Holly." Sahara gave a smile, every bit of her a tangle of nerves.

"So, a few days away then, Sahara? Aiden asked. "I only ask because I had plans for a surprise for you. And I'll be gone again when you get back. So I won't see you for a while."

"Surprise?" Both women exclaimed at once.

Aiden laughed; glad to have the tension eased in the room. "Yes, I think it will be a surprise that both of you will like, but it's for Sahara, and I've been planning it for a while. We'll need the day."

"A whole day?" Sahara relaxed and her mind played with the idea of receiving a surprise from Aiden. It made her warm and safe, knowing that he had spent the time to think something up for her. She looked at Holly who was clasping her hands together and whose eyes glistened with happiness for her.

"What could possibly take a whole day?" Sahara asked.

"You'll have to wait and see. I was going to take you tomorrow, but now we have dinner planned and I don't want to rush the whole thing. We'll go when I get back again."

"Yes, but how do you expect me to think about anything else now? What is it?"

"Never mind!" Aiden laughed. "You will wait, and obediently, I might add."

Dessert wound down and Holly found her way to her favourite spot under the stairs, cuddled into a comfy chair to read, Yo Yo Ma's Appalachian Suite playing softly in the background. She had only a couple of hours left before she'd need to head back. It made her sad, leaving this place. It felt more like home than her apartment today, but that was probably because that place had only ever held her, and now her being had expanded to hold two others in heart space. She wondered if she would feel lonely now, at home.

All her reminders of France were also reminders of Julie, and with some surprise, she realized that over the last two days, she had released the pain around her French lover. Perhaps she would see her French antiques and treasures with new eyes? Perhaps they would no longer feel like a way back to Julie, but a road to her love affair with Europe. In the past, she had pushed away thoughts of going back to take another pastry course, but maybe now, it would feel right?

Aiden's and Sahara's voices filtered in from where they sat on the couch. She watched the two of them curiously. Mostly they sat silently, looking out at the forest beyond, arms intertwined. They were breathing each other in, as well as the peaceful setting on the other side of the window. Her eyes closed. They all slept, and when they awoke, the woods outside were dark.

"What time is it? Aiden!"

"Damn, Holly, I'm so sorry...we all fell asleep." Aiden moved about, adding logs to the fire, turning on lights.

"Shall we come out to the café with you? Do you need any help?" He cursed himself for leaving her in this position. Sahara went out to start the car.

"No. Please, stay here. I'll be fine. I'll need a couple of hours to prep for tomorrow morning. I'm just surprised by the dark, that's all. And we'll see each other tomorrow."

"Till tomorrow then," Aiden whispered to her.

He held her tightly to him, kissing her eyes, her lips. "You'll call when you're safe at home?" He hated letting her go, and the idea of her travelling home alone in the dark, but he knew that he was being ridiculous. She would be fine. She'd managed all this time without anyone worrying over her.

"You must be hungry," he added. "It's supper time."

"No. Hungry? Well, maybe a little." Holly winked.

Aiden's heart turned over as he let her go into the arms of Sahara who embraced her with kisses. He watched them as their tongues met. Stunning! His lips itched to join theirs.

Sahara walked Holly out and waved her down the lane, a smile on her face. But her heart was troubled as she walked back into the house.

Aiden stood with his back to the fire. His face was riddled with questions, as clearly as his cock was set for taking her. She would tread lightly. There was too much to lose.

"Wine?" she asked, hoping for some liquid courage. Aiden took off his sweater as he moved towards her, his cock raging. He was bigger, she thought, more toned, his waist punctuated by those well-defined oblique's. It was madness how appealing that part of him was; where his waist dipped to his hips. She wanted him to say something, but he was silent and brooding.

He opened a bottle of wine and poured them each a sizable amount.

"I'll never drink that much," Sahara protested. Aiden shoved it into her hand. "You will," he answered brusquely, and pushed her down to her knees.

"You won't kiss me first?" she asked, her pussy already running wet, her nipples screaming for escape. He thought a moment, and sank to his knees also, offering his lips. She moaned as he forced his tongue into her mouth, kissing her violently. She bit him. He gripped her by her hair and kissed her neck, returning her bite. She moaned her pleasure as he stood once more and she ran her hands over the strain of his cock in his jeans.

Aiden's mind raced back to Sahara moving her tongue into Holly's mouth. Eyes closed, he felt her open his belt, and take it slowly from his jeans. She looked up at him and said *please*. And then Aiden lost himself to the exquisite feeling and sound of Sahara's mouth on his erection.

He would be rough tonight; she saw it in the tension on his face. She came before he ever touched her, sliding her lips over him, and sensing the energy of another woman in his aura.

So, she thought as her body rocked itself through the orgasm, *you also have something to explain, my love.*

Sahara's confidence returned as she imagined his cock in another's mouth. She could do better, she was sure.

Aiden looked down at the woman he loved, her mouth bringing him the pleasure he craved.

"Louder, Sahara. I want to hear you enjoying my cock in your mouth. Damn it, Sahara, do as I say!"

She moaned. She loved his dirty talk, and the way he owned her when he was this aroused.

An idiotic sense of manners bade Aiden not to fuck her mouth too hard, she didn't need encouragement anyway. She was moaning and sucking vigorously, making all the noise he had asked for. She licked his tight balls expertly, as she pumped his cock with her hand. He had to retrace his memories to see if anyone had ever sucked him off better, but he couldn't remember another. He could smell her and craved her honey on his tongue. He praised her and lifted her to kiss him, her face flushed and her breath coming fast.

"Was that better than the woman who blew you before you came home, Aiden?"

Sahara's words hit Aiden in the solar plexus, but she just kept on kissing him, an innocent look on her face.

"Better," he answered smoothly. "Take off your clothes."

"Tell me who it is Aiden." Sahara mumbled between his kisses and wrestling herself out of her jeans.

"Later, when you tell me about your friend the witch...what's her name?"

Sahara hesitated. Her arms tightened around his neck.

192

His hand slid down, brushed lightly against her nub. There was no mistaking the fear in her grip. He picked her up in his arms and carried her towards the sofa to grab a blanket, her legs wound around his waist, her pussy wet and hot against him. She was light as a feather, Aiden noted, Sahara's ass in his hands, nipples rubbing against his chest. He threw the blanket down on the kitchen island, and laid her down upon it. He spread her wide. She arched her back and ran her hands over her breasts, down to her slit, feeling how swollen she had become, ready for entry.

Aiden stood looking at her, his hands holding her open, eyes focused on her nub, how her hand pulled and played with it. She was smooth as silk, her fragrance meant to trap him to her.

"Take your hand away," he insisted. "I want to look at you, you're so devastatingly beautiful, my love."

Aiden stared at her, his eyes penetrating her desire. She writhed a little, trying to get away from his intensity. She knew that he was angry, because she had lied to Holly, and that he was trying to control his emotions.

"Stay still, Sahara, or I'll tie you open."

She cried out, her memories of a distant time now becoming clearer, the cruel passion of a skilled lover washing over her.

He lowered his face closer, his breath hot on her inner thigh. She closed her fingers over her nipples, and tugged. The look on his face made her spread as wide as she could manage, her stomach rising and falling with anticipation, he was wonderfully powerful in the shoulders and arms, eyes full of lust. She shoved her hips up towards him, willing him to take the first lick.

Aiden brushed his lips against her thigh. She screamed at his touch. His hair fell over her, as his tongue lay hot and electric on her clit. Slowly, slowly, he swiped at her slit, tongue maddeningly light.

He would lose his mind, he was sure, she tasted so divine; her smooth folds like a drug that he could never have enough of.

"I love you so very much, Sahara. You are like a dark pool that I'm willingly drowning in."

He said it as he pulled her clit into his mouth. She lay very still now, waiting for the exquisite sucking that only he was capable of. He knew how to take her towards orgasm in waves, almost there, and back, a little closer, and back.

"What's her name, Sahara?"

"Whose?" Sahara asked through a haze.

"Your witchy friend. From Denver."

"She's no-one."

"Liar." He breathed over her, searching for her nipples. "I hate that you're lying to me. And more that you lied to Holly. I felt your energy shift when Holly mentioned the magic store. What are you not telling us?"

He found them and licked around the pursed up areola, Sahara's breasts lost in his big hands. Taking a nipple in his mouth, he sucked softly, pulling on it and ending with a little nip.

"Harder, damn-it, Aiden!"

"Name."

"Aiden. Please." Sahara's eyes filled with tears.

"You're afraid. I will know her name," he insisted.

He slid back down towards her slit, kissing every tender spot along the way. His mouth found the magic of her inner thigh. Love bites that became more urgent as he changed sides left her begging for his cock.

"Name! If you want me to bury my cock inside you..."

"Iona."

The name slipped out and their world shook as the connection was made in the Underworld.

Iona felt it in her heart; pain so deep that she wept bitter tears as she stood praying at her altar.

Aiden plunged himself deep into Sahara, rocking her with his length and his width, hitting her in that wondrous place where ecstasy hid. He saw her tears, his heart broke open to her pain; although he could not know what it was all about.

He obeyed her calls for more, taking one hand to rub her clit. This time he knew it was coming, from the way her body tensed for that split second before she let herself go to the depths of pleasure. Her small hands gripped the blanket, her back arched, he could feel every ripple inside her, as her muscles clamped down on him and her goddess water washed over his cock. Still, he held himself; he would wait for his own release.

"Good girl. I love it when you soak my cock with your cum."

Aiden's words were erotic but his voice was still hard.

She shook in the aftermath. He took her in his arms and carried her closer to the fire. It wasn't over, she knew. Hungrily, she met his mouth, and asked him what he wanted.

He turned her around, lifting her ass for his eyes to feast on. She trembled as he ran his fingers over her slit, moving her wetness around, gently sweeping it all towards her back opening. He bent over her and kissed her ears. His lips caressed down her spine, to her tight, toned bottom.

Her passion stirred up once more, she moved her ass back towards him, urging him on. He was afraid to hurt her, but he would do this, he needed this.

"I'm going to fuck your pretty little ass, Sahara." Aiden licked along the seam of it.

She moaned and rocked on her hands and knees.

"Tell me you want it, whore."

She wobbled towards the floor with his words; he steadied her and lifted her up again.

"I want it. Aiden, I want it! Take whatever you want, I'm ready."

"Say please, Sahara. Beg for my cock in your ass." He added, more to himself than to her, "So impossibly small..." He slapped her bottom hard, as she yelled "Oh, Oh, please, more!"

Aiden lubricated himself with her wetness, flowing freely as she waited for what he would do. His hand moved to her clit, fingers insisting on raising her arousal. When he sure that she was fully wet and willing, he slid his finger into her tightly puckered bud, Sahara moaning her consent, gently priming her for his very stiff prick by adding another. Withdrawing his fingers, he dropped some spit on her opening and entered her ass with a slow, gentle movement of his hips.

Sahara's breath hissed out. But she was not new to this; she knew how to welcome him, urging him on to faster strokes, deeper penetration, relaxing as his words coaxed her into surrender.

This was not like anything that Sahara had ever felt before, his prick so hard that it offered no respite, too wide to take to the end of him. She heard his groans as she said the words he wanted to hear, asking for his hot cum on her slit, her ass, her back, anywhere.

"Cover me with it," she begged..."and tell me who sucked your cock." He didn't hold back this time, Sahara's ass in a tight, erotic hold of him.

"Diane," he answered with a tortured breath, and pulled out to spray her ass with his seed. Sahara screamed her pleasure and relief.

They stood in the shower, each waiting for the other to speak. The warm water washed over them as they embraced the silence. He washed her hair; she lathered his chest and his back. It was only when he turned away to rinse that she noticed the marks on his back, faint

195

now, but there, never-the-less.

She traced the lines with her finger, kissed them tenderly.

"Diane was my lover before we met, I built her a house," Aiden confessed, his back to her still, hands against the shower wall. "I saw her once just as you and I met; and then again this week. I needed to end it with her in person. I'd just kissed Holly, and...well, you know how that goes." He turned around and gave her a wry grin.

"I'm not concerned, Aiden, just curious. I know who you are. She smiled and moved closer under the running water. "She used a whip on you."

"Hmmm, yes. I need that sometimes. Diane was never afraid of anything I asked for."

"Will you ask me for those things, Aiden?"

"Will I be asking for too much?"

"I've done it before."

"With Iona then?" He watched her face very carefully. "Tell me about Iona, Sahara."

"Can it wait until I get back from Denver?"

"Will you see her?"

Sahara nodded. "I will explain everything, but first I need to tie up some loose ends. Please trust me; it will be better this way."

They dried each other off and went downstairs to find some food. He'd said that he trusted her, it could wait. He called Holly, and yes, she had left a message saying she was safe. He was surprised, because they'd not heard the phone ring, and Holly had laughed. She knew, and she said she wouldn't have answered the phone either.

"I know that I shouldn't be all that surprised, Sahara, because I know Holly to be an incredibly open hearted and sweet person. But really, she surprised me today with her willingness to explore love with us. Don't you think? How did it go anyway, when you brought it up?"

"I'll tell you this, Aiden. You were right when you told me I would like her when we first met. Remember, when I was so bent on not having any friends?"

Aiden nodded.

"But she's tender at heart, honest, open, and so alive! She's won me over. At times when you think she'll be shocked by what you're saying, she looks like she's waking up to a truth that has been buried deep within her. She wasn't put off by my words, or for that matter, by any of the things that we did in bed. She has a side that is young and innocent and then this other side that is knowing, and brave."

"I fell in love with her pureness of heart so long ago," Aiden admitted. "She was this very young thing struggling to make the café work, and I bought everything she was selling." He laughed. "Ok, I'm still buying everything she's selling! She's always purely herself. I think it's been hard, she's been afraid to make close friends, to be found out. I was such a buffoon, I couldn't see past myself to see how uncomfortable I made her by wanting to date her. You're the one that brought us together. It was you that gave her the first sense of being able to truly blossom. Was she really not that shocked when you told her that you wanted us both?"

"I think she was surprised, yes, but not really shocked. I think some part of her has been looking for a chance to be unconventional. And she's so trusting, Aiden. We have to care well for her heart."

His raised eyebrow told her that he was more worried about her breaking Holly's heart than him.

Aiden moved their dishes aside. "Bed, Sahara? Let's go upstairs, we can read. I'll tidy up, and follow you there."

"Don't be long," she said and headed up the stairs to his room.

She slipped into the cool, white sheets, stretching out into the luxury of his fine linens, the enormity of his bed. He would want to know how Holly felt, how she tasted. Sahara couldn't wait to feel him wrap himself around her; to reach around and pull her in towards him, to feel his cock straining against her back.

But by the time he got there, she was fast asleep. He slid in, trying not to wake her, and lay on his back, listening to her soft breathing.

She felt his warmth, and slid herself on top of him, arms and legs akimbo.

He put his arms around her, her body a pleasure to his languid touch.

She moaned, and hugged him tight.

"Love you, Dagr," she whispered.

Aiden's heart leapt, nausea rose up to his chest and clamped down like a vice. His arms gripped her involuntarily. He loved her, he reminded himself; he would trust whatever explanation there was.

"I love you too, Sahara."

In the dark, he could not have known that she had opened her eyes, but her tears gave her away, dropping silently onto his chest. He held her even closer, barely breathing now. It was an evil hour that finally brought him sleep, with Sahara curled tight into a ball beside him.

She found no peace within her heart as she attempted to reach a memory that would bring her closer to understanding her mistake. There was no choice but to brave the mists of time and poach an answer from the past. A foray into another century was always fraught with danger, especially one that involved Iona. Aiden entreated her to remain in his arms, but she turned away and folded into herself.

"He's from the past," she offered quietly, "but I don't know much more than that."

"Sahara, I trust you. There is nothing for you to feel bad about. It's torture to have you this close and so removed from me. Please let me hold you."

But she didn't want his strength, or his understanding even, she wanted to be lost in the typhoon of emotions that buffeted her fragile soul. She heard him breathing evenly now, and turned to look at his handsome face. It did not demonstrate one iota of peace. Her heart broke and she lifted a hand to smooth his brow.

He moved towards her touch. He whispered her name.

Sahara sighed and wound her way back to the safety of his mighty chest.

When she awoke, he was staring out the window, one arm under his head, the other curled around her. She lifted up to lick his nipple, kiss his chest.

He jumped at the warmth of her lips. His face a mystery of emotions, Aiden pulled her up on top of him.

She wanted to sink beneath his skin, beneath the hard exterior of his muscular body, into his heart, into his soul. Her face nuzzled in his armpit, in his neck, breathing in the scent of his hair; it seemed like the only place of solace.

His hands ran over her back, through her hair. She stretched and purred, tension releasing from her racing mind.

"I'm so sorry, Aiden," she whispered.

"No more apologies, Sahara. I know that what you said came from somewhere very deep. I'm not hurt, but I am concerned that you feel so sad today. What can I do to help you?"

She sat up on top of him, her breasts such a delicious sight that he had to smile. Aiden put his hands on Sahara's waist, and held her there.

"I can't make dinner with you and Holly now. I hate to leave you and her like this last minute, but you probably can imagine that I could not concentrate on a normal evening now, I can't go home and write, I have to set out to Denver right away. I'll call Holly and explain. Or, give an excuse, anyway."

"That's fine. But should I worry about your safety? What do you think will happen when you see Iona?"

"We have a lot of unfinished business. I have a lot to tell you...oh Aiden. Maybe you should just get out now. Your life would be much less complicated."

Aiden scowled, and moved her aside to sit up in bed. He pulled her back on top of him and looked her in the eye. "Can you answer my question, Sahara, please? What will happen when you see Iona?" His eyes and grip were insistent.

"We'll travel back in time, at least in the form of a regression, not truly back. Iona will help me awaken some memories, and then, knowing Iona, we'll begin to negotiate."

"Negotiate? Sahara..."

"Please Aiden, let me go. I don't know much, and telling you bits is only going to make things more confusing. But I do need one thing."

"Of course, anything."

"This will sound strange."

Aiden cocked an eyebrow at her. "In comparison to what my love?" he asked.

"I need your energy on me. To bring to Iona. She'll need it, and well, I'd like to bring it to her. She'll want it." Sahara slipped off of him, and sat on the edge of the bed.

"Do you mean, because she knows me? Are you offering her a taste of the past? Who is Iona to me, Sahara?"

"Please, Aiden. Trust me if you can. I can't tell you until I know more myself."

Sahara spread her legs and waited for him to understand what she wanted. Aiden got out of bed and slid to his knees before her.

"My lady," he uttered, before he opened her wider and bowed his face to her delicate sex.

<hr/>

Sahara left Aiden at the edge of the aspen wood, knowing that she had worried his heart, although he offered assurances of his trust and love. She'd have to disappoint Holly and cancel their dinner date.

Holly answered on the first ring. Sahara could hear the smile on her face and winced, hating to dash her hopes.

Holly wished her well, and asked if she should cancel with Aiden until Sahara got back. Sahara thought no, Aiden would be delighted to have her to himself, but she picked up on the hesitation at Holly's end.

"I want you to see him Holly, if that's what you want. He won't bite," Sahara laughed, "unless you ask. I think that he's anxious to talk to you."

Goodbyes were said and love words exchanged.

Sahara called Kathryn next. Could they meet this afternoon instead of tomorrow? Kathryn would have to move some things around, but it could work. Could she make plans for dinner? No. Sahara said she had research to do, and it would take all evening and the next two days. She was sorry, but this trip would have to be short.

"Oh, well, that's kind of exciting then," Kathryn conceded. "I don't mind giving up time with you if it means more bestsellers! You're terrible at keeping your word lately. Are you sure you're not in love, Sahara? You're sounding awfully strange."

"I might be. I'll see you this aft." Sahara replied and hung up before any more questions could be asked.

The next call was to Iona. Sahara left her a message at the store. She was coming in. She would stay the night, could they meet at eight? She hung up knowing that Iona would move heaven and earth and some of the between to make room for Sahara's visit.

There was only one thing left to do. Leave a note for Aiden in the mailbox.

CHAPTER 24

"Are you sure you still want me to come over, Aiden?"

"I'm not answering that."

"Ok," Holly laughed. "What are you making me for dinner?"

"Oh. Now you're being bold? Never mind what. By the way, don't bring wine, I have something new for you to try...but I won't say no to one of your desserts. And I'm picking you up."

"But I can't stay over!" Holly protested.

"Don't worry, little girl, I'll bring you home."

"But why? I can drive myself."

"Allow me to be a gentleman, please."

"Will you be a gentleman all evening, Aiden?"

"Are you teasing me?" Aiden smiled at Holly's flirt.

"No," Holly answered, laughing out loud. "I'll see you at six."

Six o'clock seemed excruciatingly far away and Aiden busied himself with work details and chopping of wood. He never felt nervous around women but Holly threw his equilibrium like nobody else.

He walked into the cafe at five thirty, picked up a few items, and ordered a pound of Peruvian beans. The girl behind the counter smiled up at him, and asked if he was having a good day. He answered, charming and polite, smiling at her youthful blush.

A customer looked up to see where this was going. The man was perennially alone.

Holly's familiar voice broke into the room as she came down from her upstairs apartment.

Aiden scanned her from head to toe and ignored the sudden tightness in his chest.

She was wearing a flowered dress cut just above her knees, white with red poppies, topped by a black cardigan. Black leather boots hugged her slim legs, blond hair twisting down her back. She wore perfume. Her breasts peaked out cheekily from the low v neckline. She grinned at him on her approach.

Aiden stood from his stool at the counter and reached for her hand. He kissed her on the mouth.

"Wench!" he whispered into her hair.

"You smell like the forest," she replied.

If she had wanted to make an impression, she had succeeded. Holly turned to the astonished girl behind the counter.

"Lilith, I'll see you in the morning. Seven a.m. sharp. Thanks for everything."

And then, ignoring the heads twisting in their direction, she walked hand in hand with the shamelessly victorious Aiden to his truck. That he opened her door first was not lost on the now openly gaping group in the café window. The two most available people in Riverbend had finally been caught...by each other!

He got into the truck and looked at Holly who was biting her lip, a question in her eyes.

"How long do you figure before texts are sent out?" she asked. "Do you think everyone will talk?"

Aiden started the truck and leaned across to steal another kiss. "I hope so," he replied. "That was one of the best moments of my life Holly. You look amazing." His eyes settled on the round of her breasts.

She gave him her hand to hold. "Have you always been this handsome?" she asked.

"I tried telling you," Aiden laughed and drove them to his forest home.

She pulled her boots off at the door. Aiden's jaw tightened as he appraised her outfit, her bare legs under her dress. He added to the fire and opened the wine. She padded after him towards the kitchen.

"I'm nervous," she said.

"Me too." He put the veggies in the oven to roast. "Dinner won't be long."

"Why are *you* nervous?"

"Remember when you confessed that you weren't interested in men?" He took a long sip of wine.

"Yes. But it seems that I was wrong." She laughed. "That night seems ages ago."

"Hmmm, yes. Well, that night, I was crushed to find that the woman I had set my heart on was completely out of my reach...for heaven's sake, Holly, aren't you going to drink any of that wine? Look, the bottle has a chicken on it, and it's from France!"

"Pushy man!" She laughed. "Now, about your being nervous."

"I'm incredulous that we're in this new place together," he said, shrugging his shoulders, "and hoping desperately that you're not going to say it's all some kind of a mistake."

"And Sahara's not here."

A shadow flickered over Aiden's eyes. "And Sahara's not here, right. Would you be more comfortable if she were? I can behave you know."

Holly took a most unladylike gulp of wine. "No, it's not that. I'm not scared of you in particular."

Aiden raised a doubtful eyebrow at her.

"Ok, I am a little bit afraid of you, and where we're going with this, it's all happening so quickly...not that I mind. Okay, I'm rambling."

Aiden pulled her close. "We have all the time in the world to discover what will be. Come, sit with me."

He walked her to the sofa, and sat facing her from the opposite end. She curled one of her legs under, sipping more wine.

"Tell me, what do you hope for in the next few years?"

"Well, I'd like to solidify my business, perhaps take on an apprentice, and make an effort to take another course in France."

He nodded in approval. She was practical, ambitious.

"You've taken on a big responsibility with the café. There were a lot of ways that it could have gone wrong, but you've done well. I'm proud of you."

He reached to tap her glass and they toasted to her success.

"My father helped in the beginning. I had some money set aside for college, but since I ran away to Europe and took a relatively inexpensive course, he still had a sum to forward to me."

"You haven't talked about your parents much. I assumed you weren't close."

"My mom is very sweet, but she never understood why I was so eager to leave home. Dad is a bit more flexible. They love me. I seem to have disappointed them. You know how parents make their plans."

"Yes, I do. Similar scenario here, but now that I've managed not to ruin myself by 'whittling sticks' as my father once put it, I seem to be redeemed."

Holly looked around. "Well, you don't seem to be starving anyway."

Only for you. Aiden thought, his blood humming just to be sharing his sofa with her.

They sat lost in thought for a moment. Holly sighed.

"Aiden, if you and I, I mean if Sahara and you..."

He reached out his hand and she snuggled into him. His hand ran over her hair, and traced along her neck. She gave in to the shiver that tingled along her spine.

"Aiden, if we were together, all of us, who would live where? Sahara would never abandon her cabin, you need all kinds of space to just be you, and I live in town. I know that I seem like a very independent sort, but I've been lonely, you know?"

She looked up into his eyes. Aiden scowled.

"Come here, sweet thing."

She sat facing him now, straddling his legs, arms wrapped around his neck. She reached to pull him closer, and dropped a tentative kiss on his lips.

"What's wrong, Aiden? You look upset."

"You tear my heart out when you say that you've been lonely. The details will work themselves out, don't worry. I doubt that Sahara would live here with me, on a full time basis anyway. Later, perhaps, you could keep the apartment for emergencies, or let it out to the apprentice you hope to have, and just keep couch surfing rights if there's bad weather and I'm not around to fetch you. I have an idea that you might like anyway."

Were they really sitting here discussing living arrangements? He was so afraid that the bubble might burst.

"What?" Holly warmed Aiden's long, muscular legs.

"I thought I'd add on to the house at some point."

"Add on? But, you already have two bedrooms!"

"Yes, I know. Hey, how can I concentrate with you heating up my lap and nuzzling around in my hair?"

"I love your hair." She bit his ear. His hands tightened around her. "You were saying..."

"A place of your own...damn it woman, keep still, I'm trying to make a declaration of my devotion."

He gave in. There was no escaping her lips, the softness of her touch, her heat on his legs. Hands tangled in her hair, he kissed her as his cock rose without apology. He found his way under the hem of her dress, her bottom fitting enticingly into his grip, her g string offering very little in the way of modesty. She moaned into his mouth, and tightened her legs a little to keep him away.

"I'm willing to go at your pace, but you'll have to admit that you're a terrible tease," Aiden smiled.

"Anyway," she sighed. "You were saying about adding on to your already capacious house?"

"Yes." He kissed at her collar bone, making her writhe like a snake. "I was thinking that I could add on a space for you to bring your favourite things here. Everyone needs a place of their own. I could visit you in your room."

"Oh, so this is all about you living out some kind of fantasy?"

"Well, yes. A man needs a harem and all that." Aiden caressed along her inner thigh, as she let him in a little further. "But one day, we might need more bedrooms anyway."

"For extra wives?" Holly parted the neckline on her dress, her nipples poking at the delicate lace of her bra.

"Nooo...the extra room is for the children I hope to have one day."

The idea of children rose on the air like a feather borne lightly on the wind. It suspended itself between them.

Aiden's words caught Holly in the pit of her stomach, awakening a yearning that she had abandoned along with her dreams of finding a lady love. Trying to hide her surprise, Holly put her hands to her face. But it was too late, he had seen her reaction, and mistook it for dismay.

"I've said much too much, Holly. Forgive me."

He cursed himself silently, his face turning hard.

Holly shook her head as her eyes filled with great tears that rolled down onto her breasts. He bent to kiss them, pulling the white lace aside suddenly, exposing her pert nipples to his lips. She gasped at first contact, her hands in his hair, pulling him closer into her.

"No, Aiden, you don't... oh, oh...please."

He laid her down on the sofa, her breasts filling his hands. She spread a little for him. His mouth tugged on her nipples, hungry for her, both body and soul.

"*Holly*. Damn, woman, you taste incredible."

Aiden's hands found their way along the outside of Holly's thighs, pushing her dress up.

Holly's breath caught as he stopped just short of exposing her fully. Her legs tightened once more.

Aiden waited for instructions. He was sure she was intent on killing him with anticipation.

"Tell me what you'd like, my love. I'm yours."

He sat back on his heels, his hands pushing back his hair, a vulnerable look on his face as he beheld her in such a compromising pose, just barely glimpsing the area covered by a sinful scrap of lace.

"You may have a look...just a little, something to look forward to," Holly replied, shaking now.

He noticed that she didn't open any further, waiting for him to place his hands on the velvety skin of her inner thighs, and push her legs wider. They were playing the fine line of control given and control taken, Aiden surprised that she understood the subtleties of a game that he loved to play.

He groaned and lifted the end of her dress, steeling himself to re-sist the need to taste her. How often had he imagined this scene; the first glimpse, the first taste, the fragrance of her sex? And now she was before him. It was entirely surreal. His fingers slid gently around the edge of her g string, and carefully, ever so slowly, he exposed her to his hungry eyes. She purred; a long and satisfied sound.

"Do you like it, Aiden?"

He had trouble answering. His brain was on fire. She was not acting quite the innocent that he had imagined. Already she had taught him how she liked to be approached, what stirred her desire. He noticed the subtle and not so subtle differences between her and Sahara's sex. The little tuft of manicured hair on her mound to offset the smoothness of the rest of her, how her inner lips peaked out like a pink silky flower, the way her clit stood high and erect, where Sahara was completely bare and tightly tucked in, more like a flower still in bud. They were both so very enchanting in their own way.

"Beautiful. Holly. Please, tell me that I may touch you."

"One touch, we'll save the rest."

She trembled as she waited, not sure if he meant to touch with his hands or tongue. When she felt his finger take its slow and tender slide down her slit, she moaned and called his name. She sat up sud-denly and kissed him hard, moving to straddle him on the sofa. He had that crazed look that she noticed from time to time. It still scared her, but if she was bold, then maybe he wouldn't notice her fear of his intensity. She took his hand and kissed it, pulling a finger into her mouth, sucking hard.

Aiden closed his eyes. He felt her breasts graze his face as she swept her nipples across his lips, her perfume making its mark on his memory.

She scanned across the expanse of his chest, his wide shoulders, muscles rippling down his belly towards the strain of his jeans. She reached down to his cock, and gave the length of it a light stroke. His eyes flew open, to see her other hand on her breast, rolling her nipple and smiling.

"About the extra rooms, Aiden. Are you saying you want to make babies with me?" Holly asked. After all, he had brought it up. *He* wasn't afraid to be real, why should she be?

He stared at her, his mind and body reeling between the intense need to throw her to the floor and take her, to the seriousness of her question, no matter how lightly she seemed to address it.

"This is how you tell me that you'd consider having my children?

Teasing me with your beautiful bits and not letting me have more than the tiniest taste? Oh, you are cruel. I should take you over my knee and spank you."

"I hardly think I've been bad enough for that."

She pouted and slipped a finger inside herself. She offered it to him and laughed when he begged for more. As much as she ached for his fingers inside her, to discover what it would feel like to have his face lower to taste her, she wanted to wait. But if she did not leave his lap, she was afraid that she'd come right then and there, her clit already aching and throbbing.

"I want *food*, Aiden!" she said, and slipped off to the kitchen, leaving her panties behind. "Aiden, the veggies are burning! Where are your oven mitts?"

"Shit! I'm coming, Cruella."

"What? So you tease me to distraction and burn my dinner, then call me Cruella?"

"*I* tease *you*?" He strode over towards her, stiff cock still trapped in his jeans. I'll have you know, young lady, that I have *never* been left this wanting. Ever. And here, put on your scanty underwear, before you accuse me of pilfering them."

She grabbed them from him and stuffed them in her purse.

"You intend to eat dinner like that?" Aiden asked.

Holly ignored that and stuck her head in the fridge. "You go put on the grill, I'll make some salad. I'm starving. Any more wine?"

He couldn't stand it one minute longer. He yanked her out of the fridge.

"I love you, Holly. I love you. I know it's soon for you, but I can't bear to not say it out loud. I need you to know that I love you. Not only for today, or for the day when you finally let me into your charming bed, but for as long as you'll have me."

She stood so still that he had to resist the urge to shake her. He buried his face in her hair, holding her to him. She was shaking.

At long last, she spoke.

"I know now that I have loved you also, Aiden. I just couldn't see it, didn't want to see it. I was waiting; waiting for Sahara to fill my life and my heart. She brought me to you. And when she showed me her love for you, I was able to recognize my own."

"I'm falling deep into you, Holly."

Aiden let his mouth graze her lips, his tongue sliding into her mouth, delicious licks followed by an insistent thrust that caved her knees.

"*Je veux tomber plus profondement dans vous.*"

Aiden's arms tightened, his hips moving towards hers, she felt his arousal as sharply as she felt her own.

"*Don't!*" Aiden said when Holly offered to translate. "I want to wear those words on my heart exactly as you said them."

A small cry escaped her. Aiden's emotions ran deep, and he wasn't shy to expose them. She shivered realizing how close she had come to not ever knowing who he truly was.

She kissed him softly on the forehead, and busied herself with dishing out dinner. She really was starving.

"Aiden?" she asked.

"Yes, sweet thing?"

"Do you remember the time at the patisserie when that guy was asking me questions, trying to figure out if I was taken?"

"I do. Very clearly. What about it?"

Holly noticed how swiftly his soft look switched to a hard stare as soon as she mentioned another man.

"I remember how you changed seats from your table to the counter as soon as you saw that I was uncomfortable. You gave him one of the coldest stares I've ever seen, I had no idea you could even look like that. He backed off right away, and you hadn't even spoken a word to him."

"Even then, Holly, I thought of you as my own. I'm not territorial by nature, but with you..." Aiden broke off, his eyes holding her to him. Holly reached her hand over. His shoulders eased.

"I'd forgotten to thank you for that, Aiden. He'd made me feel cornered."

Aiden nodded, hand gripping his fork a little tighter.

"I'm not easily given over to jealousy, Holly. As a matter of fact, it's a bit of a foreign concept to me. But I'm sharing you with Sahara, and that's it."

She mentioned that it would be time to go soon, and looked for her hair brush in her purse. He offered to do it for her, and sat her on a kitchen chair.

He lifted the brush to her hair. Holding a fistful in one hand as he ran the brush through with the other, he realized a sudden dimming in his eyes and a loud ringing in his ears. He shook his head to make sense of the sensation. But the memory was upon him like a searing hot brand before he could shake it off. Another time, another maiden, her hair in his hands, his loins on fire.

"Aiden, I don't think you ate enough." Holly's voice broke

through. "No more wine for you. I'll make some coffee." She probably shouldn't have tortured him like that. Aiden looked shaken.

Holly opened windows to let in crisp forest air, blithely unaware of the wood fairies that quickly made their way in, settling on a shelf of books by Aiden's side.

No need to worry, they determined amongst themselves, Aiden seemed to have recovered sufficiently from his trip to the Oracle Wood. But they would stay a while, as instructed by Pan.

Aiden took the coffee from Holly's hand, sitting in one of the chairs under the stairs, a single candle lighting the cozy space. He had no words left to say to her, lost as he was to the memory. Questions were all that he had left. He drank in silence, watching her watching him, content to embrace the quiet between them.

Holly sipped her coffee and studied his face. Deep in thought, impenetrable, his features set to that hard look he got when trying to make sense of something that irked him. It made him all that more handsome, and it gave her pleasure to be part of his mystery. She knew that he wouldn't offer any explanations for this sudden mood.

Stretching out his legs, he let out a sigh and held out his hand to her. She put down her cup, and came over to kneel at his knees. But he pulled her into his lap, against his heart.

"I'll take you home," he whispered, and they both felt the pang of disappointment at having to part due to Holly's early morning at the bakery.

"I wonder what Sahara is doing right now. She's probably exhausted from her meeting and falling into bed," Holly whispered as she wrapped her arms around his neck, lips searching for his.

"I wonder," he replied, welcoming her soft moans as her tongue met his, heat searing through his veins. But he really didn't wonder, because he knew that Sahara *was* falling into bed, with a woman that he was also strangely entangled with. He felt an overwhelming urge for violence, and his grip on Holly's arms tightened.

She pushed on his chest and peered into his eyes. He relaxed his hands, quickly apologizing.

"I'm not a little girl, you know," she said defiantly, her clit tingling from his grip, correctly gathering his assumption that she wouldn't like a heavier hand in bed. Another time, that statement would have put an amused smile on Aiden's face and pushed him to test her words. But tonight, the oddly familiar phrase only made him frustrated as hell. He had no business feeling this damned irritable, with Holly in his lap. Aiden looked up as a sudden gust of wind made a window slam shut.

"Do you smell that, Aiden?" Holly asked, sniffing the air like a cat.

Aiden had already made out the message sent on the wind. The whole house smelled of pine forest, a damp mossy aroma spiced with the essence of freshly trodden needles. It was Pan, Aiden was sure of it. Pan would protect Sahara, and this was his sign. He relaxed his shoulders and led Holly to the truck.

"I'm home for two more days," he told her. Please let me make up for tonight. Would you come to Telson with me for dinner?"

"Telson? In public, you mean, like a date?" she teased.

His hand gripped hers tightly. "Don't tease me, Holly. I'm ready to rip your clothes to shreds."

He drove into the night, dreading the moment he would leave her at her door.

"Should I be afraid of the other Aiden, the one who's not a gentleman?"

"You're still teasing me, you wench! And yes, you should be afraid," he answered, looking straight ahead.

She felt his words on her spine, an electric shock that left her weak. Tomorrow could not come fast enough.

CHAPTER 25

Aiden.

There's never enough time to say all the things that I want to say, and maybe that is just as well. I know that you're concerned. There is a chance that this note will make you even more concerned. Please try to understand that the time with Iona is meant only to help me uncover memories. Without them, you and I have no chance of remaining in a sane relationship. I now know for certain that you and I have shared another lifetime together, and as much as I wish that it all could remain in the past, Iona simply will not allow it. I need to know why. It's obvious to me, if not to you, that you are capable of magic, probably more than just a little. This journey has begun, and there is no way to avoid it.

I'm going to ask Iona to regress me to my/our previous life. There is no danger in this, I have been regressed before. What I am concerned about is if we agree to time travel. I've never done it, and with it is a chance of no return. Iona travels...Aiden, I was afraid to tell you...Iona is a powerful sorceress, capable of many things that I am not.

I wish there had been more time for me to teach you about my world, but as it stands, you are left in the position of having to trust that these strange words I am writing to you are not the ramblings of a mad woman.

I like to be prepared. I am leaving you a hand written note detailing wishes concerning my estate should anything happen while I am away. I've also mailed a copy of the note to my lawyer, who will be drawing up a proper will. I can almost see your face as you read this; feel the tension in your hands. My love, 'all shall be well, and all shall be well, and all manner of things shall be well', as was once said. Please do not abandon all your plans and drive out to Denver in search of me. Protect me by staying calm. Certain connections may be made while I am away, but these will not be new to you. I'm speaking of Pan, who is everywhere, covering me and you with a degree of protection. You'll know if he's been around.

This is going to color your time with Holly, I realize, and for this I am sorry. I'd repeat myself and say that there is still time to get out if this is all too intense, but know, even as I'm saying it, what is going

on in your heart, and that you will not leave me. I love you. Kiss Hol-
ly for me. I will be in touch as circumstance makes it possible.

Until we meet again,
Sahara.

Aiden stared into the fire. He unfolded the next note.

"I, Sahara Taylor, bequeath the whole of my estate, including
proceeds and interests from my published works, to Aiden...

It was signed, dated, and noted that a copy had been sent to her lawyer.

He sat for a long time, not moving. He realized that he didn't know very much about her. She had left her whole estate to him, not to her family, not to a long-time friend. He didn't even know if her parents were alive. They had met, fallen in love, shared intimacies, dragged Holly into their world, and he didn't even know who to contact if something happened to her. She was, indeed, a dark pool of mysterious depths.

His chest felt tight and his breath was short. There was no denying that he loved her; loved her to distraction, leaving no room for turning back or even needing to know who she was. Whatever happened, he knew that he would not turn away from her. She was under his skin.

"Fuck, Sahara. You'd better come back, and explain the mystery that we're in."

He poured himself a scotch, and picked up his cell to send Holly a text.

"Sweet dreams, Holly."

She replied right away. "And you. Can't wait for tomorrow. Heard from Sahara. Good meeting with the agent apparently. She's having dinner with her friend now, Iona, but you probably already know. I miss her."

He gulped his drink and considered pouring another, but decided against it. He knew why she had sent word through Holly. It was easier for her to keep his energy separate from her task. Pacing the floor, he paused at the door, thinking that a walk might clear his head. But no, he'd have to walk for miles. The fire called him again.

Tomorrow night might be tricky, he thought. All his desire for Holly, his frustration at not being able to help Sahara would come out too violently for comfort. Maybe he should set the ground rules for the date before they met; he had few reserves for control left, where Holly was concerned.

The memory of his glimpse of Holly's sex, set against the backdrop of Sahara's note produced a low, agonized growl from the normally collected Aiden, and he threw open the front door to the cold wind. He found himself at the woodpile; axe in hand, his body ready for a battle that he could only wage with himself. It felt good to hit something with this much force, to see it split and fall beneath his power, to ache inside and out, to release his rage. His body awoke to a sensation of grace in motion, much like a swordsman would feel in battle, where all thought was erased and the body took over the ballet of the kill.

When he was spent, he found his way back to the fire and his box of herb. He took it carefully from its' pouch and rolled himself a joint. He closed his eyes and remembered the words Sahara had spoken the last time they'd smoked. He asked for wisdom, for strength, for understanding. He took a long drag and inhaled magic and sacredness. The house was dark now, only the shadows of the flames played upon the walls. Slowly, he found respite as the plant world opened up to him and fanned him with peace. He caught the scent of pine again in the room, and knew he was not alone.

There was nothing to do but rest and wait. He had no choice but to work on plans tomorrow; and his mind needed to be clear. He decided against sleeping in his bed, it would seem too big. Throwing a few logs on the hearth, he settled down into a blanket on the sofa and fell into a dream filled sleep. A tall and willowy girl, with flowers in her hair, led him by the hand into a forest deep and dark. He knew that soon they would be lost, but he didn't care. He would go anywhere with her.

CHAPTER 26

"Explain to me again why you're cancelling our perfectly good dinner plans?" Richard asked, changing out of the shirt he had just put on and trying on another.

"An old friend is coming into town and I'm having dinner with her," Iona said.

"Right. And that flimsy excuse you gave me about why I can't join the two of you?"

"Richard! I've already said. I need this night alone with her."

Richard turned to look at her, his face unreadable. "*All* night then, my love?"

"I didn't say that." Iona paced the room and fidgeted with her hands.

"You're not saying much. And you're acting like a cat caught in a trap. I'm just curious, that's all. What kind of woman can make my tightly controlled lover this flustered? I'd like to meet her."

Iona took his hands in hers. She put on her sweetest smile. "You will, soon. But not tonight! Now drop it." Her look turned determined.

"Alright, but tell me this. Do I know her, from before? You've been so bloody vague about our past life together, and I've been extremely open and patient, but there will come a day when I'll press you for more information. I won't be kept in the dark forever, Iona." He grabbed her ass and squeezed hard, pulling her closer, knowing that his hands were a drug for her.

"I will tell more, but not today," Iona breathed.

She tried to look as innocent as she could, but he could read her, and knew even now that trouble was brewing. It made him hot as hell. Any woman who could throw Iona off this much was worth his meeting. He turned away to hide his growing erection. There was something in the air that alerted his uncommonly sharp senses.

"I'll be at my apartment. Let me know about tomorrow night." He peered into Iona's closet. "I really need to keep more clothes here," he announced, scowling at his choice of apparel.

"That's ridiculous," Iona replied. "You have more clothes here than me. Get out." She kissed him and shoved him out the door.

Iona drew a bath, and aired out her flat. She stripped her bed and put on clean linens, the best she had. She replaced the burned down candles in their holders and pulled a large box from her closet. She checked inside. All that she would need was safely tucked inside. Her tarot reading table was clean and set. She placed fresh herbs on her altar in the mortar and pestle, arranged the figures of the Goddess and the Green Man, and poured herself a glass of wine. It had been over six hundred years. Tonight had to be perfect. There was a lot to lose if something went wrong.

In what seemed like mere seconds, Sahara stood in Iona's arms, a stunning reminder of love gone wrong.

Iona took Sahara's coat and hung her own as well. She lit some candles, while Sahara poured them some water. The room was heady with the scent of incense. Sahara toured the room, hand trailing the reading table, a perfectly round crystal globe gracing its center.

Iona watched her prowl around, her heart filled with love and regret. They drank the water, settling on the sofa, facing each other.

"You look beautiful," Iona whispered admiring Sahara's simple black dress and the way her breasts pushed their way out of the scooped neckline, a hint of black lace peeking through, nipples pushing at the gossamer like fabric.

"As do you, Iona," Sahara replied. Iona's hair spilled onto her bare shoulders, the cream sheath of a gown hugging her slim figure tightly, breasts bare beneath, wrists covered with silver bangles.

"I might need a drink after all, Iona. Just a little, for courage."

"I have everything you might need," Iona purred. Would you like a little bit of herb? It's excellent, organic, grown bio-dynamically. I think it might help us on our journey. I've been incubating it in my little pyramid container over there." She pointed.

"I've always loved your connection to the plant world. You're the best I know." Sahara took the tiny crystal goblet of wine that Iona offered.

"I know you, Sahara, you respond so quickly. This will be all you need."

Sahara watched Iona roll the herb for them to share, whispering incantations as she worked.

"Shall we begin?" Iona lit the joint and took the first inhale. She opened herself up to the wisdom floating on the vaporous essence of the plant, her eyes closed, and every fiber of her alert to the energy of the room. When she opened her eyes, they were glowing with the ethereal light of the Fey.

Sahara fell into the light and inhaled.

The Fey opened the portal, the King of the Fairies sat up on his forest throne, ears perked. There was no turning back from the journey now.

Iona leaned in and brushed her lips against Sahara's. Sahara moaned, her mouth aching for Iona, their kisses light and tender, whispering love words.

"It's time," Iona said into Sahara's ear, leaving a trail of electricity surging over Sahara's trembling body. They walked hand in hand to the little table, where their memories would be revealed.

Iona nodded, and they laid their hands on the crystal globe, glowing with a light blue hue.

Sahara felt herself lifting out, and for an instant tried to hold on to the reality of the room.

"Let go, my love," Iona urged.

They floated through layers of mist laden time, nothing left now but joy. The view opened up to a sun drenched field, a sea of grass waving in the wind, and two young women running towards the turbulent aquamarine of the Atlantic, their laughter drowned by crashing waves. They fell to the ground, wrapping their arms around each other, kissing passionately. The tall grass afforded them the privacy they needed. Away from prying eyes and gossiping lips, they could express their love, breasts bared to the wind that licked at their straining nipples.

"Will you always love me?" asked the girl with the sun bleached hair.

"Forever," replied her lover, lowering her dark tresses to the others taut belly, gently sweeping across, tickling her skin.

They lay in their oasis as long as the sun was high, warming their bare bodies in the comfort of their grassy bed.

"We should go," whispered one of them, as the shadows lengthened over the landscape.

"We must. Dagr will be worried."

They stood and gathered their clothes, helping each other dress, kirtles pulled over their heads, slippers hunted for amidst much laughter. They set out towards the village where they lived, the wind now sharp. A figure on a horse appeared on the hill, scanning the horizon. They yelled and waved their arms at where the figure stood, and smiled at each other as the horse made its way towards them. He was coming to collect them, always so aware of their needs and his desire to provide for them.

They looked up at him, his blond hair whipping around him. He towered over them on his war horse, a man of great strength and stature, his large hands swallowing the reins as he held tight to his mount. His heart shone through his eyes as he jumped down to greet them.

He kissed one. "Arinn." He kissed the other. "Brigida."

They moved into his chest, breathing in his scent. He lowered his face to their hair. He could smell sex on them. It stoked his passion.

"You must be hungry," Arinn surmised, lightly brushing against his erection.

He laughed a deep, throaty laugh, and ran his hands through his hair. "That I am, my lady. That I am. For home then?"

And he threw them up onto the back of his steed, leading their way back to the manor house.

Iona gave the signal and the guardian of the gate stood ready. The King of the Fairies sat back on his throne, grunting his displeasure.

Sahara felt herself slipping forwards through time, her head turned to the past, grasping for more images. The portal entry misted over and disappeared from sight. She slammed into the present, her hands tight by her side, tears streaming down her face. She opened her eyes.

Iona sat watching, the light in her eyes a warm glow, her heart on her sleeve.

"Hello Brigida," Iona whispered, as Sahara laid her head on the table, her body heaving with her sobs, Iona's fingers in her hair, gently stroking.

"I want to go back, take me back, Iona, I need to see more." But she knew that it was all Iona would allow for now.

"You're still in love with Dagr!" Sahara cried, a precious few memories awoken. She understood clearly now Aiden's attraction to Holly, Arinn's essence so familiar, and her own instant connection to the man that Iona coveted. She crawled over to Iona, heartbroken to the love that bound the two of them together.

"Arinn! What happened to us Arinn?"

"You will see, in time. No more tears tonight Sahara, we have other things to tend to. We'll journey again tomorrow. She refilled their goblets of wine, and bade Sahara drinks hers.

"Will I need more courage tonight, Iona?" Sahara asked.

"More than a little, my love." Iona replied.

CHAPTER 27

The sun rose as it did every day, stretching itself out over the horizon. Sahara felt the warmth of it through the window pane, slowly opening her eyes to unfamiliar surroundings. She felt a slight bit of panic before realizing where she was. Cocooned in the deep pillows and luxurious linens of Iona's bed, it was difficult to make out the ample contours of the room, the tall windows dressed in European lace, and the massive posts of the carved oak bed.

She sat up, and observed the silence around her. Her wrists and ankles ached. A slight stinging on her back called her to slip out of the high bed and pad over to the full length mirror on the bedroom wall. She turned her head to peer at her bottom, the telltale signs of the whip so barely visible that she had to stare to find them.

Iona found her standing there, hands on her breasts, curiosity on her face. She carried a tray with a pot of steaming tea and a bowl of berries. She was resplendent in a diaphanous chemise, a gracious smile on her innocent face.

"Good morning Sahara. I've brought you some tea, and I'm running you a bath. Sleep well?"

Sahara contemplated the woman before her. What she knew of her as a sorceress no longer matched the vision she had glimpsed the day before. That girl she had loved, Arinn, had been innocent and devoid of any proclivity towards darkness. Iona, on the other hand, held a smoldering power, she knew how to walk between worlds, how to work magic and alchemy. So much must have transpired between the scene they had visited yesterday and the end of that lifetime. She shook as she stood there, more vulnerable than she had felt in months.

Iona set the tray down and pulled Sahara into bed with her.

"Come, my sweet, it will not do for you to catch your death of cold. Sit here like a good girl and drink this tea. She lifted a raspberry to Sahara's lips.

Sahara took it obediently in her mouth and wrapped her hands around the delicate china cup.

Iona arranged herself to face Sahara on the bed. "You'll feel better after your bath."

Sahara nodded, sipping her tea. "I ache all over," she said. "And I don't remember anything about our..." she held out her wrists, to show Iona a bruise.

"Yes, that. I can explain. I gave you some sleepy time tea." Iona shrugged looking completely un-apologetic.

"That explains my lack of memory, although I'm sure it was more than just 'sleepy tea', but it does not explain these bruises." Sahara tried to avert her gaze from the pretty picture that Iona's breasts made draped as they were in the chemise, but it was impossible.

"I was protecting you, Sahara." Iona replied, defensive. "You slipped back in time a little from the games we played, and the memory scared you. I've erased it."

"I'm not comfortable with you having that much control, Iona, I'm not Brigida anymore. I'm capable of taking care of myself."

Iona's eyes flashed a deep hurt.

Sahara looked down and smoothed the duvet. "I'm sorry Iona. That was unfair. But we have to make new rules for this life together."

Iona nodded, and when she lifted her eyes, they were once more the limpid pools of serenity that Sahara had such a weakness for.

"May I have my bath now please, Iona?"

Sahara lay in the hot water, soaking in the oils infused with plant essences. Iona washed her hair and gently caressed an exquisitely fragranced soap into her skin. Sahara closed her eyes and spread her legs for Iona as her hands slid closer to her sex.

"I love you still, Sahara. Forever," Iona whispered into her ear.

Tears prickled behind Sahara's eyelids, and she let them fall. Was every lifetime to be complicated then? Was there no respite for her ravaged soul?

Iona pulled her out of the bath and dried her off. She led her to the bed, and motioned her to lie down.

"I have some oils for your back, you'll go home without any trace of our play last night."

Sahara could only stretch herself out and purr her answer. She closed her eyes, sinking into the pleasure of Iona's hands on her skin, tracing her fingers along her spine, towards the appetizing curves of her bottom. She raised herself a little on her knees.

Aiden checked his cell. No message from Sahara. He planned his day, contemplated his work, and spooned some ground coffee beans into the bodum. The phone rang and he felt a rush of energy. "Sahara!" he thought.

"Good morning!" Holly's cheerful voice confused him momentarily.

"Well hello. How are you?"

"I'm well. You?"

"Looking forward to our dinner tonight. Actually, I'm glad you called. I wanted to let you know that you'll need to dress for tonight. I won't be in jeans."

"Oh. Ok"....

"Is that alright, or shall I change the reservations for somewhere else?"

"It's fine. You caught me thinking about my wardrobe. I haven't done that in a while."

"Shall we go shopping?" Aiden suggested. "My treat."

"What? No! Don't be silly, I have to work and so do you," Holly laughed. "Besides, I don't want you to spend money on buying me clothes."

"You may not have a choice in that. I can be very persistent," Aiden countered.

"Really?" Holly remarked. "I hadn't noticed."

She asked if he'd heard from Sahara, and he said no. They agreed that she must be buried in piles of details with the agent. Aiden felt a tug in his heart at not being completely open with Holly. It wasn't his style, but he supposed this was Sahara's secret to tell. He made breakfast and arranged his work before running over to Sahara's to feed Willow and let him out. Maybe standing in her space would be some comfort. He missed her, and was more than a little worried.

⟶ ❊ ⟵

Holly told Lilith that she'd be back momentarily. She ran up the stairs to her apartment and threw open her closet. She hoped she still fit into the little black dress she had bought in Paris. She tried it on, it fit like a glove. Too short maybe, she wondered? She inspected the curve of her bottom in the dress, and rummaged around in the drawer for some stockings. Shit! Where were those stay-ups with the bow on the back? She hadn't had reason to wear anything remotely like this since her life with Julie. She smiled as she contemplated Aiden's reaction to her in stockings; how surprising this was, looking forward to an evening of teasing a man. Holly had no illusions as to Aiden's intentions from now on.

When he picked her up that night, Holly saw an entirely new side of him.

"I get the feeling that you're surprised about something," Aiden said.

"You look sooo good!"

She hadn't anticipated how incredibly stunning he would look in expensive tailored pants, or the fitted shirt that accentuated his broad back and muscular shoulders to perfection.

"This is a surprise? I distinctly recall you telling me the other day how handsome I was," Aiden joked.

"You are! I'm just remembering the boy who took me to prom," she laughed. "He had to get dressed up, of course, and showed up in these ridiculous pants that were a bit short, and too wide, and his jacket didn't fit...I guess that image stuck in my head. But here you are, in these slim, well-tailored trousers, and your shirt fits you exquisitely. And your shoes are nicer than mine!"

"Well, I am neither a boy, nor incapable of dressing myself. But speaking of shoes and dress, where have you been hiding those legs?"

He pulled her in for a kiss, his hands strong around her waist. He had his hair tied back with a black ribbon, she noticed, and it gave him the look of a rogue playing the role of a prince.

"Are you ready for this?" he asked as they drove towards Telson.

Holly kept staring at the way his muscular legs strained the fabric of his pants. How happy and sure of himself he looked, one hand on the wheel, the other on the gear shift.

"Holly!" Aiden looked over at her, legs crossed in a provocative pose, her face pensive.

"Sorry. Yes. I'm ready. Wait! Ready for what?"

"I have quite a few clients in Telson. We're bound to run into some at the restaurant. I'm usually alone when I go there."

"Usually?" Holly teased. "Will it just be old clients?"

"There's someone I built a house for, her name is Dianne...we later became lovers. I'll tell you more another time if you want. In any case, if I see her, I won't pretend not to notice. She was a good friend, and I think she might still be hurting a little. Would you be open to saying hello if necessary?"

"Of course." She took his hand. "I understand completely."

He gave her hand a squeeze, and brought it to his lips. "How may I introduce you?"

She was warmed by his manners, his desire to make her feel comfortable.

"You may introduce me as your good friend, which is what I am."

"I love you." He leaned over to kiss her, one eye on the road. She smiled at him and kissed him back, her tongue spreading fire.

"Aiden?"

"Yes, my love?"

"When you go there next, with Sahara, let's say, well...how do you hope to make this work?"

He drew in his breath. "The next time I go there, it will be with you and Sahara. We're going to meet this thing head on. I love you both, and I'm not going to hide it. I hope you're ok with that?"

She could do nothing more than nod. She loved his strength. It made her want to weep.

CHAPTER 28

As Aiden had anticipated, more than one person stared as they entered the dining room. He nodded politely at people he knew, holding tight to Holly's hand. She made a tantalizing picture beside him, black dress moving with her curves as she walked, French heels accentuating the athletic lines of her legs, blond hair in waves to the small of her back. It was clear that she was younger than him and that he was completely taken with her. Aiden didn't see Dianne anywhere; they might just get away without having to speak to anyone. The host walked them to his usual table for two.

He ordered wine and met Holly's eyes, his protective side plainly visible.

"I'm alright. I had no idea that you could cause such a stir in a place," Holly said.

"I assure you, it is not I who is causing a stir, my love." He reached his hand across to her. "You're stunning. I'm so delighted to be here with you."

Holly would have answered but someone was standing beside them, and Aiden was getting up, introducing Holly to Dianne.

Holly looked up into the face of a woman she could only describe as darkly captivating, with genuinely friendly, if slightly misted eyes.

"Hello," Holly smiled.

Dianne shook her hand warmly, complimented her on her dress. She said she had to get back to her table of friends, but that it was very good to meet her.

Holly watched as Aiden pulled Diane in at the waist ever so slightly as he whispered something in her ear, and placed a kiss on her cheek. Dianne's eyes closed as the kiss met her, and then she was gone.

It was the first and only time that Dianne had been seen with Aiden in public, and her friends knew immediately that they had been secret lovers, from the transparently controlled smile on her face. Dianne guessed correctly that this was serious for Aiden. He wouldn't risk gossip otherwise. And how could she blame him? Holly was a natural beauty. Dianne had seen her before, at that little French café in Riverbend.

Aiden sat down, ignoring the stares of the women at Dianne's table. The rest of Dianne's dinner would be ruined, fielding questions and speculations. She'd receive his flowers tomorrow, thanking her for her graciousness towards Holly, and repeating his whispered words to her, that he treasured their times together. He didn't expect her to lie to her friends about their involvement now, but he was sure that she wouldn't divulge details.

"She's still in love with you," Holly stated simply.

"Yes." Aiden looked at her, his eyes steady. "We had an agreement, but the heart will do what it will do. And I only ended our relationship recently. You're being very understanding, and I'm truly sorry if this is awkward. It's just not my way to avoid things."

Holly watched him pour their wine, his jaw set. It was no wonder that Dianne had difficulty letting him go from her heart. Aiden was an enigmatic, striking man.

They barely heard the bustle around them, the restaurant full of well-heeled regulars. They were difficult to ignore, the golden demoiselle and her rakish seducer.

"Are you having a good time, my love?" Aiden asked as dinner progressed, leisurely and dotted with discreet caresses.

"The best!" Holly sat on her hands, trying to keep herself calm.

He had stirred up her excitement. She had forgotten how much fun it was to be out enjoying life, there had been too much time spent working and worrying. She felt naughty, setting the room to gossip, with Aiden's intense energy focused entirely on her happiness.

"Will we have dessert?"

Holly shook her head, blushing.

"Your desserts have spoiled me anyway, for any others," Aiden said, thinking ahead to the rest of the night.

He paid the bill, and stood to take her hand. They left with the same turbulence that they had entered with, Aiden's hand to the small of Holly's back as he ushered her out the door into the cold mountain air. Standing behind her, he opened the truck door.

She turned at the last minute, a thank you on her lips, leaning in with a whisper of a kiss. His cock rose as he walked around to his side, hidden well by the dark and his superbly tailored dinner jacket.

"You're pretty hot dressed in a suit," Holly admitted, still bowled over by his elegance and the graceful way he moved for such a rugged man.

"We'll have to go out more often then," he said.

"You'll run out of money," she said jokingly.

"I promise you that I won't." Aiden's jaw set.

He looked straight at her and put his hand under her chin, rubbing her lower lip with his thumb. They drove to the café with hands held, the night tight around them.

"Ask me in, Holly." Aiden said with a grin as he walked her to the door.

"Are you planning on dessert now?" She fumbled with her key and he took it from her, making short work of the lock.

He pushed her into the stairwell, and buried his face in her hair.

She tried to get away from him, heading for the stairs, but he pinned her to the wall, tongue warm on hers. His hands swept under her short dress and found her bottom, bared by the lace g-string and stockings. He groaned.

"What do you plan to do with me?" Holly asked between breaths.

"Whatever I can get away with."

He took her hand and leapt up the stairs, forgetting that she was in heels. She ran after him, heart pounding out of her chest with anticipation.

She poured them some water while he opened the wine. His jacket off, she could clearly see the raging erection in his trousers. He started to roll up his shirt sleeves but changed his mind and took his shirt off. Her breath caught, imagining herself beneath him. What a dashing picture he made, his pants hugging his slim hips, his chest hard and defined. He made an adjustment to his cock.

Aiden threw back his wine while she sipped hers. She was already past the point of making clear decisions. Holly stood obediently as he unzipped her dress and pulled it off, unclipping her bra while he bit around her ears, urged on by her whimpers. He whipped her around to look at her ass, hands grazing the bows on the back of her stockings, insisting she keep her heels on.

"I won't be much of a gentleman tonight, Holly," he admitted as he kissed her deeply, his hands on her breasts, rolling her nipples deftly.

She was gasping, trying to hold on to her breath. She was already wet, melting to his touch as he felt on her inner thigh, stroking the softness of her skin.

"Put me over your knee, Aiden," she begged, her lips now to his ear.

"Why Holly. You wicked girl." He wasted no time and grabbed hold of a chair, sitting and facing her down over his lap. He felt his energy gathering, and his hands heat up. He hoped to hell that she wouldn't push him over the edge.

"Why do I get the feeling that you're not as innocent as I had imagined?" Aiden asked as he caressed Holly's delightful bottom, his soft touch the calm before the storm.

"I've had a lot of time to think and read," Holly replied, fidgeting in his lap, hands reaching for the floor.

Aiden laughed heartily and without warning brought his hand down smartly, leaving a mark.

She cried out and asked for more.

He told her she'd have to let him know when she'd had enough, spanking as he talked, a little harder now. But she didn't ask him to stop. His fingers curled in her hair and he gave her a little yank, signalling her to stand up.

She faced him with tears in her eyes, and shoved her tits in his face, sitting in his lap. Her natural longing for a woman pressed her to make love to his nipples with erotic gentleness, sucking on them with great skill. He moaned and pulled her up again.

"You're so very good at that. Tell me, did I hurt you just then?"

She nodded. He smoothed his hands over her bottom, kissing her tears. "I'm sorry."

She shook her head. "I like it. Sahara and I...."

He groaned as he kissed her, her mouth tender and pliant, imagining Holly playing rough games with Sahara.

"I can have a heavy hand, Holly. Stop me when I've forgotten myself."

"I don't want to stop you," she said her hands on his belt. "May I see please?"

She offered an innocent look. He lifted her off and stood up to undress. She sat down, legs spread, arms wrapped around the back of the chair, giving her breasts a jaunty look.

Aiden's breath left him in a rush. Sitting like that, with her nipples aroused and her hair hanging down around them, she looked nothing like the innocent that he had her pegged for. He stepped out of his trousers, aware of her eyes on him, his cock raging to escape his briefs.

She shook her head as she stared at his erection.

He laughed. "Courage, Holly, one step at a time."

He sank to his knees before her.

She pushed herself open a little wider, closer to the edge of the chair.

He sought out her nipples, sucking them as she had done his, but a little harder, pulling them tightly into his mouth, until she cried out and rocked on the chair. He pulled her stockings off, taking one to tie

226

her hands behind her. He put a small pillow between her spine and the rails of the chair. Then, lowering himself to his knees once more, he allowed himself the pleasure of pulling aside her scanty g-string to see what he'd be getting before taking it off altogether.

She ached to put her hands in his hair, now loose of its ribbon. She struggled a little, but he had tied her well.

"I've been thinking about this moment for so long Holly. I've been dying to taste you. You smell so good."

He held her legs open, his thumbs stroking close to her sex. His lips travelled along her inner thigh making her cry out, and ask for his tongue. She was soaked with desire, her clit erect.

"Your pussy is dripping wet," he observed; jaw clenched with need.

"Lick it up then... let me taste it on your lips."

Aiden stilled, his face now set into a lust induced hardness.

Holly blushed when he looked up at her, but pushed her legs a little wider anyway.

"You surprise me Holly. I like it," Aiden growled.

His fingers ran over her perineum, pushing some of her wet around.

"I don't look like Sahara, do I?" Holly asked. "She's so tightly put together, everything tucked in."

He groaned thinking of Sahara's tight cunt and how erotic it was that Holly was thinking of her.

"You're exquisite." His fingers opened her more; he was dying to feel inside her. "Your clit is hard. I want it in my mouth."

"*Aiden!*" Holly thrust towards him. "I'm so turned on seeing your beautiful face down there. I want to see your face in Sahara's pussy too. To watch you lick her dry. I want to see your fingers inside her, to see you make her come on your hands." She fidgeted, trying to loosen the tie on her wrists once more.

Aiden lunged for her lips, his tongue demanding.

"I had no idea that you'd have such a filthy little mouth, Holly. Keep talking like that and I'll come in it." He bit her lip and she cried out.

"On your knees, boy," she whispered as he slid back down.

When his tongue finally found her, she yelled his name. His mouth devoured her; she moved herself against him.

"You're delicious...I love you so fucking much," Aiden whispered.

She hadn't known that a man's tongue could be so precise, so delicate at times. She came violently when he slipped his fingers in while his lips pulled roughly on her clit. He swiftly untied her and laid her on the bed. She lay breathing heavily, hands covering her face.

"Hiding from me, Holly?" Aiden rumbled around in her bedside drawer, for what he knew would be there.

"I didn't know, I had no idea..." She blushed but reached her hand to her clit, rubbing herself.

Aiden held up the sex toy he'd found. "You won't mind?" he asked, not really asking permission.

She nodded, her fingers on her nipples. He bent over to kiss her and rub the dildo across her lips. She slipped out her tongue and gave the tip a lick.

Aiden thought that he might pass out.

He turned it on and slipped it gently along her belly, towards her clit and along her slit. She tried to move away but he held her down roughly, his tongue once more on her clit, moving the toy inside her.

She gasped and pushed forward.

"More, little girl?"

She bucked her hips and cried out for more, harder, faster.

He leaned one leg on the bed and whispered in her ear. "I'm going to give you more, but you have to trust me."

Not knowing what he meant, she looked into his eyes and saw the man she had always thought too intense for her. He looked possessed. She shuddered and nodded at him, somehow willing to go wherever he led.

With a turn of his wrist, he had found the angle at which to tease her magic spot, she'd let him know soon enough if she'd felt this before.

Holly tried to keep from making the noises she knew must be too loud, but her body urged her on towards letting him know that she loved the place he was pressing on.

"I'm going to pee!" she breathed, her hands clutching the sheets. *Jesus. Aiden!* Oh, keep doing that..."

"You won't. Trust me. Cum for me. *Now* Holly!"

She bathed in the heat that rushed over her entire body, escaping through the crown of her head, shaking as she squirted on his arm. It was the best orgasm she had ever had, her brain foggy still when Aiden lay down beside her.

He gathered her in his arms, holding her tight to his chest. She kissed him fervently, laughing and crying at the same time.

He grinned with satisfaction.

"I could get addicted to seeing you fall apart like that Holly." Aiden wrapped them up in the covers, his cock hard against her.

"Thank you." She smiled. "You rocked my world."

They lay together a while, not speaking, until she got up to bring over the bottle of wine.

"Your turn," she said, as she took a swig straight from the bottle for courage. He looked at her, amused.

"I hope you won't accuse me of causing you to drink too much."

She kissed him with lips drenched in wine. Soft, coquettish caresses, and dragged her hair across his chest. He held his breath as she removed his snug briefs, peeling them over his ever present erection. She passed her lips in a hot swath along his length, and he grabbed her hair instinctively.

"Holly."

"May I suck your cock, please?" she asked, remembering what Sahara had taught her. She'd practiced on her knees with the strap on Sahara had used to please her with.

He closed his eyes, his stomach tight, still having trouble believing that she was here, doing this. "Suck it, my pretty little whore."

The words slipped out before he could stop them, and as her tongue took a hot, clean swipe across the bottom of his tight balls. His hand went to his erection; he held it in a firm grasp.

She nipped along his belly, pleased to see how well-groomed he was, his cock delicious beneath her exploring tongue, encouraged by his smutty words, moving his hand away.

"Start softly, Holly." He felt her run her hand gently along the length. She tried to close her fist around the base, but her fingers wouldn't meet. "Come up here and kiss me. Put your tongue in my mouth."

"No. I prefer my tongue on your cock." She licked delicately along each side, her tongue curling along as it swept left to right.

"You're gorgeous." She breathed onto his cock. "And taste delicious."

"Your mouth is delicious. Are you sure you've not done this before?" Aiden thought about how sexy it was to see a girl taste her first cock.

"Yours is the first cock I've had in my mouth...except for the one Sahara was wearing the other night," she answered, taking the tip of him between her lips.

"You're trying to kill me," he groaned, the image of that scene hot on his brain, and tried to push his way into her mouth. She resisted and swung her leg over to straddle him, her pussy close to his face.

Aiden lost all control and pulled her in to him, licking her from her clit to bud.

She struggled away, slipping her mouth over his length and sucking vigorously, his hands grasping her ass, her moans on his skin. She didn't need tutoring; she knew how to draw out his pleasure as she moved her mouth upon him, and becoming increasingly wet as her own excitement mounted.

"Next time I see you Holly, I'm going to fuck your snug little cunt," Aiden bit out, his breath shallow as he tried to hold on to his need to explode.

Holly moaned and arched her back towards him. He slid one finger along her slit. It was softer than velvet.

She sucked harder, pulling on him as her tongue swiped along to keep his cock wet, her one hand stroking his balls. He was on the verge of coming, how she knew she wasn't sure, but it was something in his energy that gave her the clue.

"Fuck my mouth, Aiden. Please."

He felt her tighten around him as he slid his fingers inside her, his thumb on her clit. She moaned her pleasure loudly, heard him commanding her to move with strangled breath...that he was ready to come.

"Goddammit, Holly, move!"

But she held on tight, and listened to his roar as he came in a rush to the back of her throat.

His arms wrapped around what he could reach of her.

"Holly, you...you should have moved. You're spectacular."

She nodded, and slid herself out of bed, her eyes smarting from her effort to please him. She smiled at him over her glass of water, wiping her mouth with the back of her hand.

"I guess that was dessert." She'd never felt naughtier or more triumphant.

He called her to him and held her close. "I hope you're not going to kick me out, I want to hold you all night," he murmured. "I love you Holly. I'm not letting you go. Ever."

She set her alarm and turned out the lights. He was already asleep, looking impossibly big in her bed. She kissed his forehead and whispered goodnight.

"Doux reves, mon amour."

CHAPTER 29

Once the seal was broken, there was no way of keeping the memories from flooding in. Time, that quirky, non-linear human construct was behaving in the most peculiar way, as far as Sahara was concerned. She had slept most of the day away, exhausted from the regression and whatever play Iona had engaged her in the night before. Fitful at best, slumber only proved to be a jumble of recollections, and worrisome images.

When Iona brought her a cup of fragrant tea, she also announced that it would be time for supper. This confused Sahara greatly, as she was certain that she had just laid down a couple of hours ago.

"You've been sleeping all day, my sweet," Iona said. "You must be starving; you've had barely any breakfast and absolutely no lunch."

Sahara sat up in bed and stretched. "You're right, I am starving. What's for supper?"

"I'm cooking soup. We have cheese and olives, and also some excellent rabbit terrine."

The word 'rabbit' made Sahara's eyes open wide. "I remember rabbit. I mean from before."

Iona, of course, knew very well why she was serving rabbit.

Sahara asked Iona to hunt down her purse. She checked her cell, but there were no messages from Aiden or Holly. She sent them both a text, all was well. She smiled thinking about how Aiden must be enjoying this time with Holly, all to himself. Iona was back in the kitchen, making preparations for dinner...only the table was set for three.

"Are we expecting company?" Sahara asked, feeling a twinge of apprehension. "I thought we were going to do another regression."

"I'd like you to meet someone," Iona purred, coming over to gather Sahara into a hug.

"Who? I'm not in the mood." Sahara felt annoyed and trapped.

"It's someone who will help you remember. Someone I'm involved with now. Someone I love."

"Someone from our past," Sahara surmised. "What a tangled web. I'll get dressed." She left for the bedroom.

Iona followed her in, a tiny box in her hand.

"I have something for you," she said. "A small present."

Sahara smiled and tried to relax. She took the box and sat down on the bed. "Will I like it Iona?"

"I'd like you to like it," Iona replied. "It's something you used to love before."

Curious now, Sahara lifted the top off the tiny box. She peered inside. Two small, adjustable gold rings. She looked up at Iona who sat watching expectantly.

"Are these what I think they are?" Sahara's nipples rose quickly as she lifted the delicate rings out.

"May I?" Iona looked hopefully at Sahara, and began unbuttoning the shirt she had lent her to sleep in.

Sahara realized that her nipples were sore, even before Iona lowered her lips to wet them.

They stuck out impertinently. Iona slipped the rings on.

"Beautiful," Iona purred. "Will you wear them for me through dinner?"

"I'm sore," Sahara confessed. "But if it pleases you, Iona."

"It pleases me greatly. Now go get ready, our guest will be here any minute."

Now that she thought of it, Sahara was curious. Seeing Iona with someone did have a certain appeal, she would be showing her vulnerable side, something Sahara found intriguing. In the last minute, she decided to rinse off quickly in the shower. Oooh, how delicious the light pressure from her new gold rings, she liked these kinds of games.

Iona had turned on some music, and was singing in the kitchen, her voice clear as a bell, raising energy in the room, pulling in the four directions to play with them. So, a night of magic it promised to be. Sahara smiled as she applied her eye makeup and a hint of red to her lips.

Throwing caution to the wind, she topped her jeans with a silk blouse, omitting her bra. Her nipples poked at the fabric; there was no mystery as to their length. Satisfied with her appearance and ready for an evening of unchartered waters, Sahara walked into the kitchen to find Iona in a passionate embrace.

Lightning hit them both simultaneously. The man in Iona's arms turned to look at Sahara with a smile on his face, ready to greet the woman who had Iona so enraptured, eyes swiftly noticing the boldness of her breasts.

She looked into his midnight eyes, at his raven hair, handsome features, and tattooed arms. He was shockingly desirable. They extended their hands towards each other. Their fingers touched.

Richard looked confused at first, before a memory cleared his vision.

"Brigida!" he uttered, shocked.

"*Richard*," Sahara whispered, and fell to the floor in a faint.

Richard bent over Sahara, picking her up, carrying her to the sofa. He shot Iona an incensed look. She was rushing a glass of water to him laced with rescue remedy, eyes cast down.

"How incredibly irresponsible of you!" Richard hissed. "Did you plan this?"

"I thought we could spend the evening with me guiding the two of you back in time, and that you'd figure it out gradually. I had no intention of it being like this. Just how much do you remember from that one look?"

"Bugger all!" He spat the words. All I know is that when I saw her, her name was clear and that she meant something to me. You've got a lot of explaining to do, Iona."

"I will explain, of course I will. Please, let's just help her come to."

Iona looked at how Richard cradled Sahara, his hand stroking her forehead, concern on his face. Even if he didn't remember her directly, his body was very aware of his connection to her. His arms held her proprietarily. His legs welcomed her warmth. It wouldn't be a long trip for him to recognize Sahara as someone he'd loved. Iona bent over her, dropping light kisses onto Sahara's lips.

"Sahara, my sweet, wake up. I'm here."

Sahara opened her eyes and looked up at Iona and Richard hovering over her. She covered her face with her hands, and shook her head. She wasn't as ready as she had thought. It was more than she'd bargained for this weekend.

When she looked back up at him, Richard's eyes were penetrating hers with hawk like intensity. She peered back defiantly, and it made him smile.

"Sit up!" His voice was commanding, yet richly interlaced with kindness. She slid off his lap and sat on the sofa drinking the water Iona had brought. "Are you feeling better...I seem to have shocked you."

Iona brought over a blanket and Sahara wrapped herself in it, pulling her legs in under herself. It was a move Richard recognized from a haze of distant memories. He frowned with frustration.

"Sahara," Iona began to apologize. "I can see that my plan of introducing you to Richard like that was a mistake. Please forgive me, I hoped to take us all into a regression and you'd come out knowing each other. I should have known better. You're both much better at breaking through time than I gave you credit for."

She ran her hand over Sahara's face. Sahara leaned in to her touch, aching to be held. Iona cocooned Sahara to herself.

Richard watched them with great interest. Their bond was undeniable. He stood and left for the kitchen to open a bottle of wine for them, then poured himself a scotch.

Sahara followed him with her eyes; he carried himself with an uncanny mixture of elegance and power.

She welcomed Iona's lips on hers, aware of Richards stare from where he stood.

"Iona," she begged between kisses, "please feed me, I am so hungry. And please tell me who Richard is. I am overwhelmed by his energy, and a memory I cannot quite grasp. If you love me, please make things clear."

Iona broke down in soft tears. "I do love you, Sahara...please know this. Come, let us eat, when you're feeling stronger we'll go back. I promise you that Richard is someone you can trust. Come."

Richard pulled out a chair for each of them and offered to serve. He had another scotch. It warmed him and offered a small bit of solace in this confusing scenario.

Iona drank her wine gratefully, but bade Sahara eat first before she drank hers. Sahara felt their familiar pattern, she the apprentice, Iona the experienced wise woman.

"Sahara hasn't eaten all day," Iona said to Richard by explanation.

"Oh?" Richard questioned, his voice rough, placing bread and soup before them. "I wasn't aware that it was your custom to starve your guests."

He sat down to join them. Sahara shivered at his closeness, his aura was immense.

"We've had a lot of catching up to do," Iona replied smoothly. "Sahara needed sleep."

Richard looked at Iona sharply. He knew what *that* meant. In the beginning, until he had gotten used to her energy, he had also been knocked out by her love. So, they were lovers. It made no difference to him, as long as she was able to keep herself honest.

Iona looked into his eyes, a touch of hurt behind her usually calm look, and he felt himself already relenting. It would be easier if she wasn't so deceptively fragile in her loveliness. He was always confused by how someone so intense could also look so breakable. And obviously, Sahara was under the same damn spell.

They made small talk; Sahara slowly coming out of her shell, warmed by her dinner and the glass of wine she was eventually permitted. Richard told her that he owned a gallery in town, and she told him that she wrote.

Iona explained that Richard was very well read and had, in fact, helped to fund several libraries overseas.

"Europe?" Sahara asked, wondering what kind of resources one might need to fund libraries anywhere.

"I deal in art. Europe is the natural place to be. Actually, I'm most at home in the UK."

As soon as he'd said it Richard realized that he'd just stumbled upon a clue to his past life. He offered more wine to Iona who accepted but, who also, by an almost imperceptible look at Sahara, declined for her. Iona caught the amused look on Richard's face; he had their dynamic figured out.

"Have you known Iona long?"

It was a silly question, and they all laughed, but underneath it, they were aware that this was all just stalled time until they began the regression. Iona made coffee, and they moved on to the warmth of the chairs by the fireplace.

Sahara welcomed the soothing aroma of the hot drink. It was difficult to control her emotions. All at once, she was frightened and aroused, her misbehaved nipples giving her away. She had caught Richard staring at them without apology and it only threw her more off center. Apparently it hadn't been a good idea to tempt the situation and she regretted it now.

Iona left them alone as she swept off to prepare the table for the regression. She turned down all the lights and lit the candles. A drift of incense perfumed the air. Sahara tried desperately to hang on to a feeling of Aiden and Holly, for security. But Richard's arm, as he reached to hand her a chocolate, left her staring at his tattoos, where she caught the word 'Dagr' in swirling script alongside an image of a warrior facing the rising sun. She touched his arm.

"What does it mean...Dagr?"

"A new day." Richard answered, eyes radiating heat.

"What made you get it...if you don't mind?"

"I had a dream. And I couldn't forget it. The image felt like it belonged to me."

Richard felt sad for the frightened bewilderment in Sahara's eyes. She was so very small, but something about her, maybe her smooth muscles and healthy glow made her seem capable of great strength. She had an incredible ass, he noted, and those protruding nipples were simply maddening. She moved like a cat, stretching often, with a curious habit of pulling her short hair to ease her tension. But it was her smile, the winning way she had of showing an empathetic heart that made him melt. He didn't even try to avoid the hope that Iona would share. He'd never been much on beating around the bush, he thought it best to come right out and find out what he was wondering about.

"Do you live in Denver, Sahara?"

"No," she answered, offering no other clues.

"Is someone waiting for you at home?" He looked straight at her, acknowledging his own forwardness.

"Yes, as a matter of fact." She decided to give him more than he would expect. "Two someone's."

He smiled at her, a dark yet respectful look crossing his face.

"I see."

"Do you?" Now she was gaining the floor. He was interested, and she'd only made him more curious.

"Well, at least now I know where I stand."

"I'm sure you don't," she countered.

He laughed and raised his cup to her. She'd won.

"Everything is ready." Iona stood beside them. She led them to the table, a diminutive pot of tea and three tiny cups in the middle. She poured.

"This will help us to remember," she said.

Sahara sniffed to make out the herbs. Richard raised an eyebrow at Iona, but took his and drank.

They joined hands, the tea making its way through their consciousness, Iona guiding them with her words. The room spun away from them and they were tumbling towards the mist.

Sahara tried to recall if she'd seen Iona drink her tea...

CHAPTER 30

Richard paced the floor of his chamber, watching the kitchen boy struggle with the larger pieces of wood on the hearth. Surely they'd be back soon, bringing news of the fight. He had ordered the rooms next to his to be aired and the fires lit. The beds had been made with fresh linens. Richard was determined to honour Dagr's request, no matter what questions were raised about his unusual treatment of those captured. There was no way of knowing who had escaped. His orders had been clear. Dagr's women were to be brought unharmed to the castle. He could hardly have asked for Dagr's life to be spared, but asking for his women to be captured for questioning wasn't unreasonable. Word was to be sent ahead via a messenger. There had been plenty of time. His fury rose with each step around the room. He poured some wine and drank liberally even though his head ached from the night before.

At last! A cry from the courtyard alerted him to the activity below. It was mere moments before a loud knocking sent him racing to the door, letting in the exhausted rider.

"Speak!" He ordered with undisguised frustration. "What of lord Bretel?"

"He escaped, my lord."

The man near collapsed to the floor, having ridden the night through, chased by demons real and imagined.

"Escaped! To where?" Richard's heart leapt with relief. Dagr safe. It was the only thing that really mattered.

"To the wood, my lord, that demon infested place where only the possessed can roam."

The rider hoped he would be offered some water but no such offer came.

"And no-one followed him in?" Richard asked incredulously.

"No one dared. Some were slain trying. It was of no use, the devil himself drove them back."

Richard stared at the rider.

"What of the captured? Who is being brought back?"

"One maiden, one of the handfast. Everyone else is dead, except for the Pagan and his other woman."

The rider's throat was dry. Every muscle ached. "My lord, could I be so bold as to ask for a small drink? You see..."

To his surprise, before he could finish, Earl Richard Dumont had

237

poured him an especially large beaker of wine and sent him on his way to get bread from the cook, with a pat to his back for good measure. He left scratching his head, trying to determine whether the Earl was assuming, as everyone else had, that the Pagan would perish in the haunted woods. Perhaps that was the reason he had been so generous, instead of whipping him for the bad news of the man's escape. He secretly felt sorry for the girl they had captured. She certainly didn't look like someone who would knowingly anger God and King. But that wasn't his business after all. He sat in the kitchen and told the flabbergasted cook the entire tale of the demon worshipping village and how the Pagan had awoken all hell to help him escape. Indeed, he had seen several of the demons himself.

When the soldiers returned, a haggard and bewildered group, Richard was standing in the courtyard, ready to honour Dagr's last request. Whoever this girl was, he would find ways to protect her. It would require some skill, but he was privy to certain resources as Earl after all. He had hope now. Dagr was alive. And from what he knew of Dagr's birthright, he knew that there wasn't a devil that would harm him in those woods. He pulled aside the first man to ride in.

"What news of the battle?"

The soldier shook his head. "Punish me if you must, my lord, but I will not wage another such battle for you. I am now a murderer of innocent women and children."

He walked away with Richard's astonished gaze glued to his back. But there was no time to re-butt and speak empty words about those not being his orders but orders from the King, because she was here.

Brigida lay on the horse, her face pressed to his neck, her hands clutching the mane. Even as dirty as she was, her clothes covered in blood and her hair in a tangle of knots, she was startlingly attractive; her dark eyes velvet pools of haunting sadness. She bared her lips at him as he came forward to see to her dismount. She had spirit. She reminded him of a captured cat. He gave instructions to have her deposited in the appointed rooms, and disappeared to his own.

The attendant maid would look to the girls' bath and meal. The rest could wait till tomorrow. He could rest now, knowing that Dagr was alive as were his beloved. The rest of the madness he could sweep from his brain for the time being.

Brigida allowed herself be lowered into the hot fragranced bath. Her eyes scanned the surroundings; it was clear that she was in the Earl's rooms, by the rich weave of the tapestries and the generous fire. She winced as the cuts on her legs and arms met the water. The servant offered to bathe her, but she shook her head. Brigida waved her away to the corner, sinking beneath the water.

Brigida wept. Ignoring the fretting maid waiting to dry her, she wept bitter tears of loss, recalling the terror of the last few days. In her madness, she had run from her hiding place with Arinn, although she had heard Arinn screaming her name. She had seen Dagr frantically scanning the village for her, as he fought to preserve his life. She had sat frozen to the spot, traumatized by the brutal actions of the man she called her own. He had warned them that this evil would come to them.

But he had promised that the Earl Dumont would protect Arinn and her if he were to be struck down. The Earl Dumont? What had the Earl to do with them? It had all made little sense, and she hadn't believe him anyway. She wished that she had never seen him in battle, had never seen her handfast so brutally fearsome. When she had felt the press of a hand on her shoulder, she was sure that it was Dagr come to get her. The village was quiet, deathly quiet. She had turned and was quickly disappointed. They dragged her screaming and kicking, the ground tearing at her skin, her hands raw from clutching at anything that would keep her from being taken away. She could no longer hear Arinn calling for her. There was only the quiet talk amongst the soldiers. It seemed they were divided on what had happened here. One of them had untied her, and given her a horse to ride, one that had lost its master.

"My lord said *unharmed*" she had heard him hiss. Let us leave this place. It is cursed."

The water turned cold and she lay shivering. The maid crept closer, concern on her brow.

"My lady, you must come out of the water now. The Earl has ordered bread and meat for you, and some fine honey wine." She chattered while she dried Brigida gently. "It is best if you sit by the fire now." She led her to a stool by the hearth.

"There are some fresh linens and a dress hung for you. I do not know that it will fit you, but it is what we had left from...umm, left."

Brigida burst into fresh tears as the maid picked up a hair brush. The memory of Dagr brushing her hair made her ache strongly for home. If only she could know where he was, and why he had left her behind. But of course, he must have tried to find her. If only she had stayed with Arinn!

She lifted her arms to allow the nightdress to be placed over her head. She did not argue about being tucked into bed, grateful for the hot stone at her feet. The day crept to night and she drifted in and out of fitful dreams.

Brigida felt a coldness so deep in her body and spirit all night, that she was startled awake when a hot liquid pooled between her legs. She lifted the covers curiously, wondering what to make of the strange sensation. The maid woke with a start at Brigida's scream.

Richard jumped from his desk where he had been pouring over a letter, as sleep would not come. The maid howled in fear when Richard broke through the chamber door.

He was beside Brigida in three steps, eyes on the linens stained red. Brigida looked at him in horror before she fainted, an anguished moan filling the room.

Richard turned to the maid, who was pacing the floor and talking loudly to herself, averting her gaze from the bed.

"Quiet Sarah! Run quickly to the still room! Wake the woman there, and tell her to bring her potions. RUN!"

He threw more wood on the fire, and put a pot of water on the hook in the hearth. A fine thing this was, if anyone were to see him, playing nursemaid to a captured wench. He remembered Dagr with his heart on his sleeve, as he had asked him for protection of his women and his lands. One day, when he found Dagr again, he would tell him that he had done all he could, and it would be with an honest heart. Nothing could be done for the child that was lost, but he would be damned if he let the girl die also.

The old woman hurried her way up the stairs. What did the stupid girl mean; blood in the bed? Probably another one of those mishaps when her lord got a little carried away in the bedchamber. The Earl Dumont was a strange one. But he was good to her, always had believed in her ways. Well, she would find out. She should have made the girl carry her basket of tinctures and herbs. It was getting heavier every year.

"Old woman," Richard addressed her as she hurried now to the bed. "What can be done? Do you have the right potion?"

She lifted the covers. Richard turned away.

"The room needs to be kept warm. Here, Sarah! Bring the pot of water, do not spill it you fool! I think it best for m'lord to wait in his chamber. I will tend to the...the..." She waved her hand at the bed.

"This is not my doing," Richard whispered to her under his breath.

"I am not a judge of what goes on here. Now, leave me to it, if you want her to live."

She gave him a reassuring look and lifted her chin showing him the door. She could afford to be informal at her age, especially considering all the secrets she had kept for him.

She woke Brigida with a firm tap to the face, waving a small vial under her nose. Brigida sputtered as she drank a disgusting liquid pushed toward her. The bitter herbs would signal the womb to stop the flow of blood. The woman cleaned her with a soft cloth that she had dipped in scorching hot water and something with a strong stench of alcohol.

"When dealing with things of this nature," the old woman instructed the pale faced maid, "it is best to keep things clean. More would be saved if the doctors listened to me, the ignorant fools."

Brigida whimpered as the cloth touched her. She drank some of a different kind of tea, and did not complain as the old woman laid a poultice on her aching belly. They changed her nightdress and laid her back down in clean sheets.

"There, there," the old woman chanted. "You will survive. You are not the first that has lost a babe. You are young. There will be others."

She sighed and shook her head. A candle lit her way as she circled the room, incantations rolling off her tongue.

Sarah stuffed herself into the furthest corner of the room. It was true what they said in the kitchen. The old woman from the still room was a witch!

Brigida was weak at daybreak, but the old woman was certain that she would recover well. No fever. She left instructions with Sarah for Brigida's care, leaving the pouch of dried tea, and the other herbs for soaking into her washing water, wrapped in tiny linen pouches. A small vial containing spirits was to be used sparingly in the wash water as well. No letting her in the tub until she was good and healed. She should come later to the still room for a special tonic. She would order the girls food from the cook herself. Broths and greens only. She knocked on Richard's chamber door.

"All is well, my lord." She looked at Richard's tired face. "Here you are. Add these powders to your tea. You will sleep. There is nothing to worry about now."

He bowed his head to her. She ran her fingers through his hair. It had been this way always, since he had been a boy and had hid in the still room, eating her warm crusty bread with herbed butter, and listening to her sing as she pounded dried plants with the mortar and pestle. She had her own oven, and her bread was filled with delicious seeds, the best ones were the ones burnt right onto the crust. It had been Dagr's favourite place too...his mother had been in Richard's fathers employ then, and she had often worked in the still room as well.

"Thank you. You have put my mind at ease. Is there anything you need that I can provide for you?"

"What does an old woman like me need? Maybe some lambskin to put in my shoes. I feel the cold more now. That will be all, my lord."

"You shall have it, and enough for your cot to sleep on as well."

"Your kindness is always taken to heart. I will not forget! But mind you take better care next time my lord. Some girls cannot take a rough man."

She left the room laughing under her breath, as Richard shrugged his shoulders and waved his hand to dismiss her words.

<hr />

Brigida slept for days it seemed. She obediently took the tonic even though it made her mouth cry out for water. She drank her broth as instructed, chewing the steamed greens. As soon as she had taken her meal, she would close her eyes again and drift off. She was searching for a dream. A dream of Dagr, of Arinn, of their home. But the dream never came and she wondered if losing the child meant she was cursed with dreamless sleeps. Rest and forgetfulness, these were hers in abundance.

Richard came to see her when she slept. Her colour had returned and her hair had been brushed out to a dark mahogany. He could not help but notice the full tenderness of her lips, nor the way her lashes lay upon her face as she slept. Once, she had opened her eyes suddenly and peered at him with furrowed brow. And in that moment, Richard had felt a stirring in his heart. She was more than fair, she was mystery, and that was a dangerous elixir for a man like Richard,

242

whose appetite for new discoveries overshadowed his good sense.

"Have you learned her name yet?" Richard asked Sarah, who was terrified to have him speak to her.

"Yes, my lord. Brigida. But she has not said anything else," she hurriedly added to discourage further questions.

"Brigida. A Germanic name. Fitting, I suppose."

Sarah had no idea what he could mean and sat quietly watching him from under her eyelids as he sat by the bed, now and then pacing towards the mullioned window. He could be handsome, she thought, his hair grazing his shoulders, so starkly black against his white shirt, if he did not look so frighteningly stern. He had the build of the young and strong. She shuddered. Imagine having to attend his bed? He was probably vile and acted like a beast. She had heard that he asked things of his lovers that were too disturbing for words although she could not think of what that might be.

Richard thought about having to leave at daybreak. He would leave instructions with the old woman. She was the only one he could talk to about this sensitive situation.

"Sarah."

"Yes, my lord?"

"I will be away for a week or more. You are not to leave Brigida unattended, but if you do need to leave the room, lock the door behind you. The old woman will know what to do if there are problems. Do not, hear me...do not go asking anyone else what needs doing. Am I clear?"

He knew that he frightened her, but it was better this way. If she was scared she would be less likely to gossip. He held back the annoyed feeling creeping over him. He had very little use for females who could not keep their courage around him.

Richard leaned over the bed and touched Brigida's head lightly in parting. He whispered something to her. She opened her eyes, and surprised him with the emptiness within, before slowly turning her head towards the wall.

Richard felt an odd impulse to offer her a tentative bow. "My lady," he said simply, and was gone.

Something about that look...Richard tore down the stairs to the still room. He felt a cavernous hole in his chest. It was overwhelming and took his breath away.

"Old woman," he said in greeting as he entered the still room. "I will be away for a weeks' time, you will be in charge of the girl...Brigida. If anyone asks, only you and Sarah are to attend her."

He sat down in his customary seat by the fire and she handed him some mead and bread.

"She has shaken you, my lord," Hannah observed. "Well, it is not surprising, coming from the Pagan's house."

He looked at her sharply. "What do you know of this?"

"Kitchen talk only, my lord." She offered a tooth-gapped grin. Richard relaxed.

"Strange, I was saying goodbye to her, whispering, and she opened her eyes and gave me a most disturbing look. I felt a great emptiness right away."

He drank his mead; his legs stretched in front of him, and set his cup down for more.

"Aahh. She is able to talk without words. Now you know how she feels. She has told you."

Hannah shook her head at him. "This is not a wench for you to play with. Leave her alone."

"You assume too much, as usual, old woman. I am merely keeping her in my care for the Pagan."

"Do you think I do not remember... the gifted, golden son of the most attractive couple at court?" Hannah stood recalling a memory. "He is the only one you have ever been able to trust your life to. I know you, my dark, handsome lord. It will not be safe for you to shift your love for him to her. I can see a broken heart, and for that I do not even need my Sight."

"Ridiculous! It is you who should be careful," he chided, but gave her a teasing smile. Besides Dagr, Hannah was the only one who truly knew who he was and to whom he could speak plainly.

"Is there anything you can give me, some tonic that might be useful for healing wounds? And some powders for dreams." He knew that she would guess what he was up to; there was no need to explain.

"You might bring winter garments as well," she advised. "The seasons are changing."

He nodded, as always, her wisdom made him humble. She had always looked out for him *and* Dagr. Friends like Hannah were rare at the home of a powerful earl. A noble like him had no-one to confide in, and if he did do, he would find himself quickly betrayed. When he called her 'old woman', only they knew that he was addressing her as 'friend'. It was their long time code. She handed him a small parcel and sat down heavily, a sigh on her breath.

Richard smiled and knelt on one knee for her blessing. "I will be careful, Hannah, and bring back news."

She nodded. She was used to his comings and goings. If only he could choose less dangerous habits. But that was part of his appeal.

He rode like hell fire to the sea. Another day, he would brave the images of the burnt out village, but not today. For now, he would satisfy his guilt by dropping supplies for Dagr in the cave that had served them in their childhood years. If Dagr was alive, he would know to look there, out of necessity. There was no other safe place nearby to look for provisions. Richard scrambled down the rock face until he reached the cave, a place safe from the wind and intruders. He found remnants of the last fire they had lit, a bittersweet memory now, but one that still had the power to tremble his frame. Laying the provisions towards the back, he stood undone as he thought of Dagr standing before him. He would kill to bring that moment back, to have Dagr safe in his embrace, forgiveness on his lips. Or better yet, a whip in his hand.

For the few days that he visited the manor home of one of his knights, discussing various details pertaining to quelling rebellion, Richard was, at best, distracted. All his thoughts returned to what he might find in the village on his way toward home. He had ridden out alone, but someone from the manor house would escort him back.

It would be reported that Richard Dumont was seen making a tour of the burnt remains of the cottages, and that he was satisfied with the work the soldiers had done. The Earl was not one to suffer the Old Religion well; he had done his duty and stamped out the festering wound of an uncompliant pack of Pagans for the King. He had even left the mark of the cross and a drawing of a road leading to hell on a scroll, for anyone to see, staked to the remains of the manor. He was eager to leave the place it seemed, teeming as it was with tortured ghosts, because he rode his horse hard until he was within sight of his castle. Richard's enemies had one less thing to point their finger at as far as his loyalties were concerned.

Richard knocked gently on the door of the room next to his upon his return. He knocked harder yet, a reply not forthcoming from within. He tried the lock. Open! Inside, the bed was made and the fire was out.

He raced down the stairs towards the still room. His heart pounded as he imagined the worst. Brigida had taken fever while he was away and had died. Feeling sick yet from the sight and smell of Dagr's ransacked village, he ran into the still room paled and with troubled brow.

Time moved slowly as he observed the usual calm of the still room. Hannah stood at the table, bottles arranged ready for filling with tinctures and vinegars, the air ripe with the heady smells of pounded herbs and seeds. She turned towards him, the smile on her face turning to concern as she looked into his dark eyes.

"My lord," Hannah bowed ever so slightly. "Whatever is the matter?"

"Where is the girl?" He looked at her, willing her words to be other than what he feared.

"Why..." Hannah began her answer, but was interrupted by a loud clatter at the garden door.

"Hannah!"

Richard heard her voice through many layers of relief. There she stood, a wooden bowl crashing to the floor, calendula flowers in a race to catch up, her face radiant with a smile, if only for an instant.

Brigida curtsied and lowered her gaze. She looked then to Hannah who was reaching to take her hand, and hold Brigida to herself as the girl took to trembling with a vengeance.

"Now look what you have done, my lord!" Hannah clucked. You have upset my still room." She smiled as Brigida hid behind her.

Richard stood stuck to the floor, his face completely readable. What he had not counted on was that she would have such a delightful smile; or such light in her face. So she lived! He tried to look his most receptive, but he knew that the surprise of seeing her had arranged his face into something far more alarming.

He moved to help Hannah with the flowers, but she waved him away. Sometimes he truly forgot his place, she thought.

"Now my lord, you will not be troubled with this. See here, Brigida has recovered well, my tonics have done the trick."

Brigida stared at Richard bending to help the old woman; it reminded her of Dagr clearing their supper dishes, a most baffling habit.

He recovered himself and stood looking at Brigida as she tried to fade into the walls. He made her uncomfortable, and he could hardly blame her. He sat as he was bid by Hannah and took her offer of mead. Sometimes he also wanted to fade into the walls. He was suddenly tired and cared not what anyone thought. None of them spoke for a long while, the powerful Earl sitting with wine in hand, watching the movements of the girl he thought too beautiful to have to lend a hand in anything but love. She fit into the dress that had been found for her as if it had been tailored. She was slender and lithe, her dark hair hanging down her back in a braid, with a ribbon laced throughout. Her breasts pushed at the edge of the neckline, skin bronzed yet smooth as silk, boasting the sheen of oils. That was a trademark of Dagr's, Richard knew. She seemed at ease in the still room. He wondered if she was in training; or maybe an assistant to a wise woman already.

Brigida trembled where she worked. What manner of noble was this, at home in the still room, Hannah holding some kind of power over his ability to thwart her familiarity towards him.

What would he do with her, now that she was clear of falling to fever? What would her future hold? Would she ever find her way back to the man and woman she loved?

"Will you eat, my lord?" Hannah shoved some bread and butter on the table, and a bowl of broth.

"I will, Hannah, thank you." He looked towards Brigida and Hannah motioned him to invite her to join them.

"Come eat with us Brigida," he commanded.

It was not an invitation as such, but it would do.

Brigida turned abruptly when she heard her name on his lips. Her eyes shot fire, but she came obediently to the table and sat. Was she to break bread with the Earl then, in this strange twist of events, where Hannah seemed to have him tamed to an acquiescence unbefitting of a noble? It seemed so, because there he was, handing her a piece of bread torn with his own hands, his eyes burning through her, leaving her in a quandary between a consuming fear and a most unwelcome desire.

"Are your rooms to your liking?" he asked her.

Brigida nodded, shy to make her voice heard.

He wanted to ask more questions, but Hannah took over the small talk and told him of Brigida's skill with plants, and that she would appreciate having her help from now on, if he had no other plans for her keep.

He had no plans and said that it had been settled then, Brigida could work in the still room during the days, and he would meet with her in the evenings, as his schedule allowed, to hear of her progress. He was glad that Hannah would have company once more. And he understood the importance of having an apprentice to take over.

"Are you planning to keep me here forever?" Brigida asked boldly, although her eyes held fear.

He smiled and threw her off guard. "Time will tell, my lady. Only as long as you need protection, and that is yet to be determined."

"I should think you are the one I need protection from," she replied, her eyes now searching his face. "Until few days ago, I was well protected, and free from fear. Do you mean to be my captor and my protector at once?"

Hannah shook her head and got up from the table.

Richard stood and leaned over the table towards Brigida. She held her place. His lust had risen suddenly and he felt weak. A bold maiden was his ultimate challenge.

"I will see you in my rooms tonight."

He swallowed the rest of his mead in one gulp and gave Hannah a peck on the cheek.

"Send some herb, Old Woman, my man will come to collect it, and some more of those sleeping powders."

He left with a flourish and a slam to the still room door.

Brigida laid her head down and wept.

Hannah boiled some water for tea. It seemed everyone one of them would need help from the plant world today.

CHAPTER 31

When Richard opened his chamber door to her that evening, he had a plan firmly in mind. She would stay as an apprentice to Hannah, and he would move her to the room assigned to still room help. Hannah would tend to her comforts and protection. The still room was an essential part of the castle, the herb garden as well. Under the guise of assisting the physician, Hannah was considered irreplaceable, her knowledge of preparing salves, tinctures and teas allowed the doctor to focus on the important matters of healing the noble family.

Richard's father had been fortunate to have Dagr's mother, Lara, as his mystic. She also had acted officially as the apprentice Hannah was training. Dagr's mother's skills included reading the stars and some alchemical work, but these were practices that Richard had only observed when Dagr had let him into his mother's rooms, where she taught Dagr her craft.

It was a small, close knit group, Richard's father practically obsessed with creating a safe place for Lara to do her work, hidden from the prying eyes of the clergy. As a boy, he had been comforted by the closeness between his father and Dagr's parents. They had spent days on end hunting, just the three of them, a joyful group of friends. Now, with the perspective of a grown man, he understood why his father had taken such interest in the handsome couple. And he could hardly blame him; his tastes in bed were inherited.

As Hannah reached her frail years, she would need a new assistant, and if Brigida proved to be skilled, he could justify her stay. He would instruct her to say that she had been the unwilling victim of Bretel's ways; she could plead to be kept, for where could she go, her community wiped out? It would be his duty to find her a place in his employ. The old gardener would not mind some spry help either. There, it was settled in his mind. He was sure Brigida would agree.

She came in pulling the scent of the still room behind her. She was flushed with anxiety, her face hot as his eyes roamed her body without a hint of gentlemanly manner. He caught himself as he looked into her eyes and pointed to the table where he hoped she would join him for a late meal. She nodded and sat with her back to the wall. He acknowledged her fear with a scowl, and poured her a goblet of wine.

"Will you drink with me, Brigida?"

She took the wine and watched him over the goblet as she drank.

The liquid must have given her courage, Richard decided, because her expression became bolder. He was on fire for her and it made him angry. This was not what Dagr had meant to happen, he was sure.

"Will no one question how I have come to share your meal?" she whispered, eyes pointing to the boy tending the fire and looking furtively in their direction.

Richard gestured towards the boy, who shot up like a hare from where he had been kneeling.

"Leave us."

The boy bowed and exited the room as fast as his legs could carry him.

Richard paced the room before deciding to sit down. The room was warm, he wished to undo his shirt, but that would most likely scare her more.

"I would like to explain the reason for your stay here." He took her silence for agreement. A bead of sweat had risen on her upper lip, as the wine, the fire and stress no doubt had warmed her blood. Richard had a thought of kissing it off.

She raised her eyebrows at him, signaling him to continue.

He drank, not sure how to make sense of the collapse of her world, which words to use.

"You have suffered at my hand," he began. What happened, to your village, was something that I can hardly explain, except to say that there was little choice in the matter." He could see that she doubted every word that he had spoken. "One could say that the politics of a land are not always in the hands of an Earl."

"You do not take responsibility then?" She looked at him blankly.

He wondered at her courage. Perhaps she felt that she had lost so much that there was nothing left to lose?

"I take responsibility, my lady. As the lord of this castle, and closest friend to your handfast, I can confess to you that I am responsible."

He watched her face as she worked out her emotions.

"Friend?! Have you left your senses? Does a friend dispossess one of their village, their family, their life?"

She was standing now, her breast heaving and her eyes burning through him.

"You forget yourself, my lady. You're speaking to someone who has the power to have you...well, never mind."

"I know nothing of how to speak to you, and have little care left for what you do with me. Kill me. Please. I am good as dead without the people I love...my child. Dagr taught me to bow to no man, unless he commanded my respect."

She sat down, tears pouring.

Richard ached inside for the man he also loved. That was the part of him that was sane. The other part, the one that had little value for propriety, wanted to rip her bodice and expose her breasts, and have her tied to a bed post for his lustful pleasure.

He pushed his hair from his face and sat down beside her. She did not look up, but continued to sob.

"When you address me, you will say, 'my lord', unless we are alone, and then if you wish to. You will curtsy, you will pretend that you are afraid of me. You will play the part of the servant. This will keep you safe. If you do not, I cannot protect you. Do you understand?"

She nodded; her head in her hands. "Why am I here? Can you tell me, or am I to continue wondering?"

Richard sighed. He would tell her but was sure that it would make no difference to her grief.

"Dagr and I grew up in this castle together. Our lives have been intertwined in battle and in court life. Dagr was my knight, he may have told you?"

She shook her head.

"We shared similar thoughts on life, but the one place where Dagr made his own life dangerous was in his adherence to the Old Religion and his views on...women."

He stopped and saw that she was listening attentively. This was information about her beloved that she was not privy to. Perhaps there had been no need to burden her with stories of life at court.

"As I said earlier, there are political battles in England that prohibit me from always having my own way, and this is true of every man sworn to the King, our power is loosely held. I have enemies and they watch my every move, including my tolerance of Dagr's practices. I was held to protecting the laws and religion of the land, and what happened to your village, was something I could not prevent."

"I do not know about these things, but surely there was something you could have done? There must have been a way for you to help us, to help Dagr?"

"I did what could be done, my lady. I came with a warning, I begged him to save himself."

Richard shuddered as his memory of Dagr that day re-surfaced.

"But, as I knew he would, he refused to abandon his people, to abandon you, and he faced the battle like the honored knight that he is. Believe me; I have wept my own tears."

Richard stoked the fire and stood with his back to her.

At long last she found her words. "I have lost his child. And it is your doing."

He winced and turned towards her. "Is there anything that I can do to make up for your loss, my lady?"

"What can you give me that will replace the love that Dagr buried within me, or the time lost from my beloved Arinn?"

"Arinn. She is Dagr's other handfast?"

Brigida nodded. "She is also my handfast. We were a family. Not what your religion would consider marriage, or proper, but I love her...and him."

Richard stared at her, trying to comprehend the life that Dagr had led with the two women, and the kind of love that had bound them despite their fear of being found out.

"How long must I stay here? Can you help me be re-united with Dagr and Arinn?"

"I do not know. It will be tricky for me to look for him, and to make contact. My movements are rarely secret. He will have to be the one that gives the signal to send you back. He will know when it is safe. I am watched and you will be too. Time will tell."

She looked so utterly downcast that he almost abandoned all good sense to reach for her. But he knew she was nowhere near ready to receive his touch.

"You can do something for me," she said finally.

Richard's eyes turned hopeful, there *was* something!

"You can find a way to help them survive. If you love him, do not let them starve. There will be nowhere now that he can go to be safe. That much I know. I could not bear the thought..." And she broke into fresh tears.

The next few weeks flew by for Brigida as she settled into her life as Hanna's assistant. Her day began early, in the garden. There, she would follow the old gardener about, who taught her about the herbs she did not know already, what to harvest and when, which weeds were for eating, and which for pulling, what to deadhead, what to cut all the way back.

Hannah saw to her move into the tiny room next to hers, Richard had sent a tapestry to cheer the old stone walls, and an extra sheepskin for her cot, matching the one he had sent for Hannah. There was a new dress for the garden, one for the Lord's Day, and a cloak to keep her warm. She had never slept in better linens except when she had stayed in his apartment.

Richard had brought her things to the room himself. He trusted no one to the chore. When she unpacked her parcel of clothing, she had found a brush gilded in silver wrapped in a new kirtle. She looked up at him, a tentative smile on her lips.

"A brush fit for a servant girl?"

"It pleases me to give it to you," he replied. "Will you accept it?"

"Yes. Thank you...for all the comforts you have afforded me. I know it is not customary, I am..."

Her voice trailed off, and he knew that although she was grateful she would rather be naked and destitute with Dagr at her side than dressed like a queen at his. Well, there was nothing he could do about that. They were both aching for something they could not have.

"I will be gone for several weeks, longer maybe. I bid you goodbye, and look forward to hearing about all the new things you will have learned upon my return."

He turned on his heel and was about to open the still room door when he had a thought.

"Do you read, Brigida?"

"Some. I could learn more, if there was need? To help in the record keeping for Hannah, perhaps?"

She was sharp, he realized. She would learn and understood that it would not be wasted on her if there was not a real purpose. She had no standing any more, after all. He winked at her.

"I might be able to procure an old herbal."

The brilliant smile that she gave back in gratitude would have brought him to his knees before her if he had dared. He left before he made a fool of himself.

For her part, Brigida opened her heart just a little. Maybe he had had no choice after all in her capture. Maybe his heart was not as fierce as his countenance.

Brigida loved the activities of an herbalist. She took great pride in pounding the seeds just so, relieving Hannah of the hardest of the work. Preparing and decocting tinctures by the cycle of the moon was especially satisfying. She memorized the incantations that Hannah spoke over the salves and simple medicines. They would be stronger this way, Hannah had said.

The two women agreed on what Dagr had always done, by attending to one's daily grooming. Lara, Dagr's mother, had always smelled fresh with the scent of flowers in her hair. They prepared rinses, making heavenly scents which Hannah put into small vials for Richard to give as gifts when visiting nobles and their wives came to stay.

By the time Richard rode back into the courtyard after travelling far longer than he had planned on, he found Brigida firmly entrenched in still room schedule. She was away on a gathering trip for wild roots with the gardener when Richard ran down to the garden to see her. Hannah told him that her life had never been easier, the girl could outwork a man, and her memory of recipes and certain procedures was truly impressive.

"Will you give this to her, Hannah?" he asked as he handed her a parcel wrapped in plain paper.

"Why not give it to her yourself?" Hannah winked at him mischievously.

"Put it in her room...please." He grinned at her. "I will see her after supper. Has she been well, Hannah?

"As well as could be hoped for. She carries her sadness more lightly now." She gave him a sideways glance. "She is not yours to keep, my lord."

"I am not a complete fool!" he barked. "Just send her up, old woman! I am too tired to argue with you."

Richard ordered a hot bath. He had been travelling for days, and his body ached from all that time in the saddle. A supply of wine by his side, he languished in the hot water and yelled for more. He had found a vial of fragranced oil by the tub. He sniffed it and was brought up short by a memory. The smell of Dagr's skin, opulent with forest plants. He poured some into the water and wondered correctly if Brigida had infused it.

He allowed himself another memory, one of him and Dagr bedding a particularly winsome girl, her mouth on Dagr's cock, his own handsome prick deep in her cunt. It would have been perfect if he could have reached his hand to pull Dagr's face to his for a kiss, but Dagr, smiling, had shook his head. Dagr had taken pleasure in teasing him, it was as far as he allowed himself to go with Richard in those days.

254

The memory stoked his fire and he found his hand on his erection, the oil in the water making his skin slick and easy to bring himself close to orgasm. He held back. The thought of Brigida in the room while he longed for release was something he could look forward to. Sexual tension, even if it was only on his own part, would be delicious.

By the time Brigida arrived, he was dressed in his finest clothes. He knew that he was striking, his raven hair fragranced and held back with a blue ribbon, his legs and buttocks accentuated by the fine cut of his riding leathers, the shirt starkly white against his olive skin. He was in a fine mood, and cheered on by the wine, he greeted her with more gallantry than he afforded even the most welcome of female suitors.

She stood in the doorway in her best dress, her hair in its customary braid, her skin aglow from the days in the garden and riding the hills. She held his book, and her face was lit by a smile. She did not want to be happy to see him, she wanted to see him for the rogue that he was, the man who had torn her from her family and home. But when he swung the door open to her knock, she was taken aback by his fierce beauty, and the smell of his skin made her weak with confusion. It had been a mistake, infusing oils with pine and bark, for he smelled so much like Dagr that it made her think of wanting his skin on her tongue. They stood in silence for mere seconds, but in the space of memories, seconds stretched into minutes.

"Welcome," he said, bowing his head and extending his hand to her.

She took it and trembled at the shock of his energy. Startled as well, Richard stared hard into her eyes. She lowered them and pulled her hand away, but they both stood on the edge of sanity, arrested by lust.

"My lord," Brigida said to Richard's complete surprise, and dipped into a low curtsy.

CHAPTER 32

Iona signalled and the mists of time receded. She talked them through the journey back, gently reminding them that they would remember everything, every nuance of the moment they had just experienced. They were nodding, their eyes still closed, hands clasped together. When she told them to, they looked up to the pain and joy of recognition. Richard forgot everything but the need to kiss Sahara's lips, and she instantly understood that her life had just gone from complicated to impossible, and that at least in this moment, she didn't care.

He was at her side in an instant, pulling her out of her chair, his hand under her chin, looking for her mouth. There was no need to check what Iona was doing. Richard knew that she had planned this down to the moment, and that it would somehow serve her to see him undone by Sahara. But he would think about that later.

Sahara cried out as Richard ripped her shirt to threads, violently exposing her straining nipples to the soft light of the room.

He carried her to the bedroom and threw her on the bed, Iona steps behind.

Sahara, fingers rubbing her aching nipples now bound tightly by the gold rings, begged him to kiss her again. He threw his shirt to the floor and bent over her to make love to her lips, the lips he'd been longing to kiss for centuries. She moaned and offered her nipples to his mouth, asking him to slip the rings off, which he did, with determined teeth and a skilled tongue. She yelled his name, she held her hand out to Iona who had nothing on but a brilliant opal pendant hanging tantalizingly between her supple breasts.

Her love for the two of them lighting up her elfin eyes, Iona sank to the bed and dropped soft little bites on her neck, coaxing Sahara into giving herself to them without reservation.

Richard had no intention of waiting for an invitation. He would take Sahara, and he wouldn't be gentle. He had her jeans off in seconds, his eyes devouring every bit of her bare slit, his cock demanding its pleasure.

Sahara lips formed into a perfect "O" when she saw Richard's sizable cock, with its thick and velvety tip, veins running the length of it; not quite the length of Aiden's but exquisite in form. She was already wet, and Richard didn't want to miss out on a taste of her. His tongue on her clit exploded a series of sensations. She rocked her hips and pushed herself into his face.

Richard could smell Iona's scent close by, she was pushing her ass towards him and he knew what she needed. He lifted his hand and spanked her soundly; she deserved every bit of pain for being so clever in bringing them all together. He was torn between anger and love. Iona had brought him face to face once more with a side of himself that had been long buried, and she'd done it with the degree of cunning that he was beginning to expect.

But now Sahara was calling to him, her fingers spreading herself, showing him the place she needed him to enter, that delicious bit of cunt he was hungrily eyeing. She was ready and he thrust hard into her. Over and over, he pounded her tight slit, her moans urging him on.

"Come on me, my lady, come all over my cock, or I'll keep pounding you until you break."

Sahara shook her head.

"I said, come! Say, "I'm coming for you, my lord." Something of the past tore into Richard's memory, a wild longing to see Sahara at his mercy.

Sahara looked him in the eye and recognized the cruel but attentive lover from her dreams and she whispered, trembling violently – "I'm coming my lord"...drenching his cock with her pleasure.

He waited until he couldn't feel her muscles contracting around him anymore then pulled out to direct his attention to the breathless Iona on hands and knees, waiting her turn. He roared as he entered her, every ripple of her clamping down on him, and fucked her while Sahara kissed Iona's tender mouth.

Richard came like a king, deep into Iona's silky folds, his hands pulling her hips hard to him, knowing that he was bruising her.

She howled like a wolf when she came, and they both felt her powerful magic fall upon them, bewitching them to each other.

Afterwards, Richard brought them tea in bed and a plate of cheesecake, which they accepted happily. He couldn't remember another evening of greater pleasure. Occupying a comfortable chair by the bed, a bowl of herb in hand, he watched the two of them find release in each other's arms. Then they called him back to join them.

Later, Sahara cried softly in Richard's arms until they fell asleep, for what could she tell Aiden? How could she protect him from the fallout of their destiny? What could she tell Holly, who was the innocent in all this?

Richard woke up suddenly at four in the morning. The women were curled into each other; Sahara's face nestled to Iona's breasts.

He smiled. They were indeed beautiful, peacefully sleeping like two wood nymphs completely comfortable in their nakedness and their love for each other. He ran his hands over their silky skin, his fingers itching to find their moistness, but he settled for a stroke of their breasts. They moaned in their sleep and pulled closer to each other, Sahara's lips finding Iona's nipple to take in her mouth.

Richard's cock was fully erect, and he thought of waking them. Better to let them sleep, he decided, he would hope for their attention at a decent hour.

He went silently to the bathroom and ran a hot shower. His hands found his manhood too insistent to ignore. There was no point in avoiding his own needs, all of him now lathered up with Iona's delicious smelling soap, the one she always insisted he use. His strong hand slid gracefully along his thick erection, remembering the taste of Sahara on his lips. He wouldn't think about whom Sahara had waiting for her at home. Right now, he wanted her to himself, to think of how expertly she had taken every drop of his cum in her mouth, and it had been more than he had spilled in a while. His hand gripped tighter.

When Sahara woke, it was to the smell of coffee brewing. Richard sat in the living room, showered and dressed, the day's paper in his hand. He had the look of a man who owned the world, and was quite comfortable with the fact.

"You've been out already?" She rubbed her eyes, and pulled on her hair, standing naked before him.

He smiled a dazzling smile and offered to get her a cup.

"Good morning Bri...Sahara. You're beautiful." She stood there allowing herself to be roamed by his greedy eyes.

"I'll have coffee, yes."

She came over to him and he laid the paper down. She sat in his lap, his legs hard under her soft skin. Cuddling into him, she looked at his face, such a darkly handsome countenance, so different from all the things she loved about Aiden's kinder look; and yet so familiar.

"How can I serve you coffee with you sitting in my lap?"

"You can't, not this minute. I promise I'll get up soon."

"Please don't," he whispered into her ear, his one hand sliding under her bottom, the other hand holding him to her.

"I'm dying to fill you with my cum again."

Richard's boldness made him irresistible. Sahara shivered and

felt her sex tighten. Her nipples perked longer. She smiled at his blatant stare, and the way his tongue slid over his lips.

"We have so much to discover still," she said. "Yesterday I found
out why Aiden is such an intense part of my heart, and now there's
you…I…"

Richard reached for the blanket and wrapped her in it. "Aiden is
the man you love?"

She looked at him, surprised that he had not put the pieces together, but of course, he knew nothing of Aiden.

"Aiden is the man you used to love, Richard. Aiden is Dagr."

He sat with jaw tensed and his mind reeling from image to image, thought to thought, realizing that his heart was pounding. His
hands tightened around her and she moved to ease the grip. He
looked down at his tattoo.

"Dagr, a warrior, of course." A memory began to form in his sub-
conscious, but he couldn't quite grasp it.

He went to the kitchen to pour Sahara some coffee. There were
no co-incidences, he knew that, from his meeting Iona, to her strong
hold on his heart, to the things they had discovered last night; the
three of them re-uniting in this lifetime. He was open to so many
things that Iona had awoken in him and had taught him.

Today, many of his tastes and desires made more sense than they
had before the regression. His need for the richness of life, his desires
in the bedroom, his love for Europe and England; his natural ability
towards the businesses he ran. But one thing he had not known, and
that was about Aiden. Sahara was right, there was much to discover
yet. What he wanted to explore most right now though, was the love
between Iona and Sahara, and who was the *other* person waiting for
Sahara at home?

By the time he brought Sahara her coffee, she was wrapped in
Iona's arms, a small fey creature happily catered to by Iona's attention. How would he survive the instant desire they brought to him?
They were so bloody playful and passionate. He could watch them all
day.

"Darling," Iona purred, "any left for me?"

"Of course," he smiled, and kissed her, his tongue running over
her lower lip languidly. "I'm going out for pastries; I suppose there's
no use in saying 'behave yourselves'?"

"No, no point," Iona replied. "She's too yummy for me to ignore."

"I'd have to agree," he said with a laugh. "I'm having trouble
keeping my hands off her as well." He brought Iona her demitasse of

coffee and left for the bakery.

Sahara turned to sit in Iona's lap. Facing each other, they explored each other's eyes, their kisses sweet.

"Mmm. Richard is rakishly handsome, so much like he was, but softer, a little. I'm not good at denying myself delicious men, Iona."

"And you shall have him," Iona promised. "He is awake now to his memories, and I guess he's made it plain that he wants you. You were a great love of his life before. He's a very intense man Sahara, and he has many of the same desires that he had previously. You used to be scared of his requests...although you grew to love even those. I think that we should explore slowly."

"But why? Why do we have to find out slowly? I don't understand why you know and I can't. Iona, you're hiding something from me! What can't I know?"

"It's complicated darling, please be patient."

"I can do it myself, you know," Sahara stated defiantly. I know how to go back."

"No! Don't, Sahara! I'll take you, I promise."

"What are you afraid of, Iona?"

Iona turned her face away. "I just think that you might land somewhere you don't want to."

"But what does that *mean*? You're being obstinate and it makes me think I can't trust you."

"Do what you want then!" Iona got up and went to the kitchen. But she knew that Sahara couldn't go back without her. She had already made sure of that.

"Iona! Please don't spoil things. I'll wait. I promise."

Iona's smile made it all worth the giving in. "Come Sahara. Shower?" And she pulled Sahara to the bathroom where she took great care in washing her hair and rubbing oils into her skin; Sahara forgetting her worries and cares, allowing Iona's hands to please her. By the time they got out, Richard had brewed fresh coffee and the table was laid for breakfast. He *was* spectacular.

"I've got to go home," Sahara said.

The sadness in her voice was not lost on either Richard or Iona.

"If I may ask," Richard began, "you've mentioned Aiden, but who is the other person that waits for you?"

She looked at him and her pain was clear. "Holly."

His breath caught. A woman. This was going to be more complicated than he had thought. Somehow he had thought that she'd say she'd been joking, that there was no one else.

"Is Holly?"

"I love her," Sahara interrupted. "She's not like us Richard. She's young and trusting and has nothing to do with our past lives together, or our mystics habits. I don't want to hurt her. Aiden is completely besotted with her. If I hurt her, I hurt him. What a mess!"

"Of course," he nodded. He wondered how she would explain their connections…or would she?

She read his mind. "I'll be honest, somehow, sometime. Aiden already has some idea about Iona, but really, even he doesn't know much, yet. Aiden, however, is a man of open mind and heart. Holly has only just been introduced to a polyamorous relationship and to tell her more now would…well, I can't tell her yet."

Sahara put her face in her hands and sighed. "Why, oh why, can I never do anything that doesn't hurt someone else?" Iona put out a comforting hand.

"I'm going to concentrate on my writing," she continued. "I must. I suppose it makes no sense for me to worry ahead, does it?"

"No darling," Iona said smoothly.

Richard caught the fear in Iona's voice. She was not clever enough to fool him, although Sahara seemed to believe the soft, placating words. He removed himself to another room, letting them work out the details of their lives. He had a million questions. Questions about Aiden…Dagr. Questions about what had happened between him and Brigida. Where had their relationship gone? And the most obvious place that his mind went to, Arinn.

How had he come to know Arinn? Could he Iona as easily with Aiden as she had shared him with Sahara if the occasion arose? Perhaps that was the most important question of all.

Richard knew Iona's persuasions well. After two days of maneuvering them through the quagmire of lives and lies, she would be craving the things he had the courage to offer her. He turned the key to the lock of the spare room. Iona had left everything as they liked it. Before he left for Europe, he would acquiesce to her desires, and she to his. Did Sahara know of this room, he wondered. His cock rose as he thought of Sahara by candlelight, secured tightly to the cuffs on the wall, Iona on her knees before her.

He heard Iona calling to him. He locked the room and found Sahara in the kitchen, ready to leave.

"Richard." Her hand extended towards him. He took it and kissed it, then met her lips eagerly.

"Safe travels," he murmured. "I look forward to more discoveries, when I return, perhaps?"

They both looked at Iona who nodded in agreement.

"I know that you're facing some difficult decisions, Sahara. But I'm not sorry about anything that's happened. That's my truth." He smiled rakishly and her heart turned over.

"Are you going away?" she asked.

"England." He said simply. And they all knew where in England he meant.

She left and they missed her immediately. He told Iona that he'd be back that evening, cupping her sex in the warmth of his hand. Richard was building up an appetite for Iona begging him for mercy.

"Go get the warming oil, Iona. You know the one." His hand left her and she moaned her disappointment.

"Not all day, Richard?"

"All day," he insisted.

She slipped off to get the oil, returning into his arms with soft, pleading eyes. She knew how difficult the day would be. Richard uncorked the small vial and ran a little of the oil onto his finger.

"Spread your legs a little more, sweetness," he whispered into her ear.

Iona groaned and spread, anxious to feel his touch. Richard ran his finger deftly along her clit, applying the oil. It began to warm instantly and she leaned into him, his hands already in her hair.

"Call me if you need to, but I forbid you to touch yourself, except to apply more. I'll need you to come for me as soon as I get here." His arms held her tighter, Iona was slipping to the floor.

"Please Richard. I'll need a shower."

Richard loved this side of Iona, the side that let him control her, that gave in to his commands. As much as she needed to be in charge of her life, it was a sweet pleasure to let go and let him give the orders.

"I'll call you when I'm on my way Iona. You can run a bath then. It will be my pleasure to bathe you my love, *after* I've fucked you with my fingers and you've come all over my hand."

Iona growled, eyes flashing, her teeth bared, ready to bite.

"Give me one small pleasure before you go, Richard. Tell me what you'll be wearing when you bathe me. I'll look forward to it."

"Of course."

He pulled her in closer, knowing that the heat of the oil was beginning its slow, sweet torture of her clit. He spread her legs with his, and lifted the edge of her chemise. Even the soft brush of air on her sex would make her writhe. He cupped his hands on her bottom.

"I'll wear all your favourite things, my love. The slim black trousers I had tailored in Italy, you know the ones; they hug my ass so well. The belt you bought me...the one that hugs your ass so well."

Iona's hands gripped his arms, her nails dug in.

"A fitted white shirt. My best Breitling watch. Are you getting the picture Iona? That pair of black shoes I picked up in Monaco, and the sandalwood cologne. Will that do it for you?"

"*Richard.*"

He felt along her inner thigh, it was wet.

"And will you leave your shirt on when you bathe me or take it off?"

"What would give my sweet whore more pleasure? You know that I want to please you more than anything."

"Off. With the taste of scotch on your tongue."

"Anything else?" Richard grazed his lips on Iona's neck.

"Bring something from your wine cellar for me. Something very expensive."

"Very expensive, Iona, or *very, very* expensive? Don't forget, I know your taste for luxury." His mouth found her ear.

"Oooh, Richard. The *most* expensive."

"Done. But you know what it will cost you."

"Anything, Richard."

Richard's hands pulled her head back, her flaming red hair tangled in his fist, as his lips travelled down her neck towards her breasts. He stopped short of her left nipple which was straining for his touch. Iona's hips moved towards him.

Richard let her go abruptly, his eyes blazing with cruel desire.

"By the way, darling, thank you for last night. Sahara is so very much to my taste. I want more." He wasn't asking.

"*Jusqu'a ce soir, belle!*" And then he was gone.

Iona lay crumpled on the floor, tears stinging her eyes, the long day stretching before her, the oil and her memory of Sahara and Richard painfully swelling her clit. But that was nothing compared to her memories of Dagr and the rasping sound of metal on metal as he slipped his sword out of its sheath, just before he cut her loose from the bonds that he had put her in.

CHAPTER 33

The miles stretched endlessly, it seemed, between her and the memories of the weekend. Although the sun was beaming warm through the truck windows, Sahara felt nothing of its comfort. In fact, the closer she got to home, the colder she felt. She touched her forehead. It was burning. She must be coming down with something, but she was rarely ill. Of course! Her body was reacting to her anxiety. She had to keep a clear head. This priority was no more important than the conversations she would have with Aiden, who would, undoubtedly want to begin his own regressions and discoveries.

She knew him, he would want details, and if she understood his passions the details would fuel them on. Sahara wasn't afraid that he wouldn't understand her indiscretions with Richard. If he did find her re-miss in not asking him first, he would probably find his way around to accepting it. But Aiden would, she was sure, be incensed about her putting Holly's emotions in harm's way. And she herself felt that the situation was impossible.

What possibly could be said to Holly to have her accept, on occasion, two other people into Sahara's already crowded bed? To ask her to believe in past lives, time travel, and a shape shifting sorceress? How to warn her about a jealous Iona, who would do anything to keep Sahara's love?

It was only a matter of time before Aiden and Iona would cross paths, this she knew for sure now. Aiden, so honest and , would feel obligated to spill his truth to Holly. The burden fell on Sahara, to protect her sweet natured and trusting lover. The heat in her head and the nausea in her stomach told her that it was too late, and that she was once more in the middle of a web so tangled that there was no way out. No way from escaping whatever work her, Aiden, Richard and Iona were to conduct in this lifetime and no way of denying that her heart had opened to the fourth person in their circle. Richard was already under her skin.

Goddess protect them all! She needed to call on her guides, and her constant companions from the fairly realm. Yes! She had resources; she had momentarily forgotten that she too had powers handed down over the centuries. She would need to work her magic. Feeling a bit bolstered by her thoughts of the Fey, Sahara drove into Riverbend and parked her truck in front of the café. She recalled the first time she had done this, and her heart was warmed by the sight of Holly behind the counter, pouring someone a coffee, a smile on her lips. There was nothing to do but face her. She peered in the rear view mirror. Her eyes were wild. She carefully put a calmer look on her face and walked into the café.

Holly ran out to hug and kiss her from behind the counter as if she hadn't seen her for months.

"I've only been gone four days!" Sahara laughed, trembling a little.

"I know! But it's been a month of four days it seems."

"Has Aiden not been paying you any never mind?" Sahara sat on the only stool available and took the coffee offered by Holly with gratitude.

"Yes!" Holly whispered and blushed profusely. "But Aiden is not you, as charming as he is."

"I want to hear all about it. You'll divulge all the details?"

Both were aware that curious ears were tuned in to their conversation. Both knew the limits of hints dropped. They wanted to be open but not careless. Sahara had maintained her solitude well, although word had leaked out who she was when the library approached her for a book signing. Holly had just transcended her life as an available bachelorette to having snagged the most desirable man in these parts. Walking the tightrope to living openly in a polyamorous relationship would require some grace.

"Have you spoken with Aiden yet?" Holly asked between serving customers.

"Not yet. I've just driven in, and to be honest, I need rest. I'll message him to say I'm home."

"He's missed you, I know that much."

Holly desperately wanted to lean in and steal a kiss. She was tingling with naughty thoughts. Sahara made the tiniest gesture to discourage her; she could feel the tension and the intent.

Holly smiled and acknowledged their secret longing with her eyes. It was amazing how Sahara had just known what she'd been thinking. Holly loved that about her.

"Are you free later?" Holly asked.

"Yes and no."

"What? Which is it?"

"I think I'm overtired because I'm feeling kinda hot and cold and I need to sleep. I might be a bit of a bore if you come over."

"Sahara! As if I need you to entertain me. Tell me if you're not up to it, otherwise I'm coming over with your dinner."

"Holly." Sahara reached her hand out. Holly resisted holding it to her cheek.

"Please bring me dinner. I think I'll go home now and sleep until you arrive."

"Are you sure you're ok?" Holly handed Sahara a small box of bread, cheese and pastries. "You look more than tired." She waved away Sahara's money.

"If you don't let me pay," Sahara said, "I'll stop coming here. And don't bother playing detective, I'll tell more about my weekend later." She placed her money on the counter.

"That's ridiculous. I don't want your money."

"That's too bad," Sahara whispered. "You'll take it and whatever else I have to give you."

———※———

Sahara read Aiden's message while getting out of the truck at home. He said that he was desperate to see her, and to allow Holly to take care of her.

She'd forgotten that now that it was three and not two of them in a relationship, information would flow faster than before. She smiled. Their love for her might keep her on a straighter road yet.

Willow rubbed himself along her legs as she unpacked her groceries and supplies bought from Iona. She scratched his head and apologised for leaving him, although he didn't look worse for wear, Aiden had probably over fed him.

She opened the door and let him out. Goodness, it was good to be home. The wind was fresh and the cabin welcoming, the scent of incense perfuming the air already. She started a fire and ran a hot bath, touching this and that, to gain a foothold in her space again. She felt so much stronger here, so much safer. Her mind was clearer, but her forehead was still hot. Perhaps a hot water with lemon and honey would do the trick.

Holly tried not to worry and hurried out to Sahara's as soon as the café closed. By the time she arrived, Sahara was burning up with fever, and muttering in her sleep.

"Sahara!" Holly whispered urgently. "Wake up. I think you're having a bad dream."

She stroked Sahara's forehead, wondering who 'Richard' was, and why Sahara thought that she needed help with deciphering an herbal.

266

"Sahara, it's Holly, wake up!" Sahara's eyes flew open and she looked around wildly.

"Holly! Oh... I must have fallen asleep."

"You've been more than asleep. You're burning up with fever and are asking Richard to help you decipher an herbal. Who's Richard?"

"Richard? An old friend." Sahara struggled to get out of bed.

"You're not getting up, Sahara. Tell me what you need, I'll get it."

"I need some tincture for fever from the kitchen, and open the window in here to let the sick humors out." Sahara rubbed her eyes.

"Humors? Is this herbalist talk? What are humors?"

Sahara smiled weakly. "Sorry, it's an old medic term, I must be pulling up memories. Don't pay attention to me, Holly, I'm delirious."

"Please stop apologizing. I'll ignore your rants if you promise to stay in bed. Shall we call the doctor?"

"No, no. I have everything I need here. It's just overwork. I'll be ok tomorrow. Just get me the tincture and then you should go home, I don't want you to get sick."

"Right. I'm not going anywhere until the morning. Now, what is the tincture called?"

"The label says 'fever', and there is another called 'balance'. They're in the cupboard with the herbs and teas. Also, there is an essential oil called 'heal-all'. I need to put that on the bottom of my feet."

Holly hurried down and found the items needed in the herb cupboard. It smelled like the apothecary section of Iona's store. Comforting. She was dying to ask Sahara about seeing Iona, but obviously that would have to wait. She ran back upstairs and found Sahara asleep again. She rubbed a few drops of the heal-all on the soles of Sahara's feet, then woke her gently to offer her water and tinctures. Sahara stayed awake long enough to sip the medicine, then sank back down under the covers.

Holly looked at her phone. She wanted to message Aiden. But suppose Sahara didn't want to worry him? Well, he would want to know; it could do no harm.

Aiden, at the cabin now. Sahara has a fever and is a bit delirious. I'm staying the night, and will come back tomorrow after work. I'll call you if we need anything. Love.

Aiden paced the floor of the hotel room, face in a frown. He'd wait until the morning, and if things were not better, he'd send for the visiting nurse. Sahara would hate that, he had a feeling, but in lieu of being there himself...

He dialed the number to Holly's phone. She picked up on the first ring.

"Hey sweetie. Do you need me?"

"*Aiden*. All I needed was to hear your voice. I think as long as the fever doesn't last too long we'll be ok. I can handle this, don't worry about anything. I'll call you tomorrow as I'm leaving here, or will that be too early?"

"No, call me whenever, anytime Holly. I'm here for you. I wish I could come home this minute. I can call a visiting nurse I know."

"I've already offered to get the doctor; she declined. But she is talking to Richard about reading an old herbal, maybe we should call him?" Holly laughed.

Aiden stiffened. Instinct told him that Holly had witnessed something Sahara would not have told her if she hadn't been feverish. Sahara didn't say things that revealed more than she intended on purpose. A desire to protect Holly surfaced immediately.

"You're right, the fever is making her delirious. I'll take the blame if we have to call the nurse, but I'm sure you can cure her with just your love."

"You're sweet. I'll try. It's just me and the witch's larder to make her better. She's already taken some tinctures, I'm sure we'll be fine. Goodnight Aiden...love you."

He hated the click of the phone, the distance between them. He wanted nothing more than to have them curled safely around him in bed. Painful, love. But he relished every aching moment. He wouldn't trade it for anything.

Holly went downstairs and banked the fire the way Sahara had shown her before. She called the cat in and locked the cabin doors. She filled a pitcher of water and brought it up to Sahara's bedside. Soup could wait; it was obvious Sahara wasn't going to have any anyway. It was dark and she was tired anyway. Stripping off her clothes she slipped into bed beside Sahara, stroking her forehead, offering words of comfort.

"Arinn, hold me," Sahara muttered.

268

First 'Richard', now 'Arinn', whoever they were. Holly wrapped herself snuggly around Sahara and whispered in her ear.

"I do love you, Sahara. I do."

And they slept like kittens in a bowl of wool until Willow jumped up on the bed and woke Sahara out of her stupor. She felt her forehead. Cold. Holly lay sleeping beside her, a frown crinkling her brow. She looked out at the crescent moon shining high in the sky, a million stars festooning the heavens. Sahara was in trouble and she knew it. Her dreams had been too vivid to be anything but astral travel. She wondered how much there was to explain. She pulled Holly to her and kissed her neck.

Holly woke instantly. "Sweetie, your fever is gone!" she exclaimed as she felt Sahara's forehead. She turned so Sahara could spoon her.

"I'm so sleepy. What time is it?"

Sahara looked at the clock. "Two."

"Still time to sleep. Hold me, Sahara. I've missed you."

"You were frowning in your sleep."

"Oh. You called me Arinn. I'm jealous. I'm planning to flog you in the morning," Holly mumbled and pushed her bottom into Sahara.

"Can we wait for floggings until I feel better at least?"

There was no answer. Holly snored softly. Sahara set the alarm on her phone and closed her eyes. She knew better than to think she could lie her way out of this. Slowly and surely the truth would come out.

When the alarm rang, Sahara had already made a pot of herbal tea and stirred up the fire. She hugged Holly to her as they stood by the car. They held on tight, both of them knowing that they were hopelessly lost to the other.

"I'll expect to see you here later on. We missed dinner last night."

"Ok. I've got tomorrow night off." Holly looked hopefully at Sahara.

Sahara laughed. "There's nothing I'd like more," she said and waved her lover down the lane.

Her senses were on fire. It would be a good day of writing; she felt the familiar inspiration when Iona was calling in energies for her. A life more complicated. Is that what she had wished for?

The cabin was alight with magic, waiting for her energy. She was suddenly famished and warmed the oven to crisp up the croissants, putting eggs on the boil. Coffee! That's what was needed. Stripping the bed, she thought about how much she would enjoy hanging laundry on the line.

She ate her breakfast reading Culpeper's Complete Herbal; she looked forward to making new tinctures in the spring. When light broke over the horizon she put on her rubber boots and a warm woolen sweater. The book she had bought for Aiden was wrapped in plain paper, and tucked under her arm. She headed for the mailbox at the fork in the road. Snow would fly soon, she could almost smell it. Had it already been more than two months since she had moved here?

Her nose sniffed out the familiar forest aromas; rotting leaves, decaying mushrooms, damp pine needles, moss. She called to Pan. He appeared as quickly as her thoughts, curious about the parcel she was carrying.

"It's a book, for Aiden."

"For Dagr as well," Pan smiled mischievously.

"Of course, for Dagr. But I am not that familiar with Dagr yet, can you bring him to me in my dreams more often?"

"As you wish Brigida."

Sahara looked at Pan. Was it that easy to blend her and Brigida together?

"There is only one of you," Pan said, reading her thoughts, "living in two separate dimensions; she is living in you and you within her. And so it is for Aiden and Dagr."

"But when I think of Aiden, I feel one love and Dagr, another. They feel different, they are different. One was a warrior and one is a pacifist."

"Two sides of the same coin, as it were, although Dagr was really a pacifist at heart. How would you know an aspen if you hadn't seen an oak? The differences expose the specifics of each. Dagr awakens one kind of love because you need to feel violence to experience peace and Aiden awakens the peace...you can see what I mean? Both men live within you, showing you the beauty of opposites.

"Therefore, I cannot love one without loving the other?"

"Exactly!"

"But what if one becomes jealous of the other?"

"Becomes jealous of themselves? Rather complicated don't you think? Why don't you think less and just let yourself fall into the beauty of it all?"

They walked in silence for a while.

"What's the book about?" Pan asked.

"I found it at a used book store. It's a history of Arthurian legends."

"Knighthood, yes. An important aspect of man's consciousness, bravery, honor, and all that. Your kind are fairly obsessed with it."

"It's good, right? To be brave, to have honor?"

"Yes, Sahara, it is good, I am only teasing you. Dagr was a man of honor, remember?"

"I've remembered some. Iona will take me back again, to find out more."

"There you go again, forgetting who you are," Pan said with a sneer and was gone.

But she knew that he wasn't too angry. He was used to human beings taking centuries to learn one lesson.

She lifted the lid of the mailbox and slid in the book. She hoped he'd like it. Heading down the other fork, she soon found herself at Aiden's. This was a good walk, a triad. The beginning, the middle and the end, the trinity spoke of unity. She pondered how she, Aiden and Holly were something that came from one plus two, each of them their own entity, but now, somehow, together, they created a new reality, a third perspective. Sacred geometry, evident everywhere in nature and natural processes, even in this relationship.

Sahara found the key Aiden had hidden inside a tree. She let herself in and breathed in his essence. The house could use fresh air, she opened some windows. She stripped his bed as she had done hers, and put the linens in the wash. She wondered where his clothes line was. She walked into his closet and was overwhelmed by an urge to lie in a pile of his clothes. But that would never do. He was very neat, she noticed. He'd know if she'd been mucking about with his things. Instead, she stole a scarf for herself and a sweater for Holly. She wrote him a note, and left it in his closet:

"Stolen: one scarf, one sweater. Please see the laundry fairy for return." She drew a little heart.

She sat under the stairs, waiting for the laundry to finish, wrapped in a blanket and remembered the first night they had made love here. He had been so confident, so handsome in his lust. She loved his easy passions, he had no reservations that she knew of. Interestingly, the man who eschewed violence in life had a penchant for it in bed. Some of what Pan had talked about perhaps? Aiden and Dagr being one?

The washer sang its swan song and she got up to find a basket and clothes pegs. Impossibly organized this man! Everything placed on uncluttered shelves in orderly fashion.

All windows shut, she locked the door behind her, and picked up the basket of sheets, Aiden's scarf around her neck and the extra sweater tucked under one arm. She hung the laundry and walked home, her fingers itching to type the words that filtered in from the Between. Maybe Pan was right? She thought too much. Today she would simply live.

She left Aiden a quick text.

"I'm alive. I think you should buy Holly a nurse's outfit. Have washed and hung your bedding. I'll need pay."

⁎

Aiden's foreman watched his boss's face change as he read his phone message. Thank God...good news, he really couldn't take another hour of that penetrating silence. He had noticed a marked difference in Aiden lately. Aiden's intensity and dedication to his work was the same, there was no doubt as to why he was the most sought after builder around. But his personal habits had shifted. He was driven to doing more of the work himself, as one who needed hard labour to exorcise his demons. He was even quieter and more brooding. He checked his phone more often. The gossip was that Aiden was in love. A flurry of talk had lit up the phone lines after he'd been sighted with a stunning blond at the local haunt of the well to do. Some of what he'd heard was that Aiden had had an affair with the widow Harper, but details of that were slim.

One thing was sure. Aiden would be the last to talk about his personal life. He was private to a fault. Drew knew that there was no point in asking any questions, Aiden would talk when he was damn well ready, if ever. But there was nothing to complain about. Aiden was respected for his skill within the community. He paid fairly and treated his workers well. There was a waiting list for his homes and for the opportunity to work on his crew. Drew was surprised that it had taken Aiden this long to find love; it wasn't like there hadn't been plenty of women interested. But perhaps a man like Aiden would be difficult to pin down. He had a specific manner about him, almost what one would attribute to being old fashioned, what Drew would call honor. Aiden's word could be counted on. He would want a woman whom he could trust with his privacy, and that was in perennial short supply amid the local society. If only Aiden knew the talk that swirled around him!

⁎

Aiden was determined to head back early. There were home fires to keep burning, and he was burning up for the two women that counted on his love. He needed every minute of time he had spent working with his hands to keep his energy moving. Otherwise, he would explode, from the fantasies that filled his head, and the deep well of emotion filling his heart. His intuition told him that there had been a shift in Sahara. Whatever the regression had revealed had left her weak, and that felt to him like reason to protect Holly. He trusted Sahara to do what she needed to make her life work, but that might not necessarily translate to being something Holly would understand. A part of him was angry; knowing that he was responsible for whatever hurt might come to Holly as a result of this unconventional tryst. He would protect her if it killed him. But there was no way he would let go of the love he was building with the two of them. He wanted it with every fibre of his body, this was his to nurture and enjoy.

His recalled the last few nights as he worked to clean up the job site. His dreams had opened portals to the past. He had called on Pan who had told him that he had once been able to contact the world of the Fey for assistance in the work of a magician.

That news had wedged itself into Aiden's brain as something quite extraordinary, but it did explain in part some of his affinity to the natural world, and his interest in alchemy. Aiden smiled wryly thinking about the kind of picture him and Pan presented sitting in a luxurious hotel room, Aiden with a glass of scotch to his lips, and Pan fitting himself into a chair by the fire, his frame giant against the backdrop of the room.

"I don't need to sit," Pan had explained.

"Yes, I know, but I'm sitting and staring up at you all this time would be uncomfortable for me."

Pan's advice was to trust Sahara. But when Aiden pressed him for information on Iona, Pan said that he already knew, and to do his own digging for memories. However, that night, after a tightly rolled joint, and a meditation to meet the Fey, he had slipped onto a memory of running through a dark forest, a sword strapped over his shoulder, and a woman who looked strangely like Holly held in his arms screaming at the top of her lungs in fear.

He decided after waking up in a sweat, that he had mixed up his longing for Holly with a memory of his previous life, and went back to sleep hoping to catch another glimpse of that time. But sleep brought only the rest that he needed.

He would call Sahara tonight, maybe she would have more insight, and he was aching for the sound of her voice. But after that dream, he understood why at times he had an urge to close his hand around a weapon, or why thoughts of violence made their way into his bed. Obviously, he had been some kind of a warrior before.

He recorded his thoughts and dreams in his journal. He imagined that if anyone got a hold of this thing, there would be an inquisition into his sanity. Warrior indeed. Aiden hated war.

CHAPTER 34

Sahara saw Aiden coming from her upstairs window as he strode past her shed and towards her front door. Her heart leapt to her throat. She was not expecting Aiden until tomorrow night. She was at the foot of her stairs when he crashed through the front door without knocking.

"You need to start locking your doors at night," he said gruffly as he came towards her, his hands already on his belt.

Sahara's knees weakened and her heart began to pound. Her hand went out involuntarily towards him, palm open, in a gesture to keep him at bay. Would she ever get used to his rugged beauty and this insatiable desire to be possessed by him?

"Don't worry, Sahara, I won't whip you this time." Aiden looked as fierce as she had ever seen him and she recognized his similarity to Dagr in that instant. She thought she might pass out, but there was no time because he had already grabbed her to him and was turning her around. He pulled her short nightie up and threw her over the end of the couch.

Aiden's head swam and his throat closed as the sight of her exposed before him exploded all the love and lust that he harboured for her. She was wet, and trembling.

"Aiden! Please. Let me kiss you."

"No, my pretty little whore. I'll kiss you after I've had my way with you, and after you tell me whom you've been fucking."

She heard him stepping out of his jeans, one hand on her back, keeping her from getting up. The rip of a condom foil surprised her and hurt her, yet she could not blame him...it was Holly he was thinking of. She lifted her bottom a little to signal him that she was ready, but then, he wasn't going to wait for her to give permission, was he?

She felt his large hands spreading her open, checking that she was wet enough. She burst into tears as he rammed his cock into her, not because he hurt her, but because he could whisper "I love you" so tenderly while he nailed her so unforgivingly, and it made her want to be able to say that he would always be enough.

"Did you fuck Iona?" He bent over her and one hand went to her throat.

She nodded.

"Out loud, Sahara! Say it out loud."

He continued to pound her soft flesh, and she couldn't find her voice, it felt so damn good.

"Say it!" he roared.

"I fucked Iona!"

His hands moved to her breasts, her nipples in a tight tug between his fore finger and thumb. "And? Whom else, my lady?"

He turned her around and sitting down on the couch, he placed her back down on his cock, a curious smile on his lips. She leaned in to kiss him, her legs dripping with her juice, but he moved away.

"No, Sahara. Tell me first."

He gave a hard thrust and she was lost for words again, the heat of a gathering orgasm beginning to flow up her spine.

"Concentrate, my love. Tell me who else you gave your pretty little cunt to."

He grabbed her face and looked her in the eye, his hips moving rhythmically towards her.

"Iona's partner, Richard," she breathed, not caring now about anything but that he bring her to the crest of what she was feeling.

"Richard!" Aiden spat the name out. "And did Richard fuck you there?" He pushed with his thumb against her slick bud.

"Oh, oh! Aiden please!"

"Did you give him that beautiful ass of yours? Please tell me that you didn't Sahara."

His cock rammed deep inside her, she stammered out her words between her tears, shaking her head no.

"Louder, damn it! Tell me that you saved one little thing for me. And tell me if you liked it...his cock in your cunt, fucking you like I'm fucking you now."

She was almost there, her head thrown back, her lips parted, her nipples pointing at his face, urging him on.

"No, Aiden, I didn't give him that...oh...but I wanted to. And yes, I liked it, loved it! And I'd do it again."

She rode him like the stallion that he was, tightening herself around him, drawing out the pleasure for them both.

"Ah Sahara, it's honesty that I need from you, not to possess you," Aiden said as he pulled her face to his and kissed her sweetly while his hips rocked them into release. She tasted his tears. He puzzled her and it grew her love for him.

"Aiden, Aiden, Aiden." She repeated his name over and over, her arms around his neck, while he grazed her shoulder with his teeth.

"Welcome home, my love," they said in unison.

CHAPTER 35

"Have you had breakfast, coffee, anything yet?"

"Just you," Sahara said.

Aiden pushed the coals around in the fireplace, hoping to find enough to start today's fire.

Sahara made her way into the kitchen and ground some coffee beans. "Can you make a fire in the cook-stove as well? It's freezing in here! I'm going to wash up in the tub quickly and warm up."

"Take your time, I'll make breakfast. Do you have eggs?"

"Always." She ran her hands over him as she went towards the bathroom. He turned into her and hugged her close.

"I've missed you terribly, Sahara. I couldn't wait to come home to you. That's why I'm early. Can we spend the morning?"

"I'm done my book, Aiden! We have lots of time."

"Done...but it's only been a couple of months! Why don't we celebrate tonight? I'm so proud of you. And dying to read it."

"Want to go to town together and tell Holly?" Sahara winked at him and knew that he would have his own ideas of what "celebrate" meant.

He grinned at her and agreed. Going into town to surprise Holly sounded good, and they could work out plans for the night. His energy stirred up once more, he set to starting fires and feeding them.

"Aiden?" Sahara yelled from the tub. He found her stepping out, towel in hand.

"Here, let me." He took the towel and dried her carefully, paying attention to all the parts that intrigued him, kissing her belly on the way up. She put her hands in his hair.

"There's so much to tell, Aiden."

"I know. And I want to hear all of it. Coffee first though." He patted her bottom. "Tell me about your meeting with Kathryn, and do explain leaving me your will. I almost had a heart attack. That was an especially clever way of worrying me. And please tell me that everyone has a clean bill of health?"

Sahara nodded and blushed. "They do."

Aiden was sure she had checked *after*, and had gone with intuition. He downed one cup of coffee and held his mug out for more. They ate quickly, somehow anxious that there wouldn't be enough time to tell all.

"I left you my will because it was my way of telling you that you are the most important person in my life, and I knew that you would take good care of this land. I was going with the intention to do a regression into my past life but sometimes what one thinks they will do with Iona turns into something else, and if we indeed did do time travel, there was a chance I might not come back. I know, that sounds strange. But, you know me.

"Hardly. I'm quite sure that I know very little about you," he said, but he extended his hand to her in encouragement.

She pouted. "My meeting with Kathryn went well; I had to tell her that I was in love; she could tell by my writing. I've just sent in the last of the revisions, and Goddess willing, a real live book will come out of it."

"You say you're in love? With whom?" Aiden laughed and Sahara threw her crust of bread at him.

"When you got home and were sick, I knew that what had happened in Denver might have been overwhelming, and also, I worried that enough was found out to make a difference in our relationship with Holly." Aiden gave Sahara a determined look. "I don't want to hurt her. She's going to find all this extremely unbelievable."

"I know. I was worried sick as you heard. But, Holly is stronger and more open minded than you think. I can't promise that this will be easy, but we're in it now. It's too late to tell her not to love us. She's a determined girl anyway."

"This might be jumping ahead...but, how did Richard get in your bed?" Aiden tried to sound nonchalant, but she knew that he had felt the sting of another man bedding her.

"It is jumping ahead. Richard is Iona's beloved. He's also a direct part of our past lifetime. He ended up in my bed because of a cleverly led regression by Iona, who knew that we would recognise each other and fall into an old pattern. His name was Richard then as well."

"Iona owns the magic store, as I recall," Aiden said. "What does Richard do? Is he a wizard?"

"Funny. Richard is an art dealer. He lives in Europe part time; and partly in Denver. Richard Montfort...Aiden, what is it?"

Aiden had paled and was looking at her with disbelief. He put down his fork and swallowed the last of his food.

"Richard Montfort, my dear, is the man for whom I will be building a house next year." Aiden stood up and went to face the fire, hands in fists.

"No! Aiden, do you know him?" Sahara felt the chilly finger of fate running along her spine. It couldn't be.

"I haven't met him, if that's what you mean. I was recommended to him by an architect I work with, and he agreed to hire me based on my portfolio. Apparently he's very busy and had no time to meet right away. I agreed to build for him because the design for his house is especially artful, and it stirred something in me. It's more small castle than house, really. It will be a three year project for sure." He turned towards Sahara.

"I can see that there will be no avoiding this. We are tangled in each other's lives, and in itself, that's not something I'm afraid of. But with Holly in the mix. Bloody fucking hell! Sahara, what are we doing? How will we explain all these past lives and lovers to her?"

She came to him and bade him sit with her by the fire. He was silent for a long time. They were both shocked by this turn of events. Oh how well the Universe wove a web.

"Tell me, Sahara, I need to ask this. Did Richard love you well? Were you happy in his arms? I'm not asking because I'm jealous, but because I need to know that you are treated well. Sharing you only works if you're happy."

She met him with fresh tears in her eyes. How she loved his sensitive heart. She curled into his lap.

"Yes, my lord. He loved me so very well. In a way you would appreciate. My body knows him...from before. So it was easy, natural. I'm not hurting you by saying this, am I?"

"No. I love Holly after all. I'd be a hypocrite if I couldn't accept it. Still, I didn't expect this."

His lips found hers. She melted into him.

"Tell me all, then, I'm ready. And by the way, I love my book. I love you." He laid his head to hers. "I've been meeting with Pan," he added. "I'm further along with my memories, and have had some pretty revealing dreams, but when I ask him to tell me about the past, he says to do my own digging. Bloody frustrating."

"Yes. I had the same conversation with him. He believes in people standing in their own power. His words are wise."

"Is it too early for a joint Sahara? Do you have any herb? I'm feeling overwhelmed."

"Of course." She stood to fetch it. "You roll it, I'll get us some water to drink."

She watched him roll and again thought that his hands were the most powerful she had ever seen, but then, so had Dagr's been. She took them and kissed them. They took a long drag each and waited to hear from the herb deva. She would help them face the journey ahead.

And together, they walked into the past, as Sahara told him what little she knew, of Dagr, the King's knight and magic worker, his love for two maidens, Arinn and Brigida, and the Earl Richard Dumont. She recounted how Richard had had them burned out of their homes, and that even his love for the man he called friend could not save them all from their fate. From what Sahara remembered of the regression, she assumed that somehow she had fallen in love with Richard after being separated from Dagr and Arinn. She told him all she knew but it was clearly just the beginning, they had far more to discover.

"So," Aiden said, "I'm not new to loving more than one partner, and I see now why my hands sometimes itch for holding a weapon. My interests tend towards the same, my love of the forest. But before, my love, when you were Brigida, did you look much the same as you do now? Is that why I recognized you in this lifetime?"

"I did, but had long hair. And it was Arinn who had nipples long as these." Sahara tugged at hers, smiling as Aiden's eyes turned dark. "But what I find so very interesting, is that Holly is the spitting image of Arinn, and now I understand why you were so drawn to her in the first place. Like the painting upstairs, Holly has Arinn's ethereal beauty and spirit. But she does not belong in our past directly. She's definitely a newer soul."

"If I met Iona, would I recognise Arinn?"

"Not by colouring, Iona is as fair as can be but her hair is flaming red. She is stunning, oh Aiden, I think you would love her. She is terribly beguiling, she can cast a powerful spell. She is a gifted alchemist after all. Besides you've already seen her in a way."

"I have? When?" Aiden was intrigued.

"The raven. She shape shifts. She's dangerous, because she loves Dagr fiercely still and sees you as hers."

Aiden put his head in his hands, he remembered the raven well. "I can barely grasp it all. I trust in what you say, because I trust you and also because it's sounding familiar." He looked down at his hands. "I've killed before. What a departure from whom I am now."

"Except in bed, my love." She took his hands in hers. "I love these hands, and what they do to me."

"And Richard, I'm almost afraid to ask, does he love you still?"

"Yes, in a way. Now that we've connected, he's recognised the love we once shared. But Richard is not dangerous. He lives and let's live. But Iona...there are things that I don't know about us. Something happened to the three of us at some point that turned our love around. Iona won't tell. I need her to access the past. Although Pan thinks otherwise. But I'm afraid. There are places I won't go in magic that Iona will."

"But if Richard loves you, and Iona loves me, wouldn't it be better to leave it all alone? Just leave the past where it lies and continue on as separate people? How will we ever tell Holly about you and Iona and Richard?"

"No! Aiden, we can't tell. At least not yet. To throw her into the web now, before she knows me better and understands something about past lives, magic, it would be very dangerous. No." She looked at his distraught face. "I know Aiden. You would rather die than lie to her. But it truly wouldn't serve her to tell her now. And no, we can't step away from this now; there is a reason for us reconnecting. We've got to discover what that is and do the emotional and spiritual work surrounding it. "

"When can I meet them, Iona and Richard? I mean, I'll have to, before I do the build for him. Who knows if we'll be able to work together anyway, considering everything? Anyway, maybe for a regression together? I want to experience it, not just hear about it. I want to meet Brigida and Arinn."

It was Sahara's turn to look distraught.

"There's no other way, Sahara. I need to know now. You say that Richard and I were friends, maybe we could be in this lifetime, and I could find peace about his emotions for you. And possibly your love for him? Sahara, how much of your love for him do you still feel?"

She hid against his chest. "It's true. Oh Aiden. I do love him still. Not like with you, to spend a lifetime with, but it is love nonetheless. And more. I wanted him so badly after the regression, there was no stopping it. But Aiden, in that lifetime, Richard loved you more than a friend. I could tell during the regression that when he spoke of you he spoke as one who longs for a lost lover. We never got far enough to see if you returned that kind of love, but we could find out."

"Jesus, Sahara! Every word you speak makes me wonder more about who I am or at least was. Enough now, enough for today. I need to process all that you've told me."

He lay down and pulled her on top of himself. He wanted to close his eyes and go back to the day when he'd first met her, her smile lighting the fire in his heart. Her weight on him made him feel safe. She sighed and snuggled down deeper. He pulled a blanket on top of them.

"Sahara?"

"Mmm?"

But he was already asleep. It was his only escape. She kissed his chest and made a mental note to not sleep more than an hour.

CHAPTER 36

Sitting in Aiden's truck as he drove to town, Sahara thought about how surprised Holly would be to see Aiden home early. She dialed the café. Holly answered in a rush.

"Hi, I'm coming over for lunch," Sahara announced. "You sound busy."

"Crazy busy, but I'm not complaining. This idea of leek and Gruyere soup has made everyone nuts. Come here before it's all gone."

"Maybe it's *too* busy? I can come over tomorrow." Sahara laughed into the phone. Aiden smiled at her, his hands tight on the wheel.

"Are you insane?" Holly answered. "Get over here! Gotta go."

Aiden looked over at Sahara. She returned his look. They both knew that this would be their first time in public as lovers. And if they knew anything about Holly at all, she would come running to them with unrestrained welcome, especially since she was not expecting Aiden.

"I'm thinking, let's be open to whatever but keep things fairly respectable," Aiden suggested. "There's no way I'm going to keep from giving her a hug and kiss, but I'm not going to pretend about you either."

"You know what? I think that people might not be all that interested in our shenanigans. They might talk at first, but maybe we're overthinking it."

"That's very optimistic. But giving that Holly's place is the hub of town, and you are a local writing celebrity, and I have a certain reputation as a business person, your theory might not be that sound."

"Well, we'll see." Sahara grinned and leaned in to kiss him. "I've heard all about what you did to Holly while I was away. You made quite the impression on her."

"What do you mean, 'what I did' to her? I simply took her to dinner and we had some fun getting to know each other."

"I mean the coming in her mouth bit." And with those words Sahara broke into peals of laughter while Aiden tried to maintain a straight face. "What a way to break in a girl new to men! Really, Aiden." She winked her amusement.

"That was not entirely my fault, I tried to get her to move, but she

283

was determined. And she's not as innocent as I may have made her out to be." Aiden smiled. "God, Sahara, she's so delicious! But I guess you'd know."

Sahara nodded. She knew. "Ok, I'm sorry, I'm teasing you. Whatever you did do to her, she loved it and you've managed to sweep her off her feet. All that charm you unleashed on her made her eager for me, so for that, I thank you."

"Glad to be of service," Aiden observed wryly. "I can only imagine what the two of you got up to." He looked at her as she undid her seat belt, getting ready to step out into the street. The café from what Sahara could see, was packed.

"We haven't..." Aiden began.

"I know."

"I'm dying to. Holly wants you there."

Sahara looked down at Aiden's jeans. Hic cock was as hard as could be. She shook her head. "You can't go in there like that. Let's talk about something else for a minute."

He nodded, took a deep breath and adjusted himself. The trouble was, he couldn't stop thinking about it. They stood by the curb letting traffic go by. Then, quite deliberately, Aiden took Sahara's small hand in his, and leaned down to kiss her lips. For all his words of respectability, he wanted the world to know. And he was too much in love to care what was said. This was stepping deep out of his comfort zone, allowing prying eyes to observe his life so openly. Still, he felt the urge to just stand in his truth. Come what may.

When they stepped into the café, Holly let out a whoop of joy and ran into Aiden's arms. He leaned into her, kissing her lips, and stood by with an amused smile as Holly planted a tender smack on Sahara's mouth.

They barely noticed the silence that had fallen on the café, or felt the determination of the astonished diners to drink as much coffee as was needed to figure out this curious scenario. Had they not just seen Aiden giving Sahara a kiss outside? What were these three up to?

Holly sat them down at a table and said she'd be back with their lunch. She ran away in a flap grinning from ear to ear. Sahara looked at Aiden and raised her eyebrow at him.

"So much for keeping things on the down low," she whispered. "You've just told the world that you're a most unrespectable rogue." She smiled deeply. "I'm proud of you...and you look impossibly large in these café chairs. How tall are you anyway?"

"Six three. You know what? I suddenly realized that I just don't care what people think," he whispered back, taking her hand. "I truly feel good to be open about it. I might regret it, but in this moment, I'm happy to let the world know that I love you both."

They knew that ears were straining, and eyes were glued to them. Holly arrived with their lunch, and apologized that she couldn't sit down, she had to make more coffee.

"I don't think anyone is going to leave for a while," she whispered as she leaned over them. "I'm so happy to see you both here, you have no idea what this means to me." Her eyes filled with sudden tears and she walked away quickly to the kitchen.

The part time girl arrived with their waters. She gave them a pointed look. Aiden looked her in the eye and she skulked away, hands in her pockets.

Sahara looked at Aiden as he ate his soup and baguette, a steely look on his face. She could see more of Dagr in him today. Her beautiful man. She was totally and devastatingly in love. He could not be more perfect if he tried.

"I still have my surprise coming?" she interrupted his thoughts.

"Yes! Want to go tomorrow?"

"What is it?"

"Are you going to keep asking me that, hoping to trick me into telling? You'll have to wait."

"Ok, if Holly is free tomorrow, let's go. I can't imagine what it is!"

"I know. But you'll love it."

"Are you sure? What if I don't?"

"I'm sure," Aiden insisted.

Sahara thought he had never been more endearing, sprawled out in his chair, his eyes intense and his smile so sure. He couldn't keep from following Holly with his gaze as she moved about. Every now and then Holly would look their way and shower him with her dazzling grin. Sahara could see how much Holly had let Aiden into her heart in these short weeks. She trusted him.

Holly sat with them an hour later when reluctantly, some of the diners had left, not much more in the know than before. She sighed.

"You guys are good for business."

Aiden took her hand. "Can you come for dinner tonight, my place? Sahara is finished her book, we can celebrate."

"Yes, yes, yes! Dinner to celebrate sounds wonderful. What can I bring?"

Sahara laughed. "Just yourself, silly girl. You've done enough work for today. No more thinking about what to bring or bake or anything. You need to hire more help."

"I will, sometime. I need to pay off some operating debt first. Then I won't feel so trapped to be here every second."

Aiden looked at Sahara and knew that they had had the same idea at the same time. She nodded at him. They could tell Holly later. He winked at Sahara in acknowledgment. This was a new gateway to the past, being able to communicate telepathically.

"What about tomorrow? Can you come with us to get Sahara's surprise?" Aiden asked.

"No. Sorry. But don't wait anymore. Go together. But, in good news, if you wait another hour in town, I can come out with you then. I'll just need a ride back either in the morning or later tonight."

And so, with plans made, Aiden and Sahara left to buy groceries and wine.

By the time they picked Holly up again, news had travelled from Riverbend to Denver to Aspen and back, that Aiden had been seen with both Holly and Sahara, and the speculation was that they were having some kind of a kinky ménage because neither girl seemed to have the sense to be upset about his roaming affections.

Dianne was one of the first to hear. Well, she had always known that he was out of the ordinary; he had that air about him that made one wish they could figure out his mystery. She wondered how long before one of the women had their heart broken. Aiden was not so easy to forget or fall out of love with.

But he couldn't have two women at once, after all. Could he?

Coming soon...

The Raven and the Aspen King

The magic continues in Book 2 of The Dark Pool Trilogy as Sahara, Aiden and Holly embark on a relationship that defies all the rules.

Can Holly ever be safe to love two such intense, erotic people or will she fall under a spell cast by a witch whose love for Aiden threatens to destroy them all?

ABOUT THE AUTHOR

Monika Carless is an incurable writer and a solitary practitioner of the Wise Woman Tradition. She is a lover of the natural world and the mystery of life. Mother to two nomadic daughters and partner to a magical man, Monika is keen on adventure and has completed several long distance walks across England, which she considers her spiritual home. Born in Poland and now living in Canada, this free-spirited rebel is interested in challenging social norms and dispelling taboos. Monika has been published in several magazines on a variety of topics. This is her first novel.

Follow Monika's writing at *www.elephantjournal.com* and on her blog **Simply Solitary**: *https://simplysolitary.wordpress.com/*